EMPYRE∆X

THE RISE OF CÀ RÁ

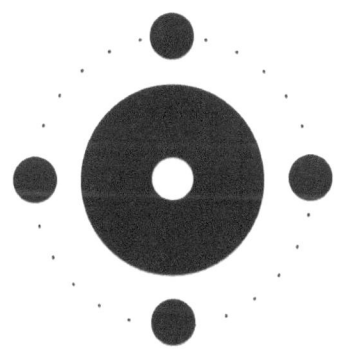

SCOTT FROST

GIZA SCROLLS

· PARALLAX DAWN ·

Published by PARALLAX DAWN an imprint of GIZA SCROLLS, LLC

ISBN (paperback) 979-8-9921779-0-9
ISBN (ebook) 979-8-9921779-1-6
ISBN (hardcover) 979-8-9921779-2-3

1st Edition January 2025

Cover Design by Andrew Gherman & Scott Frost
Edited by Amanda J. Spedding - Phoenix Editing

www.SCOTTFROST.com

www.GIZASCROLLS.com

MATTER

0 - BIG BANG
1 - DEAD CAT ALIVE
2 - FIRST VICTIM
3 - GRAND UNIFICATION
4 - THE NECKLACE
5 - IMPONDERABLE OCEAN
6 - INCIDENT AT STONE CREEK
7 - APRIL 18, 1955
8 - THE DOOR OPENS
9 - THE SPHERE
10 - ATTACK ON CAM RANH BAY
11 - THE CANNON
12 - COSMIC ENTANGLEMENT
13 - ENTER NQCO
14 - CEMETERY
15 - THE FATHER, THE SON
16 - EXOTIC MATTER
17 - ENDANGERED
18 - BARBED WIRE
19 - THE WELL
20 - THE TEMPLE
21 - BOOBY TRAPS
22 - HOLOGRAMS
23 - DEUS EX MACHINA
24 - DARK ENERGY
25 - NEURO COLLAPSE
26 - THE SACRIFICE
27 - RUMBLE
28 - ANNIHILATION OPERATOR
29 - CREATION OPERATOR
30 - QUANTUM SOUL
EPILOGUE

FOR HAYDEN

WHY IS A MOUSE WHEN IT SPINS?

· BIG BANG ·

A red key on a ball chain slid into the lock of safe deposit box number: 69-105. Trembling fingers with blistered, tissue-paper skin twisted it open. William 'Bill' Young peered inside then tucked a silver box, leather satchel, and a small white envelope into it. Sweat dripped to sting his eyes, gaze fixed on the envelope addressed to Jack.

Blood trickled from his nose, and a cool pinch scraped inside his lungs, forcing a deep cough. The silver bracelet on his left wrist beeped and flashed a sequence of blue symbols.

"Damn." His voice cracked through a calm exhale. "Please, not yet." He locked the door and slid the chain around his neck. The key glided down the chain to clink against two military dog tags.

The entrance to the vault buzzed open, and Bill stumbled shoulder-first into the bank lobby, clutching his left arm. His eye caught a digital panel on the wall.

9:23am. Monday. August 26, 2019.

A female teller on her phone paused and covered the mouthpiece. "Mr. Young, are you all right?"

"Me?" Muscle spasms wobbled his legs, but he found his footing and straightened his back. The bracelet gripped tight against his wrist, beeped. "Fine, Alice. Doing fine." He tapped his neck with his finger. "I've got this neck thing, old war injury."

"But you're bleeding."

"Oh." Blood smeared on his fingers when he rubbed his upper lip and dripped into his white beard. "Huh. Look at that. Guess it's gonna be one of those days."

A stab of pain pierced his foot and he shambled with a limp to the front door.

"Are you sure you don't need any help?"

"I'm fantastic. Have a splendid day." His words trailed into a cough and he pressed his back against the glass, giving her a quick wink.

She hesitated, gave a slow nod, and returned to her call.

Spinning through the exit, harsh sunlight blasted Bill's face. A tremor in his left shoulder paused him at the top of the concrete stoop. Through bloodshot eyes, he scanned the empty streets of downtown Stone Creek, Virginia. A bird chirped from a nearby dogwood. The fetid aroma of chicken coops and cow fields wafted on the light breeze, biting into his sweat.

His eyes locked on a grassy park across the way where a Civil War-era cannon sat between two benches. He'd sat in the park on several occasions, studying the weapon's craftsmanship, wondering about its history, the memories it held.

More blood ran from his nose, sputtering away when he coughed. A deep inhale crackled from his blood-filled lungs.

Gripping the stair handrail, he limped down each step and veered into the bank's narrow side alley. Finding respite behind a dumpster, he leaned against the crumbling brick wall and caught his breath.

Bill reached for the bracelet and tapped its smooth silver surface. A sequence of numbers and symbols flashed until they locked into place. The sultry, digital voice of a woman signaled their completion. "Oh, yeah."

The space before him undulated and refracted light into an irregular hexagon-shaped doorway. A beam of blue plasma pulsed around its completed edge.

Bill pushed from the wall and stepped toward the portal. The bracelet beeped, flashing a strobing red light. As he cast a distracted glance at it, the shadow of a figure flashed over him and smashed him against the wall.

His head bounced off the brick and he slammed to the ground.

A man stood over him, a deep scar running from his forehead down his right cheek. The man wore a steel-gray fishing vest over a white shirt. Glossy black eyes glared back at Bill.

With one arm, the man picked Bill up, lifting him into the air. When the stranger tried to speak, only an incoherent string of words and sounds came.

"You're too late." Bill laughed through a cough of blood that spattered the man's face. His heart pounded with deep concussive beats.

The man punched Bill straight in the chest and vibrations from cracking ribs rattled bone-on-bone through his torso.

Bill dropped to the ground but ignored the pain, tapping a sequence of symbols on the bracelet.

As soon as the man reached for him again, a massive jolt of electricity and blue plasma arcs shot out of the bracelet and snatched onto the attacker's arm, spreading throughout his body.

The man stood above Bill, convulsing in the sizzling current, then staggered away.

Bill rolled onto all fours, gazing at the man, whose face contorted under the energy surge. For a brief instant, a glowing, translucent skeletal figure revealed itself and fought to escape the net-like field of sparks.

The bracelet beeped and started a countdown timer that snapped Bill's attention.

Ten. Nine.

Clutching his chest and wheezing, Bill struggled to pull himself toward the portal. His fingers clawed at the ground, muscles cramping with each movement.

Eight. Seven.

Blood rushed to his head, and pain seared across his face. Just a few feet from the portal, he glanced over his shoulder. The electricity's cackles faded and the man stumbled forward.

Six. Five.

The entity's human face returned, black eyes rolling back into place. With a shake of his head, his gaze locked on Bill. The creature found his footing and sprinted straight at Bill.

Four.

Bill turned, scrambling along the ground. Faster. Faster. Trying to escape.

Three.

The man closed in, his right hand morphing into a metal claw.

Two.

With a final push, Bill sprang to his feet in a surge of pain.

One.

The man leapt, swiping the claw, but Bill fell forward into the portal.

Zero.

The bracelet beeped.

Bill disappeared.

The portal shimmered and collapsed, leaving the scar-faced man behind.

Jack Young stood at the far end of the coffee bar inside the Dragon Wing Café. Forty-two and still single, he hadn't been on a date in ages, but here he stood, trying again.

He leaned up against a high bar and glanced toward the front of the café.

His date, Rebecca, sat with her back against the aqua-green wall, her face down, engrossed in her phone. Her brown hair draped over the baby-blue blouse of her right shoulder; her white skirt a perfect contrast.

The rumble of a coffee grinder shot through the air, followed by the whir of an espresso machine.

Rebecca never looked up.

Jack's eyes drifted to an old woman sitting at a nearby table, her blue Adidas tracksuit conflicting with the purple streak through her gray hair. When he caught the woman's intense stare, he darted his eyes to the order-status screen on the wall.

"Jack," a female barista called out from behind the counter while placing two coffees on a wooden tray.

He stepped up, smiled, and gathered both coffees. "Thank you. Where is the sugar?"

The barista pointed at the wall behind him. "Right over there, sir."

"Great." He plucked a packet of sugar and a stirring stick.

As he carried the coffees to the table, he passed the old woman, who looked up at him from the corner of her eyes.

Jack slid into his chair, placed his phone on the table, and handed Rebecca her coffee.

"Here you go. Dragon Tear latte with a pump of vanilla."

"Thanks." She smiled and rotated the cup on the table with the lid opening facing her.

Jack glanced at a dragon mural painted on the wall from floor to ceiling. "It's my first time here, so the dragon theme. That seems pretty cool."

"Yeah, it's interesting." Her doe-brown eyes took in the café. "It's close to my office, so convenient."

Jack took a sip of his coffee. "You said you worked in HR, right?"

"Yup, I run HR for a small tech company. You?"

"I work at an architecture firm building computer models for clients."

"I've never met anyone who did that. What's the job title?"

"They call me a Visual Designer, but it's just engineering drawings of buildings, parks, stuff like that."

"I see." She placed her elbows on the table and cupped her fingers around her coffee. "Do you have kids?"

When her eyes locked on him, he couldn't get past a hollow façade staring back.

Jack wanted to like her, but something gnawed at him. He let out a meager laugh. "No. You?"

"Two. Fourteen and sixteen. They've lived with me since my divorce last year."

Jack couldn't imagine divorce; he'd never even been married, let alone engaged. Not that he hadn't tried, but the women in his life never seemed to click, and when they did, something always seemed to interfere...Dad.

"So they're in high school?" he asked.

"Yeah, my oldest is a pitcher for his school's baseball team. He's looking to play in college..."

While she spoke, his gaze was drawn to a painting on the wall above her head, and he froze.

Her words slowed and drifted into a muffled monotone.

The painting had a gray wood frame and showed a gnarled tree with two young boys playing. One boy sat near the tree trunk; the other sat high above, waving down.

He should've focused on Rebecca, but couldn't.

The painting reminded him of the time he fell out of his treehouse as a kid, landing hard. Jack and his brother Roger named it Star Nest. Towering high up in a four-trunk great oak, it gave them a clear view of the starry night sky.

Jack's head swirled with distant memories, and he blinked. A freefall sensation swept over his body, the sounds of the café fading.

Now, there was only the rush of air beneath him; Star Nest becoming more distant as he fell.

He landed with a thud, and the memory shuddered his arm, jolting him back to the café, and knocking over his coffee.

"Whoa." Rebecca scooted back in her chair.

In a daze, Jack righted the cup. Coffee streamed across the table and dripped off the edge onto her white skirt.

"Shit," Jack said. "I'm so sorry." *What a disaster.*

Rebecca slid to the side of her seat and tried to avoid the waterfall of brown liquid.

Jack's phone rang at full blast and vibrated on the table. He fumbled for it and turned off the ringer. Trying to scoop coffee away from Rebecca, his eyes froze on the screen.

'Incoming call from Dad'.

He pressed the send to voicemail button.

Jack stood to find napkins. When he turned around, everyone in the café was staring at him. The old woman had changed seats and faced him with an icy glare, her lips pressed together.

He headed to the counter and grabbed a wad of napkins. "Ma'am, do you have a towel or rag? I spilled my coffee."

The barista looked back at his table. "Yes, sir, be right over."

"Thank you."

When he returned to the table, Rebecca shook her head with stony eyes and wiped her blouse and skirt with a small tissue.

"I'm sorry about that." Jack handed her a wad of brown napkins and tried to soak up the coffee.

"I just bought this blouse. I'm sure it's ruined," she said. With feverish dabs, she tried to blot away the stains.

"I'll pay for dry cleaning."

She didn't look at Jack. "No, just forget it."

"Okay. Just trying to help." A couple laughed from behind him,

Jack's phone vibrated on the table, sending ripples across the puddle of coffee.

'Incoming call from Dad'.

Rebecca's eyes dropped to his phone. "Do you need to take that?"

Jack hesitated, then nodded. He picked up the phone and turned away from her, holding it to his ear. "I'm in the middle of something. I'll call you back."

He hung up and turned back to Rebecca, who had shifted her chair far from the table, put her phone in her purse, and pushed her coffee cup to the side.

The barista arrived and laid a large towel across the table that soaked up all the coffee.

Jack lifted the two coffee cups in the air while she cleaned the tabletop and surrounding floor.

"Ma'am, would you like some soda water and a fresh cloth?" she asked.

"No, thank you," Rebecca said.

"We can make you another latte."

"That won't be necessary. I'll be leaving soon."

And there it was. "I'm so sorry about this," Jack said. "Any chance I can make it up to—"

Jack's phone vibrated again.

'Incoming call from Dad'.

What the hell? Jack hadn't heard from him in years, and the man decided to call right now? At this exact moment? Typical.

Rebecca glanced down at the phone and then up at Jack.

"Excuse me one moment." Snatching his phone from the table, he stood and turned to walk to the bar. "Dad, seriously, I can't talk right now."

No response.

He spun, facing the coffee order screen. "Hello? You've got to stop calling me. I don't have time for this. I need to go."

No response.

Jack ended the call. When he turned around, only an empty chair glared back at him.

"Goddammit," he muttered.

He glanced toward the old woman's table, but only a white coffee cup sat alone in the silence.

Jack retrieved his coffee from the table, and threw down a crumpled napkin. He flicked his eyes to the treehouse painting and leaned in to examine a tiny detail he missed before: a dragonfly hovering beside the tree.

An electric jolt shot up his spine.

His phone vibrated in his hand.

'Incoming call from Roger'.

1

· DEAD CAT ALIVE ·

9:46am

In southwest Virginia, at the Pocahontas State Correctional Center, Damien 'Demi' Carver lay back on the lower bunk of his steel-barred prison cell, reading a biography of Andrew Carnegie.

Bifocal glasses hung on the tip of his nose and he scratched his white, stubbled chin. When he turned the page, he angled it to catch sunlight from the cell's only window.

The main cell-block door clanged, he laid the book flat on his chest and glanced at a hand-drawn calendar.

Black Xs marked each day until August 29th, but it was the word '*Release*' on Monday, September 9th that drew his gaze.

On Friday the 13th, the bold word '*Free*' beckoned him.

He'd made it into his seventies, so two more weeks in this pit would be easy, but the interruption of the door at this time of day was out of place.

Distant footsteps, perhaps two or three sets of boots, grew louder. One softer, a shuffle.

Jeers and cackles stretched down the hall of prison cells. A new prisoner?

Demi sat up, flipped the book closed. Pulling himself to the edge of the bed, he set the book on the bolted shelf next to him. He took a pile of geometric sketches he'd been making and shuffled them into a neat stack.

The footsteps grew closer, and he removed his glasses, closed his eyes, straightened his posture, and his spine crackled.

The footsteps stopped in front of his cell.

"Carver," Corrections Officer C.J. Cook barked. "You've got a new roommate."

Demi opened his eyes to find a handcuffed bald man with muscular arms garnished with black tribal tattoos standing outside the cell bars. A second officer stood behind with a shotgun trained on the man.

"Did you think I was getting lonely?" Demi asked.

Cook motioned his finger in a circle. "Get up, turn around, hands on the bed."

Pain throbbed in Demi's leg when he stood and grabbed for a plastic medical cane.

"Nope, gimme the cane," Cook snapped. "Can't have that in here with this guy."

"But my leg isn't healed yet."

"Not my fault you got shot. Besides, it's for your own good."

Demi passed the plastic cane through the cell bars. "I didn't know you cared."

"I don't, but the warden seems to."

Demi hated Cook. The past three months had tested his will but he endured – he had bigger things to focus on.

"Hurry, old man. We ain't got all day," Cook snapped while Demi placed his palms on the top bunk.

The new prisoner shook his head. "Hey, man, why are you putting me in with this old guy?"

"Shut it, Rivera," Cook said, then pressed a radio to his lips. "Open up on twenty-six."

A loud buzz echoed, and Cook pulled on the cell door. It opened with a metallic clunk, and he motioned the man to enter. "Alex Rivera, meet Damien Carver, resident nut job. Hands up on the bed."

Demi nodded at Rivera with a smile. "Good morning."

"What the hell is this bullshit? I don't wanna be put in here with some pervert." Droplets of spittle hit Demi's cheek.

"Shut up, Rivera," Cook said. He bent down to unlock the chain around Rivera's ankles.

Demi smiled and studied the tattoos running up the leathery skin of Rivera's neck, wrapping around the side of his head. "What are you in for?"

Cook barked from below. "Straight ahead, Carver."

"Don't talk to me, old man." Rivera glared at Demi.

Cook stood. "I see you two ladies are going to get along just fine. Give me your hands." The officer removed the handcuffs from Rivera's wrists. "Hands back on the bed."

Cook stepped backward until he was outside the bars. He slammed the door shut, turned the key, and shook the bars. "You girls can relax now."

Demi slid back onto his bunk.

Rivera gripped the cell door bars. "Why the hell am I in here? I need to be with my boys."

"Warden's order, not my call." Cook turned and walked away. "Carver's only got two more weeks, if you can make it."

"What the hell? Get back here!"

Someone yelled from another cell, "Shut up, asshole!"

Demi leaned back against his pillow, folded his fingers, and thumped his thumbs on his chest. "Well now, that was fun, wasn't it?"

Rivera stomped to the shelf and swiped the papers across the room. "You keep this shit away from me, man."

"That wasn't very nice." Demi raised his eyebrows. "Is that any way to start a friendship?"

"We ain't friends," Rivera snarled, metal crowns on his teeth glinting in the sunlight. "What you looking at, old man?"

"Your tattoos." Demi squinted.

"Huh?"

"Why do you have them? Covering up a sin? Hiding some pain?"

"I ain't got no pain. Stay the hell away from me."

"Oh, we all have pain Mr. Rivera. Some are just better at hiding it.

Behind tattoos, perhaps."

Rivera waved away Demi's words. "Horseshit."

"Okay. Here, look." Demi sat up and pulled up his left sleeve to reveal a tattoo on the underside of his wrist. "I've got one too."

A larger, black-filled circle was surrounded by four smaller, obsidian orbs at each 90-degree mark. A series of tiny dots connected the centers of the orbs in four arcs.

Demi shot Rivera a smile. "Want to know what it means?"

Dr. Andre Tarkos leaned against a metal pole on the D.C.-bound, orange-line Metro train and reached up to scratch the back of his graying hair.

Morning sun cut through tree branches and glittered through greasy window smudges.

A giggle rose from the far end of the car and his eyes darted to the source.

A young woman tickled a boy, eliciting the child's laughter, and Tarkos caught her eyes with his own, giving her a half-smile. If it were any other day, he'd talk to her, even if she looked half his age. But not today.

She didn't respond, pushing her disheveled hair behind her ear and ignoring him. How could he blame her? He wasn't anyone special.

He peered at his watch; already late for the 9am meeting. Good. He grimaced as his mind raced into unpleasant territory. A new deputy director meant fresh budget cuts and his program would have to give up a pound of flesh.

Tarkos pivoted against the pole toward the double doors to glance outside. A mosaic of trees, steel, and concrete streamed by.

None of it mattered anymore.

His role had become a dead-end position in a bureaucratic apparatus created to grind aspirations of greatness beneath an infinite loop of the mundane. They'd destroyed any possible legacy he might once have achieved. His passion for 'Soulgazer' flamed out months ago amid the monotonous routine.

Tarkos sighed heavily. He needed change.

The train car rumbled and shook when it changed tracks, penetrating the dark void of tunnels under the city.

His eyes darted to the clear reflection of the young boy in the now blackened mirror-like glass. Would this kid leave a legacy one day?

The train trundled to a stop, and the doors slid open. Passengers hustled through turnstiles and up escalators, but Tarkos kept a distant, casual pace that separated him from the routine crush of bodies.

He emerged from the underground Farragut West Station and the gastric stench of Washington D.C. wafted in his face.

Damn, the sewer gas is bad today. He wrinkled his nose with disgust.

Turning onto 18th Street, he headed down a parking garage ramp where two attendants standing outside a small vestibule, waved at him.

He nodded back and reached the rear concrete wall that held a door with a white- and red-lettered sign: '*Maintenance Only*'.

A janitor stood nearby with a mop and bucket, sloshing the concrete floor with water. "Morning," he said.

"Good morning." Tarkos pressed his thumb on a black box next to the door.

After three clicks, he pushed the door open and stepped inside a pitch-black room. The door slammed shut and a locking mechanism whirred with an engaging clunk behind him.

A single, green laser beam pierced the darkness and scanned his entire body. When it finished, a glass panel in front of him flashed red.

Tarkos pressed his palm against the glass. When it turned green, an elevator door opened and he stepped inside. The panel had three buttons and he pressed the bottom one.

Another glance at his watch as he rode the elevator down.

9:51 am. Maybe they finished the meeting already.

The doors opened, and two armed guards dressed in black fatigues greeted him.

"Morning, Jackson," Tarkos said. He stepped into a millimeter-wave full-body X-ray scanner and raised his arms above his head.

"Good morning, Doctor Tarkos," Jackson replied.

As the machine scanned him, he stared ahead at a seal on the wall of two gold rings with thirteen stars arced above an American Bald Eagle flying over an olive branch. The eagle sat within a mathematical ket symbol that read National Quantum Coordination Office.

Damn NQCO. "Where's Sam?" Tarkos asked instead.

"His wife just had a baby," Jackson said, "so, he's on two weeks leave. We've got Miggs down here now."

Tarkos looked up and grinned. "Miggs."

"Good morning, sir!" Miggs stood at attention, holding his rifle, blocking the scanner's exit.

Tarkos smiled. "A baby, huh? Aren't you guys like twenty-one?"

Jackson laughed. "Well, you never know when your ride's up. I've got two myself already. You gotta knock 'em out while you can. Scan's clear."

Miggs stepped aside and let Tarkos exit.

Jackson turned in his chair. "Have a good day. If you need any help, give us a shout—she looks pretty serious."

"Who?" Tarkos raised his eyebrows. A woman hadn't been down here in ages.

"Have a nice day." Jackson pressed a button and a hallway door in front of Tarkos opened to the reverberating voices of a man and woman in a heated argument.

Tarkos tried to decipher the muffled banter but his footsteps obfuscated the words. One voice was his partner, Dr. Bruce Hon, a geologist who had been working with him for the past four years. But he couldn't place the woman.

Stepping into the open doorway of a dome-shaped dark room, he paused, staring at a woman standing over Bruce, her finger pointing all around the room.

Bruce caught sight of Tarkos and jumped out of his chair. "Andre, thank God you're here. Will you tell her the breakthrough we're about to have?" Today, Bruce wore a gray sport coat and beige pants. Nothing ever seemed to coordinate.

Tarkos leaned into his French accent. "Morning, Bruce. I don't think I've met our guest. You are?"

"Carmen Vasquez." She held her hand out but Tarkos walked past it and placed his bag on a desk.

Vasquez crossed her arms, scowling. In her gray pants, light-blue button up and a navy-blue blazer, she epitomized bureaucracy.

Tarkos glanced at a series of camera and monitors and sat in a swivel chair in front of a computer. He grabbed a pencil, placed it between his lips and typed into the keyboard.

Bright light cast a cold glow from an adjoining lab separated by a wall of thick plexiglass. Caution signs and spinning lights above the wall flicked a faint red glow across the room.

"Bruce, any deviation in amperage or kelvins?" Tarkos asked while he typed at a fervent pace.

"Not yet."

Vasquez stepped forward. "Dr. Tarkos, I was—"

"One moment, please." Tarkos kept typing, shielding the screen from the others.

"Change in moles or candelas?"

"None," Bruce replied.

"Okay." He tapped a few final, playful strokes. "That about does it." He slapped his index finger on the enter key. "There." Tarkos spun in his chair and faced Vasquez. "Now, Ms. Vasquez, what is it you wanted to discuss?"

"Let's cut the theatrics, gentlemen. Your Soulgazer program has failed."

Bruce glared as she spoke.

"General Davis has ordered a new team to take over next week in the interest of national security."

Tarkos leaned back in the chair and crossed his arms. "So, you're shutting us down?"

"No. Not shutting you down. You're being replaced."

"Replaced?"

"Yes."

Tarkos huffed and glanced at Bruce.

"This is exact bullshit I'm so pissed with," Bruce said.

Tarkos loved when Bruce faked anger and skipped words. It never came out quite right, but it threw people off. Maybe that was his tactic. Tarkos leaned forward and the chair creaked. "Ms. Vasquez, I don't think you or the general understand what we have down here."

"I know what we don't have," she said.

"And what's that?" Tarkos asked.

She smiled. "Someone who knows what they're doing." She uncrossed her arms and grabbed her leather briefcase.

Bruce threw his hands in the air. "Everything. They're taking all that we've worked so hard—"

Vasquez cut him off and waved two envelopes in the air. "The U.S. government owns all rights, title, and research that you have performed to date, and you are under top secret non-disclosure with penalties up to and including incarceration or other forms of punishment."

"Is that a threat?"

Bruce was right, this was bullshit and Tarkos didn't like it.

"We want this to be an amicable separation, gentlemen," she said. "You'll be paid one full year's salary on condition of a clean hand-off in two weeks. You'll also get a recommendation letter for the next employer of your choosing. I argued against it, but someone must like you." She tossed the envelopes on the desk and turned to leave. "Have a safe day."

Her leather shoes slapped against the hallway floor until echoing to silence.

Tarkos snapped the pencil.

Bruce picked up the envelope that held his name and slammed it on the desk. "It's bullshit. All that work for nothing. What are we going to do?"

Tarkos drew in a deep breath. "I just resigned. They can keep their fucking money. I'm leaving." He stood and grabbed his briefcase, dumping its contents onto the desk.

"Resigned? What? I can't do that. I need that money for my family." Bruce pointed to the photo of his wife and son on a youth soccer field.

Tarkos shook his head. "I just emailed my resignation."

Bruce sighed. "That's it? Just like that? All of this for nothing?"

"We're done, Bruce. You can stick around and close shop but I'm leaving. There's nothing else we can do. Not unless you want to commit suicide with two self-inflicted gunshots to the back of your head."

Bruce didn't respond.

Tarkos walked to the glass wall of the lab and peered into the opposing room. "The world will never know our secret."

Beyond the protective plexiglass wall, sat a large machine with a series of computers floating above a circular reflective table. It housed an interconnected array of optical fibers, mirrors, and sensors. Four robotic arms surrounded the machine, each equipped with hyper-sensitive metrological gauges. Interferometers bounced green lasers around the table, measuring micro displacements. Thin wand sensors perched in patterned alignment connected to a quantum seismometer to detect particle-level vibrations. The walls of the room formed an anechoic chamber with dampened acoustics to detect negative decibels in a vacuum of silence.

At center stage of this technological symphony rested a coaster-sized, gold-coated disc. Six inches above the disc, a one-and-a-half-inch diameter crystalline sphere hovered motionless in mid-air. Glossy, concave dimples adorned the center of each of its pentagon- and hexagon-shaped faces. A half-inch metallic orb floated inside the exact center of the sphere.

Tarkos had spent the past four years studying this thing. It shouldn't be here. On Earth.

The sphere floated in the middle of his blurry reflection, as if it had grown from within. Perhaps another legacy awaited him.

2

· FIRST VICTIM ·

Monday, September 9th, 2019

Stone Creek Sheriff Tom Meeks opened the door of his SUV and swung his legs out, pressing his boots into the marshy ground. He stood with minimal pressure on his left leg to avoid pain in his worn knee and peered at his team over a far embankment.

His Deputy, Sean Finn, stared at something on the ground next to the creek, obscured from Meeks' vantage. A female Medical Examiner in a baby-blue jumpsuit stood opposite and snapped photos.

Meeks grabbed his blue-corded, white-felt hat from the back seat and fit it to his head before trudging through brackish mud. Damn air was thick and humid from September's final hot day.

Crickets chirped a rhythmic drone of dread. Tall grasses grabbed at his legs, and wind blew the stench of bloated death in his face, catching in the back of his throat.

Human.

Every carcass he had seen—man or beast—gave off a unique aroma; always a familiar acidic musk, but never the same.

Meeks stepped up to the group and confirmed his suspicion. A pair of pale feet in open-toe leather sandals rose from a puddle of murky groundwater.

Finn stood over the body of a middle-aged man, and scribbled on a notepad. "Morning, Sheriff."

"Finn, morning. Sarah, Travers," Meeks rasped in a southern drawl.

The two Medical Examiners nodded. "Morning, Sheriff."

He scanned the body and shook his head. "Helluva way to start the week."

Sarah spoke through a white N95 mask strapped tight around her face and red hair. "Yeah, and it's Friday the thirteenth this week."

Travers handed Meeks a mask. "I suppose."

The scrape and burn in his knee stung when he knelt by the body, forcing a grimace to his face. "Joe Parks, right?"

Sarah held up a plastic bag that contained a driver's license. "Yes, sir. Joseph Alvin Parks of Deer View Lane."

Meeks gave a dejected sigh. "I knew him. Any idea what happened?"

"No visible signs of blunt force trauma," Sarah said. "No blood, no open wounds. Possible asphyxiation. Lots of empty beer cans. Someone else was here with him, fishing. Maybe an argument of some sort?" She held aloft a different bag with another ID inside and handed it to him. "We found a second wallet from an Arthur Duncan, home address in West Virginia."

Meeks donned his glasses and studied the expressionless face of Arthur Duncan on the license. His knee cracked when he stood and surveyed the fishing tackle sprawled at the edge of the creek. "Never heard of him." He handed the bag back to Sarah. "Finn, let's get an APB up to the State Police on Duncan."

"On it," Finn said.

Meeks rubbed the back of his neck. "Did we get any prints?"

Sarah penned notes on a chart attached to an aluminum clipboard. "Prints are everywhere. Travers took what he could. Based on decomposition, I'd estimate the body's been here at least a week. Wallet, cash, and cell phone are here, so not a robbery."

Finn put his pen in his shirt pocket and closed the notepad. "I'll secure a search warrant, check out his address, pull phone records, contact next of kin."

Meeks walked to the head of the body. "Joe didn't have any." He took a long look at the swollen face and frowned. Something wasn't right. "What's wrong with his eye?"

Sarah dangled the camera by her side. "What do you mean?"

"His left eye. Why's it black?"

She knelt and grabbed Joe's head with both hands. "I didn't get to that yet." She twisted it to the side and his neck creaked like a taut rope. Brown slime dripped out of his mouth.

Sarah used two fingers to pry the eyelid wider. "Subconjunctival hemorrhage."

"English."

"The blood vessels in his eyes burst and irrigated the white of his sclera. See?" Her finger moved from his eyelid and hovered over the eyeball.

"Okay, but why are they black? I've never seen that."

"Anemia can turn blood dark. It's almost always a chemical reaction from drugs."

"Heroin? Fentanyl?" Meeks asked.

"Not sure. I've never seen it this thick before. Maybe combined with necrosis..." She trailed off. "Travers, make a note we'll need toxicology." She separated the lids on the right eye and confirmed the same gloss-black color.

Meeks dropped his chin to his chest. "Joe had issues, but I never pegged him as a junkie." He lowered his mask and surveyed the creek bank butted against the edge of the forest. A warm breeze flowed up from the hills and held four vultures in an updraft overhead. A fifth descended to a scraggly ash tree to join three others, keeping overwatch of the carrion at his feet. He glanced at Joe's body. "Why haven't the animals touched him?"

"We were talking about that before you arrived," Sarah said. "No idea. Maybe something inside spooked them. The lab will give us a clue."

"Well, it's damn peculiar if you ask me."

Finn nodded. "Yessir, it is."

"Who found him?"

"Myers boys," Finn said. "They skipped school to go hiking, found the body, and called their parents. Said they didn't see anyone else."

Meeks swatted at a fly. "Sarah, that guy you brought in from up on Black Wolf, when was that?"

"Week and a half. Why?" She leaned over Joe's body and snapped a close-up photo of his face.

"His eyes, same thing?"

"No, that was a heart attack."

"Hmm. Okay. Move him when you're ready and bag all this evidence." He waved his hand over the crime scene. "Get me those labs. The last thing we need is another surge in overdoses right before the holidays."

Finn's cell phone rang, and he stepped away to answer it. "This is Finn. Yeah, he's here." He turned to Meeks and their eyes locked. "Okay, we're on our way." He ended the call. "Someone reported another body at Whipple Farm. Carter said Channel Three is already there."

"Damn. Tell her to keep the media out, and Finn, see who we can get down here from the State. This may get worse." Meeks glared at the vultures. "Friday the thirteenth, huh?"

Sunlight poked Jack's skin and he squinted at the broken clouds that scattered sporadic shadows across Woodlawn Cemetery. Light and dark, except for splashes of faded color from dying flowers near gray and mottled headstones. A cool, northerly breeze chilled his skin.

The funeral director, who functioned as a minister, stood in a cream suit and prattled on in monotone about his father and the infinite loop of nature; the cycle of life and death.

"The great tension between them is our existence. A precious wonder during both times of joy and moments of sorrow. The creator gave us the life of William Young, who brought Jack and Roger into this world, and he served them well. He would not want us to stand here and weep; rather, celebrate his existence, and cheer for our future. We now give William back to Mother Earth to be reunited with his beloved Elisabeth, together as one in the dust of eternity."

As if the man ever knew him. Jack wondered if this guy would be saying the same things had he deciphered the confused inner workings of a crazy man.

All the time spent tracking down paperwork, shipping his body, getting authorization, funeral planning. Even in death, an endless list of clean-up tasks just to lay his father to rest. Jack couldn't look at the picture of Bill smiling. That was a long time ago, and now, a cloud of chaos still loomed over Jack.

He nodded to his brother, who stood holding his wife's hand as his two boys fidgeted in dark suits by his side.

Their father's sister, Rose, stood next to Jack, using a white silk cloth to dab tears flowing through her thick makeup.

He glanced at a framed picture of his mother leaning up against his father, one of the few photos of them together he could even find. Bill hugged her tight while they both grinned back, with a camera flash sparkle in their eyes.

"Stop," Jack's eldest nephew, Lucas, cried out to his younger brother Nate. Roger put a big hand on Nate's shoulder and squeezed until he stood motionless.

The minister closed his book and bowed his head in silent prayer.

Roger shook his head. "As screwed-up as he was, I'm gonna miss him."

"Yeah," Jack said, stiffening at Roger's words. What else could he say? Good riddance? Maybe. More like relief from the burden.

He endured a hug from Roger's wife and offered a tissue to wipe her streaked face.

"I'm so sorry, Jack," she said. "If you need anything..."

What could anyone do for him? But he smiled and nodded. "Thanks, Laura."

The two boys laughed while playing a raucous hand-slapping game.

Now, to chat with Aunt Rose and her slippery silk handkerchief. She held a black and white picture of her and Bill as teenagers in one hand and hugged Roger while keeping her red-rimmed eyes focused on Jack.

She sighed at a portrait of Bill next to the urn. "That was a nice ceremony, Jack. Thank you. It's the way he would have wanted it, to be with your mother."

"I'm sorry, Aunt Rose," Jack said. He patted her on the back with light, awkward taps.

"Your father, bless his soul," Aunt Rose prattled, her jowls glistening with sweat in the heat, "was a very troubled man." She snuck a furtive glance at the urn and made the sign of the cross. "At least now he's at peace."

"Let's hope so." Jack followed the path of a blue-dasher dragonfly that glittered in a ray of sunlight behind Aunt Rose's head.

Red lipstick tracked vertical cracks in her lips. "Jack, when are you going to settle down?"

"Jack will be fine, Aunt Rose," Roger said, his blank face not fooling anyone. "We should get going."

Jack understood the reason for butting in, though, and tried to let the stiffness out of his neck.

Her red lips stretched into a smile. "That's good. You always were so smart. And the ladies?"

"Haven't met the right one yet."

"That's okay. Someday."

Lucas called out, "Mommy, I'm hungry."

Roger ushered Rose to his car. "Why don't you take Peter to the car, and we'll grab lunch."

"Yes, that would be nice. Maybe a martini too," she said.

"Laura, can you pack everyone up please? I need to chat with Jack."

"Take care, Jack." Aunt Rose hugged him. "Thank you again for such a nice ceremony."

"Goodbye, Aunt Rose. You behave now." Jack dared not let go until she wriggled away.

"I always do. Be sure you come up and visit me."

"Sure thing."

Rose hobbled away to the car.

"Listen." Roger grabbed Jack by the upper arm and guided him under the shade of an oak tree. "I really appreciate you handling all this. We've just had...well, kids, you know?"

"I know." Jack gave the same response he always did. He didn't blame Roger, couldn't blame anyone. Nobody wanted to deal with Bill, not even the doctors.

Beads of sweat dotted Roger's forehead. "So, the lawyer said he finished reviewing all of Dad's finances. There wasn't much left other than the cabin. He said they'd finalize numbers on Monday and can cut a check minus fees by the end of next week."

"Okay, that's fine."

"The only thing we need to figure out is—"

"The cabin."

"Yeah. He figures a grand an acre, maybe more from a timber company. Five or six hundred thousand, maybe."

Laura called from the car window. "Roger, can you turn on the A/C, it's getting hot in here."

"Okay, be right there."

The funeral director approached carrying a cigar box and handed it to Roger. "These are the personal effects we removed from your father. We'll wrap up here and be in touch next week. Again, we are so sorry for your loss."

"Thank you," Jack said.

Roger opened the cigar box, examined the contents then shut the lid and handed it to Jack. "I know it's still fresh but the sooner we sell it the better. That money could go a long way for us."

"I know Rog. We'll figure it out." He loved his brother but yet again, Jack would be the one cleaning up his dad's mess.

"Listen, I'm just glad he's in a better place now, you know? It's been tough the past few years and I know you didn't—"

"Let's— It just needs to be over." He looked down and took a deep breath.

"He was in a dark place at the end," Roger said. "You know he didn't mean all those things he said."

"I'm fine with it."

Nate cried out from the car. "Daddy, Aunt Rose is melting."

"I'm coming, son."

Jack smiled. "I'll take care of the cabin."

"You sure?"

"Yeah."

"Laura and the kids, we can come up and help but not for a couple of weeks."

Jack shook his head. It'd be better without them. "Nah, I need a break. I'll call you once I know how it looks."

"Dadddddy."

Jack half-laughed. "Get out of here."

"Okay."

"I'm coming, I'm coming." They hugged and Roger shuffled away. Both of his boys screamed in unison. "About time."

Jack watched his brother leave; watched long after he was gone.

What's in the cigar box? Jack lifted the lid and peered inside.

A gold wedding band, a silver bracelet, and a pair of Army dog tags. He shuffled them around and found a red key that hung on a ball-chain under the other items.

The chains on Demi's shackles coiled to the ground like a loud, clinking snake. An armed officer led him through the last barred door of the main prison hall and into a corridor. He leaned heavily on the cheap plastic cane, limping with each step.

A buzzer sounded, and the officer ushered Demi through the final door. The blue, fluorescent light of the locked hallway turned into a warmer glow of sunlight through barred windows.

A female clerk behind a plexiglass window shuffled paper. "Damien Carver?"

"The one and only," he replied.

"Let me get your possessions."

Demi's voice quivered. "Thank you. Eh, please be careful with them."

The woman shot him a short smirk and rolled her eyes. "Yeah."

Twinges of pain shot up from his thigh. At his age, the limp would be permanent so a new cane would be in order. A proper one.

A plastic bag and metal box slapped down on the counter beneath the window. The clerk slid it towards him and pushed a pen across the paper. "Sign here."

Demi ignored her, pulled a black sport coat from the bag, and put it on. With an anxious breath, he flipped open the metal box, removed his wallet and three rings, which he placed on the fingers of his left hand.

The rest of the box appeared empty. A moment of anxiety filled him. Could it be missing?

He angled the box up and a crystalline sphere rolled down, bathing Demi in relief. He snatched the sphere and placed it in his right coat pocket with a cautious eye on the clerk.

The clerk struck a louder tone. "Sign here."

Demi complied and the clerk stamped the paper.

She pointed away from him. "Exit to the left and out the main gate when the officers open it. You're a free man now. I don't want to see you back here, you hear me?"

He grabbed a black hat from the bag and tipped it on his head. "Thank you, my dear."

Demi stepped through the door and into the sunshine.

Officer Cook stood waiting. "Came to say goodbye, Carver."

Demi ignored him and continued on to the front gate.

Cook followed behind. "I hope we taught you some lessons while you were here. Be a good citizen and all. But knowing how fucked in the head you are, I'm sure we'll be seeing you back here real soon."

Demi kept limping to the gate. "I don't think so."

"Tony, open the gate," Cook said.

The barbed-wire gate screeched and clanked as it slid open.

Cook scoffed. "You know what? I've changed my mind. I give you a month until you're pushing up daisies. Just another washed-up old junkie still living in the past. Can't stay off the heroin."

Demi stopped and turned with a smile. "I don't need heroin, but thank you, Officer Cook. I'll miss our little moments together. It's not often I get to interact with primates."

Cook smiled up at Demi. "Now's your chance, free man. Take your payback shot."

Demi stared at Cook.

"Do it!" Cook snapped under his breath.

"Not today." Demi turned and walked out of the gate. "But I do suggest you start treating our friend Mr. Rivera with a little more respect."

A run-down black 1962 Lincoln Continental waited at the prison gate. The rear suicide door opened and a man in a black suit wearing sunglasses climbed out of the car.

"Takashi, how are you?" Demi asked.

Takashi nodded back in silence.

Edgar and his twin brother Miles sat in the front seats. Edgar poked his head out of the driver's window while Takashi helped Demi into the car.

"How's it feel to be a free man?" Edgar asked.

"Very good, Edgar, but the three months were fleeting."

"Yeah, that's right. I remember my first stint. Went by fast. The second one? Not so much."

"But you ain't ever going back," Miles said.

"You know it," Edgar said, and chomped down on his bubble gum with an open-mouthed grin.

Demi struck a somber tone. "But we have bigger things to set our sights on and we don't have much time. Is everything prepared?"

"Yes sir. Friday the thirteenth!"

Takashi got into the rear passenger seat and closed the door.

"Good," Demi said. "When they arrive, we need everyone at the temple and ready to go." He looked out the window at Cook and waved as the prison gate shut. "See you soon," he whispered.

Back in his cell, Alex Rivera sat motionless on the lower bunk.

He stared in silence at a sketch on the wall.

A sketch of Demi's tattoo.

• GRAND UNIFICATION •

3

Tarkos leaned his foot against a large rock atop the southern cliff edge of Raven Gap Quarry just west of Stone Creek. Heat radiated through his shoe.

Deep shadows sliced across the quarry's striated walls and lulled his eyes out of focus. He rolled his tongue against the corner of his lower lip.

This quarry was where it all began, where they found the sphere. Buried deep in the bedrock. From there it was whisked away to a top-secret agency, and into the hands of scientists. His hands.

The workers who discovered it died of stomach cancer. Or so the agency said. They classified the sphere as *unknown origin*. A matter of national security, they said.

Tarkos had even named it Project Soulgazer, but the world would never know his work.

A round, white stone glinted in the sunlight, and he picked it up.

He threw the stone as hard as he could toward the far side, expelling a loud grunt that echoed through the quarry.

Gravity pulled it down in silence, in freefall, until it hit the water far below.

Tarkos exhaled a calm breath. Now he stood alone.

Past the quarry, through winding forest roads, Stone Creek Manor rested atop a rocky outcrop overlooking a wide section of creek bed.

Tarkos drove his silver Audi sedan into the circular driveway and over a single-lane bridge that joined two sections of rock wall.

Small rapids splashed miniature white caps that rippled past the hotel. He stepped out of his car and the wind shifted, drifting an odor of livestock and chicken coops that stung his nose. A pungent but comforting smell of farm country. He had stayed here twice before with his ex-wife. Maybe he'd enjoy it more this time.

Grabbing his suitcase and laptop bag, he headed into the hotel. An elderly man sat on a bench in the lobby and stared at Tarkos.

"Good afternoon." The old man's voice stretched with a guttural, southern drawl.

"Hello," Tarkos replied, and stepped up to a dark-oak front desk where a young woman greeted him with a smile.

"Good afternoon. Welcome to Stone Creek Manor, are you checking in?"

"Yes. Andre Tarkos."

"Yes, sir, Mr. Tarkos, let me pull up your reservation." She scanned a computer screen below the countertop. "Here we go. We have you staying for five nights with us, is that correct?"

"Yes."

"Very good. And you'll be in our king suite facing Black Wolf Mountain. I just need a credit card and driver's license please."

He handed them over and glanced back at the old man whose head hung low, fingers crossed against his chest.

The receptionist's voice pulled his attention back. "Here you go. And here is your room key, the elevator is just down this hall to the left."

"Thank you." He tucked his wallet into his coat pocket. "And the restaurant is open at what time?"

"Six o'clock."

"Okay, great. Thank you."

"My pleasure. We hope you enjoy your stay, let us know if you need anything."

With a nod and smile, he gathered his bags and made for his room.

The taut bedspread rippled under the impact of his luggage and he threw open the blinds to a wooden balcony. The glass door slid open and he leaned against the railing high above the creek. The dark silhouette of Black Wolf Mountain stood stark against streaks of raspberry hues accented with ribbons of pink and blue rolling clouds. Tarkos soaked in the moment and drew in a breath. The farm smell had disappeared, or he had adjusted to it, either way, he savored the breeze.

He turned back toward the glass door and rested his elbows on the rail, casting a long, dead stare at the laptop bag.

His attention broke when the lamp on the desk inside the room flickered. It strobed an instantaneous prism-like flash in the glass door that blended with the peak of Black Wolf, then disappeared. He glanced back at the mountain and furled his brow.

The time had come to share his secret with the world. Consequences be damned.

On the far side of Black Wolf Mountain, Jack drove his black Toyota 4Runner along the hidden gravel trail, ignoring the large 'No Trespassing, Authorized Personnel Only' sign overgrown with creeper vines.

At only five in the afternoon, this side of the mountain had already cast an early darkness for the crickets to sing.

Driving through the open pipe gate, Jack let out a wry chuckle, and wondered how many people ignored the sign. How many had his dad chased off the mountain?

The headlights pierced the pitch black of the forest, lighting his way up the rough road. Thick vegetation scratched up against his 4Runner, and divots in the road bounced him around.

The trail to the cabin was just under one mile up the side of the mountain.

The 4Runner hit another rut that jolted the front end. His cell phone flipped off the dash, smashing against the shifter with a loud crack before tumbling into the passenger footwell.

"Shit." Jack pumped the brakes and shifted into park.

When he picked up the phone, he cursed at the sight of the shattered screen. Though it lit up, webbed cracks obfuscated everything. He banged his hand on the steering wheel and glared out the window at the dark woods.

With a deep breath, he shifted back into drive, and proceeded on the overgrown path up the mountain.

Near the end of the trail, it opened to a large clearing shrouded in a veil of pitch black.

He looped around the final bend and the headlights cast a wide beam of light upon the cabin.

Pulling to a stop, he looked through the windshield. Even though the headlights illuminated the outside of the cabin, the inside seemed even darker. The moon had risen and cast a bluish glow behind a sea of dark clouds.

Stepping out of the 4Runner, he walked through the swath of light, his long shadow stretching against the side of the cabin. It reminded him of an old horror movie he watched as a kid. Not that Jack believed in ghosts or monsters for that matter.

Up on the front porch, he fumbled with a flashlight and flipped through a set of keys, trying several before he found the right one. He reached inside and flicked the light switch.

Nothing. He flicked it again.

Jack shined the flashlight down the front entrance into the living room. Light sliced through the darkness as whirls of dust particles sparkled in its beam.

He returned to his vehicle, backing it up to a shed about fifty yards away. Inside, the flashlight illuminated dull chainsaws, rusted axes, and shovels with split handles. He navigated a hoarder's path of gasoline cans, propane tanks, and boxes filled with spare small engine parts. He bumped into a bench, nudging a bucket off that crashed, spilling metal parts that clanked across the floor.

"Dammit."

At the far end of the shed sat a homemade solar-power inverter with a battery storage array. He flipped on the master power switch and light flooded the property.

When he stepped out of the shed, the cabin had come to life—a warm beacon in a sea of darkness, and he paused to soak it in.

The cabin had two floors along with a basement, and sat on hundreds of acres of land. Although near the top of Black Wolf Mountain, it rested on a large plateau overlooking the valley.

The mature trees that surrounded it hid most of the view in the summer but in late fall, the view was spectacular. A wooden-post fence framed a trail leading from the rear of the cabin up an inclined slope to a red-gabled barn. A single light glowed above its large, double-door opening.

It couldn't be any more remote and isolated, which was the way his father had wanted it. Jack wished he'd been back sooner, but they had passed the point of no return years ago.

He latched the shed door and turned the light into an open slant roof carport attached to the shed. A brown tarp fluttered in the breeze and he pulled it back to reveal a seventies-era Triumph motorcycle. His father had taught him how to ride this bike. As beat up as it was, it held a lot of memories.

When he aimed the light at a puddle of oil beneath the Triumph, a loud growling broke through the chorus of insects, shooting the hairs on the back of his neck straight up.

Jerking the flashlight to his left, he scanned the dark edge of the forest, trying to focus through the thick, nocturnal chorus of bugs in the direction of the sound.

Stepping back towards to the 4Runner, he opened the passenger door and retrieved a 9mm H&K handgun from the center console. With a quick rack of the slide, he held it low and ready, and cast the flashlight into the trees again.

The growl snarled just behind him and he jumped back, spinning around with the gun raised.

"Jesus Christ!" His voice echoed through the forest.

A ragged dog stood before him. One he knew.

His finger tensed but didn't pull the trigger.

With a whimper, the dog licked his lips and laid down at Jack's feet.

"Newt."

Kneeling to pet the dog's head, Jack wondered how the old boy could still be alive. He thought Newt had died years ago. Aunt Rose had given his dad a Belgian Malinois puppy in the late nineties who he'd named after Sir Isaac Newton. The crazy stories this dog must have heard from his old man. But that was Newt, loyal to the end.

Newt whimpered under Jack's touch.

"How the hell are you still alive? Huh, boy? Come on let's get you some food."

Jumping up, Newt followed Jack as he grabbed his bags and returned to the cabin.

Edgar turned the Continental onto a dirt road that led up and over a small hill. They passed through a wooden arch gated on both sides by a weathered buck-and-rail fence. A sign above the arch read, *Temple of New Hope Welcomes You*, in white paint above the same black symbol of circles tattooed on Demi's wrist.

"I bet it feels good to see that," Miles asked.

"Yes," Demi replied.

They drove past a non-descript wooden shed and rumbled by several small barns. Men and women walked out of the buildings and followed alongside the car.

They reached a two-door gate and two men armed with hunting rifles, opened it. The car drove through and stopped in front of a Victorian farmhouse.

Situated at the center of the large farm, the white building called back to an historic era with tall windows, gingerbread-trimmed eaves, and a wraparound porch. Scalloped roof shingles had warped and splintered from a century of storms but it stood as a survivor, a long companion to Demi and the generations of Carvers before him.

In the courtyard, a group of fifty people had gathered. Takashi exited the car and opened Demi's door.

When he stepped out, the crowd erupted in applause. Leaning on his cane, Demi scanned the crowd and gave them a gentle nod.

He raised his voice, "Friends, I have missed you all a great deal and I am warmed by your welcome home. I am eager to share some exciting news with you. Let's meet in thirty minutes in the temple. Prepare yourselves. Something wonderful is about to happen."

The applause increased, woven through with whispers of wonder before they meandered away from the farmhouse. When Demi had inherited the home, his father passed on the secret of the sphere, as his father did before him. And from the sphere grew the temple.

He stared beyond the crowd at a large barn that dwarfed the farmhouse. This building—the temple itself—had commanded all resources and towered over the farm with an immaculate glow.

Designed to bring people together from diverse walks of life who believed in something more. Something special that only the sphere could bring, but what?

As the sphere consumed him, so did the temple.

Two women wearing plain burgundy dresses walked up to Demi and he turned to greet them. They bowed their heads in unison, "Welcome home." The brunette, handed Demi a black, wooden walking cane with a sterling-silver handle. "A gift for you, sir."

Demi smiled and tossed the old cane away, admiring the new one in both hands. "Ahh, majestic." He squeezed the silver handle, pressed the tip into the ground as he leaned on it. "It's good to be home, ladies. Elena, Lyssa, how have you been?"

"Good," they replied. The blonde, Lyssa, opened a rosewood box lined with purple velvet fabric. Demi reached into his pocket and placed the sphere inside.

Lyssa's eyes seemed to widen and he took note of the expression.

"Lyssa, is something wrong?"

She glanced away. "No, sir. I'm just tired."

"Then let's have Elena put this away and you go get some rest."

Lyssa darted her eyes up to Demi. "No, sir. It's fine. I can do it."

Demi pursed his lips, taking a deep breath through his nose. "Very well. Take the sphere to the temple and wait with the others."

"Yes, sir."

The women turned and headed up the inclined path to the temple.

He looked at Takashi and flicked the cane up. "Bring him to me."

4

· THE NECKLACE ·

Moe Harper scooped marinara spaghetti onto a plate in the kitchen of his double-wide mobile home on the south side of Stone Creek. The dim light of a neon sign outside flickered through a cracked, dusty pane of glass in the front windows. Moe's Salvage Yard.

His Doberman, Zeus, ate the last of his dried mini-chunk dinner. The thick chain around the dog's neck clinked the side of a stainless-steel bowl with each bite it took.

Moe grabbed his plate and a DVD remote, pressing the greasy play button. The opening credits to *Magnum P.I.* blasted through a mono speaker and filled the trailer with a flashing glow.

Bobbing his head to the electric guitar music, he entered the living room and settled into a worn sofa chair. His finger punched the air with each musical crescendo stinger timed with scenes of guns, explosions, and kissing.

He shoved a fork of pasta into a slice of garlic bread, and Moe's eyes widened when Magnum's red Ferrari 308 GTS streaked across the screen. There couldn't be a more perfect dream car, and he'd wanted one ever since he was a kid.

Zeus stretched and dropped to the floor, his heavy collar hitting the linoleum tile with a thud.

At the start of the show, Moe quoted along with Higgins, whose bickering at Magnum culminated in a snarky, pretentious barb.

When the punchline landed, Moe laughed, sauce dripping from his lips. "I love you, Higgins." His thick southern twang let out a chuckle.

He sipped his beer and wiped his face with an oversized napkin.

Zeus perked his ears up, let out a low growl, and stood with his head angled at the front door.

"Easy, boy." Moe flapped his hand toward Zeus with a dismissive wave.

The growl intensified, and Zeus bared his fangs, lifting stiff legs in a guarded stride toward the door.

"I just let you out." Moe flicked his head at Zeus, then back at the television, smiling and quoting again. "Magnum, you are clad only in your undershorts—"

A shrill series of barks from Zeus pierced through the room.

"Goddammit, Zeus!" Moe pressed the pause button, and the room fell silent. He pushed the tray table out of his way and wriggled to stand, throwing his napkin on the chair.

Limping to the chained door, he peered out the window and flicked a light switch. A bright spotlight illuminated the empty front lot. Moe scanned the yard.

A guttural growl from Zeus startled him.

"I don't see anything. You smell a fox?"

Moe snatched a Detroit Tigers hat hung on the wall, and when the door creaked open, Zeus bolted through and sprinted toward the junkyard.

"Zeus!" Moe grabbed a flashlight and pulled open a drawer for his revolver. Whatever the noise—a fox, rabbit, or thief—he'd be ready.

Stepping outside, he caught sight of Zeus darting up one of the dark paths of stacked vehicles.

"Damn dog." Moe shook his head. The flashlight lit up the ground, and Moe pointed it in the direction of Zeus' disappearance. Easy to tell which one, with all the crazy barking and growling echoing off the graveyard of steel vehicles.

Zeus' bark escalated with ravaging growls that echoed behind the cars.

"What the hell?" Moe stopped in his tracks when a blue light shot up from behind the vehicles, flaring into the sky.

With a cautious step, he drew closer, but the barking stopped, and Zeus let out a loud yelp.

"Hey boy, what's wrong?" His stride quickened. *That's no rabbit.* The flashlight shook with his frenetic pace.

Rounding the corner of stacked cars, he froze at the sight of blood.

Zeus staggered to him, whimpering. A gush of blood hit the dirt, and Zeus collapsed, one leg caught under his chest.

Metal clanged ahead of Moe, and he traced the blood trail with his light. It settled on the silhouette of a man standing with his back to Moe.

The stranger stood in front of a car's engine bay that cast a blue light, rippling shadows across the wall of junked vehicles.

Moe pointed the revolver at him. "What did you do to my dog?"

The man didn't move.

"Hey, I'm talking to you! Turn around!"

With a slow turn of his head, the man glared back at Moe.

Just behind the man, a blue orb of plasma spun in a rhythmic pattern over the car. Bursts of energy spliced pieces of rusted metal onto an oval-shaped, football-sized drone that hovered in the air.

The man stepped forward, the light catching his face. A deep scar ran from above his right eye down his cheek. His eyes flashed with a red glow.

"What the...?" Moe trained the gun on the man, who took a step forward. "Don't come any closer!"

The blue plasma orb stopped spinning, turning into a bright, white light that blinded Moe. An arc of electricity shot from the orb to the rusty drone, and a magnetized chunk of metal attached to the top of its body like a striped Mohawk.

The orb went dark, and the striped drone turned in Moe's direction. A red light glowed on its front face.

"Screw this." Moe turned to leave but a second silver drone hovered in front of his face.

An amalgamation of scrap car parts, its yellow lights cast a menacing light that threw Moe off balance.

A metallic dart fired from a hole in its chassis, stabbing into his neck and delivering a high-voltage charge that had Moe's limbs twitching into shock. His fingers contracted, forcing the gun to fire into the dirt. The Detroit Tigers hat flipped off his head. The pain masked his fear.

His body tensed and he fell back, crashing to the ground in a plume of dust and dander. He peered through half-closed eyes as the drone floated above him.

The man approached Moe and straddled his chest. He retrieved a small square device from his pocket that had a series of rusty gears and greased levers encasing a shiny silver body. When the man pressed a button on its side, clicks and beeps preceded the appearance of a long, thin, glass needle tethered to a translucent wire.

The man pricked the needle into the skin behind Moe's lower left ear, and it glided up into his head like a sword in a sheath. A stab of pain fired on the left side of his brain, and the device's gears started to spin and whir.

Waves of energy pulsed inside his brain, and Moe's eyes rolled back into his head. A torrent of memories streamed across his mind. Images of people he'd long forgotten. Places he'd been to as a kid. Secrets and promises he kept and broke. His entire life flashed as if he had experienced it all over again.

A light glowed across the man's face and his eyes flashed blue.

The pulses stopped and the man removed the needle.

Moe exhaled with a trance-like moan.

As the man stood and stepped away, the striped drone flew in by his side.

A panel on the drone opened, and a sharp metal blade emerged. Glints of light reflected from the blade like a laser pen into Moe's eyes.

The twang of the drone's metal blade hovered over him.

Moe's heart pounded, a relentless and confusing terror that coursed through him. "Higgins," he mumbled.

The drone accelerated down at his neck in a single, cold slice that thrust Moe into a void of darkness.

Hot steam from the shower laid a blanket of condensation on the mirror over the sink. The reflection blurred Tarkos' naked body into a phantasmic specter of refracting water droplets streaking down his face like crystal blood.

The swivel-mounted mirror behind him echoed the main mirror, reflecting his eye into an illusion of fogginess. He swiped a cloth over both mirrors and positioned himself in their infinite loop, none of which hid the cold, hard-blue of his gaze.

Would the world even care when he exposed their secret? Probably not. Maybe he'd fuel conspiracies among fringe Area 51 fanatics, but it wouldn't leave a mark.

Cleaned and dressed in a steel-gray sports coat, he headed down to the hotel restaurant. Three stools lined the short side of the bar, where a white-haired man dressed in black sat in the middle.

Tarkos pulled the left stool next to him and sat. He waved at the female bartender who nodded back. His stomach growled and he scanned the bottles of liquor sat in front of a mirrored wall behind the bar. When he passed over a bottle of Bombay Sapphire Gin, the white-haired man's eyes caught his.

The square from a white band poked out from under the man's collar.

"Good evening, Father," Tarkos said.

The man looked up at Tarkos with a huff. "Reverend."

"Excuse me?" The response caught Tarkos off guard.

"Most folks around here call me Reverend, but my name is Harrison Fletcher. You must not be from around here."

"Well, no, not really. Just a tourist, a few times."

"Hmm." Fletcher took a sip from a brown beer bottle.

Tarkos glanced at the drink menu and up at the bartender, who leaned onto the bar and smiled. Her brunette hair dangled over a gold name tag tucked into the folds of a low-cut black top. *Teresa*.

"Evening, hun. What can I get ya?" she asked.

"Do you have a wine list?"

She handed it to Tarkos and he gave it a quick study. "A bottle of Cabernet Sauvignon, please."

"A whole bottle?"

"Yes, please." He wanted—no, needed—to drown in alcohol tonight.

"Coming right up."

Fletcher tilted his beer and picked its label with his thumb.

"I didn't know members of the clergy could drink?" Tarkos asked.

"Wha...?" Fletcher's eyes widened and he bellowed. "Would you look at that? I thought I ordered a bottle of water. Tess! Didn't I order a water?"

Tess glanced back and nodded. "The lord works in mysterious ways, Reverend."

"He sure does. Or she, for that matter." He smiled and tipped the bottle with a toast. "Can I ask what draws a tourist back to Stone Creek, Mr...eh..." Fletcher winced, obviously trying to remember.

"Tarkos. Andre Tarkos."

Tess placed the bottle of wine and a single glass in front of Tarkos. He held it up and examined it for stains.

"It's clean," she said, frowning before she turned away to help a man at the other end of the bar.

Tarkos smiled. "Sorry, old habit." He poured the wine and its crimson, high-tannin legs trickled down the sides of the glass. "So, you asked what's brought me back to Stone Creek? I'm looking for something."

Fletcher tilted his head, and his speech slurred. "And what could you possibly be looking for here?"

Tarkos sniffed deep of the wine in the glass and savored the fragrance of a smoked pepper bouquet. If they only knew the things he'd seen. "The truth." He tipped the glass and sugars from the wine flooded over the tip of his tongue. Bitter flavors of smoked currant drizzled over its back and sides, dancing across its taste buds.

"The truth?" Fletcher shifted in his chair and straightened his back, letting out a frail, raspy cackle. "Haha, my boy." He raised his beer bottle for another toast. "Here's to the truth. And when you find this truth, it shall set you free!"

They clinked drinks and sipped.

Tarkos swallowed. "John, chapter eight, verse thirty-two."

"Ah, so, a student of the gospel as well," Fletcher said.

Tarkos laughed. "I grew up in a Catholic school in France. And I'm sorry to tell you, but I fell away from the church a long time ago. Old memories die hard, I suppose."

Fletcher cleared his throat, and his smile disappeared. "Notre-Dame de Paris." He rubbed the lip of his beer bottle with his thumb. "My wife always wanted to go there."

Tarkos cracked a smile. "And I didn't know Reverends could marry."

Fletcher didn't respond.

"You should take her someday, it's still a beautiful city."

Fletcher's thumb stopped. "She's passed. And I'm too old."

Tarkos winced. "I'm sorry, I didn't mean to—"

"That was a long time ago. Maybe I should have taken her. There never seemed to be enough time or money for that matter." Fletcher leaned into Tarkos and smiled as inebriated folds of aged skin creased across his face. "And to answer your question, I wasn't always a Reverend." He gave Tarkos a wink.

Tarkos set his glass down, careful not to disturb a bible bound in a cracked black leatherette cover resting on the bar. A silver chain poked from between its pages and draped into a puddle of condensation from the beer bottle. "Well, to be honest, I don't have fond memories of my school being run by puritanical French Orthodox nuns. It was, let's say, quite strict, and I never fit in. I guess I asked too many questions, and the sisters didn't like that."

"And now you're all grown up, far from the beaches of France, still asking questions."

"Right."

"Well, it's getting late and I've got confession in the morning," Fletcher said. He downed the last of his beer, rose from the stool, and fumbled to put on his coat.

Tarkos turned in his seat to face the man. "For what it's worth, from a science perspective, your wife is still with you. Her matter, her energy, that is. So even though she's gone, she's still here."

Fletcher locked a sullen stare on Tarkos while buttoning his coat. "I would very much like to believe that. It was nice talking with you, Mr. Tarkish."

"Tarkos."

"Tarkos. Yes, excuse me."

Tarkos smiled and stood. "Let me pay for your tab."

"That won't be necessary."

"I insist."

Fletcher swayed. "Well, thank you, my good Frenchman." He gathered his Bible and held up his finger, circling it in the air. "And he shall repay him for his good deed."

"Proverbs... ehh, nineteen-seven?"

"Close enough. Seems you must have been paying attention to those pure French nuns after all. Good night."

Tarkos smiled and swallowed the rest of his wine.

Laughter from a young boy echoed across the restaurant and startled both of them. A cold flush fell over Fletcher's face when he glanced at the boy and froze.

Tarkos looked at the boy, then tracked Fletcher who turned and shuffled away, disappearing through the restaurant doors.

"Put his drinks on my tab," Tarkos said to Tess.

"Oh, the owner doesn't charge him anymore."

"Why's that?"

"He was just diagnosed with cancer. The Reverend's had a pretty rough life, so she helps him out where she can, occasional meals and a drink or two."

Tarkos looked back at the empty entrance of the bar. "That's too bad." He took a final gulp of his wine.

Tess draped a white towel over her shoulder. "How long are you in town?"

"Just the week."

"Family vacation?"

A smile shot across his face. "No. No family. No work."

"Well, we don't get many Frenchmen in here, so maybe I'll see you tomorrow?"

"Are you making a pass at me, Miss Teresa?"

"That depends," she said. "Would it be good or bad?"

"There's no such thing."

Tess's white teeth cut through a broad smile and she bit the tip of her thumb. "You're getting far too deep for me."

A warm rush of blood throbbed up his neck and he paused. He didn't need a distraction, but here she stood. "I can go deeper," he beamed.

They both chuckled and looked away from each other.

He dragged his hand through his hair. "But I'm afraid I would be bad company tonight. Tomorrow maybe?"

She rubbed the towel on the bar and looked up at him. "Yeah, I'm off tomorrow."

"Well then, I'd be delighted to meet up. How do I reach you?"

Tess threw the towel in the sink, grabbed a pen and jotted her number on a hotel business card. She flipped it up in her fingers and held it out to him.

When he took it from her hand, her index finger rubbed along his knuckle. The warmth of the wine kicked in and blood rushed to all the right places. "I look forward to calling."

"I look forward to answering."

He leaned back in the stool and ran his hands through his hair. "What do I owe for tonight?"

Tess smiled and rang up his tab. "By the way, I think it was real nice of you talking to the Reverend like that. Most people don't talk to him anymore."

He scribbled his signature across the bill.

A sparkle reflected up from the floor and caught his attention. He reached down and picked up the necklace that had been resting in the bible. A silver pendant about two inches long sat looped on the chain. It weighed almost nothing as he ran his thumb over a series of striated grooves on both sides of the pendant. Its polished metal surface reflected light up into his face.

"Looks like the Reverend dropped his necklace."

"Huh." Tess glanced at it, leaning across the bar. "I can give it to him next time he's here."

"Where's his church?"

"About a mile west of here."

"Okay, I'll take it to him in the morning."

"I'm sure he'd like that."

Tarkos tucked the necklace in his coat pocket. "Good night, Tess."

"Good night, Andre. Dream well."

5

· IMPONDERABLE OCEAN ·

Newt savored the last morsels of dried dog food from his red dish. A glaze of saliva and crumbs coated its plastic bottom, and he lowered his head to lick it clean. His tongue curled and lapped water from a stainless-steel bowl, its surface dulled by a patina of countless scratches. A comforting sound echoed off the kitchen cabinets as his collar hit the bowl with a familiar ping, a routine that brought a sense of security.

It had been two weeks since he drank anything clean, but that didn't matter in this moment of content. Warm water and saliva dribbled from his lower jaw and he took several deep breaths.

A squeal from the hinges on the cabin's front door turned his attention, and he moved to the entryway, his toenails clicking across the linoleum floor.

Jack entered the cabin with unfolded cardboard boxes bundled under his arm and turned into the living room. He tossed them onto another stack of boxes, and shot a quick glance at Newt. "What do you think? More boxes or more trash bags?"

Newt tilted his head with perked ears, panted, and rounded the corner to leave.

"Maybe a match would be easier." Jack scrutinized the cluttered room and tried to count the mounds of magazines, crates overflowing with electronics, and tools littered across the wood floor. The sooner they sold this place, the better.

The cabin had once been a beacon of healing for both him and Roger after their mother died. Bill had worked tireless nights and weekends to finish it, fueled by her memory. The boys played hide-and-seek throughout its split-level floors while their father disappeared to work on a never-ending list of projects.

An upper level with a wood-burning stove witnessed many tales told over singed marshmallows while they watched the sun stretch and set across the valley. Whispers of ghost stories swirled from their bunk beds, and they cowered at the sound of the wind. They'd sometimes cry out for her, and Bill would rush to their side.

But as they grew, so did the distance from their father, and just like the cabin, he turned into something they no longer recognized. As time passed, they spent more of it with their Aunt Rose and less of it with him– a painful rift in their bond.

The door to the third bedroom creaked open and Jack stepped inside flicking on the light. This room had a larger footprint than the others but lacked the same volume of clutter. A drafting table sat opposite a floor-to-ceiling bookshelf with a myriad of electrician's tools lay sprawled across its surface; precision drivers, wire strippers, hex keys, a soldering iron, a voltage meter, wires, insulators, and screws.

A shoe box of plastic propellers and aerodynamic model-airplane fins teetered on the edge of the desk.

Several sheets of lined grid-paper with hand-drawn electronic schematics decorated the walls. He ripped them down and crumpled them into a black trash bag.

A framed quote on one of the bookshelves read, *'Without Victory, there is no Survival. ~Winston Churchill.'* Trash.

A wood-framed 5x7 photo from the Vietnam War sat next to it. The faded and washed-out ink showed his father standing between two men in green Army fatigues, their arms over each other's shoulders, with wary smiles on their faces. Trash.

The shelf above it sagged from the weight of dozens of stacked black-and-white notebooks overflowing with wrinkled sheets of paper. He pulled one off the shelf and flipped through its pages. The light above the desk flickered. The pages stopped at a crease, and he angled the notebook toward the light. A series of dots outlined a spiral shape with handwritten text below it.

April 7th, 1996. Visited Zygma 12. Stunning.

The next two pages contained an outline-sketch of two round heads connected by a wavelength pattern.

Instant Communication – Theta Waves. Symbiotic consciousness needs throttled translation.

One of the heads had a leather BDSM-style face restraint on with squiggle lines surrounding it. A power cord ran from the top strap into what appeared to be a meter that read 120v.

"What the hell?" A grin lit up his face, and he suppressed laughter with each page-turn.

December 17th, 2001. Dex says Tora Bora lacked a wider tactical bomber flank to prevent enemy escape. Flaw in the Grid Shield design. Risk. Need to seal exfils...Aerial???

A ripped fold in the journal's worn, cardboard jacket forced it to the last page.

March 25th, 2002. Snow melted. Broke ground for the Grid Shield. Jumping back to Arios tomorrow. Cà Rá needs more time – there isn't any.

Bewildered by the nonsense, he tossed it in the trash and it crinkled against the tattered schematics. Without hesitation, he reached up and swept all the journals off the shelf and into the trash.

The box of propellers tipped off the desk's edge and dumped its contents onto the floor. As he knelt to gather the parts, he noticed a 2019 classic car calendar dangling from a push pin on the wall behind the desk, and stood to examine it.

Every day in August had a large black X marked out until the 26th, the day his father died.

He pinched the lower page and flipped it up to September. On Friday the 13th, Jack's name had been written and circled in thick, red ink.

Four days from today.

Saturday the 14th, each day, and every month after, had been torn out of the calendar. The lamp's glow cut a shadow over his hand into an arc that highlighted the red ink.

This was exactly what the doctor said would happen as his father slipped further away. He'd create these artifacts of insanity. And now, here Jack stood, tossing the inner workings of his father's mind into the trash.

He tugged the calendar off its hook and pressed it down into the trash bag that had already filled to the top. When he lifted it, the black plastic stretched and ripped, spilling the journals across the floor.

"Goddammit, Dad. Such a shit show." Disgusted, he left to fetch another bag.

As he stepped into the hallway, a creak and popping noise startled him, and he froze. The lights dimmed, shrouding the far end of the hall in darkness.

"Newt."

No response.

The bulbs flickered to a dim glow for a brief moment, then brightened.

As Jack stared down the hall, a second creak from the living room shot through the darkness.

A chill gripped his spine, and he leaned both hands against the entry's wood trim, searching in silence.

"Newt. Here boy."

Another creak pierced the silence, and he rounded the hallway's corner.

The door to the basement was ajar. Adrenaline raced through his body, and he grabbed the handle, yanking the door wide.

He leaned into darkness of the stairwell.

Empty silence.

Jack switched on the basement light and descended with cautious steps. "Newt, you down here?"

When he reached the last step, he paused. Newt sat at attention in the middle of the concrete floor feet tucked behind his knees, spine erect, ears perked up. The dog's gaze was locked on the blank, cinder-block wall.

"Newt."

No response, not even a flinch. Just a silent gaze at the wall.

"What is it? A mouse?"

Jack stepped off the stairs and when his foot hit the concrete floor, broke Newt's attention.

"Come on." Jack motioned Newt to go upstairs.

Newt pushed up on his legs and looked up at Jack then stared back at the wall. If dogs could sigh, Jack was sure Newt had done so when the dog turned and ambled up the wooden treads, toenails tapping each one.

"Time for bed."

Jack glanced over his shoulder at the wall, paused a moment before heading up and closing the basement door behind him.

6

· INCIDENT AT STONE CREEK ·

Demi stood with his eyes closed at the edge of the temple's main stage. The doors had been opened and a breeze pressed against his skin.

He inhaled deeply, and his mind raced with traces of memory fragments passed on from years of handling the sphere. Flashes of glowing entities swirled, cut into by barren land, rocky terrain and rushing water.

Snow.

A snowy landscape filled with the doldrums of war and chaos.

Smoke. Fire. Explosions.

Union and Confederate soldiers engaged in bloody carnage and the rage of death.

Blood-soaked snow.

Images flittered and flashed through his mind.

A Union soldier—likely his great-great grandfather, Henry Carver—hiding behind frozen horse carcasses.

Confederates crying out and shooting at him.

Running, falling, rolling down an embankment.

Voices yelling, echoing across the rocky creek. "Here. Over here. Yankee spy in the gully."

Carver splashing into water, limping on his broken leg.

"I see him! On the rocks!"

Leaning back on a boulder, his face—Demi's bloodline—reflected in icy creek water.

A flash of light in the silt bed, drawing the man's gaze to a crystal orb. The sphere.

Grasping it, squeezing it in a moment of death.

The crack of a gunshot from a soldier's revolver, point blank in front of him.

The sphere saving his life.

Demi opened his eyes and the aroma of torch fuel carried by a wisp of black smoke, drifted across his face. The memory of his family's secret had played countless times in his mind.

A dream, among many he didn't understand, that the sphere had shown him. It drew a direct path from his lineage to his destiny, a triumphant vindication to his skeptics. Demi savored the thought.

The gentle breeze shifted direction and sputtered the flames of metal torches that formed a ring around the wooden stage he stood upon. Sparks of fire flicked into the inky night sky.

Every member of the temple sat in the amphitheater, bunched together on terraced rows of railroad ties. He scanned the group in front of him; an eclectic bunch of all manner, shape, and style. Young, old, bearded, shaven, long-haired, bald, tall, and short. He had tested each of their convictions for his cause and now had news that would delight them. A smile crested on his face.

"Friends. Fellow travelers. I stand with you this evening, to inform you that our time has come. The navigator has arrived!"

A current of joyous whispers spread across the group.

"And I have seen her. I have touched her." He held his open hand up toward the crowd, and their eyes widened with delightful applause.

Takashi, Edgar, and Miles stood in an arc behind him.

Demi leaned on his new cane and staggered to the front edge of the stage. "As you know, the government tried to stop me, and locked me away. But through your conviction and will, I'm back. And I promise each of you, that we will soon begin our journey to the next world."

Edgar clapped and the audience followed his lead.

"Each of you carries a unique glow, a light that shines on our community. Some have come to escape the depths of darkness. Violence, abuse, drugs, alcohol." He paused and closed his eyes, forming a new daydream that echoed against his words. His heartbeat slowed and drummed a deep percussion in his chest.

Thump thump.

A flash of Pocahontas State Correctional Center with Officer Cook ambling past his old cell. An image of Rivera lying face down in a pool of blood. A muted cry from Cook at the guards to open the cell door.

Demi's voice continued. "You were lost. Wounded and weak. Searching for a place to be reborn."

Thump thump.

Inside the dream, Cook turned Rivera over. Blood poured down the big man's face and Cook checked for a pulse.

"There, on your wrists. The sphere shows you the universe and your tiny place in it. Truth, Purpose, Control, Wonder. The four tenets of our Temple, to which you have pledged your unwavering devotion."

Thump thump.

A guard ran down the hall past a row of cells and an inmate slid a bed frame pole between the bars that tangled the guard's legs, toppling him forward. The man dropped his shotgun when he hit the ground. Distracted by the noise, Cook turned for a moment. Rivera opened his eyes and they beamed a stark white against the mask of red blood.

"There will always be many, *many* detractors trying to stop you. But you must persevere. Adapt. Survive."

Thump thump.

Rivera pulled out a shiv and sliced Cook's throat. Blood sprayed from his jugular against Demi's sketch of the circle symbol on the wall.

Demi smiled at the mere thought of it. "They took me away because I know the truth and they tried to stop me. To stop you."

Thump thump.

He let his mind drift to the end of the dream. A swarm of inmates rushed into the halls, and overpowered the officers. Shots ricocheted as Rivera smiled, wiped blood from his face and escaped, disappearing into the night.

"And so, our journey awaits us. I ask each of you to follow your assigned duties. Everything must be perfect. One tiny mistake by anyone, can ruin it for us all.

"But before we leave, I do have some unfortunate news to share." Demi turned as Edgar and Miles dragged a man in jeans and a white t-shirt who now had a potato sack over his head, to center stage and pushed him to his knees. "We have a traitor amongst us."

Miles pulled the sack off the man's head. His blond, disheveled hair fell to his shoulders.

The audience gasped.

"David has committed the gravest of sins," Demi said. "He has shared many of our secrets with a journalist all in the name of money."

David cried out to the audience. "It's not what you think. Please. It's a mistake."

Demi pointed at them. "Look at them, David. You have betrayed each and every one of them."

Takashi stepped forward holding a black case, which he opened. A stainless-steel Desert Eagle 50AE handgun glimmered in the light.

Demi picked it up. "He has betrayed your dreams for his monetary gain."

David mumbled, "I'm sorry, Lyssa."

Demi froze and his eyes widened. "Lyssa?" The stark realization of David and Lyssa entwined in betrayal punched him in the gut. He glanced around the stage. "Where is she?"

"Who?" Miles asked.

"Lyssa, where is she?"

Miles shrugged.

"The sphere. Elena, bring me the sphere."

Demi pressed the tip of the barrel against David's temple. "Without truth, we lack purpose. Without purpose, we lose control. When we lose control, we cannot see the wonder."

Tears streamed down David's face and he gasped for air.

Elena returned with the rosewood box and opened it.

The sphere was gone.

"Where's Lyssa?" Demi screamed.

"I don't know, I don't know."

Undeterred by the response, Demi lifted his head and screamed into the night. When he finished, only silence greeted him. He cleared his throat, searching for control. "So, now, my friends, Lyssa has also betrayed you. David and Lyssa working together to take you down."

He scanned the audience and his voice carried to them all. "Lyssa. I will kill him. Bring me the sphere. I know you can hear me. Bring it to me and I will spare his life. The father of your unborn child."

The crowd sat quietly but Lyssa did not respond.

"This is your last chance. Do you hear me?"

David cried out. "Lyssa! Run!"

Demi pulled the trigger.

The gunshot echoed through the valley while the crowd jolted in stunned silence.

He turned with a glare and scanned the edge of the forest.

Smoke poured from the barrel of the gun and he handed it to Edgar. "Find her."

Tarkos slouched into the thick, orange cushions of a teak chair in the living area of his hotel room. Curtains flapped against the balcony's open glass door. His empty bottle of Cabernet Sauvignon wafted a sweet, blackcurrant aroma into the air.

Fletcher's necklace sat atop a pile of papers on the coffee table, weighing them down, their corners furling in the breeze.

Tarkos closed his eyes for a moment and tilted his drowsy head.

His eyes snapped open and he was sitting back downstairs in the hotel's restaurant, opposite the bar. He wore a white tuxedo jacket with a black bow tie, a red carnation pinned to the lapel.

Tess approached him carrying a round tray bearing a martini. She wore an above-the-knee bright-purple sequin dress; her makeup was flawless, and her short hair styled into spikes. The crystal sphere from the lab dangled on a silver chain around her neck. She looked gorgeous, and he couldn't have wanted anything else in that moment.

"Your drink, sir."

"Thank you." He took a sip. "Perfect."

"Is it wet enough for you?"

"Very."

He glanced over her shoulder at Fletcher, who sat with a beer at the bar, flanked by two nuns. The good Reverend stared back at him through the mirror, smiled and gave him a thumbs up with a wink. The nuns shook their heads in disapproval.

Tarkos turned back to Tess, and she drew him near to her cleavage.

"They say I make the wettest drinks in Stone Creek," she said through lips that glistened cherry-red.

Tarkos smiled. "My tongue would agree."

She sat down beside him in the table booth, ran her hand across his chest then reached up to cup his chin. "I need someone to help get me out of this town. Open up my full potential." She leaned in for a kiss.

"Spread your wings and fly?"

Their lips moved closer but didn't touch. She moved in with her tongue, but Tarkos glanced back at Fletcher, whose eyes had locked onto the sphere that now spun above the bar in front of him.

Light refracted off its crystalline faces, and it spun faster and faster.

Vasquez appeared behind Fletcher, and Tarkos jolted. She pulled out a handgun and held it to the back of Fletcher's head.

"No–Wait!" Tarkos jumped up, threw Tess to the side, and rushed to the bar.

As he reached them, Vasquez turned back to Tarkos, pressed the gun deep into his chest and fired.

A flash of light, then darkness.

His head jerked back as he awoke from the nightmare and heard a gunshot echo in the distance. *Was it real?* Wind gusted into the room. He focused his eyes on the glass door and scratched the back of his head. Tarkos leaned forward and pressed his fist against his lips as he eyed Fletcher's necklace dangling from the edge of the table.

At the junkyard, Duncan lifted his index finger that glowed a cool white, flickering a beckon call to nearby bugs. A small swarm of dragonflies approached, swaying around the light as he studied them.

Their independent quad-wings flapped and rotated as they hovered—frozen—in mid-air. Their large, compound eyes mesmerized by the cackling flicker of light. Each eye contained 30,000 ommatidia; infrared capable nano lenses that would become his spies.

One by one, he gently tapped the dragonflies with his left index finger. A flash of electricity sizzled along the body of each one, and they flew off in random directions. Duncan watched them sail high into the sky.

Snatching Moe's head by the hair, he turned to leave, the two drones joining him at his side. As he walked from the junkyard into the forest, Moe's severed head dangled by his side, remnants of cerebral blood dripping from his brain.

In the lofted rectory of his church, Reverend Fletcher lay in a deep sleep, his conscience benumbed by alcohol. The stale taste of hops brushed his throat with each breath. A wall-mounted Bulova clock ticked a rhythmic drone, filling the vacuum of darkness. His eyes twitched and he exhaled a half-toned whimper.

A young boy emerged from a dark corner of the room and glided toward the foot of his bed. Fletcher's breathing accelerated when the boy neared and whispered, "Daddy?"

Although Fletcher's eyes remained closed, the presence of his son, Daniel, filled him with profound loss.

Tears welled and flushed beneath the lids. Mumbling voices poured into the room and he tried with all his might to open his eyes.

Daniel raised his right fist above the edge of the bed, as if to give his father something. Fletcher shook his head, and the voices grew louder.

Daniel unfurled his fist, and Fletcher's eyes shot open.

He stood over Daniel, who lay motionless in a hospital bed. Doctors and nurses raced to save his life. Corrugated plastic venting intubated his lungs through surgical holes in his chest and nasal cavity. Daniel stared back at Fletcher with wide eyes. Machines cried out a flat-line hum while medical staff shouted instructions to each other.

Fletcher wailed, watching the life of his son drain away, his gaze forever lost.

Two orderlies grabbed Fletcher and yanked him back, pulling him farther and farther away. He flailed in wild desperation to touch his son one last time.

Darkness collapsed around him, and he opened his tear-soaked eyes. In a daze, his gaze drifted to the Bulova clock that ticked back at him.

7

· APRIL 18, 1955 ·

J ack and Bill sat in gray plastic chairs in an oversized gray conference room, part of a larger circle of other people. Jack had on a pair of shorts and a blue collared shirt, while his dad wore a brown camo shirt with a blaze orange knit hat sat atop his head.

This group had the promise of a last-ditch attempt to get his dad help, but Jack had given up all hope. Nothing he tried ever worked.

Bill leaned to Jack and failed at his whisper, "Everyone in here is bat shit crazy."

Several patients scoffed toward Bill, and Jack acknowledged them with his hand. "Quiet," he said to his father in frustration.

Doctor Julian Glaus entered the room and sat in the only empty chair. He opened a grid-lined notebook and readied his pen tip on the page.

"Good morning, everyone." His thick Swiss accent echoed in the cold room.

Everyone replied except Bill who folded his arms and crossed his legs.

One patient, Peter, a man in his early-twenties whispered to the woman next to him as she giggled.

"Peter, please, let's focus," Glaus scolded.

Peter held his index finger to his lips to shush himself.

Glaus addressed the group with a choppy tone. "Today's session will be a little harder than usual. Our cognitive rehabilitation journey has its ups and downs, our goal is to stimulate different areas of the brain. Today's focus is on *fear*. Your words of the day are on the card in front of you with your name. You have fifteen seconds to study them. When you are done, please hand them to Winston."

Bill picked up his card and showed it to Jack. *Garden, Please, Veil, Heart. - Young, William.* Winston passed behind Bill and he held the card back above his head to be taken.

Glaus surveyed the group. "Who wants to start us off today by sharing one of their fears?"

Nobody spoke.

"Anyone want to start us off? Maybe be a little vulnerable?"

Glaus turned to Bill. "Okay William, tell us, what scares you most?"

Bill hesitated as all attention turned to him. "People who think we're alone."

"What do you mean?"

"You know, alone, in all the universes."

"You mean like aliens?"

"I didn't say aliens."

"You said universes. Isn't there only one universe? That's all-encompassing?"

"I said what I mean."

"I'm not sure I understand," Glaus said, removing his glasses.

"Sounds about right," Bill snapped back with a curt tone.

Jack pursed his lips and rubbed his neck.

Glaus pointed his glasses at the others in the room. "And so why do these people scare you?"

"You mean, you're not?" Bill let out a bellowing laugh. "Come on!"

"I'm asking you."

"Well, you're one of them of course. If you truly believe we are alone, then you are stark raving mad. All of you."

"I believe in aliens," Peter said.

The doctor and Bill locked eyes.

"So yes, I am afraid of you," Bill continued.

The clicking sound of high heels approaching from the hallway filled the room. The door opened and a petite woman of Asian lineage wearing a white nurse's uniform walked in.

Jack's eyes followed her from one side of the room to the other. She carried a clay pot with a long-stemmed red flower. Nobody else paid attention to her and she exited the room without a sound bar the clack of her heels.

Glaus coughed and sat up in his chair. "So, sitting here right now, you are afraid of me, of us, because we do not believe in aliens."

"But I do," Peter snapped and the doctor held his hand up to quiet him.

"No, not right now. But there will be a time when you realize we are not alone and you'll be getting slaughtered as you babble on and on about how you were wrong. And as you try to stuff your entrails back into your abdomen, you'll be in my way and crying for help and I won't help you."

"Bill, will you help me?" Peter asked with a boyish anxiety.

Bill gave a solemn nod of acknowledgment. "Yes, Peter, I'll help you."

Peter pumped his fist.

"I see." Glaus tilted his head.

Bill leaned forward in his chair and shook his head. "I'm not quite sure you do."

The doctor shuffled through the stack of cards and paused on one of them. He held it up so the words could not be read. "And Bill, can you tell us the four words on your card?"

Bill paused as he stared him down. "Evil, Danger, Earth, Asleep."

The Doctor glanced at the card and flicked his eyes back at Bill who beamed with a wide grin.

"Well?" Peter cried out.

"Correct," Glaus said.

Peter smiled.

Glaus looked around at the group. "I think that will be all for today—"

Bill jumped up from his chair with a loud echoing scrape. Jack followed him through the hallway and into a small kitchenette.

"What the hell was that all about?" Jack asked.

"What the hell was what?"

"You're supposed to be in here getting therapy, not stirring the pot so they think you're crazy. At some point, they're gonna lock you up."

Bill scanned the shelves. He grabbed a box of cereal with a bowl and spoon. "Do you think I'm crazy, son?"

"No, Dad, but I can't keep doing this. I'm trying to get my life together and I keep getting sucked right back in. Every time I get a call from the doctor, it's like what the hell did he do this time? I shouldn't have to be doing this."

"Roger never gets upset with me."

"There you go with the Roger thing again. Roger hasn't done this nearly as many times as I have, and I just can't do this anymore. I sit in these rooms and listen to this nonsense. It's constant and I'm always jumping in to help."

Bill poured the cereal into the bowl. "Jack, one day you'll understand."

"I do understand, Dad. Your dementia is getting worse and you don't see it. It's ripping us all apart."

"I don't have dementia! These doctors don't know squat. I'm sharp as a tack!"

"So why are you pouring coffee into a bowl of cereal?"

Bill looked down at the bowl and his hand shook. The coffee pot fell and shattered on the floor, splattering coffee and glass shards everywhere.

Jack shook his head. "Dammit." He knelt to pick up the pieces of glass.

Bill slumped into a chair and dragged his hat off his head then stared solemnly across the room. "I miss your mother, Roger."

"Dad, I'm Jack."

"Where's Roger?"

Jack put the pieces of the broken pot into the trash. He walked to the door and leaned out looking for help in the empty halls. The nurse from earlier walked across the hall at the far end and slipped out of his view. "Excuse me. We need some help in here."

No response.

He slid pieces of glass into a pile with his foot. "This is exactly what I'm talking about. Roger can never be here so I have to clean up the mess."

"Oh, Jack, yeah. That's right, I know. Do you miss your mother?"

"Yes, Dad."

"I miss her so much. I wish she were here. She would shake her head, smile, and tell me not to listen to these doctors. They're the crazy ones. My brain is fine. Like Einstein."

Jack soaked the coffee with paper towels and threw them in the trash.

Bill froze and gazed across the room. "Did you know when Einstein died, a doctor kept his brain at home? Imagine that. Promise me when I die, you won't let them do that to me. Cut me up. But you're probably not going to miss me, after all this, will you?"

Jack put more soaked paper towels into the trash. "Of course, I'm going to miss you."

When Jack turned around, his father was gone. He stood in an empty room. "Dad?" Jack ran to the door and rattled its handle. "Dad?" He pounded the door with frantic strikes and peered out the tiny, square window. "Dad!" Jack beat the door with his bare fist and tried the handle again.

He glanced through the window one last time, and a demonic, pale face appeared. Its glossy-red eyes and yellow-stained razor-sharp teeth jolted him.

It let out a loud shriek as the window shattered, firing glass into Jack's face.

Tuesday, September 10th, 2019

Jack awoke dazed in his bed to a loud knocking on the cabin's front door. He squinted in the morning sun and sat up on the edge of the bed. Sliding on a black t-shirt and jeans, he stood and ran his hand through his hair. Newt barked at his feet while the knocking continued.

Unlocking the front door, he opened it, and jolted to an immediate upright stance. He never expected to find a beautiful brunette woman in jeans and a white top standing on the porch. It had to be some sort of mistake, but regardless, his heart hammered at the sight of her.

She held a thin leather briefcase tucked under her arm and a leather holster with a handgun strapped to her hip.

"Good morning. Mr. Young?" she asked in a smooth, southern accent.

"Yes." He opened the screen door.

"I'm Stella Hopper." She held out her right hand. "From Stone Creek Homes."

"Uh, hi. Good morning." He shook her hand. "What exactly can I help you with?"

"I'm here about selling your cabin?"

Jack leaned on the doorframe and nodded. "Selling the—did Roger call you?"

"No, I don't know who Roger is."

"Rose Fawcett?"

She shook her head. "I don't know her either." She smiled and reached into her leather folio, pulled an envelope and handed it to Jack. "We got your letter. Well, my dad did but he had to go out of town, so here I am. You said you wanted to meet at nine a.m. on September tenth, to discuss selling your property. Park at the pipe gate, walk up the trail. I thought I'd be earlier but phew." She turned her head back at the road. "What is that, about a mile hike?"

"Nine-tenths of a mile," he said, scanning the letter. At its bottom he noted his father's signature. "This is a little crazy, this letter is from my father, not me. I'm his son, Jack. My dad, Bill, passed away about two weeks ago."

Stella frowned. "Oh no, I'm so sorry to hear that. Then I guess this is a bit of a surprise."

"Yes, well no. I mean, the crazy part sounds right. But my brother Roger and I were planning to sell this place, so I came up last night after the funeral...I'm sorry, this is just strange."

"Hmm. Well, I can come back another time if it's better for you."

"No. No, it's fine. Would you like to come in?"

"Do you mind if I bring my gun inside?"

"Oh, not at all. Don't worry, you won't have to use it."

Her laugh was like birdsong. "It's not you I'm worried about, but there are plenty of bears up here, so you can't be too careful."

When she entered the cabin, she surveyed the foyer while Jack pushed aside boxes and cleared a path. "Sorry about the mess. Would you like some coffee, uh, Stella?"

"Star. You can call me Star, and I don't drink coffee. Do you have any tea?"

"I'm not sure but can check."

Jack headed into the kitchen as Star sat at the dining table.

"I gotta be honest," she said. "I didn't expect this place to be this big. Most of the time, when we visit a mountain cabin for sale, it's a dilapidated shack. In fact, my dad wanted to come because he's always wondered what was up here but he got tied up down south."

Her eye caught the dog tags next to the silver bracelet on the table. She picked one tag up as the red key slid down the chain.

YOUNG, WILLIAM J. RA1069105 AB NEG NO PREF

Jack opened a cupboard and found three identical, unopened boxes of tea. He pulled one down and read the label. "All I've got is, juniper mint honey?"

"Are you serious? That's my favorite."

"Really?" He removed two tea bags.

"As God is my witness." Star gazed at Jack through a kitchen window opening above a small two-seat bar.

When her eyes met his, a slight smile tugged on her lips, and he froze for a moment.

A warm tingle nudged him out of the brief daze and he poured bottled water into a tea kettle and set it on the electric stove.

"How long have you been a realtor?" he asked while searching for teacups.

"About fifteen years."

"That's a long time." He leaned on the bar to focus on her.

"I like it. My parents started the firm back in the nineties and we service the entire valley. I never thought I'd be doing it this long but it pays well and keeps me active. And I get along with my dad, he keeps—"

Jack stared at the dog tags on the table.

"I'm sorry," she said.

Jack waved his hand. "You're fine. I never had that kind of relationship with my dad."

The tea kettle let out a faint puff of steam and a quick whistle. "It's been years since I even saw him. He built this place after our mom died and he pretty much moved up here. Sort of shut down, gave up, I guess. I have no idea why I'm boring you with all this."

Star smiled. "My mother always says I'm a good listener. And I'm fine with it."

Jack pointed around the room at stacks of papers and books. "You see all this stuff?"

The kettle whistle grew louder.

Star surveyed the journals, sketches and schematic blueprints littering the rooms and walls.

"The inner workings of his mind," Jack told her.

The kettle screeched and Jack pulled it off the stove. He poured the steaming hot water into two mugs, brought them to the table, and took his seat.

"Thank you," Star said. "It sounds like he was lonely." She took a cautious sip of the steaming tea.

"Yeah. But now he's gone." Jack drew a breath.

They both sipped their tea and their eyes locked in an uncomfortable, silent stare.

Everything calmed around Jack. What's happening? The letter. The tea. Was he still dreaming?

Jack laughed. "Okay, so yes, we want to sell. Close this chapter. What do we do next?"

"Well, if you want me to be your agent—"

"Yes! Please be my agent."

Star smiled and removed a pen and notepad from her folio. "Okay. I need to ask you a few questions and if it's fine with you, I'll take some exterior photos in a bit. When my dad is back in town we can come back, take interior measurements when it's cleaned up. We'll work up comps and put a listing together for you to sign. Sound good?"

Jack nodded. "Yes."

"Perfect. Oh, by the way, this red key. You do you know what that's for, right?"

Jack shook his head. "No idea. They said my dad was wearing it when he died."

"That's a safe deposit box key for the bank in town."

Jack picked up the red key and the dog tags slid down the chain. "There's no way I would have figured that out."

"Yeah, I thought you might not know. The manager of the bank is a friend of ours, I can introduce you to him if you'd like."

"Sure." He slipped the chain into his pocket.

Star shifted in her chair. "Do you have lunch plans?"

"I don't."

Her fingers trembled around the pen. "Tell you what, why don't we plan to meet at the bank around noon, you can open the box, see what's inside, then we can grab some lunch?"

"Yes, I would love that. I mean if you're up for it. I'm sure the box is empty, so I don't want to waste your time."

"I have time." Star smiled. "But first, let's go through these questions."

After completing the paperwork, Jack held the cabin door open for Star but Newt darted out ahead of her and into the woods.

"Newt," Jack called out.

Star stepped down the front porch ahead and held her cell phone high to take a photo of the cabin. "Is it okay if I get the sides and back?"

"Sure."

Star dipped around the cabin's corner as Jack scanned the woods for Newt. The air had cooled and a breeze flowed through the trees creating a ripple through their leaves.

"Jack!" Star shouted from behind the house.

He sprinted to the back of the cabin, and when he reached her, his eyes darted upward and he froze.

Three circular, metallic machines floated in the air about fifteen feet away.

Star didn't move and glanced at Jack as he crept to her side. "Please tell me you know what these are?" she whispered, placing her hand on her holster.

"No clue."

The drones floated down to within five feet of them. The middle drone appeared to have a damaged fin on its left side that kept it off balance.

Jack slowly took her arm and pulled her back half a step.

The middle drone wobbled through the air, moving within two feet of Star. It had a weathered metallic body and a large, glass camera lens pointed at them. Star stood frozen while the drone studied her.

"Don't move," Jack said.

Upon hearing this, the drone turned and floated right in front of him.

Jack's face reflected in its round, glass eye. The other two drones moved in closer.

A small panel opened on the right drone and a tiny barrel protruded from its belly. It aimed the barrel at them and made a low humming sound. The drone on the left produced a pair of long, sharp, metal blades that started to spin.

Star unholstered her gun.

The drone in the middle turned to face the other two drones, then rotated back at Jack.

It spun around and flew away into the backyard as the other two drones floated to the ground. The drone with the barrel fired a red plasma beam that burned weeds. The drone with the blades hovered inches above the ground and started to cut the grass.

Jack shook his head.

Star raised her eyebrows and smiled in disbelief. "I've never seen anything like that before in my life. Will the drones come with the house?" she asked, lightening the mood.

"I suppose," he said while watching them from afar, tending to the yard and garden. "Does this mean lunch is canceled?"

Star drew a wide smile. "No."

Newt ran up and yelped at the drones. Jack reached down to rub the dog's head. "Why didn't you tell us about this?" Newt sat and looked up at them, his tongue lolling from the side of his mouth.

Star held up her digital watch. "I'll see you at the bank at noon. Oh, do you want my number in case something comes up?"

"I would but I broke my phone last night."

"Ouch."

"Yeah, but it's just a phone. It'll be nice to be disconnected for a few days. Do you want a ride to the gate?"

"Nope, it's good exercise." She turned to leave but not before he caught a large smile on her face.

As he waved, the round drone flew up and startled him from behind. "So what are you? Some kind of caretaker?"

The drone flashed a green light on its lens and let out a single electronic beep that had to mean 'yes'. "Oh, you can understand me?"

The drone acknowledged with another green flash and beep. *Yes.*

He thought for a second. "I see. Did my dad make you?"

This time the drone replied with a red light and a deeper electronic sound that signaled 'no'.

"Hmm. Can you speak?"

No.

"Are you damaged? Is that why you can't fly straight?"

Yes.

The drone rotated to show Jack its damaged aero fin that matched the fins in the office. "I think I saw one of these inside. Want me to try and fix it?"

Yes.

"Okay, let's see what we can do."

8

· THE DOOR OPENS ·

Meeks walked past a tow truck with a damaged red sports car hitched to it. He entered through the barb-wired gate of Moe's garage and into the front dirt lot. Another day, another body.

Scanning from the trailer to the salvage yard, his eyes stopped at Moe's body, covered by a white sheet, laying face up. Only he didn't have a face, much less a head according to Sarah.

Moe's trail shoes stuck out from the end of the sheet.

Sarah and the pathology team hovered over him, measuring a long, bloody trail with as open-reel tape.

Meeks approached Finn and another man, Fred Jones, near the front of Moe's trailer.

Finn had already started scribing notes and details into his notebook.

Fred sat on a stack of three tires, his knee bouncing up and down in a nervous twitch. "I can't believe he's dead. Not like this. I just talked to him yesterday." Fred's hands rested on his bouncing knees. Sunlight glinted off his greasy, unkempt hair.

Meeks placed his hand on Fred's shoulder. "Fred, I know this is hard and I don't like it either, but I gotta ask you a few questions."

"Yeah, Sheriff, whatever I can do."

"When you talked to Moe yesterday, did he mention anything. Something unusual, or someone giving him trouble?"

"No. Nothing. He didn't mention anything."

"Any arguments or recent fights? Did he upset anybody?"

"Not Moe. You knew him, Sheriff. He was a good guy."

"And you saw nothing else when you found him this morning?"

"No. I was excited to see him because we just got that totaled eighty-one GTS from a crash on forty-two." His thumb flicked over his shoulder at the wrecked red Ferrari on the truck. "Moe's been dreaming of that car since we were kids and I was gonna surprise him. Dammit, it's just not fair."

"When you arrived, was anything out of place? Take a minute and think carefully."

Finn's scratching stopped.

Fred stared at the dirt and shook his head. "Everything was fine. Reckon, I was here just before eight. His trailer door was open but he wasn't there. So I went around back to look for him. That's when I found Zeus... then Moe. The bastard even killed his dog. Why?"

Finn lifted his pen and gave a nod. "We appreciate you calling us right away, Fred. We know this is difficult."

Meeks straightened, hands on his hips, and surveyed the lot. His upper teeth mashed on his lower lip. Turning back to Jones, Meeks tilted his hat up. "Fred, Finn's gonna take you to the station for some questions and a full statement."

"Why, Sheriff? You don't think—"

Meeks waved away Fred's words. "It's just procedure, Fred. I don't for a moment think you would do anything like this."

Fred nodded and took a deep breath. "I wouldn't ever."

"I'm not saying you did. We'll get this taken care of but we have to do it right. For Moe."

"Okay. Yeah. For Moe. Just promise me you'll get whoever did this."

Finn helped Fred stand, but the man slumped toward the front of his truck and stopped. Sarah snapped a photo of Moe's body and all color escaped Fred's face.

"You know what, Sheriff?" Fred said. "I'm gonna fix up that Ferrari and do a charity auction. You think Moe would've liked that?"

Meeks nodded. "I think he would."

As Finn and Fred walked away, Sarah approached Meeks. She snapped off a pair of bloodied gloves and placed them in a hazmat bag. "Think he had anything to do with it?"

"Nope. We've got a killer on our hands, and my wager's on that Duncan fella." The sight of Moe's body filled him with unease. "So, we've got three bodies in two days. Tell me you've found something."

"Same thing, no indication of a struggle. Cause of death appears to be decapitation. Something very sharp. Single, clean cut. No sign of the victim's head."

"And the dog?"

"Puncture wound to the gut. Took place somewhere over there." She traced her hand from Zeus to the junkyard. "It likely ran to the victim and bled out right here."

"Any chance of finding Moe's head?"

"If I had to guess, I'd say we won't find it."

"Why's that?"

"When we examined Joe Parks and the Jane Doe from Whipple, we found puncture wounds behind their lower left ears." Her finger pressed into her skull at the same location. "An initial scan showed intracranial bleeding in both of them. We're still waiting on toxicology, but if these are related, then the killer is likely covering their tracks."

"That's a helluva theory."

"If they're injecting something into the victim's brain, then it's just a matter of time before we can break down the chemical composition, track down the ingredients, and find the killer. But, without the head, it's inconclusive."

"Yeah, but we've got two bodies intact. Doesn't add up."

"You're the Sheriff," she said, then slipped a fresh mask onto her face. "I'm just the Deputy Coroner. Will let you know if we find anything else."

"Thanks, Sarah. I'm gonna see the mayor. We'll need some outside assistance with…"

The rumble of a Channel 4 Valley News Network van cut through his words. Reporter Linda Fox exited the van holding a microphone. Her blonde hair folded over her shoulders while she primped it in a side mirror. The van door slid open and her cameraman shouldered his gear.

"Already?" Meeks pulled his hat down, exhaling hard.

Sarah smiled. "Good luck, Sheriff."

"Don't tell her anything. She's still gunning for her big break."

A dragonfly zipped past Meeks and pulled his attention away from Fox. It glided toward Moe's body and landed on the tip of his shoe.

Jack sat in the cabin's office and attached the final screw to a new aero-fin on the drone. "There. Good as new."

The drone beeped green.

Jack rolled the drone on its side and examined scratches and burn marks on the rear of its body. "You been in a fight or something?"

Silence.

He rolled his fingers over two smooth flat metal prongs directly opposite the glass eye. "What's this? Charging port?"

Yes.

A smear of mud covered up writing below the prongs. *'H gh i h e PO att '*

"What's this say? PO att?" He grabbed a rag and splashed rubbing alcohol on it. When he wiped the mud away the sticker read: *'High Discharge LIPO Battery'.* "Oh, battery. Makes sense."

The drone rolled right side up and floated into the air.

"So, do you have a name?"

The drone hovered in front of him but didn't reply.

"I see. Well…how about I call you PO?"

The drone beeped and flashed green.

"Okay, PO it is." He tossed the screwdriver on the desk and stood.

PO spun around and darted from the room.

"Hey, wait, where are you...?" Jack rushed out after him. He reached the hallway just in time to see PO enter the basement doorway.

Jack gave chase, and reached the bottom stairs of the basement, shadows from his body slithered through the musty room. He flicked on the light at the stoop.

PO hovered just above Newt in the middle of the room.

Newt sat motionless, ears perked, eyes locked on the basement wall that stared back at him in placid silence.

"What's this, guys? Come on. Upstairs. Let's go."

Newt didn't budge.

"Newt, why do you keep..."

A gold-framed newspaper cutting glowed from the shadows. 'Einstein Dies!'

"...staring at the wall?" Jack's voice faded into the cinder block walls. He stepped closer to the faded yellow newsprint.

'Greatest Scientist of his Age Dead at 76.'

Accompanied by a photo of Albert Einstein.

Jack glanced from the photo to Newt and back to the photo.

'April 18, 1955'

Newt whimpered and scratched at the wall.

"What the hell?" Jack ran his hand over the coarse concrete surface. Grit sifted but it felt normal. He put his ear up against it and pressed his hand against the other ear. The bracelet flashed blue light.

Jack leapt back and the blue light faded. His heart galloped and the hairs on his neck stood. With a breath, he brought the bracelet closer to the wall.

The flashes of light pulsed blue in a repeated pattern until it became a constant color. The face of the bracelet materialized a five-digit display of zeroes.

With a swiping motion, he spun each digit with his finger. Numbers and patterned symbols cycled like tiles on a slot machine.

Five digits. Einstein.

41855.

He spun the number four into the first digit and the bracelet beeped.

When he locked in each number, the bracelet flashed green and emitted a sultry female voice. "Oh, yeah."

A beam of green laser light shot out from the bottom of the wall, an ambient light flooding the basement. It ran from the floor, up the wall, turning at hard angles to form a six-foot hexagonal outline.

Panting, Newt wagged his tail and scampered around the floor. PO hovered motionless in the air.

An electronic whirring buzzed, then a mechanical grind followed by a loud clang. The hexagon shape sank back six inches into the wall and slid downward into the floor with a metallic shriek.

The sounds echoed away into the newly-formed, pitch-black doorway.

Newt darted through the opening, down a flight of curved stairs and disappeared into the void.

"Newt!"

PO rotated away from Jack and followed the dog.

Jack grabbed a flashlight from the shelf beside the switch and shone it into the darkness.

The light passed over another gang box and he flicked its switch on. Two continuous lines of blue light flashed across the tunnel ceiling then stabilized. The hum of electricity accompanied the dim glow.

A distant bark from Newt bellowed up through the doorway like an angry ghost.

"Newt!" His voice reverberated back at him,

The bracelet's face flashed green then dimmed.

Jack holstered his handgun and crossed over the threshold, descending into the unknown. His back flattened against one wall and he stepped down each rough stone step. Wheezing sounds blew wind upward and he staggered. *Focus.* A shiver crept up his back and he glanced behind. The clear daylight from the basement showed an empty space at the top of the stairs.

Jack was alone.

The slipshod stairs meandered down, cutting back and forth the deeper he went. The flashlight dulled against the thick darkness while the blue strip-lights grew dimmer.

An icy chill draped his spine when he came to a section of lights that wrapped around a bend and disappeared. He banged the flashlight and it brightened for a moment. Rounding the turn, the tunnel opened to a wider cavern and he stepped down onto a landing pad.

A metal railing sat on the edge of the pad and led to a steeper set of descending stairs. He squeezed the railing tight.

The sense of falling into nothingness overwhelmed him, and Jack fought to breathe. Pushing his back against solid rock, he molded into it and let his eyes adjust. He always wondered if he was more afraid of heights because he'd fall or because he'd jump.

There was no bottom to this pit. At least, none that he could see.

Another bark from Newt carried along the cool breeze.

"Shit."

Jack held the rail with one hand in a death-grip of white knuckles, taking slow, measured steps. He kept his eyes—and the flashlight—trained on the stairs.

He tried calling out one last time. "Hello? Newt? PO?"

Silence.

The blue lights flickered, creating sporadic shadows that further slowed him.

The handrail ended abruptly, and he stopped to catch his breath. He'd come too far to turn back now. Jack cast the flashlight down the stairs where it highlighted a large, flat surface.

Scraping the flashlight against the wall, he used it to steady himself on the final descent. At the last step, a spacious path emerged, bordered by the pit of darkness. A makeshift wooden fence guarded its edge, and Jack grasped it tight.

He passed under a vaulted entrance into a larger cave.

Newt barked again, only this time, louder. The dog was close.

When Jack stepped into the cave, his flashlight illuminated an object on the ground and a burst of red color bounced up from it.

Pages from a comic book furled in a slight breeze.

Jack picked it up and read its cover. *Solar Sniper No. 4 - The Jupiter Wars*

Bold lettering stood above a cosmic battleground with spaceships and explosions. Ships fired laser cannons at a giant robotic scorpion.

The date on the comic read July 2019 just above its website: *www.SolarSniper.com*

Tarkos opened the right-side door of the Church of the Resurrection. Two of its hinges wiggled from rusty screws bending against the soft wood of the jam. Weathered white paint flaked off into a pile on the stoop. He stepped inside onto a plastic entry mat that squished beneath his feet. The sound of the door closing rang hollowly through the church.

The dank odor of incense lingered as he headed into the main chapel, ignoring the holy water font. He walked down the aisle between two rows of pews. Light poured into the chapel from upper windows, and a life size crucifix with a statue of Jesus hung behind the main altar. A closed office door sat tucked away to the right of the sanctuary.

As he neared the front set of pews, a faint whimper came to him that echoed throughout the chapel. Tarkos found a girl on the floor curled in a fetal position, asleep and mumbling to herself.

Her breaths were as deep as her sleep, and her eyes moved in REM state. Her hand clenched something tight, and Tarkos stared at a dark circle tattoo on her left wrist.

The office door opened with a loud clang and Fletcher walked in carrying a vase of flowers.

The sound jolted Tarkos and it woke the girl.

She looked up at Tarkos in fear. "No. Please no. Get away!"

Fletcher looked at Tarkos and rushed to the commotion.

The woman cried out, "Please, help me, don't let them take my baby!"

Tarkos raised his hands placatingly. "Shh. No. Shh. You're okay, you're safe."

"Lyssa?" Fletcher said.

Tears streamed down Lyssa's cheeks and she curled up, pushing her face into her forearms. "They killed him. They killed him."

"Oh no..." Fletcher tried to help her up.

Tarkos held the necklace up to Fletcher, dangling it near his face. "I came by to give you this necklace you dropped last night. I just found her."

Fletcher took the necklace and placed it in his coat pocket. "Thank you, now give me a hand, would you?"

They lifted Lyssa's almost limp body and sat her on the pew.

She trembled and mumbled gibberish while taking stuttered gasps of air. Fletcher sat next to her and put his arm around her.

"He killed David. Killed the father."

"Who killed the father?"

She struggled to get her words out. "Demi."

Fletcher looked up at Tarkos. "We better call the police."

Tarkos pulled out his cell phone and dialed 911.

Lyssa sniffed loudly. "They're all going to die."

The operator answered, "Nine-one-one, what is your emergency?"

"Hello, my name is Andre Tarkos and I'm at the Church of the Resurrection. We just found a traumatized girl inside who says someone has been murdered."

"Sir, is the girl injured?"

"I don't know. It doesn't look like it but something's happened to her and she needs help."

"Are you or anyone else in danger?"

"No."

"We are sending police and an ambulance. Can you stay on the line until they get there?"

"Yes."

Lyssa looked up at the face of Jesus on the crucifix behind Tarkos.

"I'm sorry. So sorry," she mumbled through tears.

Tarkos turned and locked eyes with her.

She screamed and jumped up from Fletcher. "Nooo!"

The operator heard the screaming. "Sir, is everything all right?"

Fletcher tried to grab her but she struck him on the face with her elbow. Lyssa jumped over the front pew and ran to the altar smashing into Tarkos. His phone dropped to the floor as he tackled her.

The operator's voice sounded again. "Sir. Sir...?"

Lyssa collapsed to the ground. Her left hand opened, and the sphere rolled out of her palm and arced upwards, floating six inches above the floor.

Tarkos' eyes widened. Another sphere...*but how?*

9

· THE SPHERE ·

J ack rolled the comic book up and slid it into his back pocket. Pointing the flashlight ahead, he emerged into a domed cavern, its walls arcing high above, fused of metal, rock, and earth. Blue lights highlighted some of the structure while much of it remained shrouded in darkness. The stone floor gave way to a narrow path that ended in a twenty-foot-wide crevice.

Passing the light up and down the crevice, he stopped dead in his tracks with no way to cross. Newt barked once more; the sound was close, seeming to come from above a rock wall across the crevice.

As Jack moved along the edge, the flashlight caught the corner of a wooden plank sheared off by darkness. Moving closer, he positioned himself at the edge, where the light exposed it entirely.

The beam of light cut out against a hard edge of darkness and he scanned around it to find a rectangular opening.

A planked rope bridge illuminated when he pointed the light inside the opening. When he peered around the outer edge, the bridge disappeared. This had to be another dream, or some sort of crazy illusion whipped up by his dad.

Grabbing the comic book, he tossed it through the opening and it landed on a wooden plank. Testing the illusion, he picked up a small rock and tossed it outside the opening. The rock plummeted straight into darkness where the bridge should have been.

"What the hell?"

The flashlight moved through the portal opening first, followed by a cautious step onto the first plank. The bridge wobbled. He grabbed the rope handrail, squeezing its sinewy fibers, and it quivered down both sides.

A deep breath helped balance him while he avoided eye contact with the ominous pit ready to swallow him up. It measured a mere twenty feet across, but his mind estimated one hundred dizzying yards.

The next plank sagged with a creak under his weight. His stomach dropped, sending a queasy sensation over his body that reminded him of taking off in a plane. He hated flying.

A cautious step forward swayed the bridge that rippled across its span. The comic book nudged to the edge of the plank. Jack stepped again, and it slipped off, its pages flapping as it plunged into darkness.

"Whoa...Okay. Okay, you can do this."

Steadying himself, he gripped the flashlight tight and continued ahead. He skipped off the last board of the bridge and shuffled away in relief.

A curved stone path ascended the rock wall, leading to a metal platform that served as the floor of a spacious room. On the side closest to him sat a long table filled with computers, machines, and electronics. He walked past the workbench, shining the light across steampunk contraptions, industrial oddities, and mechanical curios that cluttered its surface. On the far side, Newt sat once again at attention, staring up at something.

"Newt, come here."

Stepping forward, a light from the subject of Newt's focus beamed across Jack's face.

A woman of Asian descent lay asleep on a metal table atop a large stone slab. Her arms rested down her side against a white Vietnamese Áo dài dress. An array of red lights shimmered and arced in circular patterns, forming a canopy over her body.

"Newt, what the fuck is going on?"

Newt looked up at Jack without a sound

"Hello?"

The woman didn't move. Holding his hand up to the arcs of light, tiny waves of red plasma danced across his fingertips.

He followed a series of wires connected to the metal table and traced them back to the long workbench. A computer flashed random numbers and patterns across its screen. A metal headset sat atop a foam dummy-head beside the computer.

Three round pucks, connected by a banded ribbon, stretched around the head. Two pucks covered each ear while the third rested on the back of the head. A thin glass display covered the eyes, connected by two metal wires extending from the ear pucks.

A chair sat in front of a display flashing a white light in sync with the patterns on the computer screen. It hummed with sporadic sizzles of white noise.

Jack glanced at the woman then back at the chair, a million thoughts spiraling through his mind. *To sit or not to sit?* Curiosity had always been his downfall. "Screw it."

He sat in the chair, picked up the headset and turned it over. Blurry lights flashed across the display and the ear pucks hissed a faint digital whine. Despite holding it close to his face, he couldn't discern the sound or images. The arcs of light over the woman turned from red to yellow. With a slow movement, he wrapped the headset over his ears.

The three pucks tightened against his head as a thin, clear needle from the left puck pricked into his skin behind his lower ear. A quick pinch and his body buckled with a jolt back into the chair. "Fu—"

Bright lights flashed across the workbench while the mechanical devices whirred and sputtered. Shivers ruptured the base of his skull and traversed down his spine, through the rhomboids, in a scattershot spread across his back, twitching his muscle fibers. His eyeballs rolled upward in their sockets and tugged on his sense of equilibrium, pulling him forward.

The woman opened her eyes.

∞

Lyssa's maniacal cries echoed throughout the church.

When Tarkos reached for the sphere, a swell of energy formed around it and exploded. It filled the entire chapel in shimmering pulses of radiant light that scattered across the room.

Tarkos staggered back and Fletcher gasped, holding his hands over his eyes.

The light faded and Tarkos looked down at Lyssa, but the woman had passed out.

He and Fletcher glanced at each other in total silence.

A loud digital alarm beeped, startling Tarkos. *My phone?* He pulled it from his pocket. A text message had come in: *Soulgazer vibration 1Hz, 2μm/s.*

"What the hell?"

He scrutinized the sphere where it hovered motionless above the church floor.

His phone rang and flashed an incoming call from Bruce. "Hello?"

"Andre, did you just get the text?"

"Yes."

Fletcher headed toward Lyssa, and Tarkos turned away, slinking into a pew to lower his voice.

Bruce spoke with hurried words. "The readings just started flooding in, the sphere is glowing."

"Where are you?"

"At the lab. I was packing up, next thing I know, I start getting these alerts and the sphere flashed a bright light. Something's up."

"Did you do anything?"

"No. Nothing's changed."

"Is anyone with you?"

"No. Just me."

"Okay, I'm coming back to the lab."

"You won't get in. They've already shut down your access. I was about to leave."

"Dammit." Tarkos ran his hand through his hair. "Does anyone else know about this?"

"Nobody."

Fletcher looked up at Tarkos as police sirens and an ambulance rang in from outside.

"Okay, okay. Then you need to get the sphere and bring it here."

"*What?* I can't do that."

"Bruce, I found another sphere. It's here. In Stone Creek."

"*Another one?*"

"Don't ask, just...I don't care how you do it, get that sphere and bring it down here. Something's going on."

Two paramedics with a stretcher rushed into the chapel.

"How the hell am I gonna do that?" Bruce asked, panic edging his voice.

"Figure it out. Just get here ASAP. I gotta go."

Tarkos ended the call and scooped up the sphere, placing it into his pocket.

Bruce stood in the lab, eyes frozen on his phone. Tarkos was right about one thing – everything they had worked so hard on for years would be lost, but perhaps this event could spark their vindication. He peered at the sphere through the glass window then looked across the room at a coffee tumbler mug on his desk. It read *I Lava You Daddy*.

Stepping to a main computer terminal, he punched in a sequence of commands and pressed the enter key. A series of scripted operations scrolled across the screen and red lights near the upper corners of the lab spun and flashed across the room. He looked back at the main door but nobody had noticed.

A robotic arm inside the lab contorted and rotated along a ceiling track. It hovered over the sphere with precise, controlled movements, plucking it between its metal fingers. The arm glided to the front of the lab and rested the sphere inside a box protected by a clear, sealed door that opened to the control room.

Bruce grabbed a key from a drawer and opened the box, his eyes fixed on the sphere.

Closing the flaps of a cardboard box, he walked to the main exit of the facility. The box shifted under his right arm and he used the coffee tumbler in his left hand to steady it. He placed the mug on top of the x-ray machine housing and set the box down on the conveyor belt. A soldier examined its contents and scribbled notes on a clip board.

"Is that the last box?" he asked.

"Yes," Bruce replied.

The soldier pushed the box through the conveyor belt and it slid through the x-ray machine. Another soldier looked at it on the screen and let it pass through.

"Okay, you can go into the scanner." The soldier motioned him into a millimeter wave machine but Bruce paused.

The soldier gave him a direct stare. "Everything okay?"

Bruce patted the pockets of his lab coat and pants. "I think so, just want to make sure I got everything since I won't be back." He shook his head with a satisfying smile. "I'm good."

He stepped into the scanner and held his arms up for the scan. Once completed, the soldier motioned him through and he walked to the end of the conveyor to pick up the box.

"Oh," Bruce said as he turned around. "Forgot my coffee."

He reached up and grabbed the coffee mug from the top of the scanner. As he turned to leave the soldier shouted at him.

"Hey, Doc!"

Bruce froze then turned slowly. "Yes?"

"We need your badge. Says here we gotta collect your badge."

Bruce set the mug down, unclipped his badge and handed it over. "It was nice working with you guys. Thank you for your service."

"Yes, sir. You take care and keep out of trouble. We'll get the elevator."

With a muted smile, he grabbed the mug and box and entered the elevator, doing his best not to look nervous. After he pressed the Main Level button, nothing happened. He cast a calm glance at the soldiers who stared back at him.

His finger clicked the button several times in a row but still, nothing happened.

One of the soldiers set down the clipboard and headed toward the elevator.

With one final press, they started to close, and Bruce heard one of the soldier's words. "As weird as he is, I hear the new one they're sending is a nutjob."

"Great," the other soldier replied.

Bruce reached his car and pulled a metallic cube out of the cardboard box.

His hand trembled when he popped the top off the coffee mug. Reaching into it, coffee splashed on the seat when he pulled out the sphere. He wiped it with a rag, placed it in the box and typed a digital lock code on its side. He put the box on the backseat floor, looked around the garage and began the drive to Stone Creek.

On the outskirts of town in an open field, Duncan's eyes flashed.

The sphere.

He walked in its direction. Two dragonflies hovering by his side darted out ahead of him.

A white light flashed with a burst of static noise and a stream of digital pixels flickered in Jack's eyes.

A chaotic moment of confusion ended with him standing in the quiet of a forest. He scanned the white oak and pine trees towering over him. Was it a hallucination? A virtual dream?

Pre-dawn autumn air swept from the treetops and chilled him.

The sun crested from behind a hill and turned the dark sky to an ashen gray. He tried to walk but when he stepped, the dimensional space pixelated and twitched the landscape. It appeared to be some sort of playback that created a spatial disorientation around him.

His head movements and body motions didn't align to the landscape, as if he floated within a holographic video. As he spun to explore the forest, he found a man dressed in blaze-orange camouflage sitting on a hill tucked behind a cove of pine saplings.

He motioned toward the man and the environment seemed to skip ahead, shifting through space. Everything around him continued to move forward in real time but when he leaned back and pulled his arm, it all went in reverse.

The weightlessness of his body was like swimming underwater in the deep end of a pool, floating through an immersive video playback.

He moved toward the man who sat still, scanning the forest.

Jack gasped. "Dad."

Bill sat motionless in a makeshift hunting blind. Birds chirped and a slight breeze wisped through the valley. He turned and seemed to gaze straight through Jack.

A twig snapped and diverted his father's attention. Bill paused and turned his ear to search for the source of the noise. A quick shuffle of fallen leaves rustled to his left. He turned his head and grabbed his rifle.

A pair of antlers appeared above a nearby hill about one hundred yards away. An eight-point buck moved forward.

The deer passed through Jack, and his father lifted his rifle to a shoulder-ready position, peering through the scope.

Walking with a tall, confident gait, the deer flicked its white tail every other stride.

The deer stood too far out of range. Jack watched his father focus on controlled breathing to steady his aim. A straight on shot, with its head down, would be difficult and likely wound, but not kill the animal.

The buck bobbed its head several times as it advanced.

It snorted and paused, gaze locked on Bill and its impending doom. The deer glanced to its right as if it had spotted Jack. It didn't seem bothered by this and continued to advance, moving closer with each stride. Its rack was a spectacular formation of bone and cartilage that had grown with symmetrical perfection.

Bill stayed motionless as the deer moved within shooting range and quartered toward him opening a clean shoulder shot.

Jack watched, breath held, as his father's finger crept on the trigger.

The buck stopped, its eyes locked on Bill.

His father pulled the trigger and the hammer struck the .30-06 cartridge exploding the primer and igniting the gun powder. The 150-grain bullet separated from the brass casing and spiraled out of the barrel through a fiery flash and puff of smoke searing through the gas pressure propelling it towards the deer. Jack flinched at the sound of the gunshot.

The buck turned to flee but the bullet struck its front left shoulder piercing the hide and shattering two ribs. The bullet coursed through fur, flesh, and muscle. It exited through the right abdomen in a plume of bloody hairs.

His father's hand trembled, and Jack watched the man take a long calm breath that frosted in the cool air. Bill pulled back on the bolt handle and ejected the smoking cartridge while the deer jumped over a large fallen tree, down an embankment, and disappeared.

Did he miss? He picked up the spent cartridge and placed it in his pocket.

Jack watched his father shoulder the rifle and climb out of the hillside blind.

Bill took short quiet steps toward the fallen tree and Jack followed close behind. As they approached the tree, he scanned the ground for signs of a blood. Bill stepped sideways and scraped leaves with his boot until he discovered two drops.

A few feet away, more blood and soon a trail of it to follow.

Jack followed Bill down an embankment that led to a gully. Ascending an incline, they reached a small clearing and dirt trail that bordered a rotten wooden-post fence strung with rusted barbed wire. A ragged 'NO TRESPASSING' sign dangled by a single nail on one of the posts. A newer sign had been placed next to it that read: 'LAND FOR SALE 400+ ACRES'.

The blood trail ran straight through the fence. Bill studied the 'NO TRESPASSING' sign before scanning the woods. Spreading the wire with his hand and boot, he stepped over the downed fence post.

On the other side, he picked up the blood and followed it through thick underbrush.

Jack followed his father across the boundary and paused at a bend around a two-trunk split tree. This should be the path leading up to their cabin, but it came to an abrupt end.

As they moved up the mountain, Jack caught sight of the buck's antlers poking from behind a rock formation that rested on a moss-covered knoll.

They climbed, and found the buck laying in a pool of blood.

Standing beside his father, Jack stared as Bill pressed the barrel of his rifle into the deer's neck. He knelt and picked up the head of the animal by its antlers. Its neck flopped and tongue dangled from its mouth. Thick black eyes, frozen in death, gazed up at Jack.

The crack of a twig echoed to the left of the knoll. Bill dropped the deer and stood, looking around. Without a sound, he stared across the forest tree line.

Silence.

A second snapping sound cracked in the air and Bill spun, glancing behind him. He stepped towards the edge of the knoll and a loud crunching sound swirled around him.

The ground beneath Jack's father opened up, and Bill tried to jump away. Too late. The earth opened, and swallowed Bill.

Jack could only stare on in horror as his father tried to grasp clumps of crumbling dirt, but Bill tumbled into the earth and slid down a vertical rock face. The hole narrowed, and his father caught himself for a moment before crashing down onto a hard, flat surface. The back of his head bounced off the ground.

Staring back at the distant hole above, a single beam of light streamed down illuminating his father's face.

For a moment, Jack stood above ground, shaking his head as the deer jerked back to life. It gyrated and writhed up onto its legs with a snort, twisted its head, and darted away into the forest.

Another glitch, and Jack slid through the playback next to his father who lay nearly passed out on the ground.

From the darkness, a crystalline blue light shimmered to Jack's right.

A glowing hand passed through his stomach and startled him.

A translucent, blue, skeletal figure emerged, reached down, and touched Bill's face.

10

· ATTACK ON CAM RANH BAY ·

Vietnam – August, 1969

Another white light strobed more pixels in Jack's eyes. The memory-experience streamed around him as if he were watching from inside a disco ball.

Shadows from the propeller of a Bell UH-1 Iroquois 'Huey' helicopter skirted the shoreline of Cam Ranh Bay's white, sandy beach.

Jack observed his father on the veranda of the Ngân Café with his friends Nico Tedesco and Dexter Mosely. He stood as a shadow in a dark corner of the café – a place of respite for the weary and lovelorn to escape the chaos of war and empty their wallets.

Waves of sunlight sparkled off the sapphire-blue ocean and reflected in Jack's eye as he watched his father squint against the light. Half-naked bodies of GIs soaking up surf and sun dotted the beach. A bamboo fan circulated warm air as condensation dripped from bottles of *"33"* beer on their table. The aroma of char-fried chicken and sweet, sticky rice floated around them.

Nico sipped his beer and hunched over, both elbows on the table. "So, Dex, when this shit's over, what's the first thing you gonna buy when you get back home?"

A smile broke on the left side of Dex's mouth and spread wide.

"Sports car. Something fast. Something blue."

"A Charger? 'Cuda?" Nico asked.

"I don't know what a Cuda is, but it don't matter. Whatever I can afford. You get the car, you get the women." Dex shook his head with a deep, raspy laugh.

"More like a VW Beetle on our salaries," Nico said.

"Bah." Dex waved his hand.

Bill smiled and took a long swig of his beer.

"And you, Bill?"

Dex leaned in and grabbed Nico's shoulder. "Wait, wait, don't tell me. Umm. A new mechanic's toolbox!"

Bill huffed a laugh and rested the beer on his knee. He leaned his chair back on two legs. "Nah, nothing that fancy." He paused and gazed out at the ocean. "Tickets to a Cubs game at Wrigley. Right behind home plate. Hot dog, beer, a bag of peanuts. Maybe get lucky and see Santo hit one out on the Pirates."

"Cubs? Shit, man, they'll never win a series. Ever. Yankees all the way!" Nico said. He slammed his bottle on the table, snapping Bill's attention.

"Can't stand the Yankees. And what are you gonna—" A deafening crash of broken glass and a gasp from customers interrupted him.

Stepping out from the shadows, Jack glanced at the bar.

A male server writhed on the ground in a pool of blood and shattered glass. His free hand reached up for the bar and he tried to pull himself up, but fell back in pain. The café owner rushed to his side and waved his hand at everyone. He wrapped the man's bloodied hand in a towel, and shouted commands in Vietnamese to another woman who ushered him out of the café.

The owner stood waving his hands to the crowd of onlookers, then grabbed his cigarette from the bar and took a deep drag on it before shouting to another server. "Cà Rá." His voice shot across the room and he pointed his finger at several tables.

Jack focused on his father, whose eyes had frozen with a glossy stare on Cà Rá. He'd never seen his father look at any woman this way. Not even Jack's mom.

The owner placed three bottles on her tray, and she navigated around tables toward them. The dark shade of her shoulder-length hair matched her eyes. The dim light created a bronze glow on her skin.

Looking at Cà Rá, then his father, Jack absorbed a moment he never knew existed.

"Hey-hey, Earth to Bill!" Nico waved his hand in front of Bill's face.

Cà Rá arrived at the table and set each beer down. Bill straightened in his chair, his unwavering gaze following her every movement.

She looked at him and smiled but shied away as she picked up empty bottles.

Nico lit a cigarette.

Bill reached into his shirt pocket, pulled out a wad of money, and handed it to her.

"Jesus, Bill, share the wealth," Nico said, cigarette dangling from the side of his mouth.

Cà Rá spoke in broken English. "No, no. Too much."

"Take it," Bill said in Vietnamese.

She shook her head. He placed it in her hand. "I want you to have this."

She nodded to Bill. "Cảm ơn rất nhiều," she said. "Thank you...very much."

Nico and Dex stared at Bill.

With a nod, she turned and walked away.

Dex laughed. "Sure, Cubs game. Yeah, right."

Bill smiled and ran his hand through his hair.

Cà Rá returned to the bar and looked back at Bill. He focused on her and she ran her hair behind her ear, then she darted him a slight smile and turned away.

The memory-stream accelerated, and Jack floated forward to a dirt road at the edge of a large Army barracks. Metal-roofed buildings and green tent structures lined the streets.

Bill, Nico, and Dex walked past a three-placard signpost: '6th Convalescent Center US Army Logistical Center Vietnam'. A round, analog clock on the sign ticked to 12:07.

The three men sang in broken baritone and stumbled past the chapel that sat next to a hospital building.

Nico stopped to light a cigarette. "Hang on, I gotta piss." He ducked around the corner of a tent building.

"Jesus, Nico, you're gonna get us court-martialed," Dex said, swaying to lean against Bill.

Cà Rá appeared out of the darkness, walking down the opposite side of the road carrying a paper bag. Bill belted a chord and when he tilted his head, his eyes locked onto her and he stopped singing.

Dex caught sight of her. "Ohhhhh shiitttt."

Bill pulled away from Dex and wiped his face. He tucked in his shirt and swiped his hand through his hair.

Dex laughed. "Looks like Bill's found a jewel."

Nico laughed and tilted his head back around the tent as he sucked on the cigarette.

Cà Rá lifted her head at the men and stopped. She smiled at Bill and her bag tipped, three oranges spilling out.

"There you go," Dex said.

Bill started toward her, then stopped as the faint whine of a mortar shell grew louder and drowned out the night air.

"Incoming!"

A soldier screamed in the distance and a fiery explosion ripped through the corner of the building next to Cà Rá. The percussive shockwave shredded metal shrapnel that blasted into her body and drove her to the ground.

The force of the impact spun Bill to the ground. "You guys all right?"

Dex and Nico ducked for cover as small-arms fire erupted. Viet Cong Sappers shouted as they ran between medical buildings, hurling bomb satchels into them. The explosives detonated one by one, followed by patients and medical staff screaming in agony. Smoke poured across the road and a base-wide siren pierced the air.

"What the fuck man?" Nico screamed.

A soldier on fire ran out of the building, and a Sapper fired his AK-47 striking him with multiple shots in the soldier's chest.

A shadow ran from behind Jack – Nico. He tackled the Sapper and they fell to the ground. A muffled shot broke above their bodies, and Nico rolled away, bloodied.

Dex screamed and ran at the Sapper, who turned and fired. A bullet struck Dex in the leg, but he snatched the rifle away and smashed the Sapper's face with it. He shot into the Sapper's chest and hovered over Nico's lifeless body, scanning the area.

Bill pulled Cà Rá to a sheltered area behind a truck.

Blood poured from her mouth as he knelt by her side.

Her eyes welled with tears.

Bill pulled up a section of her shirt exposing a deep gash. "No, no, no. Hang on. Hold on," Bill said. He pressed the material against her side and blood gushed from the wound.

She spoke with a weak and faint breath. "Hãy cứu tôi...save me... hãy cứu tôi..."

"Stay with me, Jesus, God stay with me."

Blood bubbled from her mouth with each breath, choking her.

Cà Rá reached up and touched his face, and Bill grabbed her hand, clasped it tight.

"Hãy cứu..." She took a breath but didn't take another, the light leaving her eyes.

Sporadic rifle shots cracked through the night and Bill cupped Cà Rá's forehead, then caressed her hair with calm, gentle strokes.

"I'm sorry."

A flash and a pop of pixels broke the silence and Jack now stood before his childhood home.

Bill awoke slumped over the steering wheel of his truck in the driveway. In a daze, he glanced around the front of the house, confused. He got out of the truck and grabbed his rifle and jacket.

Jack stood on the porch and watched his father walk up the stairs. As Bill reached the porch, his two boys ran out the front door.

"Hi, Dad."

"Hey, Dad."

They zipped by him, carrying a thin yellow bat and tennis ball.

Jack tracked his eight-year-old self, a kid without a care in the world, and watched the boys sprint down the street.

He could never forget that day.

Thick dark clouds rolled in overhead.

Jack's mother walked out of the house onto the porch, "Where have you been?"

He looked up at her and whispered, "Mom."

"I had an accident," Bill replied.

"What? Bill, are you all right?" she asked while helping him into the house.

Jack passed through the aluminum screen door and it slammed shut behind them.

She removed Bill's flannel shirt, revealing a large section of blood on his undershirt.

Elizabeth gasped. "My god, Bill, what happened? Take that off."

"I'm fine, I'm fine. I slipped on a rock and fell while tracking a deer. It's just a scratch."

She led him into the kitchen and sat him down. Bill leaned forward and winced when he touched the back of his head.

Elizabeth poured him a coffee and soaked a rag in a water bowl. She blotted blood from his hair and looked at the wound. "I think it's stopped bleeding."

"I feel fine, just a little woozy, is all." He stared down into his coffee.

"Do you think you need to see a doctor?"

"Nah." Bill waved his hand. "You know, I've been thinking. Maybe it's time to get a vacation home."

"Get some land, build something to escape with the boys, and relax."

She let out a little chuckle. "With what money?"

"I know, I know. Where I was hunting up there, it sure was beautiful. Serene. The kind of place we could do something nice."

"But also dangerous. That rock must have knocked something loose in there. Look what happened to you."

He sipped the coffee. "And quiet. They're not making any more land, you know. I found a lot for sale—"

The phone rang, interrupting him. Elizabeth set the cloth into the bloodied water bowl and grabbed the long, corded phone from the wall. "Hello?"

Jack could hear the muffled voice of a man on the other end and listened as best he could.

"Mrs. Young?"

"Yes."

"This is Doctor Greenhouse."

She sat, squeezing the phone cord tight. "Hello, Doctor Greenhouse. I didn't expect your call this early." Elizabeth looked at Bill as her hand twirled the cord.

"I'm calling to let you know that we got the results of your bloodwork back." The doctor paused. "And in your CBC test, we detected an anomaly. We'd like you to come in tomorrow or Friday to run more tests."

Jack glanced at a wooden crucifix on the wall above his mother.

"Anomaly? What-what do you mean by that?" Her voice trembled, and she looked at the floor, knotting the phone cord a second time around her hand.

"The tests show your white cell count is much higher than normal. It's likely a sign of an infection, so we need to run those tests to rule out something else."

"Okay," she said, letting out a long breath. "Is it something I should be worried about?"

Bill looked up from his coffee as thunder rumbled outside.

"No, not right now. Let me do the worrying for you. I will transfer you to one of the receptionists who can get you on the schedule right away.

"And Mrs. Young? Everything will be all right."

At that moment, both boys burst through the front door of the house and ran upstairs, yanking her eyes away from the floor.

Jack glanced at them then back at his mother as a single tear rolled down her face.

Jack's heart rate reached a feverish pulse and a tight pressure swelled through his skull. He panted, trying to catch his breath as the sharp pain forced him to cry out. He jolted, his survival instinct surging, and he snatched the headset away. Leaning forward, he rubbed his eyes with his palms, forcing calm into each breath as he waited for his sight to adjust to the darkness of the cave.

He stumbled from the chair, snapping his gaze to the table, but the woman was gone.

Snatching his flashlight, he shined it at the far side of the cave. "Newt?"

Light flicked to his side, and illuminated the woman standing next to PO and Newt. Could it be the same girl from Vietnam? Cà Rá?

"Hello Jack," she said, her soft voice echoing throughout the chamber. She rubbed Newt's head and PO's glass eye rotated.

Jack stood in silence as a thousand questions collided in his mind. "Who are you, and what the hell was that?" he asked, pointing at the headset.

"I am Cà Rá. You have experienced a memory-echo of your father."

"A what?"

She stepped forward and the light cast a soft glow around the edge of her dress. "A reproduction spliced from the memory-data of your father."

"My father is dead."

"Yes. He was my friend, and I am afraid his death means we are out of time."

"Out of time for what?"

She canted her head and looked over his shoulder into the darkness behind him.

When Jack turned, he found nothing. "What are you looking at?"

She beckoned him to follow her. "Come, I have answers." She glided inches above the ground to the center of the platform.

Jack hesitated but then followed her with Newt and PO lagging behind.

Cà Rá raised her hand and pointed at a four-foot-high pillar of stone crowned with a metal cylinder. The cylinder measured about one-meter long and ten inches in diameter. Conduit and electrical wires ran down from its base across the platform, disappearing into the chamber's dark corners.

"The Empyreax."

Newt looked at it, then at Jack.

"Oookay. The Empyreax," he said. "What is it?"

"A gateway to the center."

"The center of what?"

"All creation. At least, that's what we believe."

PO hovered next to Jack, who turned to him and asked, "Am I dreaming?"

PO flashed red and blipped. *No.*

Cà Rá continued, "Eons ago, in the center of the Tyraxis Universe, we discovered the Empyreax. Its origin and how it got there were unknown. Many tried to open it, but all failed. It became an object of great desire and endless war."

Jack ran his fingers over black, arcing grooves cut into its matte, gunmetal-gray surface. They converged at a round indentation filled with hundreds of serrated notches.

"When war reached our home-world, Calodox, a small group of us escaped with the Empyreax. Our planet was destroyed and we were hunted. Chased out of existence. We set out on a secret journey to hide it, jumping through universes and erasing our tracks. Then we came to this desolate planet buried deep in this dead universe, but our crew was betrayed. I was the only survivor and forced into dormancy guarding the Empyreax. Your father awakened me. Since then, we have prepared for their arrival."

Jack curled his lips and shook his head in confusion. "Arrival of who?"

"The Xurricans. William was preparing for battle."

"Hang on, hang on. Time out. Wait a minute. Let's start from the beginning because this is ridiculous." He took a breath, mind reeling. "My father, who was bat shit crazy with dementia, found a secret, underground alien spaceship, woke you up, and built a cabin on top of it?"

PO flashed green and beeped. *Yes.*

Cà Rá looked at PO and nodded in agreement.

Jack cast PO an annoying squint. "And he was preparing to go to war with an alien army that will destroy Earth?"

PO flashed green and beeped again. *Yes.*

"A seventy-six-year-old man, all by himself?" Jack asked.

"Now that William is expired, you must take his place."

"Whoa, whoa, whoa. I'm not. I can't." Jack shook his head.

"William was a brave warrior until his end."

"No, in fact he was a terrible father at the end. But how would you know?"

"He only did this to protect you and Roger."

"What do you mean, protect us?"

"In time, the Xurricans will find the Empyreax and destroy Earth. Now, with his plans and the Empyreax key, we can fight back."

Jack waved his hand at the technical oddities scattered about. "I mean, what the hell, all this time? This is what he's been doing?" He spun around and threw his arms in the air. "Why didn't he tell us?"

"The calculated risks were too great. Not only from the Xurrican threat, but from your own government."

Jack shook his head, trying to deny it all. "Like, seriously, does it ever end?" He yelled into the dark of the chamber and his voice bounced off the walls. "Huh, Dad? Is it ever going to end?"

Cà Rá, PO and Newt stared at him in silence.

He turned and wiped his face with both hands, drew in a deep breath. "So, if you're some kind of alien, why do you look human?"

"I took the form your father wanted me to have. An echo from his memory."

"So why don't you change back?"

"I'm fine as I am."

Jack exhaled, a laugh bubbling at its end that sounded a little crazy.

Cà Rá tilted her head at him. "Your father sacrificed himself to save me. I promised to protect you and your brother until the end."

"The end of what?"

"I told you already. The end of the great Xurrican battle."

"Right. And when will this battle take place?"

"Soon."

"Let me guess, Friday the thirteenth?"

"Correct."

"Of course. How cliché," he mumbled to himself.

Cà Rá grimaced then stumbled forward, grabbing her side.

Jack glanced at her stomach and blue sparks of light flickered from what appeared to be a wound. "Are you hurt?"

Her voice trembled for the first time. "Jack, we do not have any more time. We must find the Empyreax key before the Xurricans do."

"Okay. Let's ignore the madness of this, and pretend that I help you. First question, when do they arrive?"

"They are already here," she said, removing her hand from her side. "Xurricans can hide in your species."

Of course they can. Jack tried not to roll his eyes. "So, how would we even begin?"

"Do you have William's plans?"

"What plans?"

"He said the plans would be kept safe with you."

Jack looked down at Newt then at PO, deep in thought. Some of the puzzle pieces were starting to come together, but surely this was just crazy talk— "Wait..." He reached into his pocket, grasped the red key, and held it up to her.

Three dragonfly scouts darted through Main Street park, scanning their surroundings. They flew under a bench, dashing past a boy throwing a frisbee with his father. They separated, and one twisted through the air towards a three-story building with a sign that read: *Stone Creek Medical Center.*

It flew to the upper floor and landed on the ledge of a room, peering through the window.

Inside lay a woman in a hospital bed, an EKG machine attached to her. A nurse injected medicine into an IV drip.

Two men sat in chairs watching the nurse.

The door to the room swung open and a doctor entered. "Reverend Fletcher, good morning." He shook Fletcher's hand then reached to shake the other man's. "I don't think we've met, I'm Doctor Cilman."

"Doctor Andre Tarkos."

Fletcher leaned in. "Is she going to be, okay?"

"You know I can't say much but there's no need to worry. Do you know her parents or any relatives?"

Fletcher dropped his head. "Her parents died and after she turned eighteen, she just disappeared. Is there anything I can do to help?"

"If we can't locate any relatives, then you'll have to sign some paperwork downstairs."

Tarkos pointed to an ultrasound machine next to the bed. "So, with that machine in here, does that mean she's pregnant?"

The doctor hesitated. "I'm sorry I can't share that."

Fletcher squinted.

"For now, she's asleep and we're monitoring her closely. But I can ask you this. When she was brought in, she kept rambling about someone named David. Any idea who that is?"

They shook their heads.

"Well, she's going to have to stay here overnight for observation. Drug addicts come through here every other week. When she comes down off her high, we'll go from there."

Fletcher nodded. "Thank you, Doctor."

The dragonfly focused on Tarkos as he reached into his pocket, pulled out the sphere, and rolled his thumb over it. His eyes dragged to the window and stared straight back at the dragonfly.

∞

The image of Tarkos holding the sphere flashed in Duncan's mind.

He stood upon a hillside and looked back toward the town with narrowed eyes.

The striped and silver drones swooped down by his side, sputtering a metallic growl.

· 11 ·

· THE CANNON ·

Rivera's eye gleaned up at the sign over the Lucky Duck gas station. A beat-up Chevy truck passed by and he crossed the road, the smell of exhaust fumes wafting with him.

He looked over at a woman pumping gas into her car as she jabbered away on her cell phone. Eyeing the woman from afar, she finished pumping gas and placed the handle back. She walked into the gas station with her credit card and keys, disappearing behind a row of snacks.

Rivera walked with a brisk, slight crouch to the passenger side of her car and knelt glancing around. Upon seeing her purse in the seat, he opened the door and snatched a twenty-dollar bill from it, closed the door and slipped away.

He crossed through a row of trees and over the street to a small strip of shops into the Twin Kiss Café that sat nestled between a hardware store and pharmacy. When he pushed the door open, it struck a bell that chimed three times. The smell of coffee and maple syrup hit him, and rumbled his stomach.

Several customers paused and looked up at him. With an uneasy glance, he turned and moved to a red swivel chair against the café bar. The patrons returned to their chatter about the weather, local news, and an upcoming farm auction. Rivera sat at the bar and a middle-aged waitress placed a coffee cup and menu in front of him.

Her eyes paused on the tattoos inked across his face. "Coffee?"

Her silver name tag glinted sunlight into his eyes. *Ceci.*

Rivera nodded and she poured black coffee into the cup, steam rising. He drank it all down, clinked it back on the plate and she refilled it with her eyes widened.

"Someone's thirsty, huh?"

Rivera kept his face locked down on the counter.

"One of those quiet types too. But I'm not judging." She snapped her chewing gum. "You want something to eat?"

"Yes," he said. He tilted his head to the menu and scanned it quickly. "Eggs with spice."

"Spice? What kind?"

"Lots."

She paused, and he looked up to her nod. "All right. I think we've got some cayenne. How would you like your eggs?"

"Scrambled."

"Okay, hon. Anything else?"

"Water." He caught the eye of an older man in a cook's apron and white hat behind the serving window. Rivera stared back for several seconds, and then the cook disappeared from the window.

"Mac, need an order of scrambled eggs, extra spice," Ceci said. She slapped a paper on a spike and a plate of pancakes and bacon slid out.

The chef called from the window. "Spice? Like cayenne?"

"Yup."

Mac tapped a silver bell that dinged and jolted Rivera. Glancing around the café, he slid off the stool, and walked to a door marked bathroom.

He tried to twist the handle open but it was locked.

When he shook the handle again, a female voice filtered out. "Just a minute, please."

A woman with a small child eyed Rivera and got up to leave.

She hurried the child past him to the front door. The toilet flushed, diverting his attention.

The door opened and an older woman stepped out. "I'm done, young man. Please be more patient." She gave him a dismissive roll of her eyes and slid past him, taking her seat with an older bald man wearing a hearing aid.

He entered the bathroom and locked the door.

Rivera turned on the faucet, then stared into the mirror, cool water running over his hand. He scooped it up and let it trickle down his face. His eyes chiseled into the reflection and the buzzing of the fluorescent light grew louder. He snatched a paper towel and wiped his head.

When he exited the bathroom, he stepped past a Sheriff taking a seat at a table behind his stool with another officer.

"Morning, Sheriff Meeks," Ceci said.

Twisting onto the stool, Rivera kept his gaze down at the counter.

"Good morning, Miss Ceci," Meeks said. "You having a sparkling day?"

"Not with all these murders happening," she said.

Several customers looked up and focused on Meeks.

"Well, now. Let's not go spreading rumors. We've got a few drug overdoses and an animal attack. Probably a bear."

"That's not what I heard Sheriff," a man yelled from the far end of the café's bar.

"Oh, hell, Karl, this is exactly what—"

The cook punched the ready bell and a moment later a plate of spicy eggs slid in front of Rivera.

"You want Tabasco?" Ceci asked.

"Can I get this to go?" His face angled down at the food then he looked up at her from the corner of his eyes.

She dragged a measured glance at Meeks then back to Rivera. "Sure. You got money to pay for this?"

He slid his hand across the counter and released the crumpled twenty-dollar bill from his palm. Ceci grabbed it and handed him a Styrofoam container. She turned to ring up the cash register and he walked to the door.

The old woman from the bathroom blocked his path while she hobbled through the doorway.

He tried to slide past her but she stopped and furled her eyebrows. "Could you wait, please? Some folk don't have any patience or respect."

Three older men at a nearby table eyed Rivera. He glanced back at the Sheriff who sat with his back turned.

The woman made it through the door.

As his foot crossed the threshold, Ceci cried out to him. "Hey, sir, your change!"

Without stopping, he dashed out, the door slamming shut behind him.

The Triumph rumbled to the corner of Main Street and Eaton Hollow Park. Jack squeezed the throttle and the engine's exhaust barked one last time then fell into an idle purr. Cà Rá sat on the rear seat, arms wrapped around his abdomen.

He leaned his left foot against the sidewalk curb. "I need you to get off and wait here."

"Why?"

"Because."

"Because why?"

"Be-*cause* the woman I'm meeting—"

"What woman?"

He released a deep breath and raised his voice. "Never mind that. Off."

Surprised at his tone, she dismounted and stood facing him.

"Listen, Kara—"

"Cà Rá."

"Cà Rá. I need you to stay incognito."

"What means incognito?"

"Holy shit, is he testing me?" Jack mumbled.

"Is who testing you?"

This had to be some kind of elaborate joke. Or maybe something he ate spit him into a bad dream. How could any of it be real?

"Did you ask my dad all these questions?"

"No. Why do you ask?"

Jack chuckled ruefully. "Okay, look. I'm meeting a woman to help me use the key to get the instructions from my dad. That's what you want, right?"

"Yes. The instructions from William." A petite smile lit up her face. "Do you like her?"

Jack pointed his index finger, and she locked her eyes on it and followed the path he made toward a green park bench. "Go sit on that bench, don't move, and stay quiet until I return."

She drew a breath to speak, and he snapped his fingers in her face. "Nah-ah. Not a sound."

Her brows furled, and defeat creased her face. She glanced at the bench, then back at Jack. With a disgruntled sigh, she walked away and took her seat on the bench, hands folded in her lap.

With a throttle twist, the engine roared, and he turned down the street, away from her.

Micro-sounds from across the park echoed inside Cà Rá's ears: the shuffling of a squirrel scraping the bark of a tree with its claws; a bird pecking at insects in the grass, feathers swooshing against each blade; the high-pitched buzz of a bee collecting nectar. William had brought her here twice before and they'd sat on this very bench. She closed her eyes and bowed her head to remember.

His gravelly voice echoed in her mind. "That's a cannon from over a hundred years ago."

William sat next to her, wearing a light-blue denim shirt, white hair draped out from under his brown, distressed baseball cap.

She opened her eyes and studied the cannon that sat on a concrete pedestal in front of them. Its patina-bronzed barrel rested on a long, black wood trail that stretched to the ground. Two oversized, spoked wheels supported the cannon's body.

"What did it do?" she'd asked.

"Well, during the Civil War, it hurt some people, I suppose. But at the same time, it protected other people. They would stuff a large iron ball or a canister of balls into it that would shoot straight out at the enemy. Pfoosh!" He sliced his hand forward through the air.

"A primitive weapon that served both good and bad," she said.

"I never looked at it that way, but sure." William paused with a fixed gaze at the cannon. "You know, a multi-shot burst like that is a good idea. I think I can—"

A faint buzzing broke Cà Rá's attention, and she opened her eyes. The flaps of a dragonfly's wings slapped the air, hovering directly above her. Thirty beats per second slowed to a near standstill.

Its wings swished, and she tilted her head to study it while two bulbous eyes stared back at her. It glided down in front of her face, and her reflection flashed across its 30,000 geodesic lenses.

A blue electric light pulsed in its body, and she squinted. The grim vision of a man's face with a deep scar on it flashed in her mind and startled her. It had the signature of a Xurrican.

She raised her hand, twisting her fingers in the air toward the dragonfly. Its legs and wings collapsed inward, and the ten segments of its body contorted and crumpled together. A white flash popped with a sizzle, and it fell to the ground.

Cà Rá stood and looked over a hedge of ligustrum bushes toward the bank. The Xurrican had to be nearby.

Jack rode to the front of the bank, and parked on a side spot. Star stood waiting for him. Not wanting to scare her off, he eased the bike to a slow roll and let the engine sputter to a stop.

"That's quite an entrance."

Jack skipped two steps up the stairs, smiled and looked back at the Triumph. "Yeah, it was my dad's bike. Thought I'd give it a workout."

"It's cool, I haven't been on a bike in a while."

"Yeah? Maybe I can take you for a ride." A red blush filled his cheeks. "Or something, geez."

Star laughed, "It's okay. So, lunch or bank?"

"Huh?"

"Do you want to eat before we go into the bank or after? Never know if our appetite will be ruined."

"Oh, right, yeah, I've got the key."

Jack glanced back in the direction of Cà Rá. "Listen, I think I need to tell you something."

"What do you mean you think you need to? Let me guess, you're married?"

"No, no. God no."

"Girlfriend?"

Jack stumbled through his thoughts. Gorgeous woman in front of him. Check. Psychedelic experience in a cave. Check. Vietnamese woman who knew his father. Wait.

He drew in a breath; better just to tell her. "No. Look, something happened this morning after you left the cabin, and I'm not sure what to do. I don't know anyone in this town, and I just met you, but..."

All or nothing. "Okay, this is gonna sound strange, but I like you. And I know if I tell you what I'm about to tell you, you're gonna think I'm crazy or something."

"Look, Jack, are you on drugs because I'm not into drugs."

"No, nothing like that. I found–I found something at the cabin. Not in the cabin. Under the cabin."

"Found what?"

"It's—"

Cà Rá's voice bellowed behind him. "Jack, what are you doing?"

He jolted upright and turned. "Jesus, I said don't do that."

Star took a half-step back.

Cà Rá stepped forward toward him. "There is a complication. The Xurrican that killed your father is here."

Jack shuffled down the stairs and nudged Cà Rá away with a whisper. "I said to stay out of sight, what are you doing?"

Cà Rá spoke loudly. "Did you get the instructions?"

"Shh."

Star hollered from the stairs. "Jack? Is now not a good time?"

Cà Rá looked back at her. "Who is this?"

Jack rolled his eyes. "Star, her name is Star."

"The other woman?"

"And who are you?" Star asked.

"I am Cà Rá. I am with Jack."

"I thought you were single. We can do this some other time."

"Do you have the instructions?" Cà Rá asked Star as she passed by.

"What instructions?"

Cà Rá darted a look at Jack, then back to Star.

Jack jumped in front of Star. "Whoa. Wait, please don't leave. This is what I was trying to tell you. This is Cà Rá, a friend of my father's. She's looking for some sort of instructions from him, and we think they're in the safe deposit box. Look, let's just go in the bank, open the box, get whatever it is she's looking for then she'll leave us alone." As Star angled away from Jack, he glared with wide eyes at Cà Rá. "And we can have lunch."

He couldn't remember the last time he met a woman like Star; actually, he'd *never* met a woman like her, and it showed. "I know this is crazy. I told you. Please, I'll buy lunch."

Star paused then uncrossed her arms. "No more surprises?"

"None. I promise."

She stared at him for a long moment. "Okay. Please don't make me regret this."

He turned to Cà Rá. "Wait here, we'll be right back."

They walked up the stairs and entered the bank.

As Cà Rá's face reflected in the glass door, she turned and stared down the street at the hospital building.

The door to hospital room 206 opened, and light from the hallway sliced across the floor of the dim room. Duncan entered and walked past an IV drip-bag stand to the edge of the bed where a woman lay sleeping.

A monitor beeped and caught his attention. The name *'Lyssa S.'* flickered on its screen and a green pulse-line displayed 75bpm. Oxygen tubes ran from behind the machine to a nasal cannula wrapped around her head.

He raised his left arm and pulled his shirt sleeve back to reveal a rusted metal bracer. With a press of two buttons, a series of red symbols flashed on its face. A compartment slid open and a fine glass needle with a red, pulsating stem protruded from its side.

Leaning over the bed, he tilted her head to the side and inserted the needle into the base of her skull behind her left ear. It penetrated the seahorse-shaped hippocampus limbic structure in her brain. In a synchronized junction, both the needle-stem and the bracer flashed red with an increasing tempo. Duncan closed his eyes and immersed himself in her memories.

The monitor beeped and updated to 79bpm.

Unstructured images flashed before him. A group of children splashing in the water. Seated in a classroom staring at a boy. An older man and woman screaming at each other.

Another beep. 86bpm.

Duncan skipped through the experiences. Smashing into a car through an intersection. A group of teens drinking with wild abandon. Jumping off a cliff and splashing into water.

108bpm.

He caught sight of the sphere in a myriad of stuttered images. The sign for the Temple of New Hope. David. Tarkos and Fletcher. The crucifix from the church, awash in bright light.

The beep from the monitor echoed across the images with a fevered tone. 158bpm.

Near the end of the record, the most recent memory took hold.

The fetus of a young child inside her, the wet sound of its heartbeat mixed with the rapid beeping of the monitor.

185bpm.

A female voice broke through the heartbeat and shattered the experience. "What are you doing? Get away from her!" a nurse shouted.

Duncan opened his eyes and withdrew the needle. He stumbled back and knocked the food tray to the floor. Duncan turned, and his eyes flashed bright blue at the nurse, who screamed and rushed out of the room. Three steps behind her, he raced into the hallway and sliced his hand through the air.

The nurse buckled at the knees, and she tripped, cracking her head hard on the floor.

A male orderly rounded the corner, noticed her on the ground, and rushed to her side. "Amy, can you hear me? Somebody, help!"

Duncan walked up behind the orderly and smashed his fist down on the man's head. Vertebrae shattered in his neck, and he collapsed.

Another nurse rounded the corner behind Duncan and dropped a clipboard. She screamed, and Duncan once again swiped his hand to the side.

A pulse of energy streamed down the hallway that lifted and threw her against the wall. She slammed into the floor and blood ran from her lips but she clawed at the floor, trying to pull herself away.

Duncan moved toward her with slow, measured steps.

Tears streamed down her face, and she pushed herself along the floor, desperate to escape.

The shadow from Duncan crept across her body, and she rolled onto her side. Anguish and fear froze her face, her eyes locked to his.

He raised his hand to end her torment but another female voice shouted from behind him.

"Stop!"

12

· COSMIC ENTANGLEMENT ·

Jack and Star stared at a floor-to-ceiling wall of safe deposit boxes. He scanned the numbered placards for 69-105 and wondered how many secrets had been hidden in this room. Treasures from the past, perhaps, evidence of affairs used for extortion or even the paternity papers of an illegitimate child. All of these secrets, stashed away from the world. And here he stood, searching for his.

He found the box, pulled the chain off his neck, and grasped the red key.

"Think there's money inside?" Star asked.

"Not a chance. He didn't have any money."

The lock clicked when he inserted the key and twisted. With a slight tug, he pulled the door open, and Star leaned in over his shoulder to peer inside.

A glimmer of fluorescent light reflected off the silver, rectangular box as he pulled it out of the opening. It didn't have any seams, hinges, or a mechanism to open. He flipped it around in his fingers and handed it to Star.

Jack grabbed the worn leather satchel and its shoulder strap drooped down. Two brass clasps kept its cover secure and he slid the latches to open it. Inside, he found a black 5"x8" Moleskine journal. He thumbed the pages, flipping through a series of mathematical equations, formulas, and sketches of electronic circuits.

Star glanced over. "You think this is what she wants?"

"I don't know."

"Anything else in there?"

He reached into the satchel. "No, nothing."

Jack placed the journal back inside the leather satchel then turned back to the safe deposit box and retrieved the white envelope, pausing to study his underlined name on the front of it.

He glanced back inside.

"Is that it?" Star asked.

"Just this letter."

He ripped the top of the envelope open and a tri-fold letter slid out, which he unfolded.

West Church Graves had been typed in the very center of the page.

"West Church Graves," Star said. "What does that mean?"

"No clue."

"What's on the back?"

He flipped the paper over to reveal the word *MOON* typed in all capital letters.

Star examined the paper. "This doesn't look like a set of instructions. Unless this journal is what your friend is looking for?"

"Cà Rá. None of this makes any sense. Let's go."

He slammed the door of the safe deposit box and took the key.

Cà Rá stood in the hospital hallway, her eyes glowing a deep sapphire blue.

A scowl creased Duncan's face and his gruff voice warbled, mixed with electronic crackles. "Guardian. Back from the dead, are we?" His fist tightened by his side. "Your human friend is not here to save you this time."

She glanced back and two drones floated in behind her.

"I will sort the data from his memory, and soon the Empyreax will be ours."

She didn't make a sound.

"He liked your human form, didn't he?"

Cà Rá darted her eyes straight at him.

"Did I hit a nerve? Very strange one of these creatures liking a Calodox. No matter. His death was quick."

The striped drone fired a dart at Cà Rá and she slid to the side. The dart sailed through the air and stuck into the far wall.

The second drone fired a series of plasma arcs she deflected with a swipe of her hand. She motioned toward a fire extinguisher that ripped from the wall and smashed into the drones. They spun away and crashed through a window. Glass particles sprayed outside while patients and nurses screamed.

Jack and Star walked out of the vault room and he placed the letter and silver box into the satchel.

They reached the front door of the bank and Star pointed through the glass. "Jack, she's gone."

He buckled the first clasp on the satchel but flashed a look to the front before snapping the second. "What?" He exited the bank and stared at the empty sidewalk then around the park. "Figures she'd be just like my dad. Doesn't listen worth a damn."

"Where do you think she went?"

"I dunno. Maybe back to the cabin?"

"Okay, then let's head back there."

"Look, Star, I don't want to tangle you up in this. Maybe I need to—"

Shrieks echoed from down the street and their attention turned to a stream of bodies pouring from the hospital.

"That must be her," Jack said.

Duncan's eyes flashed red and he levitated several feet. He raised his arm and lunged down at Cà Rá with a smashing blow to her head throwing her to the ground. The force of the impact shattered a massive spider crack across the floor. She swung her legs out from under her body and kicked up at him with a savage strike that drove him back.

Patients stuck their heads out of their rooms and crept down the hall trying to escape the fight.

Cà Rá grabbed Duncan's arm and flung him into a wall, smashing him through to an adjoining room. She followed him inside.

A mother and her son sat side by side with the boy connected to a chemo infusion machine. The woman jumped up and shielded her son from the dust and debris that shot through the air.

Duncan threw Cà Rá against the wall and she plowed through it back into the smoke-filled hallway.

She tried to stand but stumbled to the floor as blue, digital sparks of plasma dripped from her stomach and dotted the floor. Cà Rá pressed herself up on one hand and kept her silence.

Duncan stepped toward her, fist raised.

Cà Rá looked up at him.

When he drew his hand back to strike, an umbrella smacked him on the back of his head.

"Leave her alone!" the mother screamed and swung the umbrella to hit him again. He didn't even twitch as he turned and let it strike his face multiple times.

The woman dropped the umbrella, raced back into the room to stand in front of her son with her arms outstretched in a protective stance. "Don't you hurt my boy."

Duncan stalked after her, snarling, and leaned back to hit the woman.

Her eyes squeezed shut. "I love you, Peter."

Before his fist reached her head, Cà Rá swooped up from behind and pulled his arm back. He gasped from the jerk backward, gasped again when Cà Rá smashed his face with repeated elbow strikes then drove his head down to the ground.

The woman peered through one eye while Cà Rá delivered blow after blow. She opened her eyes wide when his head caved and flashed with a burst of light, revealing a skull-like face with black eyes.

Cà Rá thrust a devastating strike that ripped through his chest. An electronic buzz mingled with a human scream cut through the air. She picked up his body and hurled it back into the corridor, away from the woman and her son.

"Thank you," Cà Rá said. The woman stepped to the side and Cà Rá leaned toward the boy. She placed her hand on his forehead and a sizzle of yellow light spread from his eyes, down his neck and pulsed throughout his body.

Cà Rá closed her eyes and the intensity of the pulses grew. The light turned a bright white then faded. She nodded and smiled at the boy. "All better."

The woman stood, mouth agape.

"Your son will be fine," Cà Rá told the mother, then turned to leave through the busted wall.

A nurse behind the desk in front of Tarkos yelled into her phone. "Get the patients out! Where the hell is the Sheriff?"

Two doctors ran down the stairs of the main lobby, and Tarkos grabbed one by the arm. "Hey, can you help get the Reverend out of here?"

The doctor pulled away and ran out the main entrance.

"Hey! Hey!" Tarkos screamed.

"I'm not going anywhere," Fletcher said, pulling out his bible and clutching it.

Tarkos swiveled his head to the top of the stairwell and a man in a steel-gray fishing vest floated from the top of the stairs into the main foyer.

His eyes widened. "That's not possible."

A woman in a white dress flew in from behind the—*robot? Monster?*—and smashed into the thing, their bodies hurtling through a full glass window on an upper floor.

Thousands of shards of glass showered down, and Tarkos tried to cover Fletcher as best he could. The reverend stumbled and tripped backward, hitting his head on the ground. The bible flipped out of his hand.

"Are you okay?" Tarkos shouted through the noise.

Fletcher rolled over, blood dripping from a wound on his head. "Just dandy." He grabbed his bible and slid it into his coat pocket.

Smoke and dust filled the corridor, and lights flashed above them. A loud crash echoed from the foyer and Tarkos shielded his face with his forearm.

A nurse crawled toward him, blood pouring from her leg.

"Wait here," Tarkos said to Fletcher.

"Not too long now," Fletcher replied with a grimace.

Tarkos grabbed the nurse and slid her out the front door onto the sidewalk.

Glass exploded above him and flames leaped from the windows. Sirens from a firetruck grew louder.

Tarkos raced back inside and helped Fletcher stand, then the two staggered out of the hospital side entrance and Tarkos rested the reverend against a bench.

Fletcher's eyes drooped to a close.

"I'll be right back," Tarkos said.

Cà Rá and Duncan spun through the air, entwined in a fury of kicks and punches. Sparks of blue plasma dripped from her wound and he focused his attacks on it.

With a mighty blow, he ripped a section from her stomach. Her arms and legs fell limp and she crashed twenty feet into the ground.

He paused and took a deep breath to regain his energy.

Crawling helpless on the ground with her hand covering her wound, she tried to attract objects from around the room and smashed them into him. She reached up one last time but had no energy left.

Duncan strafed in a single instantaneous flash and rendered a force that knocked Cà Rá down. A concrete column shattered and rained debris on top of her.

He floated to the ground and stood over her.

Her eyes shifted to the side as Jack ran into the room. "Hey, asshole!" Duncan turned to face Jack.

"Jack, no," Cà Rá pleaded with a groan.

"Why don't you pick on someone your own size?" Jack ran up and punched him in the face. The impact of his knuckles sent a shock of acute sharpness through the bones in his hand, up his arm, and forced him to reel back in pain.

Duncan lifted his hand and Jack floated into the air. His body arched backwards as it rose without any control.

The crack of a loud gunshot blasted through the lobby. The bullet struck Duncan in the chest and neon blue plasma energy poured from the wound and floated in bulbous droplets through the air.

Jack fell hard to the floor and looked up to see Star with her revolver in a three-point stance.

She fired again and Duncan jerked back. Four more shots and Duncan fell back, splashing into a large fountain.

Star's hands trembled and rushed to Jack's side. "Jack. Are you all right?"

"I'm fine."

Star pulled him up and he winced in pain.

"Did I just kill a man?"

Cà Rá's voice startled them. "Not a man. A Xurrican." She sat up with blue energy swirling from inside the shredded, pixelated wound in her stomach.

"Jack, you must go now." She smiled but her eyes rolled up into her head and she fell backward.

Jack turned to Star. "Get your car, quick."

Star pulled her car up and Jack placed Cà Rá into the back seat.

"Get to the cabin, don't wait for me," he said.

Star stared back at Jack with wide eyes and a trembling lip.

"It's going to be okay. I promise," he said.

He cupped her face and she tried to smile but nodded instead and drove away.

Two police vehicles screeched up next to him. Voices on the radio barked through the open window. "Finn, do not enter the building, repeat, do not enter the building. There may be hostages."

Jack kickstarted the Triumph and opened the throttle. As he pulled away, an explosion ripped out from the side of the building and showered him with glass. He slammed on the brake and jerked the handlebars forcing the bike into a sideways slide.

It wobbled, and despite the noise, he heard something fall off the bike. He turned to look but couldn't see it.

"Hey, get back here," an officer yelled.

Jack darted a quick glance at him, turned the bike full throttle, and sped away.

Tarkos stepped back into the hospital and peered around the corner of the main corridor. He glanced around the room, squinting through the smoke.

Footsteps echoed from the far side of the lobby, and he knelt behind an overturned desk covered by a fallen plant and waited, staring just over the top of it.

At the rear of the hospital, Demi leaned on his cane and walked through the smoke-filled hallway. Edgar and Miles crept ahead of him, guns drawn and pointed up the corridor. Takashi followed behind Demi with cautious steps.

The farther they moved through the hallway, the greater the damage. Shattered glass, exposed wires, medical equipment, and piles of debris littered the floor. Sparks sizzled and popped from broken overhead lights.

They turned the corner and entered the main lobby. It had been completely destroyed and filled with piles of smoking rubble.

"Find the girl," Demi said.

Edgar nodded at Miles and they both sprinted up a staircase.

Smoke swirled near the far corner of the room and caught Demi's attention. He limped forward on his cane and found the mangled body of a man half submerged in the water fountain. The back of his head rested on the concrete ledge with his eyes and mouth wide open. Takashi stared over Demi's shoulder at the body.

Demi paused and leaned closer to the man's face. A scar ran from his forehead down across his cheek, and a red light shimmered from deep within his eyes.

A loud crash sounded behind them, jerking their attention away. A metal shelf had fallen over and shattered the window of an information kiosk.

When Demi swung back to the body, a hand reached up and snatched hold of his chest.

Takashi grabbed the hand, and a burst of blue energy shocked him with a jolt that threw him backwards.

The body pulled Demi closer to its face, and the blue energy traced up through him. Demi mumbled and tried to resist the pulses but they tugged at him, ripping a shapeshifting plasma out of the body that merged into Demi. The energy pulsed one last time and flipped him backward to the ground. His cane fell to the floor and slid away.

Takashi pushed himself up and stumbled to Demi's side, rolling the man over.

Demi stared up at him. "What happened?"

Takashi shook his head.

Fire truck sirens blared in the background, and Demi glanced at the main entrance. "Help me up."

Takashi lifted Demi to his feet, steadied him before turning to find the cane.

Demi oriented his eyes to the room and inhaled a deep breath. Cool air filled his chest and seemed to run throughout his entire body. Muscles in his legs tightened. His skin tugged and stretched taut against his face.

Miles ran down the stairs, followed by Edgar. "She's here, but there's no sign of the sphere."

Tarkos stayed as quiet as he could, creeping away from the foyer and disappeared into the smoke.

Demi stared at Edgar in silence.

"Demi, what do you want us to do?"

He glanced at Miles and then at Takashi but turned his attention to a broken window high above.

Two drones floated down through the window and hovered either side of him before he turned to leave. "We must go."

Miles cast an uneasy glance at Takashi. Demi took a few steps then Miles beckoned him. "Demi!" He gathered the cane from the floor. "Your cane."

Demi turned and Miles handed it to him. After a brief pause to study it, he snapped it in two and threw the pieces away.

Something caught his attention, and he looked at the overturned desk. He scanned across the room, paused, then walked away.

Takashi followed Demi and the drones as they vanished in swirling wisps of smoke.

Edgar shuffled up to Miles. "You seen those things before?"

Miles spit tobacco onto the floor. "Nope."

"Shit's getting real, huh?"

"Yup."

Fletcher lay on a crimson-colored velvet couch supported by brass-tipped black legs. His head rested on a scallop-patterned cushion, and although his eyes stayed closed, he could see himself from afar. A focused spotlight above him cast a circular halo of shadows across a herringbone parquet floor. Beyond the spotlight, the silence of a void of darkness surrounded him. An icy chill raked his skin and tingled the hairs on his neck.

Could this be the moment of death?

His son Daniel stepped from the shadows and knelt by his side. When Daniel stroked Fletcher's head, a gentle warmth flowed throughout his body. "Daddy," his young voice beckoned. "Daddy. Wake up."

Fletcher wanted nothing more than to open his eyes and embrace his son one more time.

Daniel's hand caressed his white hair front to back.

A slight smile appeared on Fletcher's face but froze when Daniel screamed at him with the agonizing cry of a thousand banshees.

"Wake up!" His eyes flashed through yellow pupils slit like that of a cat, and his skin boiled black with evil. Claws emerged from his fingers, and he raised his hand against the swirl of a fiery hellscape.

With a swipe downward, he struck Fletcher across his face and slashed gaping wounds that gushed blood.

Daniel's voice changed. "Fletch! Wake up. Fletcher!"

He jolted awake and slumped against a bench outside the hospital.

Tarkos lightly slapped his face, and his eyes glinted open with a subtle head bob. "You still with us?"

Fletcher grunted.

"How many fingers am I holding up?"

Three fingers waved in front of his face. "Three shots of bourbon," he said, voice drowsy.

"Okay, you're fine," Tarkos said with a chuckle. "Can you stand?"

"Um." Fletcher squinted and looked around the chaos in the streets. Smoke billowed from the front of the hospital, and the wail of sirens mixed into chatter from the crowd of spectators.

His eyes focused on a black Moleskine journal that sat on the road just a few feet away from them. "What do you suppose that is?"

Tarkos went and gathered the journal, thumbed through it. "No idea."

The rumble of a car engine filled the air.

"Andre," a man called out from behind them.

"Bruce," Tarkos said.

Fletcher glanced up at Tarkos, and asked, "You ever get the feeling something was happening, but you didn't quite know what?"

Tarkos looked down at him. "Something is happening." He lifted Fletcher by his arm and helped him hobble to the car. "We need to go."

Bruce pushed his glasses tight to his face. "What the hell is going on?"

Tarkos reached into his pocket and held up the second sphere. "I was wrong about Soulgazer."

13

· ENTER NQCO ·

Meeks exited the hospital entrance and stepped over shattered glass from the sliding doors. Shards crunched under his boots. A horde of media crews scattered about, trying to get viral sound bites from witnesses; he would never understand the callous frenzy. Dozens of onlookers stood cordoned off by yellow tape, snapping pictures and recording video on their phones. He scanned up and down the piles of smoking debris that covered the sidewalk.

"Helluva sparkling day," he mumbled to himself.

Deputy Finn turned to him. "What was that, Sheriff?"

"Nothing."

Meeks stepped down the stairs and listened to a middle-aged woman speaking with Linda Fox. Another reporter stuck a microphone in Meeks' face but he waved them off.

The cameraman pointed his finger at Fox. She lifted her chin and held her microphone up to her face.

"Blake, good evening. We are live outside the Stone Creek Medical Center where authorities are assessing damage from what appears to be a terrorist event. Witnesses report hearing multiple explosions and possible gunfire from inside the hospital. I am— ma'am, over here." She tugged on the woman's arm. "I'm standing here with Rae-Ann Johnson who was supposedly inside when all this happened. Rae-Ann, what can you tell us?"

The woman leaned into the microphone and tried to take it away from Fox who tugged it back. "It's actually Rae-Ann Jackson, but that's okay," she said in a creamy southern drawl. "So I was inside the infusion room because my son Peter has lymphoma, it's a cancer, a tumor the size of a baseball in his neck. And we were sitting there doing his treatment and we started hearing all this commotion with the floors and walls vibrating all around us."

Meeks raised his eyebrows and leaned in.

Rae-Ann threw her hands in the air and the cameraman had to pull back. "Out of nowhere, the wall behind us just blew up, then this guy comes flying into our room. I knew he was going to kill us, so I did everything I could to protect my son. Then, this young girl, rushed in and started fighting him with her bare fists. I didn't know who she was, never seen her in the hospital before."

"What kind of fighting? Martial arts?" the reporter asked.

"No, just straight up like you see on UFC. Maybe, yes what's it called, Mixed Martial Arts? I'm not an expert, my husband and Peter would know. So this guy slams this little girl down with all his might, and she was strong, like you wouldn't believe how she fought back. So, I reach into my purse and grab my can of mace, 'cause I keep mace in there in case I ever get jumped by a rapist."

Other reporters had gathered around her and held microphones, cameras, and smartphones up to record her.

"And I sprayed it in his eyes and started beating him with my umbrella, which I had because it was supposed to rain this afternoon, but it didn't. He must have been high on drugs or something cause his eyes looked like they were on fire. Anyway, she picks this dude up and tosses him like a rag doll out of the room. Just like that." She snapped her fingers.

"The girl walks over to me, and she says in the calmest and sweetest little voice you ever heard, 'thank you'. Then she leaned forward and touched my son's forehead for a few seconds and poof she disappeared.

Next thing I know, Peter's tumor is completely gone, his neck totally flat. A miracle. The doctors took my son to Woodson to look at him. But I know she saved him."

The reporter's eyes widened. "And you believe this woman cured your son's cancer?"

"I don't *believe* she did, I *know* she did. She's my angel."

"And what happened to the man?"

"I'm not quite sure. After that, we heard gunshots and screaming way down the hall. A few minutes later, everything went silent. That's when we heard the police and some nurses helped us escape."

Rae-Ann looked directly into the camera and pulled the microphone to her face as the cameraman zoomed in. "Angel, whoever you are, *thank you*. Thank you from the bottom of my heart for saving my boy."

Fox nodded and pulled the microphone back. "That's quite a story, Rae-Ann, thank you for sharing." Fox looked back into the camera. "Blake we're going to try and get some more eyewitnesses lined up, and maybe an official statement from law enforcement about this breaking story. Back to you in the studio."

Shouts and screams from the horde of reporters turned to face Meeks and he jolted.

"Sparkling," Meeks said louder this time.

A female reporter broke through the shouts. "Sheriff, what was that? What do you think of her story? Where is the girl? Who is the man?"

Meeks frowned at the horde before him, and he held his hands up and waved them to give himself some room. "Look, folks. We don't have any statements to make right now. We've contacted the FBI and they are en route."

"How many victims?" another reporter shouted.

"We don't know but this is a casualty situation." He glanced back at Finn. "Finn, can we disperse this crowd?"

"On it, Sheriff. People, let's go. Now is not the time for questions. We'll have a press conference in—"

"What about the MMA girl?" A reporter yelled in a high-pitched voice. "Who is she?"

"Now, look," Meeks said, "we don't know anything yet about a girl. As soon as we have details to share, we'll let you know."

Another reporter shouted. "Anything from the hospital security cameras yet?"

"They're working on it. I have to go."

With a quick turn, he leaned into Finn and whispered. "Take Rae-Ann to Woodson with her son and see what else we can find out before the Feds get here."

"Will do." Finn stretched out a roll of yellow tape to push the crowd and reporters farther away from the hospital.

A siren squawked from the right side of the street and Meeks jerked his head in its direction.

Three blacked-out Chevy Suburbans with blue flashing lights drove past two state troopers who waved their arms trying to stop them. A lane opened up amongst the crowd and the cars broke through the yellow tape Finn had stretched out.

"What the hell is this?" Meeks said. They had just called the FBI so they couldn't have gotten here that fast. His bad knee twinged when he stepped down and stood in front of the Suburbans.

Reporters swarmed the vehicles and Finn shouted at them to move away.

Everyone paused and the crowd fell silent.

The doors of both vehicles opened.

Muscular men wearing khakis, black shirts, FDE plate carrier vests, and black caps, stepped out, lining up next to the middle Suburban. They each had a thigh-holstered Sig Sauer P320 handgun and carried a 9MM Heckler & Koch MP5A3 carbine. A coiled wire extended from their ear to under their shirt collar.

A man shouted from deep in the crowd of spectators. "Oh, hell no." Everyone stepped farther back with their cameras recording.

"Everyone turn your cameras off and leave the premises. You are now trespassing on a Federal Homeland Emergency investigation."

Meeks stumbled along the sidewalk and lifted another section of yellow tape over his head. "Hey! Hey! What are you all doing? This is a crime scene, you can't just waltz in here like this."

He glanced at a patch over the man's left chest. It had been embroidered with a yellow |NQCO> symbol on it.

The man put his hand on Meeks' shoulder to prevent him stepping forward. "Sheriff, you need to step away."

"Get your hand off me unless you want to lose it." His red face reflected in the man's sunglasses.

"Sheriff Thomas Meeks?" A woman stepped out of the open door of the second vehicle.

"That's me. Who the hell are you? What are you all doing creating a scene like this? It's not protocol."

"Carmen Vasquez with the United States NQCO."

"What the hell is that?"

"The National Quantum Coordination Office."

He leaned back to Finn. "You ever heard of them?"

Finn shook his head.

Meeks fired back at her. "My ass. Where's the FBI? We called them over an hour ago."

"They called us."

"What do you mean they called *us*? How does the FBI not have jurisdiction?" Meeks glanced past her at agents confiscating cameras while the crowd dispersed and ran away.

"We need your men to clear the area now."

"Who the hell are you to give orders? I'm in charge here."

Vasquez stepped past him and over the threshold into the hospital lobby. The agents grabbed silver cases from the Suburban trunk space and followed her.

"Goddammit. Will someone tell me what's going on?" Meeks stomped his foot on the concrete, and Vasquez paused. The pain in his knee shot up through his leg. If that didn't get him, his blood pressure would.

"We'll show you," she said.

The NQCO agents set the boxes in the middle of the foyer and opened them. They retrieved electronic devices that rested on tripods, and each agent stationed them throughout the room. As they turned each device on, red lasers scattered across the room and generated a three-dimensional scan of it on a nearby laptop screen.

"Sheriff." Finn raised his finger and tried to interrupt.

"Hold on, Finn. Listen lady, it don't matter what agency you're with. You could be from the Vatican for all I care, but I've got multiple deceased residents in less than a week. And now we're looking at some sort of terror attack on our town. So I'm not about to let political suits from D.C. start pushing us around just to get a photo op for the next election."

Vasquez stared up at him without a blink.

Finn broke the silence. "Sheriff—"

"Finn, give me a second. Please."

Before he spoke another word, Vasquez pulled a photograph out of a manila envelope and held it to his face. "Have you seen this man?"

Meeks pinched the sides of the photo in his fingers, angling it down to the light. "No, never."

"What about this man?" She slid another photo on top of the first. "No."

"Doctors Andre Tarkos and Bruce Hon. They were scientists in one of our Quantum Intelligence programs who stole something, and we have reason to believe they've come to Stone Creek."

"Stole what? Why here?"

"That's classified. But it's a matter of national security and I need your help finding them."

"What does this have to do with anything?"

"Sheriff —" Finn flashed his hand in front of Meeks, who snapped back at him.

"For Christ's sake, Finn, what?"

"They got the security camera footage back online. You need to see this."

∞

Star opened the front door to the cabin and stepped inside, the leather satchel draped over her shoulder. Newt jumped up from the floor with a bark. Jack walked in sideways with Cà Rá's limp body in his arms. Digital pulses of blue light flickered down her side and flashed across his face.

"Bedroom down the hall," he said.

Star turned on the hall light and jumped back when a loud beep with a red light flashed just in front of her face.

"Jesus."

"PO get out of the way," Jack said.

PO rotated and floated to the side of the hall away from Star.

"PO?"

PO's round eye blipped green and beeped.

"That means yes," Jack told Star. He entered the bedroom and laid Cà Rá on the bed. Newt lay on the floor and whimpered.

"Jack," Star said.

"Gimme a minute." He walked back out of the room past Star.

PO floated into the room and glided above the foot of the bed. A horizontal beam of blacklight shot out from his glass eye and scanned across Cà Rá's body. When it passed over her stomach, bright neon-red sparkles materialized and flickered like the tips of digital flames. They drifted into the air and disappeared. PO shut off the beam while a fast-scrolling calculation of numbers and symbols stretched over the curvature of his eye. The sequence ended with the number *59704*.

Jack re-entered the room carrying the electric, corded, silver head harness.

"Jack, I need to know what the hell is going on."

Without a word, he placed the harness on Cà Rá's head and strapped it under her chin. A silver hoop rested between her eyes, and two straps pulled down her cheeks clasping on the backside of her neck. He looped the electric cord off the side of the bed and plugged it in.

As soon as he did, the number on PO's display started to tick down once every second. *59703. 59702.*

"Jack!" Star's yell bounced off the walls.

"I'm sorry. I'm sorry." With a gentle touch to her fingers, he took her hand, and she fell into his arms. Tears streamed down her face, and he squeezed her tight.

"What is this? What have I done?" she asked.

"It's okay."

She fought back tears through a sniffle.

The sweet aroma of coconut flooded his senses when he pressed his face into her hair. "Shh. You did what you had to."

"I mean, it was supposed to just be a date, right? Now I'm going to prison."

"What?" He leaned back and cupped her face with both hands. He wiped warm tears from her cheeks.

"I just want to go home. I didn't ask for any of this."

"You can't go home yet. They'll be looking for us. For her."

"I killed a man, Jack."

"To save me. Star, listen. You didn't kill a man. It wasn't even human."

He turned her around and wrapped his arm around her waist. "Does she look human? Does any of this look human?"

PO's blacklight emitted again and scanned over Cà Rá's wound. Thousands of particles of neon-orange light pulsed over her stomach, seeming to regenerate the wound.

With a light sniffle, Star wiped her face clear. "What's it doing?"

"Charging. I saw this thing in one of my dad's journals yesterday."

He looped the satchel off Star's shoulder and placed it on the desk. The main pouch flap rolled open and he reached inside to pull out the letter and metal box. "Hang on..." With both hands, he stretched the satchel wide and peered inside. "Where's the journal?"

The desk chair squealed when he swiveled around and scanned with frantic eyes around the floor. "Shit. I think it fell out at the hospital."

He turned back and when reached for the letter, the bracelet on his left hand passed over the box and vibrated with a blue flash.

Jack startled but cautiously moved the bracelet closer to the box.

Lighted geometric patterns flashed on the bracelet and in unison with the faces of the box. Whirring rotors and a sequence of clicks chirped before the top of the box cracked open. He reached for the lid and flipped it back, exposing a black drone about the size of a smartphone.

A standing Lady Liberty quarter sat centered on the top middle of the drone encased in a hot-glued acrylic slab.

An affixed sticker in the corner read 'Press Me' next to a red button.

"I don't think you should press that," Star said, trepidation in her tone.

Jack hesitated and rubbed his hand across his mouth. "I think we need to." He reached out and pressed the button.

Nothing.

Jack pressed the button again.

Still nothing.

He pressed it a third time. "Well, I guess—"

Green light flashed on the drone and four, round plastic props clicked and stood upright.

Star flinched and stepped away.

The drone's blades powered on and spun with a high-pitched squeal. It rose and hovered in front of Jack for only a moment before darting out of the room.

"Hey," Jack said sprinting after it. The drone sped down the hall faster than he could keep pace. It slid out the front door and he stumbled onto the porch, watching it arc into the sky, drifting away.

He returned to the living room and Star stood with Newt and PO all staring back at him. "It's gone. All we have left is West Church Graves. Any idea what that means?"

"There's an old, abandoned church west of town with a cemetery. But what would we be looking for?"

"I'm not sure. Can I borrow your phone?"

"Why? It's dead and I need to charge it."

"I need to call my brother."

"Jack, I am *seriously* freaked out right now. I'm hoping this is some sort of nightmare that I'm just going to wake up from and be in bed with a bad hangover."

He pulled her hand toward the basement door. "Listen, can you trust me? I need to show you something."

"What?"

He darted a glance back at PO. "PO, keep an eye on Cà Rá."

His glass eye flashed green three times.

Jack paused. "What?"

A panel opened on PO's backside. A thin, black, lip-balm-sized tube slid out toward Jack. He plucked it free and turned it over in his hand. There was a tiny hole in the end of it that he tapped with his index finger. "What's this? A microphone?"

Yes.

"To talk to you?"

Yes.

He slipped it into his pocket and led Star into the basement.

14

· CEMETERY ·

Beads of condensation dripped from the outside of a glass of water sitting on an old oak desk. Demi leaned back into a brown leather chair in his study, and a blazing warmth traced through his body. Every sensation had been heightened and a nauseous wave of sickness fell over him.

The trickle of the water on the glass caught his attention and reflected in his eyes, the magnified refractions of light glowing from each droplet. Sounds from its beads gliding down the glass amplified and echoed in his ears.

He rolled his head back and closed his eyes. The faces of Tarkos and Fletcher flashed in his mind but then faded at the brash sound of a loud scrape.

Tilting his neck to the side, a cat in the corner of the room sat up and licked its fur with rhythmic sweeps of its head.

A pulse of electricity jolted his spine, thrusting him into a deep hallucination. The room shattered and fell away like shards of glass. The sphere splashed out of the darkness in front of his face and took his breath away. It floated before him, surrounded by plasma bursts of prismatic light.

When he reached out to touch it, a deep percussive boom pulled him out of the trance. Drawing a breath and finding himself back in his study, he paused and shook his head. The knock sounded again but returned to a tolerable volume. A knock at the door.

"Come in," he said.

Edgar entered, snapping a bubble from his gum. "Demi, there's a man here to see you, says he's an old friend. You expecting anyone?"

Demi paused and looked at the glass of water. "Yes. Yes, I know who it is."

Edgar chomped on the gum and leaned back toward the door. "Takashi."

Alex Rivera stepped into the room. Takashi followed close behind, keeping a trained look on the man.

Demi stood and smiled, his eyes flashing red. "You see, my friend? I knew you could do it. You see yourself free, and here you are."

Rivera nodded. "Now what?"

"Oh, I have big plans for you Mr. Rivera. But first, you need to get cleaned up. Takashi, show him to a room."

Takashi cast a frozen stare at Demi through his sunglasses.

"Now, now Takashi. Don't be jealous. I know he's a lot bigger than you, but you can still take him."

"I don't think so," Rivera snarled.

Takashi turned his glasses up to Rivera who gave him an icy stare. "What are you looking at?"

"Gentlemen." Demi's voice snapped through the tension. "We don't have time for this. Get him cleaned up and meet me in the temple."

Takashi waved his right arm toward the entrance and Rivera stepped out of the room.

Demi held Takashi back. "Before you go, we need to find that girl. She is very special and it is going to take more than bullets to stop her." He opened a drawer on his desk and retrieved a yellow taser-like gun frame that had been modified with additional electric components.

Edgar stopped chewing his gum. "Demi, do I get one?"

Demi shook his head. "No. Takashi is entrusted with this."

Takashi took it, bowed, and left the room.

A tingle surged in Demi's wrist and he grasped it with his other hand. Upon closer examination, his skin had rejuvenated and tightened.

"Are you all right?" Edgar asked.

"Yes. Edgar, I need you to find me the scientist and the preacher."

"Who?"

The striped and silver drones floated into the study through the main door and lined up behind Edgar. With some hesitation, he turned and raised his eyebrows.

"They'll show you the way," Demi said.

Meeks stood behind the left shoulder of a hospital security guard who sat in front of twelve monitor displays. Vasquez and Finn angled in on the right side.

The guard pointed a pencil eraser at the screen. "Okay, here. You see this man enter the rear of the building."

Meeks put on his glasses and leaned forward. "That looks like our guy. Duncan Hurley."

"He disappears from this camera." The pencil eraser skipped and tapped the screen of another monitor. "And then moments later reappears on the third floor where he attacks two staff."

"Why are the cameras out of sync?"

"They're not."

"Has to be. How'd he get there so fast?"

The guard shrugged. "That's above my pay grade."

Meeks pulled his lower lip with his front top teeth, watching Duncan kill the orderly and hurl the female nurse into the wall. "What the hell?"

The guard flicked his chin through his beard with his thumb. "So, then he goes downstairs to the lobby and confronts these men. That's definitely Reverend Fletcher. The other, I don't know."

"That's Andre Tarkos," Vasquez said.

"And then this lady appears and confronts him."

Meeks watched the fight and destruction unfold.

"Sheriff, what's going on?" Finn asked in a solemn tone.

"I don't know."

The guard tapped the screen again. "Then, we see this man and woman enter."

"Wait," Finn said. "That's looks like Star Hopper."

"Hopper?" Meeks said with a frown. "How's she mixed up in this? Who's the guy she's with?"

"Hard to see, but I don't recognize him."

They watched Star pull out her gun and shoot Duncan.

The guard continued. "As soon as she fires, the power surges and boom, lights out. We lose everything."

Meeks leaned back and rubbed the stubble of his five o'clock shadow. Vasquez tilted her head toward him. "We need to locate those two."

"Why?"

"Because they've been exposed to something lethal and it could spread."

"So why are we still in the hospital?" Meeks asked.

"I told you, that's classified."

Finn spoke up, "Sheriff, you want me to put out an APB with the state?"

Vasquez tilted her phone away from Meeks and tapped into it.

Meeks clucked his tongue. "No. She hasn't left the county yet. Call Mary Hopper and see if she knows where her daughter is. Tell her not to worry and we'll stop on by in a bit." He turned to Vasquez. "Okay, Miss Vasquez. I'll play along. What's next?"

"Locate Andre Tarkos and Bruce Hon."

Thick clouds had rolled in and covered the sunset, stretching a blanket of darkness across the valley. Jack and Star drove into the entrance of an abandoned church courtyard. A long, sloped hill led off into the distance, dotted with dozens of tombstones and hundreds of rocks spread out in a lined row. A sea of knee-high weeds guarded the front yard.

The church's walls harbored giant holes and cracks where plaster had been chipped away by time. Two oaks towered over it and clung to life from thick Oriental Bittersweet vines that cut a spiral of strangulation into their bark.

Jack tried calling Roger from Star's phone in his 4Runner, but only reached voicemail.

"Roger, it's Jack. Listen, I need you to get out to the cabin ASAP. I'm in trouble."

He clicked it off and handed the phone back to Star. "Can you text that number a message? Just say: It's Jack 911, get to cabin ASAP."

Star tapped on the phone. "It says undeliverable. Are you sure that's his number?"

"Yes." He shook his head. "This is exactly what happens."

"What?"

"This. Remember this morning? I told you that I always end up cleaning up Dad's mess and Roger's never around. Fuck. I'm sorry I got you mixed up in all of this."

"It's not your fault, Jack."

"It's my dad's fault. It was always his fault. And I'm sorry he did this to you." He tried not to look at her. How could he?

"I think at this point, we need help, so I'll take you home after this."

Star fixed her eyes on the church and nodded while biting her lip. "Okay."

They exited the vehicle and navigated the tall grasses into the foyer of the church. The main floor had rotted and gave way to barren earth. Spray paint graffiti and random symbols covered the walls. The deeper they moved, the darker it got. Jack flicked on a small flashlight and shone it around inside the empty space.

"I don't think there's anything in here," Star said as she looked around. "Something in the cemetery maybe?"

"Knowing my dad, I wouldn't put it past him."

They left the church through a rotted side wall and meandered to the graveyard. Tombstones sat in rows of twenty and most had tilted due to shifting earth. Eroded stone engravings were difficult to read.

Jack looked up the hillside at a symmetrical grid of rocks the size of footballs. "What are all these rocks?"

"Those were markers for unidentified soldiers. They say this place was a field hospital during the Civil War."

"There's so many."

"Yeah. The town was trying to designate it an historic site but lost funding back in the nineties. We used to joke...come visit Stone Creek, the town America forgot." She flicked her hands in the air with a sarcastic shake of her head.

They walked amongst the tombstones, shining light down on them. The sun dipped below the horizon and a diffuse purple glow colored the cloud-filled sky.

Jack glanced down at a headstone for a moment.

"Jack."

He looked over at Star who stared into the far distance at the silhouette of a man. The red glow from the ash of a cigar lit up against the horizon. "I see him."

The man stood motionless, facing them. Wind kicked up and the swoosh of leaves spread across the treetops.

A gust kicked up and whipped Star's hair into her face. "I'm not sure I like this."

Thunder rumbled in the distance and several heavy raindrops pelted the tombstones.

"Well, we aren't bothering him so he won't bother us." Jacke turned back around and walked down a row.

Star kept watch on the man while the rain fell heavier and turned into a downpour. "Jack, we need to go."

Rain soaked through his clothes and he shouted back. "Just a minute, get back to the car."

"He's coming!" Star yelled and ran back to the 4Runner.

Jack turned back at the man who turned on a flashlight and moved closer. "Shit." When he turned to leave, Jack tripped on a thick root that had grown up over a fallen tombstone. The flashlight flicked away and he sloshed in the mud. He pushed himself up and noticed the flashlight shining on a headstone.

It bore the chiseled name: '*Mary Anne Graves*'.

Graves? A laugh burst from him. *Of course*!

Lightning flashed and he turned back to see the man almost to him. Jack grabbed the flashlight, turned it off and sprinted for the 4Runner.

As he ran through the grass to the driver's side door, he slipped in the mud. Star screamed and he glanced at the backside of the church. The light swayed faster and faster toward him.

Jack threw the door open and climbed inside. The keys fumbled in his hand.

"Hurry."

He started the engine and pulled the shifter into reverse.

The man walked faster to the front of the church and shined the light on them.

The 4Runner careened backward down the overgrown path and into a small ditch. Jack swerved the wheel and floored the throttle as the vehicle bounced. Tree limbs and branches scratched against the metal and loud metallic thumps echoed inside when it scraped against a rock outcropping. They reached the main gravel road and turned onto it.

"We're not looking for something at the church. We're looking for people."

"What do you mean?"

"West, Church, Graves. They're people we need to find."

Tarkos sat at a desk in the rectory of Fletcher's church and flipped through the Moleskine journal. He studied the diagrams, sketches, schematics, and notations then paused on one page that contained the image of a cylinder.

Its title read: *EMPYREAX* with a thick line across the top. On the next page, he found a sketch of three rings with arrows flowing down through their center, as if nested into each other. The word *KEY* sat below the rings at the tip of the bottom arrow.

He pulled his phone from his pocket and sighed at the sight of its smashed screen. Nothing happened when he pressed the power button. "Damn, my phone is destroyed." The bathroom door clicked open and Bruce stepped out with a towel, patting his face. "Bruce."

"Yeah?"

"Give me your phone."

"Why?"

"I want to take photos of this journal."

Bruce looked at his phone. "Okay, but I don't have any signal." He handed it to Tarkos who handed it right back. "Passcode."

"Oh." Bruce punched it into the phone and handed it over.

Tarkos snapped photos of the diagrams and held each cream-colored page flat while focusing the phone's camera.

Bruce sat on the edge of the bed and slipped his shoe on. "I'm gonna be in a lot of trouble, Andre. Lily is gonna wonder where I am." He pulled tight on the shoelaces.

"You've had plenty of late nights, this is important."

Fletcher entered the room carrying blankets and pillows. "I don't have much, but you can spend the night."

"Reverend, do you have a cell phone?"

"No, but there is a phone in the back office you may use."

"Bruce, whatever you do, do not tell her where you are—" A terrible oversight interrupted his thought and stopped him cold.

Bruce cast a concerned look at Tarkos. "What's wrong?"

"Shit. I mean shoot. Reverend, do you have a paperclip?"

Fletcher nodded and motioned with his chin. "Desk drawer."

Tarkos pulled it open and shuffled through it. He found one and unfolded it, then ejected the sim card out of his phone. With a quick smack, he smashed the corner of his phone down on it several times until it broke into multiple fragments. "They'll be tracking us."

Tarkos popped out the sim from Bruce's phone and handed the

card to him.

"Well, why don't we just leave?" Bruce tucked the sim in his pocket.

"Bruce, I saw something back at the hospital. Something you wouldn't believe. I don't even believe it, but I'm not going anywhere."

"Andre, I can't get caught up in this."

"Bruce, just please help me first thing in the morning then you can leave. I'll cover for you and take the fall. This is too important and I need your help."

"Help you what?"

"I need to find someone."

"Who?"

"The man I saw at the hospital."

Tarkos turned back to the journal, snapped a photo and flipped the page. He froze at the image on the page. "What the hell?"

A comprehensive schematic of the sphere with numbers and symbols written around it stared back at him. "Soulgazer."

Jack stepped out of his 4Runner and into the pouring rain. He opened an umbrella to cover Star from the passenger side, and they huddled under it and skipped up the stairs into the cabin. Lightning flashed outside and he turned on the lights.

Star crossed her arms and shivered. "It already feels like fall."

"Hang on, I'll get a towel."

"My mom's gonna be wondering where I am."

Pulling open the hallway closet door, he grabbed a towel then opened the door to Cà Rá's room. She lay unmoved on the bed while PO floated above her like a stalwart guard. He rotated toward Jack in silence then turned back to Cà Rá.

Shutting the door, Jack walked back into the living room and wrapped the towel around Star.

"She's still the same. Would your mom know you're here?"

"Probably not, but she'll start getting worried if I don't call her." Star's lips quivered. "Can I ask you a question?"

"After everything we've been through? Sure."

"Why isn't there a Mrs. Jack Young?"

Jack smirked. "Oh, man. Nah. Never happened. Don't get me wrong, there was a chance at one point, but things just never worked out. And you sort of just wake up one day and here you are single in your forties, discovering aliens in your basement. Pretty normal, right?"

Star smiled.

"What about you? Where is Mr. Star Hopper?"

"There was one once, but that was a long time ago and I'm much better off. There aren't exactly a lot of options here in Stone Creek. But I'm good helping my mom—" A loud phone ring cut her off. "And that's her." She took a deep breath and answered. "Hi, Mom."

Jack lit a match and started a fire in the wood burning stove.

"Yes. I'm fine, why? No, I haven't seen the news. Really? Wow." She glanced at Jack and smiled. "I was on a date. No. Motheeer. I won't be home tonight. It's fine. Yes, I have my gun." Star's eyes widened with a smiling glance at Jack. "Okay, I'll be home tomorrow. What? All right, have fun at Bridge. Win some money. Huh? No. No, I have to go. No, I'll be okay. Love you too." She shut the phone off and laid it on the coffee table.

"Everything okay?" Jack asked.

"Yes. She's fine."

Mary Hopper sat on a yellow couch in her living room and looked down at her cell phone. She rubbed the dark glass of it with her thumbs then looked up at Meeks who put his hand on her shoulder.

A pained expression rose on her face, and she glanced across at Vasquez who sat in a dining room chair. Next to her, a man with a laptop focused on a digital mapping system that triangulated cell towers across a topographic map. He pointed his finger and stood to show Meeks who lifted his chin and studied the screen.

"Black Wolf Mountain."

The man looked at Vasquez and nodded.

Meeks spoke in a firm but gentle tone. "Mary, I want to thank you."

"Tom, what's going to happen to Star?"

"Nothing, we just need to locate her to ask her some questions about what happened at the hospital. It's for her own safety."

Vasquez leaned forward from her chair. "Mrs. Hopper, we are worried your daughter is in a great deal of danger."

Meeks shot Vasquez a look of disgust.

"She was exposed to a deadly chemical agent in that hospital explosion and she may not know she is sick. If she comes here, you need to let us know right away. She could be contagious, so do everything you can to stay away from her."

Tears welled in Mary's eyes and her cheeks trembled. "Yes, please help her, I don't want anything to happen—I can't lose her."

Vasquez took her hand and patted the back of it. "You have my word, as long as you follow our instructions, your daughter will be fine." She stood and left the house through the front door.

Mary looked up at Meeks as he put his hat on and exited behind the crew. Before closing the door, he turned back to her. "Mary, don't you worry, everything is going to be just fine."

"Tom. Please help my baby girl."

He nodded and pulled the door shut.

Meeks stomped without pause down the asphalt driveway. Rain gushed off the rim of his hat and he banged on the window of the Suburban. "Why the hell did you lie to her? She didn't deserve that."

The window rolled down and Vasquez's face beamed from inside. "Cooperation through fear Sheriff, you know that playbook, don't you? We'll have a team assembled at seven a.m. to head up to Black Wolf. Make sure your people are ready. Seven sharp."

Rain spilled off Meek's hat down his face. "I'm not taking—"

The window rolled up. "Don't you dare roll up this window on me, Goddammit."

The window closed and the Suburban sped off, its red taillights glowed against his face.

Finn walked up behind Meeks wearing a poncho and raised his umbrella over the both of them. "Everything all right, Sheriff?"

"Fuck no, Finn." He looked back at the Hopper home. "Something stinks to high heaven."

Star pressed her fingers against a photo of two young boys holding fishing rods, which rested on the bedroom dresser. Another faded photo of them in front of a treehouse sat nearby. "Is this you and your brother?"

Jack finished tucking a sheet across the corners of the bed then picked up a pillow and stuffed it into a case. "Yup. That's us."

"And this is your dad?" She pointed to a picture of Bill.

"The one and only."

"Huh. That's not what I thought he'd look like."

"What do you mean?"

"Well, you look just like him but you made him sound crazy. So I was picturing more of a mad scientist."

"He was crazy." Jack stepped back and tossed the bedspread onto the bed. "There. It isn't five-star, madam, but the best I could do."

"So do you think that Cà Rá has been up here the whole time?" Star asked.

"I don't know. Probably. That would explain a lot."

"Like what?"

"Like, why my father was up here constantly after my mother died."

Star walked past a stuffed penguin toy sitting on the nightstand. She tapped the pink bow on its head and picked it up.

Jack turned and stood face to face with her. "I'll be down the hall so if you need anything just—"

Star threw her arms around his neck and pressed her mouth to his. The penguin flipped onto the bed and they leaned back onto it, their bodies entangled.

Their lips slicked over as they tasted each other for the first time. Her mouth opened, and their tongues swirled together in ecstasy.

The warmth of her body radiated through Jack's clothes, and he spread his fingers through her hair then drifted his hands down her shoulders across her back. She moaned when he squeezed her tight and they caught each other's anxious breath.

Newt's paws clicked across the floor to the bedroom doorway and he let out a whimper that interrupted them.

Jack pulled back from Star and her hair draped across his face. "Hang on," he said, breathless.

"What?"

Newt tilted his head to the side with curious eyes and perked up ears.

Jack reached across the bed and grabbed the penguin. He tossed it at Newt but it hit the wall and fell just in front of the door. "Out."

Newt looked down at the penguin then back at Jack, turned and walked away.

On the north side of town, at the Montclare Community Home, an elderly man stood in his room staring out a large picture window. Heavy raindrops pelted the glass, and lightning flashed, filling the room with strobes of white. A single lamp cast a faint orange glow from a bedside table. Dozens of deep-space photos and newspaper clippings covered the walls.

Deep wrinkles lined in his face, and he glared at his reflection through an eye clouded with a milky cataract glaze.

Staring at the mountainous valley through the window had been his nightly ritual for two years where he stood with unbreakable patience. But on this night, the power of the storm brought with it a sense of calm.

A television to his left flashed images from the destruction outside the hospital with a graphic that read: *Possible Terror Attack in Virginia.* His lips curled with a smile and exposed his yellowed teeth.

"Simon." An orderly shouted at him through the open door.

"TV off. Lights out."

Simon waved at the man but kept his head down. "Sorry, boss. Had to stretch."

The orderly closed and locked the door.

Simon hated this place, but it kept him secure and out of sight. His focus turned to a calendar hanging above his bed with Friday the 13th circled in blue.

A streak of lightning crackled across the sky and thunder boomed that shook the window.

"I'm ready, Bill."

15

· THE FATHER, THE SON ·

Jack stared down at a round and tattered paper plate nestled into the grass. Clumps of damp vegetation wafted a sour odor of rot in the air. He double-tapped the end of a thin, yellow wiffle ball bat onto the plate and leaned back into a batter's ready-stance.

Roger stood twenty feet away with a tennis ball in hand that he bounced off the ground. "Runner on second. Two outs. Six to nothing."

"It's six to one," Jack said.

"No, that last run didn't count because of the out."

"Whatever, that's not fair."

"It's the rule."

Roger fired the ball over the plate, and Jack reacted too late with a swing and a miss.

"Steeeriiike one," Roger taunted.

Jack picked up the ball and tossed it back. "I wasn't ready, Roger, come on."

"If you're in the box, you better be ready."

Jack shook his head and tapped the plate again.

Roger leaned back and fired a direct pitch over the plate.

With his eyes closed, Jack swung the bat as hard as he could and launched a foul ball that landed on a concrete driveway across the street. It bounced up and over the top of a community storage shed to disappear behind a ragged board and batten fence.

"Foul. Strike two," Roger said. "Go get it, Jack."

"I'm not getting it, you get it. You're fielding."

"Yeah, but you hit it foul so you have to get it," Roger snapped back.

Jack's brow furrowed. "Come on Roger."

"Are you scared?"

"No."

"Well, go get it. Hurry up."

Jack turned and dropped the bat to gaze at the white cinder-block building and its rusted red-metal roof.

It did scare him.

Nobody knew who owned the garage but it had been used for decades by neighbors to store old cars, machinery, and tools. Things that would come and go without a thought or a worry. He could see it from his bedroom window and often heard voices drifting from it at night.

He looked up and down the street, then darted across the road. Thick, dark clouds crept over the sun and scuttled bright daylight to an overcast twilight.

Jack entered the gravel driveway of the garage and scurried to its left side into a ditch where he thought the ball had rolled. He scanned through the heavy grasses. Old bricks, rusted mower blades, and panes of glass littered the yard.

"Jack!" Roger yelled out just behind him.

His heart skipped. "Don't scare me."

"Where is it?"

"I don't know, it may have rolled inside."

They rounded the corner of the fence and Jack stopped, eyes popping wide. The booted foot of a person on the ground stuck out of the garage door. A shot of fear caught hold of him and he grabbed Roger's arm.

With measured steps, they moved closer, and found themselves staring at the body of old man Ralph Porter. His arms laid sprawled out on the ground just behind a blue Volkswagen Beetle. The skin of his pale head angled away from them and a smoky phenolic aroma lingered over his body. An empty bottle of whisky leaned up against his waist.

Roger tapped Jack and pointed at the tennis ball next to Ralph's leg. Jack took a silent step over the old man's knee and picked up the ball. Splotches of scalp dotted the back of his head, like islands in a sea of white hair.

As he stepped back next to Roger, he leaned in and asked his brother, "Do you think he's dead?"

Roger responded with a quiet shrug.

Wind kicked up the corner of a brown food wrapper next to Ralph's hand. A loaf of half-eaten raisin bread sat in the middle of it.

A beetle had burrowed into the bread and scuttled deeper into it as the paper swayed in the breeze.

"Gross. There's a beetle in the raisin bread."

Jack picked up a stick and pressed it to Ralph's chest but the man didn't move.

The boys glanced at each other and Jack pressed again.

The second time the stick tapped Ralph's chest, the old man jolted up and screamed an incoherent babble of profanity. "What the bitch wank mother fucking ding dong?"

Lightning flashed and thunder rumbled across the sky.

Both boys jumped with shrill screams then turned tail and ran. They sprinted back across the road, through their neighbor's front lawn and up the porch of their home. Roger threw open the screen door and sprinted upstairs.

The door's spring snapped the frame back into Jack's face. He pulled it open as fast as he could and crossed the threshold, tracking mud across the carpet.

When he reached the bottom of the stairs, he glanced into the kitchen from the corner of his eye and everything slowed around him.

His mother sat with the phone by her ear, its cord wrapped in her hand, staring at him with a pained expression. A single tear rolled down her face.

"Mom?"

Wednesday, September 11th, 2019

Jack's eyelids flipped open to complete darkness and he twitched in bed. His arm brushed against Star when he leaned over to turn on a light. She lay face down away from him and didn't move when the light clicked on.

He donned his boxers then pulled a t-shirt over his head and opened the door to find Newt who stood up, ran into the room and hopped onto the bed.

"Hey, get down," he whispered.

Newt ignored Jack, rested his head on the bed, and closed his eyes.

A calm silence filled the cabin and Jack made his way to Cà Rá's room. When he entered, PO rotated at him.

"Is she okay?"

PO flashed '*yes*' then turned back to Cà Rá. The timer on his display read *36821*.

Jack moved closer and sat on the edge of the bed. He placed his hand on her forehead and a warm tingle raced up his arm. "Who are you?"

PO beeped and a panel on his front clicked open.

Jack looked back at him. "What's that?" He reached up and pulled out a thin, red multimeter test lead probe. "What am I supposed to do with this?"

A red laser beam shot out from PO's glass eye and pointed at the top of the harness on Cà Rá's head.

When Jack tugged on the probe, a thin cable extended from the bottom of PO and he stretched it out to reach Cà Rá. Upon closer inspection, he found a round port on the top of the harness. He slid the probe home until it clicked.

A bright light burst from PO's glass eyes and filled the entire room with a rapid sequence of digital strobes. An orb of images flashed in multiple, intertwined sequences, one portion of an image flipping to the next. The images scattered across the room and paused at his father standing near the back of a flatbed truck.

Jack stepped toward the hologram. His father and another man lifted a heavy metal structure off the truck.

"I'll be back tomorrow with the last one," the unknown man said. "Just need to finish up some spot welds."

"Thanks, Sam." Bill wiped his brow and tugged his hat.

A young boy with long blond hair shuffled his worn shoes through the dirt and stood in front of Bill. "Mr. Young, sir, can I please use your bathroom?"

"Sure, Mikey, go inside and it's to your right down the hall. Don't touch anything please."

"Thank you."

Mikey dashed past Bill toward the cabin. As he ran by Jack, a rolled comic book shifted in Mikey's back pocket.

Newt barked in the background and sprinted from the red barn down a dirt path to a wooden fence post. He carried the looped end of a long, twisted manila rope in his mouth.

Sam turned and squinted at Newt. "Hey Bill, why does Newt keep doing that?"

"Doing what?" Bill lifted his hat to scratch his head.

"That thing with the rope."

"Oh, he's just playing."

Newt looked at them with his mouth open, yelped, then grabbed the loop and ran back up the hill to the barn.

Sam slammed the creaky door shut. Bill pulled a tractor around and hooked a chain to an object that he lifted from the bed of Sam's truck. He backed up the tractor and drove about seventy-five yards on the south slope where he hoisted the massive metal chamber up to a round platform that had a series of turbines and engines attached to it.

Sam shifted the chamber in place and secured it with four long bolts. Bill climbed up the column and uncovered a mirror attached to its side.

He tilted it with a keen eye's aim at another column just like it on the far side of the cabin.

Sam tracked his eyes between the two columns then into the sunlight up at Bill. "You ever gonna tell me what these are for?"

The digital images popped and with an electrified slash across the room, the playback skipped to beneath the cabin.

Light flashed against his face and Jack stepped forward to Mikey, who stood frozen in fear. A tumultuous orb of spinning light slapped large concentric arcs of electricity across the ground.

The whole of the dark abyss flattened with a strobe pattern of blue light that created an artificial floor spanning the entire expanse of the chamber. The dome of light began to twist like a corkscrew and created two halves that slapped down onto the grid-patterned floor.

With each slap, a burst of light sent rippling waves of energy throughout the dome. A loud boom filled the chamber and dropped in frequency, its notes wobbling to silence. Half of an egg-shaped dome of plasma formed around the device and the arcs rotated faster and faster until a dark portal-opening cut into the air.

Cà Rá streamed into the chamber and looked down at Mikey, then up at the gateway. "What have you done?" she asked.

Without pause, an entity of immense radiant light emerged from the opening. It flashed several times and looked at Mikey with glowing red eyes. The light contorted, shape-shifting into a giant metallic scorpion. It turned and lifted its front pincers leaning back ready to strike with its tail.

The scorpion growled at Mikey and he glanced down at the comic in his hand. The same giant scorpion lay sprawled across the page. The boy stepped back and tripped on a rock. The comic flew out of his hands and he scrambled to get up, to run away.

Cà Rá glared at the beast and rushed toward it.

The playback flashed white noise and skipped ahead.

Bill scrambled down the stairs into the chamber.

The creature stabbed its long, segmented stinger at Cà Rá, bursting a brilliant yellow light each time it missed her and struck bedrock.

Rushing to a cabinet on the far side of the cluttered electronics table, Bill knelt and opened its door revealing an M134 minigun. He grabbed an energy sphere and loaded it into a side compartment on the gun. When he pulled back on the charging handle his hand slid past the name Black Widow painted in white down its side. The gun hummed and a red light flashed near the trigger guard. Getting to his feet, he lowered the gun to his side in his left hand and rested his right index finger on the trigger.

Cà Rá smashed a fist hard into the back of the creature's head and stunned it, causing it to stagger back. She swooped forward with a burst of energy and formed an energy bolt that struck the creature in a burst of light but the particles disintegrated against its metallic armor.

The creature struck, knocking Cà Rá back against the chamber wall with incredible force.

Bill shouted at the top of his lungs. "Over here!"

The creature turned to look at Bill and he pulled the trigger on the Black Widow but all it did was click. He looked down at it and pulled the charging handle again and again.

"Shit."

Cà Rá leaped into the air and landed another blow on the creature but this time its pincers caught hold of her leg and pinned her to the ground.

Before she could react, the stinger arced over the scorpion and impaled her abdomen. A burst of energy ripped through her stomach and left a gaping, transparent section that tore away when the stinger retracted. She contorted and her light faded to a dull glow.

"No!" Bill flicked the handle one more time.

The scorpion turned and rushed at Bill.

On the last charge of the handle, the device clicked and flashed red again. He pulled the trigger and its six barrels rotated a spiraling beam of energy at the scorpion.

As the beam hit the creature, cavitation waves formed in the space around it and the scorpion shattered bit by bit. Millions of energy particles peeled away from the creature and dissipated into the chamber.

The energy bursts pounded against the chamber walls and Bill stood stoic in the cataclysmic path of reflecting flashes, arcs of electricity, and bursts of power. His skin stretched while his white hair pulled straight back in the waves of the thunderous force.

The scorpion rushed Bill again, and he tilted the Black Widow up, slicing its tail off. The stinger hit the ground and exploded into several chunks of sparkling atoms.

It fell back and spun to the ground. The beams from the weapon concentrated on its head until it swelled and burst in a flash of light particles.

The portal from which it came flashed and collapsed shut, leaving the chamber still and quiet.

The charging button on the Black Widow went dark and beeped. Dropping the gun to the ground, Bill clutched his chest and took a deep, wheezing breath. Sweat poured from his skin and he scrunched his face in pain.

Jack stared while his father staggered to Cà Rá's lifeless body.

He knelt by her side just as he had in Vietnam. "No. Please. Please don't leave me."

The bracelet on his left hand beeped and flashed symbols that started to countdown. Bill glanced at them and reeled in pain.

Jack twisted his wrist and looked at the bracelet.

"I just need more time," Bill said. He picked up Cà Rá and carried her to a platform. Turning back to a computer he punched a button and a dome of light covered her.

"Please protect my boys." His eyes fixed on her for a brief moment but the bracelet flashed red and beeped, forcing him to leave.

Although Bill exited the chamber, nothing changed, and Jack stood in silence.

In the corner of the chamber, an entity of light emerged from behind a rock ledge and took on a glowing, human skeletal figure. It walked up the stairs and followed Bill.

The video playback flashed again and Jack stood outside in the yard of the cabin.

A black portal opened there and Bill fell through it, crashing to the ground. His eyes darted back to the portal that closed behind him.

Beleaguered and gasping for breath, Bill curled into a fetal position on the gravel driveway. He struggled to reach for his phone, which had fallen on the ground two feet from his head. His fingers stretched and tapped against the corner of it, and he strained to pull it close. He pressed a button, and Jack's name glowed on the screen.

The call went to voicemail.

Bill winced and dropped the phone. Gasping for air, he once again reached for the phone. When he picked it up, he dialed Jack again.

The phone rang three times, and Jack answered in a rushed voice.

"I'm in the middle of something. I'll call you back."

Jack's eyes widened.

The call ended, and a spasm twitched Bill's arm. He shivered, his entire body now starting to shudder.

A digital pulse blipped across the playback, and Bill clutched his chest with pangs of anguish etched deep in his face. His hand trembled and he reached for the phone to call again.

Three rings sounded before Jack answered, this time in a tone of annoyance. "Dad, seriously, I can't talk right now."

Jack turned to PO and a tear streamed down his face. "Make it stop."

PO didn't move.

Bill rolled from his side onto his back without a sound; his face turned up to the heavens.

"Hello? You've got to stop calling me. I don't have time for this." Jack's voice echoed through the room, and his words sliced into him like daggers. "I need to go."

PO drifted from the cabin and hovered at Bill's feet. Newt ran up to him, laid down by his side and nestled his nose into his side with a whimper.

Jack took half a step forward to the hologram and stood over his father, watching through glossy eyes.

Bill's breathing slowed, and his pupils dilated as if he had seen something wondrous above him. His hand opened, and he reached to the sky—toward Jack. But how? It wouldn't have been possible.

Jack drifted his fingers through his father's holographic hand. An immense stab of sorrow slit open his heart and coursed guilt through his veins, tears flooding his eyes. His lips quivered, and he choked through deep, stuttering breaths. His father had died—alone.

"Dad."

Cà Rá's head jolted, and the playback from PO's eye shut off with a hard cut to darkness.

Jack collapsed to the edge of the bed, face in his hands, fighting back tears.

Star's shadow from the doorway's light sliced across the room and he glanced up at her, seeking solace, comfort.

"Why?" he asked.

Star moved to his side, wrapped her arms around him, and laid her head on his shoulder.

"It's okay. It's okay."

With a deep breath, he wiped his eyes and turned to Cà Rá. Though she did not speak, she told him everything. And he understood more than he saw.

"I need to help her."

16

· EXOTIC MATTER ·

Dawn had already passed when the Jeep carrying Meeks and Finn turned from the main road onto a dirt throughway that led to Black Wolf.

Sarah's voice rattled through a torn speaker inside the Jeep. "Toxicology shows no indications of alcohol or drugs but there is one unknown substance."

"What does that mean?" Meeks asked.

"There was a significant amount of something in the blood they couldn't identify. They'll send the samples to the state lab and should be able to pick it up then."

"Okay. Anything else?"

"Victims from the hospital did not have the same puncture mark on their necks. But one of the survivors, Lyssa Stone, did have it. One other thing. A metal fragment found in Moe Harper's neck was highly magnetized. So much so that we couldn't get it off the scalpel."

"What does that mean?"

"I have no idea. We sent it and the scalpel off to the lab."

"Okay, good work. Keep me posted."

"Will do. And Sheriff, these NQCO agents keep trying to take over."

Meeks darted a quick look at Finn. "And what did you tell them?"

"I was polite and told them to fuck off."

Finn chuckled and Meeks smiled. "You just made my morning, Sarah. Give me a call when anything new comes up."

"Yes, sir. Good luck out there."

The call ended with a double beep.

"Well, Deputy, what do you think?"

"I haven't a clue, Sheriff. Never seen anything like it. But I'm with Sarah, I don't trust the NQCO."

"You and me both."

The Jeep hit a low rut in soggy gravel that splashed mud up onto its rockers. It pulled off the road crossing a culvert and into a large open shoulder near the intersection of the main road and dirt track leading up Black Wolf Mountain.

Several Black Suburbans sat parked with Vasquez and her crew huddled together pointing into the forest.

She wore beige tactical pants and a black flak jacket with the NQCO logo emblazoned across its back. Two agents flanked her, holding tablets with digital maps that she studied. The sound of the Jeep seemed to snap her attention to them, and she nodded to one of the men.

The brakes on the Jeep squealed to a stop. Meeks opened the door and slid out, his boots sloshing into the mud. He reached back inside, put on his hat, and grabbed a stainless tumbler of coffee. "Good morning," he said, approaching Vasquez.

"You're thirty minutes late."

Steam rose from the tumbler as he took a sip and curled his lip. "We operate on a different clock down here, Ms. Vasquez."

"Well, since we lost so much time, I've already sent agents ahead to the cabin."

"Excuse me? Where's the warrant?"

"Right here." She handed him a stapled pack of papers, which he flipped through. "We operate in real time, Sheriff, so you'll need to learn to keep up."

"That's all fine and dandy, but just remember, we're not subordinate to you or anyone. You still answer to me and the citizens of this town. So you're not arresting anyone without my authorization."

"Under the statutes of the National Security Act we have every right to—"

"Aw, horseshit," Meeks said. "Will you stop with all this government mumbo jumbo? What are we really talking about here? National security, my ass."

Vasquez paused and folded her arms, giving Finn a dead-on stare. She turned back to Meeks. "Okay, Sheriff. Tell me, what do you know about Quantum Physics?"

An agent leaned in behind her. "Ma'am." Vasquez shot her hand up to stop him from speaking.

"Can't say that I know much," Meeks said. "Finn?"

Finn just shook his head and shrugged.

"Energy, dark matter. Building blocks of the universe? Any of this ring a bell from school, or don't they teach that down here?"

"I skipped school that day," Meeks said, "and I don't have time for games. What does any of this have to do with Star Hopper?"

"Higgenbotham."

"Higgenbotham? The caves with the endangered bats?"

Vasquez leaned back to the agent. "Call ahead and tell Carter we'll be at the cabin in one hour." She turned back to Meeks. "There are no bats."

"No bats? So why did they close?"

"I'll show you."

Loose asphalt from the road kicked up from the tires of Jack's 4Runner when he parked curbside in front of a faded green house. He peered past Star through the open window, scanning the weathered siding and dented gutters. "This is four-o-four Whipple. Let's see if anyone's home."

They exited the vehicle and walked up gray-painted steps to a front porch that creaked and sagged under their weight.

Jack pulled open an aluminum screen door and banged a brass knocker four times.

Star raised her eyebrows. "Think she'll have answers?"

"We'll find out."

A flash of white on a window next to Star caught his eye in time to see the face of a woman behind a curtain. He pointed at the window and Star turned to look but the woman had disappeared.

"Someone's home." He reached up and tapped the knocker again.

When the last knock sounded, a small slot on the door opened. A woman's voice rasped through it. "No solicitors," she said.

"Ma'am—"

The slot closed with a click.

Star smiled. "Not gonna be easy."

Jack smirked with a nod, and he banged the knocker again.

The slot opened. "Go away, I don't—"

"Ma'am," Jack cut in. "We're not selling anything. We want to talk to Rita West."

"Who are you?" the woman's voice cracked.

"Jack Young, and this is Star Hopper." He motioned toward Star and waited for a reply. "We need to speak to Rita West."

After an uncomfortable pause, the slot slammed shut.

"Phew." Jack rubbed his hand through his hair.

"Maybe I should try," Star said, and reached for the knocker but several loud clicks sounded from behind the door.

The door creaked open and the face of a woman with dark sunglasses appeared. "How do I know you are Jack Young?"

Jack reached into his pocket and showed her the letter.

West Church Graves. The woman's mouth opened and she took a breath. "Come in, come in. Before they see you."

Jack folded the letter and returned it to his pocket.

The woman peered up and down the street before she closed the door behind them.

∞

Takashi sat in the back of the black Continental that crunched over the gravel dirt road towards the cabin. He peered out the window through his sunglasses at the parallax scroll of trees and forest underbrush. Rivera sat next to him in the back seat, sharpening a Vietnam-era Ka-Bar knife with a whetstone.

Heavy metal music blasted through the car's open windows while Miles drummed the steering wheel and Edgar sat singing along with an air guitar.

When the car passed by a rotted split-rail fence, Takashi slapped Miles on the shoulder.

"What?"

Takashi squeezed his hand into a fist and Miles shut off the music.

The car transitioned to the dirt path leading to the front of the cabin.

Before Miles had put the car in park, Rivera jumped out the rear suicide door and sprinted to the porch.

"Aw shit." Miles shifted into park.

"There he goes." Edgar threw open his door and stepped out, spitting his gum to the ground.

Takashi exited the car, stood by its back door watching Rivera, and shook his head. A job like this required finesse, not brute force.

Miles killed the engine, got out, and stood next to Takashi. Rivera pounded on the front door. Miles squinted in the sun. "Is this guy crazy or what?"

Takashi nodded. Sunlight beamed through his black sunglasses while he scanned the yard. The wind kicked up and swayed the tree canopies of the forest like strands of algae swaying in a stream. It did little to cool the summer heat.

Miles racked a stainless Beretta 9mm Inox and raised it. "I'll check the back."

A sustained chatter of chirping bugs mixed with the wind.

Takashi moved with short steps to the front porch, looking through the windows for activity.

Rivera pounded on the door again, and snapped to Takashi, "Nobody's home."

Takashi waved his hand downward in a quieting motion and moved in behind Rivera. He leaned back, and peered into a window.

"Knock, knock," Rivera yelled. With a mighty swing of his leg, he kicked the door three times before it ripped off its hinges and fell into the entryway.

Takashi shook his head at the broken door and glanced up at Rivera, who had already stepped over it and into the house.

Miles crept up the front porch holding a pistol grip shotgun aimed and ready at his hips. He passed Takashi, who then followed both men inside.

They searched the living room and kitchen, then turned into the hallway. Floorboards creaked through the silence and Rivera bounded through the first office door and searched inside.

Takashi peered into the room and surveyed the cluttered mess of electronics, bags of trash, and papers strewn about. He then followed Edgar out of the office and down the hall.

Edgar opened a door and stepped into a bedroom. A toy penguin sat on the edge of the unmade bed, staring back at them. Edgar picked it up, smirked, and tossed it onto the floor.

"Someone's definitely here," Rivera said. "Edgar, check upstairs, and the basement."

Rivera opened the hall bath and swept it with a quick glance.

Takashi brushed past Rivera, and continued down the hall. He trained his eyes on the last door, and crept to it with guarded steps. He reached for the knob, but a crunching sound from the front of the cabin stopped him.

"Hey, fellas. We've got company," Miles called down the hall in a raspy whisper.

Takashi turned away from the door and scampered to the front windows. Three black Suburbans pulled up to the front of the cabin. Eight agents exited the vehicles, armed with handguns and MP5s.

"FBI?" Miles asked.

Takashi shook his head.

"We got here first, but if they want to play, let's play," Edgar said. He unwrapped a stick of Bazooka gum, slid it into his mouth, then crumpled the wrapper and flicked it away. He unlatched the window, slid it open a few inches and with little aim, fired off twenty shots in rapid succession.

The agents scrambled for cover behind vehicles and other equipment in the yard.

The slide on Miles' gun locked open. He stripped the empty magazine, loaded a new one, and tapped to seat it.

Gunfire erupted.

Bullets pierced through windows and walls.

Debris and shrapnel dusted through the cabin and whizzed by Edgar.

Takashi knelt to the floor and pulled out a Walther PPQ from his shoulder holster.

A shot from Miles struck an agent kneeling behind the Continental in the neck.

Blood splattered onto its windshield. His body contorted and slapped the front quarter panel, sliding away with a red smear on its black paint.

Shards of glass, wood, and insulation showered down on Miles and Edgar, who screamed with joy at every shot of return fire.

Edgar pumped his shotgun with each shell and shattered the windshield of a Suburban.

Takashi kneeled by a window and framed his gun's sights on the silhouette of an agent crouched behind a stack of railroad ties. With a slow, controlled breath, he squeezed the trigger and fired a single shot.

The agent jolted and fell back, clutching his right leg.

Wounded but not killed.

Ignoring the erratic, indiscriminate shooting of Miles and Edgar, Takashi steadied four more precision shots that incapacitated the agents.

The return-fire stopped.

Miles screamed from the living room. "Edgar, we having fun or what?"

"Yeah, man. Hey Rivera, what's—"

Takashi looked back but Rivera wasn't there.

A volley of bullets cracked and whizzed past them, striking a mirror. More shards of glass rained down and Takashi eased his head to the side. He ducked and leveled his aim on an agent's leg behind the rear wheel of a tractor.

His finger slid to the flat trigger, its pressure increasing.

A darker shadow loomed from the front of the tractor and stopped him. Rivera.

A blade flashed and Rivera plunged at the agent. He lifted the agent's head and slashed a knife across his neck.

Blood from the agent's arterial wound sprayed up on Rivera, his bloodied grin beaming in the shower. Rivera nodded toward the house, picked up an MP5, and stepped out, spraying bullets at the remaining agents.

Miles and Edgar leapt up and cheered.

Takashi breathed out in frustration and scanned the surroundings.

A wounded agent crawled into the open toward a handgun and grasped it, but Rivera towered over him and stomped on his hand.

Kicking the gun away, Rivera flipped the agent over and stabbed his Ka-Bar into the man's chest. Again and again.

Shouts of primal rage blared deep from Rivera's throat with each wild stab, blood spattering into the air. "Don't you ever tell me to be patient. Fucking bitch."

"What's he saying?" Edgar asked.

Miles shrugged.

Rivera let out a carnal scream at the sky and veins in his neck bulged. Streams of blood trickled from his bald head, across his tattoos, and down his neck.

Takashi holstered his PPQ.

Miles pumped his fist in the air. "Serves those bastards right. Bro, that was intense. It was awesome when—"

His arm jerked back with a loud pop, and he screamed. "Ahh. What the fuck."

Takashi turned to find a Vietnamese woman in the hall with her right hand outstretched at Miles. A blue halo of light radiated from her stomach.

She raised her left hand at Edgar and his leg buckled, bending at the knee. He fell to the ground screaming. "Bro, help!"

Miles' hand cracked and he fell to the ground.

Rivera ran at her with his knife but something tugged at him and kept him from moving forward. "Takashi."

She turned to Takashi and her eyes flared bright red. His body flipped up and pressed tight against the wall.

"What the fuck! What the fuck," Miles screamed.

Takashi slid his hand against the wall and reached into his pocket. He grabbed the taser device and slipped its barrel from under the jacket.

He pulled the trigger and a tethered dart fired striking her in the arm. Why couldn't she stop it?

A frenetic purple energy sizzled along the wire and jolted her body until she dropped to the ground.

Edgar fell back and Rivera tumbled forward.

Miles crashed to the floor and grabbed his hand.

"Dude, you all right?" Edgar said.

"Oh, my hand, bro. Damn, it hurts."

Rivera snarled at Takashi. "About time you did something. You could have gotten us all killed."

He punched Takashi in the face, flipping his sunglasses to the floor.

Takashi straightened his neck and stared back at Rivera.

"Tough guy, huh?" Rivera said. He swung again, but Takashi grabbed his arm.

Rivera pushed against his hand but Takashi held steady and tilted his head with a glare.

"Those albino eyes don't scare me." Rivera scowled and jerked his arm down.

"Demi was right," Edgar said.

Rivera picked up the woman and draped her over his shoulder. "We have what we came for." He turned and carried her out the front door.

Miles leaned on his brother and they limped behind Rivera.

Takashi bent to pick up his sunglasses and a low growl rumbled from the dark hallway.

He angled his head at a dog sitting on its hind legs, ears perked up, incisors flared in a toothy snarl.

The car doors slammed on the Continental and the engine fired up.

Edgar called out, "Takashi, let's go."

Takashi slid his sunglasses on and backed out the door with slow, even steps, never losing sight of the dog.

He climbed into the car and glanced back at the cabin.

He'd seen things very few would ever believe. Spirits of the damned. Demons of death. Flirting the line between right and wrong...good and evil.

None of it ever scared him.

But he knew this path was leading to a place that would outweigh it all, and for the first time, the hairs on the back of his neck stood up.

Rita West entered the living room with Jack and Star where they sat on a couch. She set the walking stick by her side and sat in a chair opposite them.

"How did you know my father?" Jack asked.

"Oh, we were friends. Bet you didn't know he had any friends, did you?"

"No ma'am."

"Bill was a special man. I met him a long time ago. We all did."

"By we, do you mean Church and Graves?"

"Yes, of course. Diane Graves and Simon Church."

"We all knew your dad. He saved our lives, you know. The three of us. Him and his angel Cà Rá. And for that, we were forever indebted to him."

"What do you mean?"

"Well, he asked me to hold onto something for you and said if he ever passed on, that one day soon you would visit me. He even said you might have a young lady with you." Rita smiled at Star.

"And here you are."

"Can I ask a question?" Star said.

"Sure, dear."

"How do you know this is really Jack?"

"Well, to be honest, I don't." Her dark glasses turned to Jack. "But his father gave me a question to ask and he said only Jack would know the correct answer."

"And what question is that?" Jack asked.

She smiled with a slight curl to her lips. "Why is a mouse when it spins?"

Jack's eyes widened and his lips opened in shock.

Star turned at him with a curious look. "What is it?"

"I haven't heard that riddle since I was a kid. He used to ask me all the time."

"What's the answer?"

Rita sat with her hands folded in her lap and Jack paused before standing and leaning to her ear.

He whispered the answer and turned back to the couch.

A giant grin spread across Rita's face. "Correct," she said, putting her hands on her knees to stand.

Star nudged Jack. "Well, what is it?"

Rita stepped to the fireplace mantle.

"What is what?" he said.

"The answer."

"Don't worry about it, I got it right, didn't I?"

Rita interrupted them. "Jack, my sight isn't good, could you please get me a book from the shelf?"

"Which one?"

"*The Old Man and the Sea.*"

Hemingway. Somehow, he knew it would be a Hemingway. A man's man his dad used to say. Fitting.

He scanned the shelves of books, pulled the book out and handed it to her.

When she opened the book, she reached into a cut-out and retrieved a metal plate. With careful balance, Rita walked to the mirror on the wall. She inserted the plate into a tiny hidden slot on the side of the mirror and the glass dematerialized, revealing a large, black void with a floating ring inside.

Reaching into the opening, she pulled it out and handed it to Jack. The ring dropped into his hand but it had almost no weight to it. "I don't know what it's for but your dad said you would."

The ring measured about six inches in diameter and had an arched ridge around the surface on its front side. Its flat, green luster caught the light and highlighted hundreds of tiny, notched grooves on the back.

Rita pulled the metal plate out of the mirror and the opening disappeared. "That's it. I wish I could help you further but I'm too old and too damn blind."

"Thank you," Jack said. "But you can still help. Where do we find Diane and Simon?"

17

· ENDANGERED ·

The black Suburban rolled to a stop before a long, rectangular pipe gate that blocked the road. A chain link fence, covered in barbed wire, flanked both sides of the narrow gateway and ran down a steep and impassable rocky embankment.

Meeks stared out the car window at a white sign with red lettering attached to the fence.

U.S. Department of the Interior WARNING
Endangered Gray Bat Colony
Harassment of these bats is prohibited by the Endangered Species Act
of 1973 Harassment includes entering this cave or
any other activities that might interfere with their colony
NO TRESPASSING VIOLATORS WILL BE JAILED

He knew about the bats in Higgenbotham but didn't pay much attention to them since the cave entrance sat just over the county line. Few people ventured out here, so he never needed to care. Until now.

Meeks watched an agent scan a digital access card against a metal reader on the fence. Motorized gears slid the gate open, and a strip of tire spikes retracted into the ground. Two cameras he'd never before noticed, rotated and tracked the agent back to the vehicle.

The magnitude of the moment hit Meeks with a sense of helplessness he hadn't felt in a long time.

Vasquez turned to Finn. "All right, Deputy, you need to get out. Agent Powell will stay with you."

Finn looked at Meeks. "Sheriff, I think I should see this."

Meeks shook his head. "Gotta get out, Finn. Let me handle this."

Without a word, Finn exited while Meeks stared dead ahead at Vasquez.

The door slammed shut, and the Suburban rolled up the road around a bend of thick tree growth. They stopped in front of a path leading through another barbed wire fence to a large steel door. A bulldozer, two bucket loaders, and a backhoe sat behind concrete barriers and rows of stacked barrels.

Meeks stepped out of the Suburban and stared at the fifteen-foot-high steel door covering the cave entrance.

Vasquez exited the vehicle and a deep whirring sound echoed through the open area. The door opened with a horizontal split, one half rising into the cave, and the other lowering into the ground.

Two men dressed in green fatigues armed with rifles stepped out and held a scanner up to Vasquez's face. Meeks watched a green laser scan her eye. It beeped then chimed.

"Sheriff, they need to scan your retina."

"For what?"

"We track anyone who comes in here. Believe me, not many people have seen what you're about to see."

The man held the scanner to Meeks' right eye and pulled a trigger. A green light burst from the device and startled him. A puff of air that pushed against his eyeball forced him to jerk back.

Vasquez smiled and walked past him. "That didn't hurt now, did it?"

As they headed into the cave, a musty odor hit him in the face. LED lights illuminated a diamond-plated ramp that they descended.

The air cooled, and a hard mineral smell replaced the musk.

"Remember the twenty-eleven earthquakes?" Vasquez's voice echoed against the cave walls.

"Yeah."

"Significant damage occurred in several locations along the twenty-seven miles of these caves."

The ramp's incline ended, and they stepped onto a flat platform covered by a steel cage.

"But here in Stone Creek, that damage revealed something that our friend Dr. Bruce Hon discovered in twenty-sixteen."

She pressed a green button on a panel, and the platform descended twenty feet down a ledge below.

"That same year, in the Raven Gap Quarry not far from here, workers discovered a crystalline sphere that we believe is related."

"And that's why you want Tarkos."

"You're very quick, Sheriff. We got word this morning that Hon stole the sphere and arrived in Stone Creek yesterday. We believe Tarkos and Hon are working together and may attempt to sell it to a foreign adversary."

The platform stopped at the bottom of the cave floor and they stepped off at the entrance to a plastic tent. Bright light from inside cast an orange glow across the walls.

Vasquez folded it back so Meeks could step through. "After you."

When he stepped inside, the warmth of bright lights hit him in the face. An array of cameras sat in an arc around the room, and multiple computers, screens, and sensors ran along the tent's perimeter.

In the center of the room sat a two-foot-tall green, metallic cylinder. Its surface resembled a carbon-fiber pattern shimmering with a black and green opalescence. The base of it sank into the limestone as if melted into the surrounding rock.

"What the hell is it?" Meeks asked.

"We have no idea. We can't even move it. It gives off an energy signature that prevents us from cutting into the stone. Whatever it is, it's not man-made."

Meeks crouched for a closer look and drew a breath. "And the sphere?"

"Nothing happens when the sphere is near it. We've tried everything."

"Okay, so why are you showing me this? What does this have to do with Star?"

"You said you wanted to know what this was all about. And based on the footage from the hospital, we believe Star has come in contact with someone, or something—"

"An alien." Meeks pressed his hand on his knee and turned back at Vasquez.

She raised her eyebrows. "Your words, not mine."

An NQCO agent beside her pressed his forefinger to the headset over his left ear. "Ma'am, they've found Tarkos."

She smiled. "Good. As I predicted. Sheriff, I can't expect you to understand everything that is going on, but I do expect your cooperation in the interest of national security. The sooner you can help us find Star, the safer she will be."

Meeks rolled his lower lip against his front teeth and nodded at Vasquez. "I'll do what I can."

Their vehicle rolled out the front gate and met Finn who stood near Meeks' Jeep. Powell stood with another agent by three black Suburbans.

Vasquez got out with Meeks, and they both walked past Finn. "Let's see who we've caught," she said.

She approached the middle Suburban, and an agent opened the door. Vasquez pulled herself up into the front seat before turning to face rearward.

The door slammed shut, and Meeks looked in through the open window.

He recognized Tarkos and Hon from the photos. They sat in two middle-captain's chairs, and didn't say a word.

He peered past them at Fletcher, who sat in the back row flanked by two agents. "Reverend, is that you?"

Fletcher raised his hand and nodded. "Morning, Sheriff."

Meeks winced at Vasquez. "Now look here, I can't have you taking the Reverend like this, people are gonna talk."

"We'll ask him a few questions and release him once we know what's going on. I need you to find Star Hopper."

The dark tinted window rolled up and he stared at his reflection. Gravel and dust sputtered beneath the wheels of the Suburban as it drove off.

Finn stepped up behind Meeks. "Sheriff, what was down in the cave?"

"Trouble, Finn. Nothing but trouble."

The Suburban caravan exited the gravel trail and turned onto the main road. Inside the middle vehicle, Tarkos stared at Vasquez who typed on a digital tablet. She folded its cover closed then leaned forward with her elbows on her knees.

"Anyone care to tell me what's going on? Are we having some sort of reunion here in Stone Creek?"

Tarkos folded his arms and glared out the window.

Fletcher coughed into his hand.

She shifted her focus to Bruce. "Dr. Hon?"

Tarkos snapped a glance at Bruce, who looked down at his lap.

"Father?" she asked as she turned to look at Fletcher.

"Reverend," he snapped back.

"Surely, a man of the cloth will confess what he knows?"

"Confessions are next week."

Tarkos hid his laugh behind a cough. He knew her game, and he wasn't about to play it, but he loved that Fletcher appeared to be on his side.

Vasquez shot a glare at him. "It's not funny, Andre. If we have an international crisis and people die, you'll be responsible."

Tarkos leaned forward and tilted his head. "Not my problem."

Bruce looked up at her.

"You do realize, Dr. Hon, this little stunt you pulled comes with a minimum of ten years in prison. I'm sure your son would love to visit you there. What would he be, eighteen when you get out?"

Bruce turned to Tarkos. "Andre."

Tarkos nodded. "Do what you need to do, Bruce."

"I—" Before he could finish, he froze, then looked down once again into his lap.

Vasquez leaned back and crossed her arms. "Well then, gentlemen, it seems we are at an impasse, and it will be too—"

The Suburban braked to an abrupt stop that jolted their bodies, and Vasquez whipped her head to the driver. "Why are we stopping?"

Tarkos and Bruce craned their necks above the headrests to look through the front window. A male voice squawked over the radio. "Bridge blocked by a truck."

Tarkos looked through the side window over the barrier of a bridge high above the creek.

The driver spoke into his headset. "Everyone, back up."

A loud rumble sounded behind them and Tarkos spotted a dump truck pulling to a stop blocking any exit from the bridge.

Vasquez shouted at the driver. "It's an ambush. Get us out of here now!"

The driver shifted the car but the whoosh of a rocket filled the air and hit the Suburban in front of them.

A ball of fire ripped from under the vehicle and splintered it into chunks of metal that burst through the air. Two agents, consumed in flames, jumped out and fell to the ground, their arms and legs flailing in terror.

"Jesus Christ!" the driver yelled. He turned to look back and floored the gas pedal. Their Suburban smashed into the one behind it and pushed it into the dump truck.

Agents jumped from the rear vehicle and scattered blind shots through fire and smoke across the bridge.

Tarkos could do nothing but watch as they made their way to the burning Suburban. Another agent sprang from it, also swallowed in flames as others tried to get him on the ground.

Shouts from the radio filled the car. "Man down! Man down! Somebody get back-up!"

Tarkos whipped his head from the front to the rear of the vehicle. "We're sitting ducks."

The driver opened his door and grabbed a rifle. "Everyone stay inside." He slammed the door and ran to the other agents.

"Shit," Vasquez said, and pulled out her 9mm handgun.

"We've gotta get out of here," Tarkos said. He tried to open the door, but the security latches prevented it.

A flash of light filled the vehicle, and he glanced out the front window.

An electrified bolt of sizzling energy shot down across the bridge and pierced through each agent. The power of the burst electrified their bodies into convulsions, and they collapsed to the ground.

A high-pitched screech whisked past the middle Suburban, followed by an explosion of the vehicle behind them. Shrapnel shattered the rear window and sprayed glass all over them.

Fletcher and Bruce ducked while Tarkos screamed at Vasquez, "Open the door now!" She jumped out and pulled on the latch to the Suburban, but the door stuck only a few inches open.

Tarkos gripped the headrest, leaned to his left and kicked several times at the door.

"What the hell?" Bruce asked.

Tarkos paused when he noticed Vasquez looking up into the sky. He trained his eyes through the front window and the figure of a man floated down from the sky through a swirl of smoke to land on top of the Suburban, rocking it side to side.

"I don't like this," Bruce said.

Tarkos kicked the door as hard as he could, and it swung open.

"Bruce, get out now," he said, then pulled Fletcher out by the arm.

As they scrambled from the vehicle, a metal spear sliced down through the roof and stabbed into the skull of the last agent sitting in the back. Its tip pierced through his lower jaw, and when it retracted, jugular blood splattered across the inside of the cab.

Tarkos, Bruce and Fletcher ran behind Vasquez, who then emptied her weapon at the man before reloading a new magazine.

The only agent left standing turned and fired multiple shots. A burst of blue plasma energy hit him in the chest and he flipped back off the bridge.

It was only that Tarkos recognized Demi standing on the roof but froze in awe at his body's transformation. No longer a frail man with a limp, he stood as a broad-shouldered, imposing brute. Black fatigues patterned with crystalline hexagons stretched across Demi's body like a suit of armor.

Gunfire from Vasquez interrupted his focus and Demi floated from the vehicle in a swift downward arc. He grabbed her by the neck, and with no effort, lifted her up across the bridge's barrier wall.

Tarkos knelt and with frantic glances around him, found a metal box that had been split open in the burning trunk of the exploded vehicle.

The sphere.

He reached through the intense flames into the box and snatched the sphere, placing it in his coat pocket.

Gasps and chokes for air filled the vacuum of silence as Vasquez struggled to pull Demi's hands off her.

He looked up across the bridge where a group of armed men had spread around its outer edge, laughing.

Tarkos motioned Bruce and Fletcher to step back behind the smoldering vehicle.

"Where is it?" Demi asked.

"What?" Vasquez asked through a broken gurgle.

"The sphere. Return what you have stolen from me!"

She kicked her legs in mid-air, desperate to reach firm ground. "Fuck," she said through gritted teeth. "You."

"Aww." Demi smiled and twisted her neck to the side. He produced a tethered needle that he jammed into her skull behind her lower left ear. A white energy beam glided along the tether and pulsed from her brain into him, his eyes glowing red with each pulse.

Tarkos stood and reached into his pocket for the sphere. He held it high and snapped at Demi. "Hey, asshole! Is this what you want?"

Demi turned and gazed at Tarkos for a moment, then retracted the needle from Vasquez.

His pale fingertips extended through a black metallic gauntlet like glove and he reached out to Tarkos. "Give it to me."

"Let her go, and I'll hand it over."

Demi tilted his head, then dropped Vasquez off the bridge without looking at her. Bruce gasped and dropped to his knees. Fletcher made the sign of the cross.

Tarkos screamed and his voice reverberated down through the chasm. It followed her body as she fell and smashed into the shallow, rocky waters below.

A rush of blood filled his neck and face. "You want this?" He reached his arm back and flung the sphere as hard as he could over the side of the bridge.

Demi's head jerked to track the sphere, and he motioned his hand towards it. The sphere drifted about one hundred feet away but it slowed mid-air and boomeranged back into his hand.

He rolled it in his fingers then stood upright, floating down to face Tarkos.

Tarkos looked up at Demi who stood about six inches taller than him. Several of the armed men walked past the burning vehicles and stood behind them.

Demi straightened his spine and poised to strike.

Tarkos drew in a breath and closed his eyes. He didn't think it would end like this. The desire to know more flooded his mind and a single image of the journal flashed before him.

He opened his eyes and held his hands up, open palms. "Wait, wait— the Empyreax."

"No concern to you. The woman gave me what I need."

"But you can't open it, can you?"

Demi paused and narrowed his eyes. "Go on."

"Here, look." Tarkos reached into his pocket, pulled out the Moleskine journal, and flipped through the pages, stopping on a picture of the Empyreax.

"There is a key. I know how this works." He pointed to the three-ringed key.

Demi's eyes widened. "And why not just take your memory?"

"I can help you. I've waited my entire life for this."

Demi motioned his arm over his shoulder and two men stepped forward with rifles pointed at Tarkos.

Another man with a shotgun stepped up behind Fletcher and Bruce, who held their hands up. The man waved the shotgun to move them next to Tarkos.

"Let them go. You don't need them, only me," Tarkos said.

Demi didn't say a word and turned to the burning Suburban. With almost no effort, he ripped its rear door off its hinges to reveal another silver case. His fingers ran across the digital lock and an electric pulse displayed flashing numbers that froze in sequence. The case unlocked and opened revealing the second sphere.

Bruce leaned close to Tarkos. "Andre, what are you doing?"

"Saving our asses," he replied.

Both spheres floated just above Demi's fingers and he clenched his hands tight around them then turned and looked at the men. "The woman showed me a cave. Where is it?"

"Higgenbotham?" Bruce asked.

"Take me there," Demi said.

Tarkos and Bruce looked at each other. The cultists forced all three men into the bed of a truck, and their caravan drove away from the burning bridge.

Meeks noticed billowing smoke just above the tree line on the road ahead before Finn did. "What the hell," he said.

Finn lifted his head from his phone. "Forest fire?"

Meeks shook his head.

The Jeep rounded the bend of the chasm, and they came upon the fiery destruction on the bridge. Black smoke poured into the sky from the wreckage and a field of debris lay strewn across it.

"My god," Meeks said.

Finn grabbed the radio and rushed words into it. "Dispatch, we've got a major ten-fifty at Boles Bridge—multiple vehicle fires. We need backup and EMT *now*. Possible casualties."

Meeks jumped out of the Jeep and drew his revolver. He stalked between the vehicles and knelt by the first body he encountered. After checking for a pulse, he stood and went to the front vehicle.

Finn, with his Glock drawn, stepped through the smoke on the opposite side.

Meeks peered inside the empty vehicle and squinted through the crackling flames.

Finn's voice cut through the air. "Sheriff."

Meeks looked up at Finn who was leaning over the side of the bridge, and the Sheriff rushed to his deputy's side and looked down. Vasquez lay still on the edge of the creek bed.

"Shit. Finn, get a hold of the mayor. Tell him to call the governor. We need the National Guard here now." He holstered his revolver and scampered to the side of the bridge, racing as fast as he could down the rocky slope of the ravine, all but forgetting his knee pain.

Vasquez lay face up on the rocky shore with half her body in a pool of bloody water. The bone from her broken femur stuck out from her thigh just above the knee.

"Hold on, Vasquez." Meeks took off his belt, wrapped it around her thigh, and strapped it down hard to stop the bleeding.

Vasquez jolted awake and screamed in pain. Her eyes rolled back in her head and she grimaced with agony. She blinked multiple times and finally managed to focus on Meeks. She grabbed his vest and whispered. "Meeks."

"Hold on."

Blood from her hand smeared across his vest, and she pulled him closer. "Phone. Phone." She seemed to gesture to her waist with her chin.

Meeks looked down and pulled a black cell phone from her belt clip. The sound of approaching sirens echoed above him.

"Cal–ca–" She couldn't get the words out.

He grabbed her hand off his vest and gave it a gentle squeeze. "Don't talk. We're gonna get you out of here. Stay with me, Carmen."

A slice of dark shade fell over him, and he looked up at a swath of thick clouds that had covered the sun. Sirens echoed through the ravine, followed by bright red flashing lights that did little to comfort him.

"Stay with me."

18

· BARBED WIRE ·

Jack pulled open the front door to the Montclare Community Home and allowed Star to enter before him. The weight of its glass and reinforced steel border forced it to close with a swift, loud click behind them. Sunlight poured in through barred windows but cast little color against the cold grays of the foyer. He approached a circular, faux-stone front desk where a woman wearing a blue sweater looked up from a computer.

"Good morning. May I help you?" she asked. A gold name tag glinted off her sweater: *M. Jones*.

Jack smiled and rested his hands on the desk. "Hi. We're here to see Simon Church."

"What's the relation?"

"He is a friend of my father. My name is Jack Young."

"I'm sorry, but only relatives are allowed to visit residents." She scratched her neck with a pencil.

Jack had been around medical caregivers and struck a modest tone. "Well, my father recently passed away and left a gift for Mr. Church."

The woman curled her lips and studied Star. "Aren't you Mary

Hopper's daughter?"

Star nodded. "Yes, ma'am. Stella."

"I thought so. Still, unless you're a relative, I can't let you all in. You can leave the gift with me and we'll be sure to give it to him."

Jack leaned forward over the counter and softened his voice. "It's actually money so, it's not that I don't trust you."

The woman tilted her head. "Mr. Young, residents are not allowed to keep cash in their rooms, so you'll need to deposit it into his account. I can let you visit with Simon for a few minutes to show him but you need to bring it back for deposit. Give me your IDs and sign in. I'll call an escort."

She grabbed a black radio on her desk and pressed a button that responded with a beep. "Max."

After a pause and a squawk of static, a male voice called back to her. "Yeah, Marge."

"I've got two visitors for Simon. I need you to escort them to his room."

"Simon Church?"

"Yes."

"Who the hell wants to see him?" The radio beeped with another static break.

Jack raised his eyebrows at Star.

The nurse blushed and leaned away from them. "Never mind that, just get up here."

"On my way," Max replied.

Jack retrieved his driver's license and handed it to the nurse. She copied his name into a ledger and did the same for Star.

Distant footsteps of hard leather soles echoed behind them. Jack turned, and a burly man dressed in a loose white shirt and pants walked up with a locked gaze on Star. The heavy smell of a cheap cologne mixed with cigarette ash wafted with him.

"Good morning," he said to Star with a wide grin. He held his hand out to greet her. "My name is Max. Welcome to Montclare."

Star shook his hand and gave him a demure but adoring smile. "Hello."

Jack held his hand out, but Max ignored it. "Good morn—"

"Haven't I seen you around town?" Max asked Star.

"Maybe," she said.

Marge slid their licenses back across the desk. "No more than fifteen minutes with Simon, please."

"Most people don't last more than three." Max snorted then laughed. "But let's go." He pressed a key card against a wall scanner and the door next to it clicked. Sliding his arm against the door, he waved his hand and ushered Star in front of him. "Ladies first."

Star entered the corridor, and Max slid in behind her, just in front of Jack. She looked back at Jack and smiled.

Max's voice echoed in the hallway. "How do you folks know Simon?"

"Friend of the family," Jack said.

"Odd friend to have."

Star turned to Max. "What do you mean?"

"You'll see. He's a strange dude."

"How's that?"

"He was in a car accident years ago. Always staring at things and mumbling to himself."

Max held up his left arm to a higher cylinder lock on a barred door. As he did, the sleeve slid down and exposed his wrist, which had a black sphere tattoo.

Jack stared at the tattoo and asked, "Why so many locks?"

"We took a shortcut. But if a resident gets out, they usually end up hurting themselves, so it's for their own good. Simon's in this wing."

Max knocked on the door and swung it open. "Simon, you've got visitors."

No response.

Jack and Star entered, their eyes scanning the room. A bed with a sea-green wool blanket and sheet sat empty.

"Aw shit," Max said. He grabbed his radio and spoke into it. "Marge, come in."

"Yes, Max."

"Simon got out again."

"Oh, Lordy. Lemme look at the cameras and call the Sheriff."

Max slipped the radio back onto his belt.

"Why the Sheriff?" Star asked.

"Guy's a complete nutjob. You think he's harmless, but there's no telling when he's gonna snap. I mean look at this shit. His brain is all over the place." He pointed above the bed.

They gazed at the wall plastered with newspaper clippings covering a chaotic range of topics: geopolitical events, local elections, farming updates, Civil War articles, and the occasional swimsuit model.

Jack spotted a calendar in the middle of the symphony of clippings, with the date Friday the 13th circled in red. Next to it, an article with an image of a rocky cliff read: *'Chimney Rock closed after tragic fall. May 2017'*.

Several sketches of the same rock had been taped in various spots along the wall.

"Look," Star said. She picked up a newspaper clipping on the nightstand. *'Local Grandma Diane Graves Fights Town Over Utility Construction'*.

"All right, folks," Max said. "He ain't here, so time to leave." As Star placed the clipping back down, Max glanced at it. "You'll have to come back once they bring him in."

The man ushered them out the door, and turned back into the room. He pulled the door partially closed. "Oops, I forgot something," he said.

Jack pushed the door open a few inches and peered in.

Max pocketed the newspaper clipping from the nightstand. But why?

The front truck of Demi's caravan smashed through the first fenced gate at Higgenbotham. Its tires blew on the security spikes, hurtling strips of rubber scattershot through the air. It swerved off the road and rolled into a ditch, flipping onto its side.

Dissonant sounds of gravel crunching under several other trucks faded when they rolled to a stop outside the fence. Armed men hopped out of the truck beds while racking shotguns and charging the bolts on their rifles.

A cultist opened the rear passenger door of a beat-up red Isuzu Trooper. Demi stepped out of it and shook his head at two men who climbed out of the crashed truck.

"Primitive," he mumbled.

The door of a dilapidated red Volkswagen van slid open behind him and latched into place with a metal twang echoing inside its gutted cab. Tarkos, Fletcher and Bruce sat with their legs crossed on a canvas tarp.

A loud siren wailed in the air from inside the fence, beyond the trees that led to the cave.

"This is Higgenbotham," Bruce said.

Demi smiled. "Good. And I trust you know what's inside."

"I do."

"What's inside?" Fletcher asked.

Demi sneered. "Something far more precious than bats."

Fletcher raised a skeptical eyebrow.

Bruce continued, "But our access was revoked, so there's no way in."

Tarkos gave a meager shrug. "He's right. Even if—" He stopped himself and waved his hand in an apologetic motion. "When you get past the guards, that door is pretty thick and sealed shut."

"Now, now," Demi said, tapping his temple. "Mr. Tarkos, you of all people should know that the mind is a very powerful key."

"And what do you know of me so soon?"

"More than you think." He turned to Edgar and Miles. "Let's have some fun, shall we?"

Demi rounded the trail to the entrance of the cave followed by a truck and a group of cultists lingering behind.

They stopped and let Demi move far ahead. When he approached the gate, three NQCO agents raised their MP5s. "Freeze!" they shouted but Demi continued to walk forward. The agents glanced at each other. One spoke into his headset. "Lock it down."

A secondary steel door slid down over the entrance of the cave.

Demi stopped in front of agents, who approached with their guns raised, and shouted, "Get down now! On the ground with your arms out!"

Demi dropped to one knee and raised his hands, eyes forward, locked on his prey.

"I said all the way down." The shortest agent lowered his rifle and retrieved a pair of handcuffs from a belt pouch and took two steps forward.

Demi squeezed his left hand into a fist. The fence to his left vibrated and rattled with a metallic twang.

The agent stopped and a rolling wave tracked along the length of the chain-link fencing, deforming and upending its posts.

The other two agents peered up from their red dot sights. "What the...?"

A long strand of barbed wire ripped from the top of the fence and whipped around the agent, pinning his arms tight against his body. The wire cinched tighter, and forced his finger to pull the trigger on his rifle.

Shots fired in every direction, and one bullet struck another agent in the neck, spinning him down to the ground. His partner ducked for cover behind a pyramid of stacked metal containers.

The razor-sharp barbs continued to dig into the shorter agent's skin, and he let out a full-throated scream.

Demi's head swiveled side to side and the wire wound tighter and tighter. The white of the agent's eyes bulged through a layer of blood that gushed from gaping wounds in his face and spilled down his arms.

The agent behind the containers yelled into his headset, garnering Demi's attention.

The barbed wire squeezed one last time, then shredded the agent in an arterial shower of blood and metal coil.

Demi stood and the agent fired a volley of shots, but they arced around his body as if rolling on the curvature of a shield.

Demi squeezed his right fist and four metal rebars flipped through the air behind the agent. They burst through his chest and lodged into the metal containers. His limp body skewered and motionless.

Without even taking a moment to savor his handiwork, Demi turned and stood before the large steel door. Even with brute force, he wouldn't be able to open it.

"RPG," he said.

A smiling cultist near the truck leaned forward and called out with a deep Southern accent. "What was that, Demi?"

Demi turned, and his face erupted in rage. "RPG!"

The man flinched and hemmed to the other men. "RPG now, quick."

Two men rifled through a box in the truck bed and one jumped out, knelt, and shouldered an RPG with a steady aim

"Okay, Demi, we're ready."

Demi smiled, and muttered. "Useless." He stepped toward a control panel on the side of the door and entered a key code sequence he had obtained from Vasquez's memory.

Taking a step back, he folded his hands in front of him and stood, watching the primary and secondary doors slide open. He glanced back at the RPG and smiled.

The door opened just wide enough to reveal five agents standing with rifles at the ready. One agent yelled out, "Contact!" A hail of bullets shot out from the entrance.

The head of the grenade shot out and a fireball from the rear of the launcher blasted back.

Demi tracked the grenade whizzing through the air straight at the men. It landed just in front of them and exploded in a massive fireball that burst their bodies to minced meat in a shower of burning blood.

Cheers erupted from the cultists.

Demi stepped into the cave, smoke swirling around him.

Several cultists followed him inside, trudging through the corridors, and down the elevator.

Upon reaching the tent, Demi stepped inside and smiled at the sight.

"What the hell is it?" one of the men asked.

"A radio," Demi said. "A very old radio."

He ran his fingers over the top dome of the cylinder and pressed a button on its side. Nothing happened. The glowing energy field continued to radiate around it.

He retrieved a square device from inside his jacket and pressed a button on its side. A holographic lenticular pattern rose from the face of the device and a whirring sound emitted from it.

The sound changed pitch, oscillating for several seconds, then solidified into a flatline pulse.

The glowing field around the object faded away, dripping down its sides to disappear into its base. Demi pressed the button on the cylinder again, and a panel slid open. He reached inside and tapped several buttons upon which legs retracted from the rock and slid up into its body. It rose four feet above the ground and hovered mid-air.

"Take it to the temple." Demi squinted, and a slight smile tugged at the corners of his lips. "Time for a call."

Meeks grabbed the rear door handles of the ambulance and pulled himself up, keeping pressure off his bad knee.

A State Trooper braced Meeks from behind until he climbed all the way inside and pushed the double doors shut.

"Buckle up, Sheriff," said the paramedic.

Vasquez lay on a stretcher, eyes half shut, an oxygen mask strapped on her bloodied face.

The paramedic tightened the Velcro sleeve of a blood pressure machine around her arm and clasped a heart rate monitor on her index finger. The antiseptic sterile aroma of plastics and medical cleansers filled the back compartment.

As the ambulance started to roll, it hit a dip in the trail and swayed. Meeks grabbed a shelf to stop from bumping Vasquez.

Everything rattled.

Vasquez's breath fogged inside the mask and she mumbled through a moan.

The medic peeled her eyelids back and traced a flashlight left and right to check her pupils. "Carmen, can you hear me?" The medic spoke in a direct, firm tone. "We're taking you to the hospital. We've given you morphine for the pain and splinted your left arm."

Meeks wiped his face and placed his hand on hers.

"Carmen, we're gonna get you help."

She squeezed his hand and moaned. "Meeks, ca—"

The medic glanced at the vitals monitor.

"I think she's trying to say something," Meeks said.

The medic shook his head. "Unlikely. She's in shock and the morph—" He glanced down at her left arm wrapped in a splint. "Shit. The tourniquet isn't holding."

Blood seeped through the splint and the pressure monitor beeped an alert.

The medic yelled to the front of the ambulance. "Charley, need to get to the hospital stat, she's losing blood."

"What's that mean?" Meeks asked.

"I need to put a new tourniquet on. Keep talking to her."

The monitor continued to beep and the medic pulled a new tourniquet from a drawer.

"Carmen, look at me." Meeks gave her a smile when her eyes met his. "I know this isn't the day you had planned, but we're gonna get you patched up and I'm gonna get the guys that did this."

Vasquez's eyes rolled up into her head then back at Meeks. "No." She reached up, grabbed his collar and pulled him close.

The medic snapped at Meeks. "Sheriff, hold her please."

Vasquez spoke, but her voice was muffled by the oxygen mask. "Meeks. Call ti42525."

He leaned closer. "Say again?"

"ti42525. Call."

She released his collar and her hand fell to her side.

"Is she gonna be okay?" Meeks glanced back at the medic who finished tightening the new tourniquet.

The monitor stabilized and the medic read over the vitals. "She's lost a lot of blood from her arm and her heart rate is very low. The hospital knows we're en route."

The siren from the ambulance blared from outside.

Reaching into his pocket, he retrieved his phone and paused, biting his lower lip. He dialed *ti42525* and he held the phone to his ear.

After two rings, a monotone male voice answered. "Hello."

Meeks stared down at Vasquez. "This is Sheriff Tom Meeks down in Stone Creek. I'm here with Carmen Vasquez. She told me—"

"One moment," the voice interrupted.

The ambulance hit another bump and Meeks steadied himself, leaning forward. After several seconds, he broke the silence. "Hello? Hello?"

The voice returned. "Sheriff, we are tracking your location stand by." The call ended.

"Wait. Hello. Hello." He scowled at the phone. "Damn."

The medic raised his eyebrows. "Everything all right, Sheriff?"

Twenty-four hours earlier Meeks couldn't stand Vasquez, now he feared he'd lose her. "I'm working on it."

Star knocked three times on the faded wooden door of a mid-century brick house. She stepped down off the porch beside Jack and folded her arms while looking up at the building. Electric lines sagged from a pole on the street and tied into rotted siding on the upper floor. The top windows showed no sign of upkeep with dirt that ran down along their splintered wood trim. A faint smell of natural gas whisked in the air and caught her attention.

"Do you smell gas?" she asked.

Jack scrunched his nose. "Yeah, I—" The fast-creaking sound of the door opening interrupted him.

An older woman in dirty, pale-blue jeans and a loose-fitting, long-sleeve gray shirt stepped out onto the porch. "Good morning. May I help you?" She reached up and scratched the back of her shoulder-length white hair.

"Hello," Star said. "Are you Diane Graves?"

"Who wants to know?"

"My name is Stella and this is Jack. Jack Young."

"Oh, yes." The woman's face lit up with a grin that had two gaps in her teeth. "Come in. Come in," she said, beckoning them inside.

Star turned to Jack, who shrugged back at her.

When they entered the home, the musty odor of damp cloth permeated the air. Dozens of photographs, some black and white, lined the main hallway. Star scanned them as she walked past.

Mrs. Graves ushered them into the kitchen to an oval-shaped wood table. Linoleum tiles creaked and bent when they stepped into the room. Faded yellow paint covered the walls of the kitchen and dated vintage appliances gave off a pop and squeak from the movement.

Her pale hands grabbed a chair and she motioned Star to sit. "Have a seat. Have a seat. Would you like some tea?"

"No thank you," Star said.

"Very well." The woman took a seat at the head of the table with Jack seated next to Star at the other end.

"Mrs. Graves, I'm here because my father is dead."

"Oh, yes. Such a shame." Spittle flicked from the woman's lower lip and she leaned forward to cross her hands on the table.

"He left me a message to come see you."

She hesitated and blinked. "And I bet I know why. Are you sure you don't want any tea? I can make it real quick."

"No. Thank you."

"Very well."

"How long did you know my father?"

The woman brought her finger to her chin. "Oh, I don't remember really. Years. Many years."

"What can you tell me about him?"

"What would you like to know?"

"Did you think he was crazy?" Jack asked.

"No, heavens no." Her eyes darted away from Jack to Star. "I mean, we're all a little crazy sometimes, aren't we?"

Star nudged Jack's foot under the table. She leaned forward on her elbows "Mrs. Graves, we really—"

A loud thud boomed from the floor above. Both Star and Jack flicked their heads up to a hanging light that swayed on a chain.

"What was that noise?" Star asked.

"What noise?" The woman raised her eyebrows and held her hand to her ear.

"That noise upstairs."

"Oh, that's just my dog Reggie."

Jack interjected. "Ma'am, I need to know if my father gave you something to hold for me."

The woman turned her head away from Star and held her hand to her face as if to hide her voice. Her hazel eyes stared straight at Jack and whispered with a wink. "It's in the well."

"What well?" Star asked.

The woman frowned and glared at Star. "If you must know, it's in the back. I'll show you." She stood and rolled her eyes at Jack. "Not sure what you see in her."

The woman pulled open a sliding glass door and stepped outside. "Let's go."

Star stood, leaned her face past Jack's ear, and whispered, "Something's not right."

They stepped out of the back door onto a broken paver patio overgrown with weeds. An eight-foot-high board-and-batten fence surrounded the property, which lay covered under thick, tall grass.

The woman scurried ahead of them and disappeared behind a section of fence that jutted from the perimeter. They rounded its corner and found the woman standing over a two-by-two-meter square concrete pad in the middle of the yard. A rusted steel door had been propped open over a metal rung ladder that led down into the well.

Star gazed into the dark pit. "What's down there?"

The woman squinted at Star. "Never been down there myself. But your dad told me it's there."

"What?"

"I don't know," she replied. "He never told me. But it's getting hot out here. I need to go inside soon. Are you gonna go get it?"

Jack cast Star a curious look and she nodded back at him—he had to go down there.

"Ma'am," Star said, turning to the old woman. "I sure could use some tea."

A grin lit up the old woman's face. "Oh, delightful. We can let uh...Jack."

She pointed at Jack and Star cut her off. "Jack."

The woman gave Star an annoyed flick of her eyebrows. "Yes, I know it was Jack, let me finish dear. He can go down in the well while we have some tea."

"I'd like that," Star said.

"I'll go start the tea kettle." The woman turned and disappeared around the fence corner.

Jack whispered under his breath. "Why do I get the feeling I'm not going to like what's down there?" He scanned the yard. "I don't like this."

"Want me to go down there?"

Jack smirked. "No of course not."

"Well then there's no other way. Don't worry I'll keep an eye on her." She kissed him on the cheek. "Here, take my phone."

"Why?"

"You'll need a light."

"Wait. Before you go, let me call Roger."

She unlocked her phone and handed it to him.

A dragonfly buzzed by her head and dragged her attention away from Jack. It perched on the top fence rail, seeming to watch her.

The phone rang three times before Roger's muffled voicemail picked up. She looked back at Jack who had crossed his arm and stared down into the pit.

"Roger, it's Jack. My phone's dead so I borrowed this phone. I need you to listen. I'm in some serious shit down here and need you to get to the cabin as soon as possible. Call me back on this number."

He hung up and a loud clunk echoed from the bottom of the well that startled them.

Jack pointed the light down the hole and glanced at Star before he stepped onto the first two rungs of the ladder.

Star looked at him with a nervous expression and tried to smile. His head disappeared below the opening, and she turned back to the house.

19

· THE WELL ·

J ack's right foot slipped off a slick rung, and he clutched the ladder tight to arrest his fall. Light from the phone flicked against the walls of the well while he steadied himself. He strained his eyes through the dark for any sign of the bottom and for a moment, a faint light reflected back. It had to be water, maybe thirty feet down at most. With a quick glance upward at sunlight from the opening above, he continued his descent.

The sound of echoing water droplets grew louder the deeper he climbed down. He reached the last rung of the ladder and leaned his body to shine the light into a murky pool of water. A half-submerged tunnel entrance appeared to lead away from the main well, but from his current angle on the ladder, he couldn't peer into it.

With a cautious step back, dangling his right foot, he lowered into the water. It touched firm ground about three feet below the surface. The cold, waist-high water stung his inner thighs, and he turned around holding the phone to light his way. An earthen smell of muddy iron filled the air.

A stone-walled corridor, flooded with water, opened before him and he paused to shine the light into it. Water ripples trailed away from him and disappeared into the dark tunnel beyond the edge of the light.

"Again with the tunnels. Come on, Dad."

He grated his lower lip with his teeth, then took a step forward. The bracelet on his wrist beeped and flashed a blue light. When he glanced at it, a loud metal screech rattled from high above. When he looked up, the steel door slammed shut, and the well was consumed into abyssal darkness.

"Hey. Hey, Star." He grasped hold of the ladder and started to pull himself up but a loud clunk echoed from the tunnel, jolting him to spin around.

"Shit." He knew he'd be walking into a trap. But Star was right, there was no other way. The gun. Hopefully she still had her gun.

The phone's icy light shone into the tunnel's entrance. His heart raced, and the water's chill had been replaced by warm adrenaline pumping through his body. With a deep breath, he stepped through the water into the tunnel and kept the light pointed straight ahead.

As he crossed its threshold, something in the water scraped against his right leg, and he flinched. He flashed the light down at the muddy water, and clouds of bright red swirled around him.

Pale fingertips rose up from the murky water, and he jumped back against the wall of the tunnel. "What the *fuck*?"

Water splashed from his frantic movement and an arm followed by a torso broke through the surface and pressed against him. The weight of the body pushed him off balance, and he slipped but managed to keep his head and the phone above the water. Before he had a chance to move away, the lacerated and bloodied face of a dead man popped up just in front of him.

"Jesus. Fucking. Christ."

Blood poured from gaping wounds in the man's face and neck while water sloshed in and out of his slack-jawed mouth. His right eye had rolled back into his head, his left eye clouded with blood. Water from each ripple spilled over his pale skin and drew more blood from each gash.

Jack's ragged breaths reverberated through the tunnel along with the splashing water. He scrambled to push the body away, and it bobbed through the ripples, floating just under the ladder as if guarding Jack's exit.

As he calmed himself, the body rolled over, exposing more of the man's left arm. He pointed the light at it and caught sight of something just before it dipped back under.

Fear still ate at him, but Jack moved closer to the body and reached for the arm. With trembling fingers, he lifted it from the water revealing the black circle tattoo on the man's left wrist. *Same as that Max guy.*

"Star."

Two loud clanks echoed from the far end of the tunnel followed by a high-pitched metallic buzz.

Jack's bracelet flashed red and emitted a loud, rapid beep that continued to speed up.

Star sat at the kitchen table staring out the sliding glass doors at the fence blocking the well. She had only been inside for a minute but for some strange reason, she ached for Jack to be with her.

A loud metal ping diverted her attention toward the old woman who plopped a stainless-steel tea kettle on the stove. The rotten egg smell of natural gas drifted through the kitchen when she turned the stove knob and lit it with a match.

"Now let's see, where did I put that tea?" She wiped her hands on her shirt and opened a wall cabinet above the counter.

Star had dealt with plenty of strangers as a real estate agent, so keeping a frail old woman occupied should be easy. But past events swirled in her mind: the hospital, the shooting, Cà Rá. How could any of it be real? She had to focus until Jack returned.

"How long have you lived here?" Star asked, her eyes shifting to the woman.

"Oh, quite a while." The woman's pale, veiny hands opened another cabinet and rummaged through the bottom shelf. "Ah, here we go. Tips PG."

Star shot her a curious look. "You mean PG Tips?"

"Yes, yes that's it." She opened another cupboard but closed it after a quick glance inside.

"I drank that when I visited England. When did you go?"

"Never been myself." The woman opened the dishwasher and looked inside. "Here they are, forgot I washed them already."

Star pointed over her shoulder into the hall. "That's funny, I saw a picture of Big Ben in the hallway. Did you take that?"

The woman paused and glanced down at the floor. "Big Ben? Oh. That's my sister Margaret. She's a world traveler, you know."

"I see." Star glanced back at the fence and hoped for a sign of Jack but found nothing. She placed her hand on the table and pulled her purse closer with the tip of her finger.

The kettle let out a faint whistle and the woman turned to face Star with her right arm behind her back. "Would you be a dear and fetch me that sugar canister on the shelf behind you?"

"Sure." Star slid her hand away from the purse and pushed herself sideways in the chair.

Where the woman's finger pointed at the wall were shelves cluttered with tins of spices, plastic containers, books, and glass jars. Nothing stood out as sugar. Star pointed at a round red canister. "This one?" she asked, keeping an eye on the woman's stiff posture, the other on the door.

"Yes, I can't stretch so high these days."

As she reached for the canister, a large metal picture frame on the shelf reflected the old woman creeping up behind her. The glint of a knife raised above her head flashed in the frame.

Star squeezed the canister in a white-knuckled grip, whirled around, and slammed it across the woman's jaw.

An explosion of white powder plumed across the room. The woman wobbled and collapsed to the ground.

Star lunged for her purse on the table but someone grabbed her from behind and hoisted her into the air.

"No, no!"

A man's gruff voice spoke through a heavy grunt and blew stale cigarette breath in her face. "Hold still, bitch."

Feet above the floor, arms trapped by her side, Star kicked the chair. She writhed and squirmed against the grip of thick, muscled arms but couldn't break free. His nasty breath choked her.

"*Motherfucker*," Star growled, and threw her head back into his nose with a satisfactory crunch.

"*Fuck*," he squealed in pain, and staggered into the living room before falling backward releasing his grip.

The momentum carried her body down on top of him, and her leg knocked a lamp off an end table that shattered on the wood floor. She scrambled to stand, but he grabbed her foot and yanked back, forcing her to the ground. Star clawed at the carpet, trying to crawl away, but he held tight to her left leg. As he pulled her closer, she rolled over onto her back.

The old woman appeared in the kitchen doorway, rubbing her bruised jaw. She waved the knife at Star and barked at the man. "Goddammit, Melvin. Hold her down."

"I'm trying, Ma!"

"I'm gonna cut you instead of her." The knife gleamed in the woman's knuckles and she stepped toward them.

"No!" Star screamed.

Melvin pinned her down but her right foot slipped loose. She cocked her knee back, and gave him a swift kick in his face.

The force of the blow knocked him back, releasing her. She sprang up and sprinted to the front door. When she pulled it open, another man with a beard and straw hat blocked her exit. He attempted to grab her, but she pulled away and raced upstairs. Her shoes slapped against the wood treads, thumping a hollow percussion.

The deafening scream of the tea kettle followed Star down the hall where she ran into a bathroom and slammed the door.

She pressed the lock on the handle and turned to scan the oversized bathroom, desperate for a way out. Sunlight poured in through a glass-block window.

Throwing open the medicine cabinet, she scanned the shelves of bottles, ointments, and soaps. She yanked open the vanity drawers looking for something, anything to fight back with.

Footsteps and muffled voices drew close to the door.

Her eyes widened and she stepped away from it, bumping into a white clawfoot bathtub. The shower curtain brushed against her arm and she turned to look back over her shoulder.

Tracking the curtain down to the tub, smears of red showed through the opaque plastic liner from the other side. She grabbed the edge of the curtain and pulled it back. The body of an old woman lay curled up in the bottom of the tub, her eyes open, staring up at Star.

The woman's matted white hair, splattered with blood, dangled over the back edge of the tub. Her throat had been slit and fresh blood trickled down her cornflower-blue sweater.

The curtain tore from the rod and Star reeled back with a scream.

A boot burst through the door. Wood splintered and exploded through the bathroom.

Melvin ran into the bathroom, grabbed her, and pinned her to the tile floor. This time she couldn't move.

A hand pressed the side of her face against the cold tile and turned her screams into muffled echoes. Tears streamed down her face and she tried to move but couldn't budge under their weight. Something sharp pricked her thigh, and within seconds, her vision blurred.

"Jack, no," she mumbled.

Her eyesight faded to darkness, and a raspy chuckle echoed close to her ear. "Nighty night."

Red light flashed against the tunnel walls and Jack held the phone's light out in front of him. Straining to find the source of the metal buzzing, he trudged through the water. A scraping sound squealed through the air behind him and a metal gate slid from a hidden groove in the tunnel. It clunked against the bottom and reverberated through the water.

Gripping its rusted and corroded bars, he tried to lift it but it wouldn't budge.

"Shit."

A high-pitched whizzing sounded, mixed with the slosh and splashes of water behind him. He turned, and glints of rapidly moving silver, diving in horizontal vortices, slapped water against the tunnel walls.

His eyes widened at the sight of a giant arm of spinning saw blades. No doubt how the dead man met his fate.

The contraption wobbled and moved forward. Rusty blades filled the entire height of the tunnel and sliced through the water, cutting wave after wave.

The red light on the bracelet turned solid and droned out a loud whine.

Jack reached for the walls but they were smooth brick with no sign of a lever or even a switch. *Fuck!* The blades inched closer and wind from their rotation whipped his flesh.

Three metal arms with spiked, conical drill-heads rotated from the top of the machine and filled the only remaining gaps in the tunnel.

Jack stepped back tight to the gate and shook his head. The grinding, crunching, and drilling sounds drowned out everything else. A tooth touched his shirt and ripped through it. Jack screamed, his back dug into the metal gate.

Blue light flared from the bracelet and it beeped with the woman's voice. "Oh yeah."

A metallic *thunk* echoed through the tunnel, and the machine stopped moving. The blades shuddered to stillness, the last of their sharp teeth stopping so very close to his mouth.

Several metallic clangs echoed in the tunnel and the giant arm pulled back toward its starting position. It locked into place at the far end of the wall where a second corridor forked to the right of it.

Jack took a deep breath then exhaled with a slow calm.

A flushing sound took over and the water level receded, leaving a thick layer of black sludge upon the tunnel floor.

The gate lifted behind him and as he turned, Jack glanced back at the dead man.

The body lay face down, legs and arms twisted.

A bright-green, fluorescent light flickered on at the far end of the tunnel, growing brighter, harsher.

Stepping forward, his feet sank into the mud with each step, and he made his way to the end of the tunnel where the light dimmed to a dull glow. Jack now stood in front of a solid wall. The light from the phone faded, and a five-percent battery warning flashed on its screen.

He scanned the walls with the failing light and a rounded shadow caught his attention. *What's that?* A three-inch circular groove was cut into a square block. The coarse rock smoothed to the metal of the block.

His fingers found several small, ridged teeth. A metal lock. And it needed a key.

He reached into his pocket and retrieved the first Empyreax ring. When he held it up, a magnetic force jerked it out of his fingers and pulled it into the groove, locking it tightly in place.

A black portal appeared several inches away from the wall.

Another damn portal. But this one with only a single stone step on the other side.

"Hello?" Jack leaned his head almost into it and the sound of his voice faded to an eerie silence.

If his dad had built all this to keep out the bad guys, surely, he'd know it was his son? Jack rubbed his stubbled chin. Wouldn't he?

The second piece of the key had to be in there.

Holding the phone's dim light up, he stepped through the portal. A second stone paver shone in the faint light. One step between Jack and a void of darkness.

Now or never. Jack swallowed, and stepped onto the paver. Instead of a shiver of cold, a warm golden light revealed more pavers. They formed a straight path of stones that led to a large, circular platform that sat in the center of a blackness too deep to see beyond the halo of light.

Eight stairs encircled it, rising up to a stone pedestal that sat at its center. Something glinted on the pedestal that shone beneath a single spotlight.

When he reached the first step, Jack hesitated. Was it real?

Another illusion? He didn't have time to waste in thought.

He placed his foot on the second step while the other remained firmly planted on the first. It was solid, real, visible. One more step and the silence became a deadly vacuum of darkness.

Jack breathed in through his nose, out through his mouth, and took the step. The next one came easier.

Holding the light lower to the next step, Jack blinked in time with the low-power warning.

The phone shut down.

"Dammit."

No light. His fingers gripped the phone tight.

Atop the pedestal, another metallic ring, smaller than the first, lay illuminated by the light from overhead.

The second Empyreax key.

Could it be this easy? Jack rubbed the rough surface. No cuts, no straight lines to indicate hidden traps. No more time to study it; he had to get back to Star.

He snatched the ring and shuffled back one step at a time, watching the stone, waiting, his shoulders hunched, anticipating danger.

Nothing.

Just like the first key, this one weighed almost nothing. He curled his fingers through it and rubbed his thumb on its smooth surface. Its opening allowed him to slide it up onto his right wrist.

The bracelet flashed red and emitted a sequence of beeps that progressed faster until a synthesized convulsing reverb bounced through the air.

The main middle platform disappeared and the pedestal fell straight down into the pit of black.

Flashes of red pulsed from the bracelet again and the distressed crunch of the synth droned into the vacuum of the dark void. The stair Jack stood on disappeared and he started to fall but he toppled onto his backside. Star's phone flipped out of his hand and landed on the third step.

Before he reached for the phone, the bracelet flashed again and he leapt up.

The step vanished and the phone dropped, disappearing below. He bolted down the platform with frantic leaps.

One by one, the stairs disappeared and the lights shut off, an invisible beast of darkness nipping at his heels. He jumped head-first through the portal and landed with a slide face down in the tunnel's sludge.

Rolling onto his back, he sat up and took several deep breaths. The portal had disappeared and only the solid block wall stared back at him.

A metallic sound pinged from the Empyreax key on the wall. It ejected from the groove and he lunged forward to catch it.

He slid the second key off his wrist, and a magnetized force nested the two rings together.

Why go to all this trouble to hide it? At what cost for its secrets?

"Star." He scrambled to his feet and sprinted down the tunnel.

At the top of the well ladder, he pushed his shoulders against the steel cover, and it flipped up on its rusty hinges. Sunlight blinded him and he climbed out of the well, rolling over onto the grass.

"Star, I got it," he said.

Squeezing his eyes tight until they adjusted to the light, he turned his head to the side and the shadows of four people stretched over him.

"Star?"

When his eyes adjusted, the old woman stepped forward, brandishing a knife above him.

"Thank you, Jack." She grabbed the two keys from him,

"You didn't know my father," he said.

She cackled and threw her head back. "Give him a prize."

Two men lifted him onto his knees and pressed a revolver to his temple.

"Hands behind your head," one of the men said.

"Where's Star?"

"Hands behind your head. Don't move," said another brute with ashen breath.

"She's taking a nap." The old woman turned sideways and pointed the knife at Star. She lay on the grass with a white gag in her mouth, her hands and feet bound with rope.

"I swear, if you hurt her," Jack snarled.

"Shut up." The man pressed the barrel of the gun hard into Jack's temple.

"Melvin, tie him up. Marco, bring the van around back." The woman raised her cell phone, dialed a number, and held it to her ear.

One of the men grabbed Jack's hands and wrapped rope around them.

The old woman turned away from them as she spoke. "This is Vera. We have the key." She paused and listened for several seconds, then turned back to look at Jack. "Okay. We'll do that."

The rope cinched tight around Jack's wrists and he smirked.

She ended the call and crouched in front of Jack. "I was going to kill you but it appears Demi wants you alive."

"Who?"

"You'll know soon enough."

A white Ford cargo van appeared from the side of the house and backed into the yard.

The old woman placed the Empyreax key into a bag. "Get them in the back and let's go." She climbed into the passenger side of the van.

The third man opened the rear doors and Melvin barked at Jack. "Stand up."

Jack didn't move.

The old woman yelled from the van. "Melvin, hurry your ass up!"

"I said stand up." Melvin reached down and grabbed Jack by his collar to pull him up.

Jack glared up at him and spotted a red dot twitching on the neck of the man.

A black dart sliced the silence and pierced Melvin's neck. He reached up to touch it.

"What the—?" His eyes rolled back into his head and he collapsed. Another two darts whisked through the air and hit the other man who dropped to the ground.

Vera looked out the back of the van. "Melvin!"

The driver's eyes glanced back at Jack in the rearview mirror and he floored the van out of the yard. It hit the curb and bounced into the street. The van bounded away from the house and Vera screamed, "Go back, go back!"

Jack huddled on his knees and held his tied hands in front of his face. Looking around the yard he caught sight of an old man peering above a broken fence with what appeared to be a mini-crossbow pistol.

The man dipped behind the fence and Jack lost sight of him. Scanning along the fence, Jack couldn't find the man—

A board on the fence fell forward and the man squeezed sideways through it. Dressed in jeans and a sea-green t-shirt, he sprinted toward Jack. His gray zippered hoodie flapped behind him like a cape.

Jack scrambled next to Star and shielded her body.

"Hey, hey, don't hurt us," Jack said.

The man stood over Jack, and sunlight reflected off his balding, white hair. He stared down through a clouded eye and smiled to reveal several missing teeth. His hand opened and he reached out. "I'm not gonna hurt you, kid. I'm Simon Church."

20

· THE TEMPLE ·

Tarkos leaned over a round wood table and dipped a folded steak sandwich into a white bowl of au jus sauce. The rich flavors of beef broth, creamy butter, and malt vinegar washed over his tongue. Had he not paused to savor the moment, the chaos of the day would have chewed at him instead. No. He wouldn't let it. He couldn't. Swallowing his bite, he looked across the room.

Bruce sat on the bottom bunk of one of two platform beds. His feet dangled off the mattress, and he stared in silence at a burning candle on an adjacent table.

Tarkos held his sandwich up, meat clinging to the bottom of soggy bread. "Bruce, you need to give me a hand with all this food. You really should eat." He waved his free hand across the spread of food. "There's plenty. And it's French." A wide grin stretched across his face and he took another bite of the sandwich. "Mmm." Juice dripped down his chin and he grabbed a napkin to wipe it.

A toilet flushed in the room's adjoining bathroom and Fletcher opened its door while wiping his hands with a towel. He stepped into the room and headed to the table to sit. "Well, the bathroom windows are barred."

"Yup, saw that," Tarkos said.

Fletcher folded his hands above his plate and bowed his head in whispered prayer. The candle on the table flickered. "Amen."

"How's the head?" Tarkos asked while waving the sandwich toward a clean bandage on Fletcher's forehead.

"Fine, I'm fine. One of their girls fixed me up."

Tarkos smiled. "I bet she did."

Fletcher smirked. "Now, now, I'm far too old for that." He bit into his own plated sandwich and chewed in small bites, just enough to speak. "Mmm. I must say this is delicious." He glanced at the carafe of red wine in the center of the table. "Have you tried the wine?"

Tarkos picked his teeth with his tongue then set down his sandwich and leaned forward. "Not yet. I wanted to get your divine opinion first." Pausing, he tapped his fingernail against the glass. "Do you think it's poisoned?"

With a roll of his eyes, Fletcher's lips hooked into a smile. "Who cares?"

Tarkos erupted in laughter, snatched the carafe, and filled their glasses. With a swivel in his seat, he held it out toward the bunks. "Bruce?"

Bruce shook his head and didn't utter a sound.

Fletcher held his glass high toward Tarkos. "To your health, Mr. Tarkos. May you still find the truth you seek."

Their glasses clinked together, and Tarkos sipped his wine and then raised his to Fletcher. "And likewise, to my new friend." He bowed his head. "The Reverend."

Fletcher let out a dry laugh and toasted again. "This poison is delectable."

Tarkos tipped his glass back and chugged the wine in two gulps. "Ahh." He smacked his lips together. "I must say it has a dense fruit flavor, a hint of blackberry, and a bouquet of strychnine."

Fletcher let out a belly laugh, but Bruce cut him off with a sardonic snap. "Are you two finished?"

The men fell silent, and Tarkos stood while filling his glass. "Bruce, what else are we going to do? Everything we've seen today? This guy Demi? I don't know who he is but I saw—*you* saw what he is capable of. We all saw it with our own eyes. So, why does he have us held up in here? I'll tell you." He extended his index finger from his glass. "He wants us for something."

"For what? Killing people? I didn't sign up for that. I'm not supposed to be here, Andre. I need to be home with my son. My wife."

There had been a time when Tarkos was jealous of Bruce for that. Having a family unit to hold him up. But then again, if he had one, his priorities would be different. Perhaps.

"Bruce, we had nothing to do with that." Tarkos looked across the room at Fletcher. "We're caught up in something that's bigger than any of us. Don't you want to know? We've waited so long for this very moment. The truth."

"The truth," Fletcher said staring deadpan down at the table. "The truth isn't always what it appears to be." His eyes flicked up to Tarkos. "You need to be careful."

Tarkos turned back, set his glass on the table, and squeezed his chair's backrest with both hands. "I'm not scared. My entire life I've dreamed of this exact moment. And here I am. Here we are. Whether we like it or not, we're part of it. All of us."

Bruce's voice quivered. "Well, I'm terrified to think of—"

"Think of what?" Tarkos snapped back.

Bruce paused and turned back toward the candle. "Think of my son growing up without me. And Lily. Alone."

"Bruce, if they wanted to kill us, they would have done it already."

"I just want to go home."

Tarkos grabbed his glass and swigged the wine. "We're not ready to go home. They're planning something for us." He looked back at Fletcher for reassurance, but the Reverend responded with a meager shoulder shrug.

"Okay, look. Do you still have the sim to your phone?"

Bruce didn't move.

"Bruce."

"What?"

"The sim, do you still have your sim or did they take it?"

"Yes, it's here."

"Okay, this is what we're going to do. We find your phone and I promise we'll get you out of here, back home to your family."

"But how?"

Fletcher cleared his throat. "The Lord works in mysterious ways."

Three knocks sounded against their door, and a locking mechanism clicked. They all froze and turned their heads toward the door as it swung open.

A young man flanked by two armed guards stepped inside. "Demi will see you now."

Tarkos looked down at Fletcher, whose smile had left his face frozen in a morose expression. He spun back around to Bruce and waved his arm toward the armed men. "See?"

The time for savoring the moment had ended.

Late afternoon sunlight hit Tarkos when all three men stepped out into the courtyard of the sprawling farm. For a moment, the sun cast a warm, soporific daze that reminded him he needed sleep. The smell of vegetation, manure, and livestock filled the air, accented by the occasional waft of hay.

The armed guards guided them toward a two-story barn that looked more like a hangar that could fit an airplane. As he scanned the farm, he caught the eyes of its workers, who drew quick glances back at him. A man stood in a fenced pen throwing pellet feed to chickens. Two women knelt in a garden pulling weeds. A figure in greased overalls turned wrenches on a tractor. Each of them stayed quiet, submissive, but curious.

As they reached the barn's main opening, Tarkos looked up at a scaffold platform where two men stood with long rifles slung over their shoulders. He glanced over his shoulder at Fletcher, whose eyes pivoted to him. Bruce walked next to him, eyes fixed straight to the ground.

They paused at the entrance to the barn and one of the armed men stepped in front of them. When he slid open the main pocket door, a medley of berries, vanilla, lemongrass, and the sweet fragrance of mint replaced every smell of the farm.

Tarkos stepped inside and took a deep breath, frozen in awe of the majestic building laid out before him. It opened up to a massive room with second-story railed platforms running its entire length. Several rooms had been constructed in quadrants under the platforms, but the corners of their walls lay hidden beneath a sprawling garden of flowering plants, fruits, and herbs. A curated pattern of colored flowers lined the walls of the barn. Crimson, lavender, pink, sapphire...every spectrum of color in a wondrous collage.

An open-air amphitheater with round, tree trunk seats spread in an array of stepped arcs at the back of the barn. A large, domed structure rested atop a rectangular stage, the main focal point of the theater. High above, a sign with a black circle and four smaller circles at each ninety-degree mark, clung to the wall.

"Well, this is something," Fletcher said.

"This way," the guard said.

Tarkos looked over at Bruce who stared back through his glasses with glossy eyes.

Several cultists moved about inside each of the rooms, pointing at computer screens, soldering wires together, and welding metal parts.

Tarkos passed by a room with bright-blue glowing lights. Inside lay the body of a young girl of Asian descent, suspended mid-air by shackles of red plasma energy binding her hands and feet. He tapped Bruce twice and nodded toward the woman.

One of the armed men stepped in front of them, blocking their view. "Keep going," he said.

They reached the far end of the barn in front of the main theater stage and two small drones with extended mechanical armatures flew past them.

One of the drones brushed Tarkos' shoulder and Fletcher jumped with a yelp.

At center stage of the theater sat the metallic device from Higgenbotham cave.

A thick, coil-pack of wires extended from its base and led to a large table filled with computers and monitors.

"What's that?" Fletcher's voice cracked.

The drones had stopped above a conveyor belt of lights, strobing in a patterned sequence. Wires from the table led to several cylinders just below the conveyor, which pulsed in rapid succession. A streak of miniature lightning flashed with a sizzling pop.

A small glowing block of white light formed on the conveyor and a drone picked it up with its metallic pincers. It rotated away from the conveyor and placed the block on an incomplete wall of the same glowing blocks that stood only two feet high.

"I bet you're wondering what that is?" Demi's voice boomed from behind the men.

Tarkos, Bruce and Fletcher turned in unison.

Demi smiled. "Anyone care to hasarder une hypothèse? Monsieur Tarkos?"

Tarkos froze. He had a French teacher who used to ask that exact question but how could Demi know? He squinted then blinked to gather himself. And just like the little kid back in school, he responded.

"Oui, une porte?"

Demi's face lit up with admiration. "Correct."

"A what?" Fletcher asked.

Tarkos mumbled, "A door. A jump gate between universes."

Fletcher shrugged. "It's not very big."

Demi's voice took a grim tone. "Not yet, priest."

Fletcher let out a deep exhale and muttered under his breath. "This guy, too? Why does everyone think I'm a priest?"

Bruce frowned at Fletcher. "What's the difference?"

"Seriously?" Fletcher asked.

"I'm just asking." Bruce shrugged. "I didn't know there was a difference."

"There's a huge diff—"

"Enough," Demi cut in.

Tarkos focused past Demi to a large wooden table cluttered with electronic parts, speakers, and a keyboard. He traced wires from the table to the Higgenbotham device, then peered over at the glowing block wall. "Making a collect call?"

"You pick up very quickly, Mr. Tarkos. I could use someone like you. Everyone on the team is just so—"

"Violent?" Bruce interjected.

"I prefer...savage." Demi turned and sat in front of the keyboard and began typing. A sequence of symbols flashed on a monitor above him.

"No, thanks," Tarkos said. He stepped toward Bruce who nudged him as he turned.

Bruce cast his eyes forward to signal Tarkos, who traced a line from them to the far corner of the table. The Moleskine journal and Bruce's cell phone sat next to a lamp.

Tarkos whispered to Bruce. "Give me your sim."

"Why?"

"Just give it to me."

Bruce reached into his pocket and handed the sim to Tarkos.

Demi moved to the Higgenbotham device, pressed a button, and a digital display appeared with cryptic markings. After touching a sequence of symbols, a panel opened, and a one-centimeter-square cubed antenna rose from its top.

"Why don't you let these guys go," Tarkos asked. He moved to the far side of the table and leaned against it.

"Oh, I can't do that," Demi said, heading to the metal case that held the sphere.

When Demi turned his back to gather the sphere, Tarkos stood and slipped the Moleskine into his pocket.

Demi pinched the sphere between two fingers, gazing into its crystalline structure. "Do you know what power is?" He turned and looked at Tarkos. "I don't mean your primitive understanding of it. I mean the ability to create and destroy."

Tarkos leaned forward and reached for Bruce's cell phone, sliding it into his pocket.

"Who are you?" Bruce asked.

"A mercenary."

Fletcher's eyebrows lifted. "Mercenary?"

Demi moved to the Higgenbotham device. "Hired by the Xurricans to hunt down a traitor. I accidentally stumbled onto this planet, but I found the ultimate power."

"The Empyreax," Tarkos said.

"Yes."

"So why save us?"

"You told me you can open it."

Tarkos looked at Bruce. "I can."

"Well, when the Xurrican army arrives, we will take you to the Empyreax and you will open it."

Demi stood in front of Tarkos and looked deep into his eyes. "Now, you can open it right?"

"Yes. But what's inside?"

Demi hesitated.

"You don't know, do you?" Tarkos flashed a wry grin.

"Untold power, Monsieur. Untold power. And when the Xurricans arrive, they will be at my disposal. At some point, I will need you as shields to delay your military commanders. I assume they will value your lives, no?"

Demi placed the sphere inside a round orifice on the device and it slid inside. An energy field draped around it, and a rotating gyroscope of strobing light appeared over the cubed antenna. The madman chuckled. "Still works. They don't make them like they used to."

Leather-soled footsteps echoed from the far side of the barn, and a black-haired man wearing sunglasses entered the main stage area.

"Ah, Takashi," Demi said. "I'd like you to meet Dr. Tarkos."

Takashi bowed low then rose gracefully, his dark sunglasses hugged tight to his face.

"He doesn't speak," Demi said. "Never says a word. Kaze Baku they call him. The Wind Demon. I'm half-tempted to probe his mind, but even I'm afraid of what I might find."

"Why's that?" Tarkos asked.

"Some things are better left to the unknown."

The main computer let out a series of beeps, and a teletype prompt of symbols sped across its screen.

Demi scanned the symbols then typed on the keyboard. After a few seconds delay, symbols continued to scroll on the screen. He typed again, and a shorter sequence of symbols appeared. "There."

"What'd they say?" Tarkos asked.

"I sent them the coordinates of this planet and told them when the jump gate is done, they can begin their arrival."

"That's it?"

Demi sneered. "Yes, that's it."

"You are to be congratulated," Fletcher said.

"And why is that?" Demi asked.

"Well, it's obvious you're just a pawn. I thought you were some important figure from another world but you're nothing more than a foot soldier."

"You humans are so simple. By the time the Xurricans arrive, I will have opened the Empyreax. They will have no choice but to follow me or they will die. And you creatures will be long gone. But Reverend, I will give you a personal front-row seat to my...how would you call it? Ascension."

"You're mad," Fletcher said.

Demi's hysterical laugh echoed throughout the barn. "Takashi, take them away. Oh, and doctor? You may take the journal and the phone. Study them hard because if you cannot open the Empyreax..."

The striped drone floated down in front of Tarkos and unleashed its sharp blade to within inches of his face.

As Takashi led the men away, Demi lingered and turned his attention to Cà Rá. Upon entering her room, he stood by her head and waved his hand in a calm pattern over her face. A sharp needle ejected from his wrist and he pulled her hair to the side, where he slid the probe into the base of her neck.

"Now, my dear. Let's see what secrets you are hiding from me."

The needle clicked, and jolted Demi's neck back.

21

· BOOBY TRAPS ·

Cà Rá stood at the entrance to Bill's cabin, a heavy drizzle falling from the sky. A blanket of steam rose from the warm ground, forming vapors of petrichor that swirled and danced upward disappearing into the cool air. She had seen this many times, but in this moment, it reminded her of home.

"These swirls resemble a galaxy I once visited. A dozen planets had been consumed by an Invertix. Each one fragmented into quadrillions of particles that glowed from the release of their core energy." She grasped a silver pendant dangling on a chain around her neck. "From afar, it was majestic. There are few things the Calodox feared, but the Invertix is one of them. Such a malevolent force cloaked in beauty."

"A black widow," Bill said from behind her.

She turned, and he leaned back in his chair. "And what is a black widow?"

"A female spider that attracts a male and then kills it after it mates. Sometimes, we use it to describe deceptive women. So your Invertix is like a black widow."

Cà Rá stepped toward him out of the shadows. "Do you think I am a black widow?"

"No, not at all. And besides, I don't think we can mate."

"But if I were to kill you?"

"And take my soul?" A smile lit his face.

"Yes."

"I suppose then yes, but there would be nobody left on Earth to talk about Cà Rá the Black Widow. So no, please don't kill me."

Cà Rá smiled.

"All right, time to go," he said, pushing to his feet.

"Yes."

Cà Rá had seen a flyer for the county fair mixed into a stack of mail Bill had brought home the month before. She made him promise to take her so she could experience something new.

As they entered the front ticket gate to the fair, an explosion of sensory detail hit her from every direction. The voices of every man, woman, and child—delight, fear, joy, glee, amusement. The cries of excitement swooshed in the background from mechanical thrill rides. The buzzing hum of thousands of colored lights echoed around her and dazzled a glow into the early-evening sky.

She could smell the earthen mustiness of straw from a petting zoo, the sweet sugar of cotton candy, and the baked, sweet, powdered-dough of funnel cake. She followed along with children, trying to beat impossible games and marveled at their simplicity.

"William, why does this exist?"

"The carnival?"

"Yes."

"To make money."

"What do you mean?"

"The people who own this carnival, they travel from town to town to make money."

"So humans pay money for this."

"Yes."

"It is wonderful."

They walked by a low-hanging tent, and a man who stood under its canopy barked at Bill. "Hey there, fella. Wanna try and win a prize for your exotic lady?"

Bill smirked his face. "No, thanks," he said while nudging Cà Rá to move along.

She stood still like a stone pillar.

The man let out a laugh. "Looks like she wants you to give it a shot. Come on now, it's easy, you just toss the ring onto the bottle."

Cà Rá nodded.

"She speak English?"

"I speak English," Cà Rá snapped.

"Gotcha. Well, let's see if your old man can get it on."

Bill waved the man away.

Cà Rá looked up at Bill with a smile and poked him with a straight finger. "Yes Bill, please, get it on."

"Cà Rá, these games are all rigged."

She raised her eyebrows and widened her doe-brown eyes.

Bill sighed and reached into his pocket. "Okay, how much?"

"Five bucks, three tosses."

He passed the barker his money and received three plastic rings in exchange. Bill surveyed the bottles and started to flick his wrist back and forth in a slow, swaying motion.

At that moment, a male voice echoed over the drone of the crowd, and caught Cà Rá's attention. She tuned her ear to the voice, and it cleared to that of a man talking to a group of people.

"No, ma'am, this is not some hocus-pocus gimmick or charlatan trick. No sir, your eyes will not deceive you. This magic is real, and as right as rain, I will make my assistant Takashi disappear right in front of you."

Bill tossed his first ring and it clinked off the lip of a red glass bottle.

"Oh, so close," the barker egged.

Bill shook his head and readied the second ring.

Cà Rá turned her eyes toward a small group of people gathering just inside a white-fenced area.

Demi stood on a three-step platform made of wood pallets that had been stitched together. His cleaned and pressed dark, Victorian suit hugged tight against his body. He reached up and removed his black hat, exposing his thin, white hair. Grasping the hat with both hands, he dipped his head and raised his eyebrows to the crowd.

"Friends, before I make Takashi disappear, I offer each of you a small token of our goodwill. These are tiny wooden carvings made by members of our community—the Temple of New Hope. They are good luck charms. Free of charge, no strings, no purchase necessary."

Miles and Edgar stepped forward and let the crowd reach into shoe boxes to pull out a unique wooden carving.

Demi's voice bellowed across the fair. "Put it by your bed and every day you wake up it will remind you to live a life of hope and inspiration."

Other people streamed in and around Demi looking for their free gift.

Bill let out a sigh of heavy disgust that jerked Cà Rá's head to him. The second ring toss ricocheted off a blue bottle while the barker smiled.

"So close, so close my friend. Last chance, make it a good one."

Bill readied his aim one last time as Demi's voice continued in the background.

"I need everyone to repeat after me. We believe. We believe. Over and over until he comes back. Okay? Do you believe?"

A few staggered voices cried out of sync. "We believe."

"I know you good people of Stone Creek can do better than that. Let's try again. Do you believe?"

This time, they found their synchronicity and a loud chorus drowned out all sound.

"We believe."

Demi started to count. "One…"

"We believe."

Bill pulled his wrist back.

"Two…" Demi's voice stretched into the crowd's chant.

"We believe."

Bill flicked his wrist forward and let go of the ring.

The ring glided through the air, hit the lip of one bottle, and flipped end over end towards another. Cà Rá blinked and stretched her five fingers forward. The ring wobbled and curled down over the neck of a green bottle.

"We believe."

"Three," Demi cried out.

At that moment, an overwhelming rush of energy forced a jolt that arched through Cà Rá's body. Her hair fanned behind her, and her eyes flashed a glossy jet black.

"Haha!" Bill pumped his fist in victory.

The crowd erupted into joyous cheers and clapping.

"Lucky shot, old man, lucky shot." The barker shook his head.

Cà Rá focused back on Bill, then glanced at the barker.

"Lucky days. What do I win?"

The barker dragged his hand on a wooden shelf of rubber and plush toys. "Right. Since you only got one, pick your prize from this row."

Cà Rá's eyes scanned the shelf and locked onto a small plush penguin with a tiny pink ribbon on its head. She pointed, and the barker snatched it and handed it to her. "I guess he got it on," she said.

The barker smirked at Cà Rá, "Who do you think you are?"

"I'm his black widow," she replied.

Bill shrugged and raised his eyebrows at the barker.

She turned back to Demi and handed Bill the penguin.

"Cà Rá, you can't cause any trouble. Nothing that will draw attention. One more ride then we go home."

"No trouble, William. Fun." She walked towards Demi and Takashi. The crowd had already dispersed, and the men stood collecting their belongings. Takashi broke down a folding table and carried it to a nearby truck. When he passed Cà Rá, he glanced down at her, and she caught her reflection in his sunglasses.

Demi handed a business card to a woman. "That's right, ma'am. Our website is www.TempleofNewHope.com. Stop by any time. We welcome anyone who needs our help."

Bill stopped Cà Rá. "Stay right here, I'm going to get some water."

As Bill left, she took a step closer to Demi. He closed the lid on a small briefcase and turned around, but Cà Rá blocked his path and startled him.

"Whoa. Hello, young lady."

Cà Rá didn't make a sound.

"I'm afraid you missed our show already. We will be back tomorrow for the last day of the fair."

Her eyes moved from his face to the breast pocket of his coat.

Demi's eyes tracked down to the same spot she stared at and a slight smile crept from the left corner of his mouth. "How may I help you?"

"I know what you have in your pocket."

His face lit into a giant grin. "I'm not sure I know what you're talking about."

"The sphere."

He narrowed his eyes at her. "You from around here?"

"No."

"Where are you from?"

"Far away."

"Far away, huh? Well, let me invite you to learn more about our temple." His fingers and thumb twirled together and a white business card appeared from thin air, which he handed to her. The circle symbol had been printed at the top of the card with four words below it.

Truth. Purpose. Control. Wonder.

www.TempleofNewHope.com

"And what is this temple?" Cà Rá asked.

"A community of farmers looking for hope. A new world, not bound by the things of man."

Cà Rá tilted her head in curiosity.

Demi reached out to grab her shoulder. "Here, let me show—"

As he touched her, an energy pulse burst from the sphere inside his coat, and his body fell limp. Lunging forward, he collapsed, and his contorted fingers slipped around Cà Rá's necklace.

Bill screamed from behind them. "Don't touch her!"

A blast of energy detonated and forced Demi away from Cà Rá. His fingers yanked the chain from her neck, and it hurtled away into the mud.

Demi's body flipped sideways, and a shockwave dusted the nearby crowd with the force of a heavy wind. A father jumped back to protect his boys, and the crowd shrieked with people running away in all directions.

Demi crashed to the ground and gasped for air. "It's...you," Demi cried while propping himself up on one knee, trying to stand.

Miles and Edgar rushed to his side.

Cà Rá turned and looked at all the three men. Her eyes flashed gloss black.

"Shit," Bill said. "Let's go. Now."

Demi gasped at Edgar. "It's her. Don't let them leave."

"Who?" Edgar asked.

"The girl. It's her." Demi pointed while Bill yanked her away.

Edgar raised a 9mm handgun towards Bill and fired.

A loud cry of fear ripped through the crowd and people streamed from the scene in terror.

The bullet whizzed past Cà Rá and pierced a candy-striped tent canopy. Cries of women and children silenced the gun's report.

Cà Rá stopped at the edge of a tent pole and turned around. Bill grabbed at her and yelled but his voice drifted into a distant roar.

Two police officers ran into the fenced area with guns drawn and pointed at Demi. Miles scrambled in the mud and jumped over the fence, fleeing the scene.

"Freeze. On the ground now," one officer shouted.

One officer chased after Miles. Takashi stopped in his tracks and peered around the corner of a tent, watching from afar.

Demi slipped and fell forward into the mud. "She's here. She's here," he yelled. When he rolled over, he reached into his jacket breast pocket.

"Don't do it." The officer took a defensive posture, then pulled the trigger when Demi ignored the order. A single shot hit Demi in his right thigh.

Demi recoiled in pain, grabbing his leg with both hands. The officer barked into his radio and took cautious steps forward.

The full strength of Bill's voice echoed behind her. "Cà Rá, we need to *go.*"

She turned and caught the glimmer of her necklace in a muddy lump of grass. Her eyes traced across the field, to a Reverend who sat crouched behind a popcorn stand, staring at the necklace.

Bill pulled Cà Rá and rushed her away from the tent. "Where's the necklace?"

"It's safe," she replied.

At that moment, the memory replay cut to black, and Demi appeared back in the temple. Cà Rá lay motionless, silent, yet seemed to be taunting him.

He leaned back, turned, and stared at the portal. A drone placed another glowing brick onto it.

The sun tucked behind Black Wolf Mountain and stretched a blanket of red clouds across the sky. Simon tugged on the broken screen door of his trailer home. He pulled out a ring of keys that clinked together and he leaned against the front door, turning away from Jack and Star. "Gimme a second. Need to disable my booby traps," he said.

Star leaned into Jack's arm and he squeezed her tight. "You need some rest," he whispered.

With half-drowsy eyes, she nodded, her head rubbing against his shirt.

Jack glanced overhead at the fire-red sky but a few loud thuds banged from the doorway. Simon's voice rose from inside. "Dammit."

Jack stared at the opening and a loud crash of shattered glass startled him. "Aw, shit." Simon's voice quivered and cracked inside the dark trailer. Jack moved closer to the doorway and peered inside. "Simon, you okay?" No response.

Star turned her head away from Jack to the door.

He lifted his arm off her and pulled open the screen door. "Wait here a minute."

Simon's head poked out and startled him. "Okay, ready."

"You okay?" Jack asked.

"Fine. Everything's fine. Why do you ask?" Simon leaned off the stoop and ushered them inside.

His neck craned up and his clouded eye rolled to the clouds overhead. "Red sky at night. Sailor's delight." He smiled, let go of the screen, and slammed the main door shut.

The last remnants of daylight slipped into dusk and the inside of the trailer home filled with dull, gray light. A hot stink of stale mildew clung heavy in the air.

"You have any electricity?" Jack asked.

"No lights, they'll know I'm here."

"Who?"

"Everyone."

Simon moved into the main living room and pulled a rug back, revealing a trap door. When he opened it, a dull, green light appeared, illuminating a small staircase built into the ground.

"You'll be safe in here." He led them down the steps to an underground bunker the size of a small bedroom. Tubs of emergency food, survival gear, and electronic equipment filled shelves across the walls.

Jack guided Star to a bed and sat her on the mattress. She lay down, rested her head on the pillow, and closed her eyes.

Simon opened a plastic tub and pulled out a ration bar. He tore off the foil wrapper and bit into it. He held the bitten end of the bar out to Jack. "You want one?"

Jack twisted open a bottle of water and waved the bar away. "Who were those people?"

"The tattoos on their wrists, did you see'em?"

Jack nodded and sipped the water.

Simon talked while chewing. "Bunch of crazies from the Temple of New Hope."

"The what?"

"One of those new-age hippie cults. It's led by a guy named Damien Carver. Demi, they call him. No idea he'd be tied up in all this."

"What does this have to do with my father?"

"Well, they want the same thing you're after. The Empyreax key."

Jack drank the water.

"We owed your dad, and he put his trust in us as guardians of the key. Rita, me and Diane. So far, I'd say we've done a pretty shit job of it." Simon's face scrunched up with wrinkles. "Diane was a good woman. She didn't deserve that at all."

"So you knew about the well?"

"Knew about it? Hell, I helped your dad build it, well the booby traps anyway, not the well." Simon leaned in, and his wide, toothless grin lit his face. "What did you think of the saw blade machine? Did it scare ya?"

"Terrifying."

A dry cackling filled the room. "That was my idea."

"Thanks."

Simon grabbed Jack's shoulders and gave him a shake. "Come on, Jack. Nothing's gonna happen to you. You've got the bracelet. Everything you need is right there."

"But what if I didn't have it? Then what?"

"Well, we didn't have time to plan for that."

"It would have killed me like it did one of those cultists."

"It did? Oh man, I wish I could have seen that. Bastard got what he deserved for what they did to Diane."

"So, we've at least got your piece of the key, right?"

Simon thumped his temple with his index finger. "I have it in a safe place."

"Where?"

He pointed to the ceiling. "At the top of Chimney Rock."

"The top of the cliff?"

"Yeah. Your dad coded the lock, and I put it up there."

"What's the code?"

"I don't know. He never told me. I thought you'd have it."

Jack glanced at Star. "It's gotta be in the box."

Simon's bad eye blinked. "What box?"

"We have to get back to the cabin."

"Are you kidding? This town is crawling with cultists and cops." Simon motioned to Star. "She needs her rest. Besides, I have to go take care of a few things tonight."

He climbed the ladder and leaned over the opening on his knees.

"Where are you going?" Jack asked.

"Don't worry about me. You're safe here tonight. Meet you back at the cabin at nine tomorrow morning." He started to close the trap door.

"Wait, Simon!"

"What?"

"How do I climb the mountain?"

"Zig-zag."

"Zig-zag?"

"Yeah, zig-zag."

The trap door slammed shut and the sound of the carpet sliding over it ended with a thud.

Simon's footsteps faded away and Jack sat next to Star.

22

· HOLOGRAMS ·

Thursday, September 12th, 2019

Bruce twitched awake and jerked his head up from the bed. He squinted when he turned and morning sunlight seared his eyes through the barred window. His empty stomach amplified the aroma of eggs, bacon, and coffee.

"What time is it?"

"Eight a.m." Tarkos leaned back in a chair at the wood table sipping dark coffee from a blue cup while reading the *Stone Creek Chronicle newspaper.*

Sitting up in the bed, Bruce ran his hand through his disheveled hair. "I was hoping this was all just a bad dream."

Tarkos blew across the edge of his cup. "Nope."

He should never have listened to Andre. For years and years, Bruce toiled in the scientist's shadow, caught up in his endless delusions of grandeur that he believed would give him his big break someday. Books, speaking engagements, enough money to set his family up right. All of it gone, while he sat trapped in this farmhouse jail in the middle of nowhere.

Fletcher lay in the far corner bed with his back turned to them and jostled with a loud snort.

Bruce stood and shuffled to the table. "How can you be so calm?"

Tarkos tilted half the newspaper over and pointed at the food. "You should really eat Bruce, it's not healthy if you don't."

"What's the point if they're just going to kill us?"

"They're not going to kill us."

"And when you can't open the Empyreax?" He'd asked Tarkos this kind of question back in the lab. A dagger of words that would no doubt ground Andre from his careless arrogance.

Tarkos locked eyes with him, popped a piece of Wasa bread into his mouth and crunched down on it without a word.

Three knocks rapped on the door and froze their conversation.

Tarkos slowed his chewing and moved his eyes from Bruce to the door.

Three knocks sounded again, and Bruce called out. "Hello?"

No response.

A click echoed from behind the door and the bolt on the lock slid open.

Bruce glanced at Tarkos then to Fletcher who still lay asleep.

Tarkos rubbed his hands together, pushed from the table, and walked to the door, opening it.

At first, Bruce's eyes focused near the top half of the doorway, expecting armed cultists to enter. Instead, his son walked in.

"Daddy!"

"Jacob!" An incredible wave of joy filled Bruce and he knelt as Jacob ran into his arms. Holding his son erased all Bruce's fear and anxiety...

Bruce twitched awake and jerked his head up from the bed. He squinted when he turned and morning sunlight seared his eyes through the barred window. His empty stomach amplified the aroma of eggs, bacon, and coffee.

"What time is it?"

Jack crawled through a tall cluster of invasive Japanese stiltgrass and crept behind a large fallen tree. He peered through its gnarled branches at the cabin where NQCO agents had arrived in two black SUVs. Signaling with his right hand, Star moved from a nearby rock and knelt beside him.

Two agents lifted a black body bag into a white box truck emblazoned with the sunburst logo of the *Beetle Bread, Co.* down its side. One of them pulled the door shut and banged on it twice. The truck drove off as two more agents exited the cabin.

"This isn't good," Jack whispered.

"What do you see?"

"Five, maybe six agents. All armed."

"Any sign of Simon?"

Jack shook his head. "No. Where the hell is he?"

"I'm right here." Simon's voice pierced the air between Star and Jack and they jolted up against the tree. An arc of golden, electric sparks sizzled in mid-air and a hand wearing a bracelet appeared from a shimmering refraction of light. The sparks spread out from the bracelet and across the shape of a kneeling body with Simon appearing out of thin air with a giant smile on his face.

"Jesus," Jack said. "Are you naked?"

Simon smiled and looked down at his genitals. "Of course. You need to be for the cloaking device to work."

"Oh my god," Star said, turning away.

"How do you think I always escape from Montclare. Bastards have no idea."

Jack whispered, "Okay never mind that. Can you get inside the cabin?"

Simon moved up and peered over the log. His right ass cheek rubbed against Star's arm and forced her to shuffle away, shaking her head in disgust.

"Piece of cake. I'll just walk right by them. What am I looking for?"

"On the living room table is a silver box with a letter. We need that letter, and if you can get to the back bedroom. There's a girl in there."

"Cà Rá?"

"You know about her?"

Simon smiled, displaying the gaps in his teeth, and winked with his cloudy eye. "Magnificent, isn't she?"

Jack darted his eyes to Star, and she furrowed her brow.

Simon stood, and his genitals flopped between their sight line.

Jack scoffed. "Dude, what the—"

Simon pressed the bracelet on his wrist, and he disappeared in a flash of light.

"Okay, I'll be right back." Grasses ruffled when Simon's invisible body moved through them.

"He's crazy," Star said, peering over the log.

"Probably why he was friends with my dad."

"Jack, look." Star put her hand on his shoulder.

"What?"

"Over there, his cloak is fading." She pointed toward one of the SUVs.

Jack squinted across the yard where Simon's device had surely started to fail.

A pair of walking legs flickered in the sunlight, disappearing when they approached two armed agents who stood watch at the front stoop.

Simon's upper body flickered on and off several times until his entire naked body reappeared mere feet behind the agents.

Jack's eyes widened. "Oh, shit."

Simon stood waving at Jack with a giant grin on his face.

"Stop waving," Jack mumbled.

Star whispered. "What the hell is he doing?"

Simon spun around and grabbed his crotch, flipping his dick several times toward the oblivious agents. He looked back at Jack and held two thumbs up with a silent giggle.

Jack dragged a hand down his face. "This situation is about to get worse."

Simon turned and shook his ass at the agents, gyrating in a taunting circular motion.

As soon as he let a giggle slip out, one of the agents turned around with the full display right in his face.

"What the fuck?" The agent raised his rifle and the other one shook his head at the sight. "Freeze."

"Uh-oh." Simon stopped shaking his ass, turned, and stood upright.

"Hands on your head, now," one of the agents barked and

sighted his optic.

"You got me, boss." Simon raised his hands, and his genitals stared back at the agents.

Jack's eyes raced from Simon to the cabin and then to Star. "Shit." He could barely make out the agent touching his headset and mumbling into it.

"Wait, I've got an idea." Jack pulled the cylinder microphone from his pocket, pressed a button on its side and held it to his mouth. "PO. PO. Can you hear me?"

PO sat motionless in his charging cradle. A tiny green light flashed on the top of his head and he let out a series of boot-sequence beeps. An electric static sound preceded Jack's voice and it echoed inside his main logic board.

"PO. Come in."

PO jolted to life and hovered away from the cradle into the dim hallway. *Yes.*

PO rotated and spotted an agent in the main office sifting through papers and collecting items into silver cases.

The agent turned and touched his headset with his right hand "Say again? Naked what? Man? Copy." His eyes darted to a corner of the room. "Peters, go see what the hell is going on."

Jack's static voice sputtered through PO's circuits. "I need you to create a distraction at the front of the cabin. We need a distraction. Do you understand?"

Yes.

PO rotated to sneak past the office door but paused one last time to rotate a look back.

Just before he moved forward, an agent stepped out in front of him, forcing him to reel back a foot.

The agent turned to the front door and raised his rifle.

PO floated just behind the agent, who went through the front door and down the steps where Simon stood naked.

"What in the hell is going on out here? Who the hell are you?"

Lifting up over the agent, PO flew just above the men.

"Answer me. Who the hell are you?"

Simon flicked his eyes up at PO then back at the agents. "Hey, listen guys. I was just up here for a walk you know. I ain't looking for any trouble."

"Put your hands behind your head and turn around."

Simon complied and his bare ass stared back at the soldiers.

"Hudson, cuff him."

"Yes, sir." Hudson stepped toward Simon and snapped one end of a handcuff to Simon's right hand. Just as Hudson grabbed Simon's left hand, a female voice shouted through the air.

"Yoohoo."

Hudson and Simon turned at the exact moment. A stunning blonde woman, completely naked, stepped from behind one of the agent's vehicles.

"Hello, baby." A bright smile lit her face and she jiggled up and down. Her large breasts bounced in the air as she waved at the men.

Hudson lost focus and the agent on the stairs barked at Simon. "Is she with you?"

"Yeah, that's right. That's my old lady."

"Goddammit. Peters, go get her."

Peters took three steps toward the woman, who kept a high-pitched giggle.

From Simon's right field of view, another female voice yelled out.

"Hey honey, can I play with your big weapon?" A buxom, nude brunette rounded the corner to the cabin.

Simon turned, and his jaw dropped open before he slipped into a wide grin.

"What the fuck?" Before the squad leader could say more, another woman cried out from behind him.

Three more women appeared all around the front yard of the cabin, stark naked. Beautiful, heavenly.

Simon's smile turned into a wailing laughter of glee.

"Hudson, go get them."

"Yes, sir."

The lead agent stormed out of the cabin onto the porch. "What in the hell is going on out here? Hudson what the fuck are you—"

"Mmm, baby." A soft, erotic voice cut into his rant from behind him.

When he turned around, a gorgeous and nude Black woman with an athletic build and a slow stride stepped out from the cabin. She slinked up to him and lifted her neck with a moan, showing off her perfect breasts and erect nipples.

Her lips wrapped around her finger and she bit the tip of it, casting her mouth into a full smile. "I just love a man with a big gun. Can you show me how to use it?"

The agent's breath stuttered, his eyes frozen with an amorous gaze. "I uh...We can't..."

She reached up to grab his lips but just before she touched him, her body morphed into a demonic creature. Tentacles sprang from her arms and slits formed in her pupils creating yellow, cat-like eyes. Her jaw opened wide, exposing fangs and rows of serrated teeth.

When she lunged, he screamed and fired his gun.

Each of the nude women transformed into demons.

Hudson and Peters fired their rifles but the bullets streamed right through them, striking the cabin, and vehicles.

"Hold your fire!" the lead agent called. "Hold your fire! They're holograms. Shit."

The creatures swiped and clawed at the men but the holographic images passed through them.

Hudson spun around, looking for Simon and the engine of a black Suburban rumbled to a start.

"What the fuck?" Hudson said.

The wheels spun up dust and dirt, and Simon darted a laugh out of the driver's seat.

The Suburban sped away and both Hudson and Peters jumped into their vehicle to give chase.

The lead agent looked around then up into the sky and spotted PO above, directing the holographic images through the yard. He pulled out his Sig-P320 handgun and took aim at PO.

He exhaled slowly and gently pulled the trigger.

The gun fired at the same time a shovel struck his head with a *thwang* and knocked him out cold.

PO rotated and Jack dropped the shovel, looking up at the drone. "You okay?"

PO beeped back. *Yes.*

Jack sprinted up the porch stairs, Star close behind. "Check on Cà Rá."

He ran into the living room and grabbed the silver box but it was empty. "Dammit."

The West-Church-Graves paper slipped off the table and he picked it up. He turned it over, staring at the word 'MOON' then jammed it into his pocket.

Star entered the living room. "Jack, she's gone."

"What?"

Everything came to a standstill. Just when he thought he could see a path forward, any progress had been erased.

"But where? PO, is she here?"

No. PO rotated and shot a beam of light to a flat panel monitor on a wall. Jack turned it on to reveal a series of security camera screens. He took the mouse and scrolled through activity from the day before. The video playback sequence picked up where Rivera and Takashi carried her out into the vehicle.

"Shit. Demi."

Newt ran into the cabin doorway and barked, turning Jack away from the monitor.

Star pulled back the front curtain and gasped. "Jack, we have to go."

"Why?"

"The agents are coming back."

The sound of vehicles approaching grew louder and filled the cabin. Jack dashed a quick look out the window and turned to the back. He glanced around the room and spotted his handgun with two magazines that he snatched up. "Okay, let's go."

PO floated in front of Jack. "PO, I need you to stay here and lay low. Signal me if Cà Rá returns. Can you do that?"

Yes.

Jack grabbed Star and they hurried through the kitchen out the back door. When they reached the bottom of the steps, Newt stopped and turned his eyes toward the opposite section of woods, to a group of twisted tree trunks. Jack paused, staring in the same direction.

"What is it, Newt?"

After a silent pause, Newt turned in the opposite direction and dashed off toward the barn across the backside of the hill.

"Newt come back here," Jack whispered, but the dog kept running.

The vehicles screeched to a stop and Star grabbed Jack by the hand, dropping her voice to a whisper. "Come on, Jack."

He frowned and stared back at the cabin one last time before turning a quick glance at the cove of trees.

Star tugged his hand and led him into the forest.

Meeks turned the steering wheel on his Jeep and rounded the corner of Timber Way. Eight vehicles loaded with families and piles of luggage passed him, heading toward the main road out of town.

He whipped into the town's community center lot with squealing tires and stopped at a barricade guarded by two Virginia State Police officers. Rows of police cruisers, military trucks, and black SUVs lined the parking lot. A blockade officer waved Meeks forward and he rolled down his window.

"Are you Sheriff Meeks?" the officer asked.

"Yes. What's all this?"

"National Guard command center. You can park next to that ambulance."

"Yup, thanks." Meeks pulled into a parking spot and Finn ran up to him. "Sheriff. How is she?"

"They've got her in surgery. Will probably lose her arm."

Finn stared at the ground and he shook his head. "Damn."

"Well, she's alive is all that matters now. What's going on in there?"

Finn pointed to the front of the community center. "National Guard rolled in about an hour ago. And so did more Feds." His finger dragged toward a row of SUVs. "But I can't tell who's in charge."

"Let's get in there and deal with it."

The sound of a loud truck and blaring horn caught his attention. A Chevy C-10 open-bed pick-up roared up to the checkpoint and the officers jumped out of the way. It smashed through the barrier and screeched to a halt just in front of Meeks.

Six men carrying AR-15 rifles and shotguns leaped out of the truck bed.

Three State troopers drew their Glock 19 handguns and yelled at the men. "Freeze."

"Like hell we will," one of the men shouted. They raised their rifles at the officers. "Don't make us shoot you!"

"I said drop your weapons and put your hands up!"

Meeks jumped in between them waving his arms and shouted. "Whoa, whoa! Goddammit! Everyone put your guns down. Nobody is gonna shoot anyone while I'm here. You got that?"

With a slight hesitation, the men lowered their rifles.

"You guys too," Meeks said to the troopers. "Down. Now. We're all on the same side."

The troopers lowered their handguns and holstered them with their eyes locked on the men.

Meeks turned to the driver of the truck who leaned on the door. "Jerry, what in the hell is this all about?"

Jerry stepped up and pulled his camo mesh hat down tight across his head. "Tom, you tell us. We've got people packing up and getting the hell out of here. Military rolled in just now shutting everything down. Are we at war or something?"

"No, we're not at war. But there's some trouble in town."

"Well, tell us how we can help. We ain't gonna let nobody take our homes."

"Nobody's gonna take your home, Jerry. You guys. All of you. The way you can help is to go home. To your families. Let us handle this."

One of the men wearing urban-camo fatigues barked back, "No way, Sheriff."

Jerry raised both his hands, palms out to Meeks. "Tom, look. You know we can scout this land better than anyone. Deputize us, we can help. If you don't, these city slickers are gonna get hurt." He spit a dark wad of chaw juice onto the ground in front of the troopers.

Meeks bit his lower lip, looked at Finn, and then sighed. "Finn, note on this day, Thursday September twelfth at—" He glanced at his wristwatch. "Three-thirty-two p.m., I hereby deputize these men into a Stone Creek County Posse for the purposes of a manhunt."

"Acknowledged, Sheriff," Finn replied.

Jerry smiled and snapped to attention. "Talon Strike Force, ten hut!" The men stomped their right foot, straightened their backs, and saluted.

Meeks led the posse into the building and down the main hallway. A soldier, caught off guard, waved his hands for them to stop. "Sir, I need you all to stop right now." A man racked his shotgun as they walked past the soldier who leaned with his back against the wall.

Upon entering a large, open room filled with suits, soldiers and police officers, everyone froze and cast their gaze at the rag tag posse.

Meeks scanned the room and the Mayor, Barry Foster, approached, meandering through the crowded room.

"Tom."

"Barry, what's the situation?"

Barry turned Meeks away from the other men and whispered.

"The Feds are telling us that Damien Carver is starting up a Waco-like situation with his cult."

Jerry leaned in between them and shouted, "Waco?"

Meeks pushed Jerry away and snapped back at Barry. "What do you mean cult?"

Barry whispered calmly, unfazed by the situation. "Apparently, it's a doomsday cult and he's planning some sort of mass casualty event tomorrow."

"Friday the 13th," Meeks muttered. "How could he do that?"

"The FBI says two scientists who were secret cult members, stole a classified weapon from a military lab this week."

Meeks raised his eyebrows. "And you believe that?"

"Yeah. They said it was an inside job. Could do some real damage."

"How much damage?"

A man standing behind them spoke louder than everyone else. "Significant damage, Sheriff."

They turned and faced a man in a gray suit standing next to a National Guard soldier with Master Sergeant insignia.

"And who are you?" Meeks asked.

"Paul Burke, I'm a Director with the NQCO. This is Master Sergeant James Parker. I believe you met some of us earlier this week, before the incident."

"You mean the alien shit," Meeks said.

Parker blinked and shot his eyes at Burke.

Jerry's face elongated from just behind him. "Alien shit?"

Burke raised his finger and circled it in the air.

An agent in a black suit standing near him, shouted, "Everyone out! Now!"

Meeks jumped in, shouting over the man. "No. Nobody's going anywhere until we get some God damn answers. I'm still Sheriff of this town and protecting its people is my God given duty."

"I knew it was aliens." Jerry pulled off his hat and rubbed his hand through his hair. "Carter, tell'em. I was just saying on the way over here, I bet we're dealing with an alien invasion."

A man with long blond hair nodded in agreement. "Yeah, that's right.

You called it, Jerry."

Burke's steel gaze burned at Meeks, who stood his ground in silence.

The NQCO director leaned back, covered his mouth with his hand, and whispered into Parker's ear. The Master Sergeant nodded.

A smile broke out across Burke's face. "All right, Sheriff. We can use you and your men. But they'll need some real weapons, not those little cap guns."

The posse erupted into a hoot of high-fives and hollers. In spite of the jubilation, Jerry locked his expressionless eyes on Meeks.

Demi stared at the sun through a glass wall on the upper level of the temple. It cut beams of light into the veranda that showered down on Takashi when he walked into the room.

"Mr. Togo." Demi stood and brought his hands together. "Is everything ready?"

Takashi nodded.

"Excellent. It was very clever of the Calodox to hide the Empyreax deep in the bowel of this universe. It amazes me how you've survived so long in such a forsaken, dismal place."

Takashi stood motionless and Demi stepped from behind his desk toward him with an inquisitive glare.

"When I took over this human form, I kept hearing one question rattling around in its brain. Who is Kaze Baku?" Demi moved close to Takashi and focused his eyes on the reflection of his face in the sunglasses. "But the question I have is, when the time comes, can I trust him?"

Takashi remained still and silent.

Footsteps echoed behind them, and Demi cast his gaze over Takashi's shoulder.

Takashi turned as Edgar and Miles entered the room.

Edgar chomped on his gum. "Demi, they're ready for you."

Demi dragged his stare from the twins, turning it back to Takashi. "It's showtime."

At the main foyer of the temple barn, Demi walked to an overhang on the upper floor. Over two hundred cultists streamed into the room and took up firearms when they each entered the pavilion, lining up in symmetrical rows.

"Children of the Temple of New Hope." Demi's voice boomed in a deep, commanding tone. "Tonight we will all learn the truth of the universe and each of you will experience enlightenment. As prophesized, the Navigator has arrived on Earth. Our ascension into the Empyreax, the gateway to the gods, is upon us. Our journey will not be easy and there will be many who are at this very moment plotting to stop us."

The striped drone flew to Demi's right side and the silver drone flanked his left.

"But we are strong in numbers and our will is unbreakable. Together, we will fight for our future and build a new legacy. A world where we can begin anew, colonize, free from the abject failures of this one.

"I have been in touch with warriors from another universe. Xurricans, who will arrive to Earth via this portal."

On the main stage platform below, two men unfurled a large, red cloth to reveal the constructed portal. It glowed with blue light then pulsed differing colors of white and green.

Whispers scattered through the crowd.

"To prepare you for this journey, we have brewed a new elixir that will free your mind and open your eyes to the new world."

Demi stepped off the balcony and floated high above the crowd. Joyous laughter and praising shouts filled the temple.

"If you are ready to join me, take the elixir. Prepare your soul for the Empyreax dawn."

The crowd cheered and near the front row, two women handed out syringes filled with a glowing yellow liquid. Cultists took the syringes and injected them into their arms. Within seconds they stumbled into a euphoric daze.

Demi turned back around to the balcony and narrowed his eyes at Takashi, who stood between both drones.

23

· DEUS EX MACHINA ·

The setting sun cast a long shadow that ran from Jack's feet to the base of Chimney Rock Mountain. An earthy odor of warm moss wafted to him.

Red and purple clouds formed a backdrop for the top of the mountain that seemed so far away. The glacial chimney towering above a massive cliff wall, jutted from the side of the mountain. A short chasm at the top of the cliff met the back edge of a narrow ravine.

Muscles in his neck stretched from the backward tilt of his head, and he tried not to imagine himself falling off the cliff.

His finger traced a backward letter Z in the air pointed at the rock wall. "Simon said to zigzag that shelf and follow it up the rock wall." He pointed at a break in the rock near the top. "Then, hop the gap to the chimney. How wide do you think that is?"

Star shook her head. "I don't know. Four feet maybe?"

"Damn."

"Want me to go with you?"

"No. Not unless you've climbed this thing before."

"No. Never. They closed it when I was a kid because—"

"Don't say it."

"Sorry."

"Where the hell is Simon?" Jack scanned the quiet field from the rock to the steep path that led to Star's car. The sunset's orange glow bounced off the wall and shadowed the far side of the cliff. He'd have to move quick if he wanted to beat the dark.

Star leaned in and kissed him on the cheek. "A kiss for good luck. Be sure you come back if you want another one."

"Well, I do, but I dunno. This...this is crazy. I'm terrified of heights."

"I know. But you can do it. This is nothing compared to yesterday."

"I'd rather be back in the well with the blades."

"No, you don't."

"What if it's not up there? What if somebody took it? A kid."

"Jack, stop. Even if someone went up there, they wouldn't know what it is."

"I don't even know what it is."

Star lifted his chin with her thumb and forefinger. "You're going to be fine."

"Okay, I can do this." He exhaled three quick breaths to center himself.

On the final deep breath, he hopped over the wooden split-rail fence and passed a '*No Rock Climbing or Rappelling*' sign. He stepped across the first two-foot-wide shelf and planted his foot. He glanced at Star, turned away from her look of assurance and squinted up at the summit.

So high. So far away.

He leaned back against the rock, bracing his arms.

The cold stone met his flesh with an abrasive illusion of safety. He took measured steps sideways at a slow pace and ascended at an upward angle on the wall's natural path.

A cool breeze met the sweat on his fingertips, sending an icy chill across his body. Pausing while his legs shook, he peered at Star and jerked his eyes away at the sight of her distant face.

"Breathe," he said.

Slow, shuffled steps brought him to the transition point. It didn't look difficult but he had to be careful. He slid his hands up until his fingers touched the ledge and gripped.

If Simon could do it, so could he.

Grabbing onto the ledge, he reached up and leaned in as far as he could to keep gravity from ripping him away.

He pulled up and rested his right knee on the one-foot-wide ledge.

As he put pressure on his knee, it slipped off the edge, and his leg dropped, scraping the side of the wall. He gasped and clawed at the rock to steady himself, avoiding any glimpse of the steep drop below.

With another push, he pressed up on the knee and kept his balance while his fingers gripped the edge. His movements slowed, and he continued on the upper-left trajectory until the second transition point near the front face of the cliff.

The red clouds had turned dark, and the blue of the horizon had all but faded to black. Jack tried not to gaze out across the rolling valley; he had to find the next ledge. It helped that most of the sky faded into the ground below and his head didn't spin.

"Come on, Dad, what the hell am I doing up here?"

The whole thing had to be a dream, and soon he'd wake up.

The bracelet beeped with a red light that flashed against the rock wall. He growled at the sound. "I'm coming. I'm coming." A gust of wind rustled his hair.

This was no dream.

Climbing to the third shelf, his foothold improved where the rocky ledge widened by a few inches. As he continued the ascent, he met the mountain's edge, where a large boulder formed a makeshift landing that gave him a momentary respite from peril.

The boulder's left side dropped straight off the mountain. He took several deep breaths, searching for calm. The last remnants of daylight sank below the horizon and everything went black except for a dim glow from the full moon above.

Damn. He should have brought a flashlight.

On hands and knees, he moved up the boulder onto the narrow peak of the cliff towering high above the town.

At the first narrow ravine, he paused to assess his next move.

It stretched maybe two feet across, but how deep? Wind powered up from the darkness.

Jack blinked, inhaled, and leapt forward. One boot landed on a patch of pebbles, which loosened a rock that tumbled down the steep slope, echoing its lethal descent.

A distant cry flew up from below but he couldn't make out the words.

"Star?" His voice echoed against the rocks but was swallowed by the wind.

Jack crawled forward on the narrow trail, waiting for her reply.

He leaned his head a few inches over the side of the cliff, and a flash of dizziness hit him. Jack jerked back and gripped the ledge tight. A whistle of wind ran over the stone path. "Star, can you hear me?"

Silence. Once again, the bracelet beeped twice and flashed.

Night took control of the sky while he inched forward across the top ledge of the cliff. The moon cast a glow of light across the path and he came to a three-foot-wide gap.

Wind howled around him and a rush of adrenaline shot through his head.

With his weight shifted onto his right leg, he took three quick breaths and jumped.

He landed and his foot dragged across gravel that spilled over the ledge. Jack pinwheeled his arms, leaned his body forward, and dropped to his knees.

With deep breaths and sweat pouring down his back, he cursed the whole thing. Why him? Why *the fuck* did it have to be him?

He pressed his knees into the path and crawled to the chimney's angled rear side. Groping forward, his fingers scraped the raw sharpness of the ledge. Stone cavities, long eroded into the ramp, helped him climb to the barren summit, where he stood bathed in moonlight.

Jack scanned the flat stone and found nothing. He tapped his right foot in a few spots for any sign of a hole, a cavity, something. But there was nothing.

"Seriously?"

He turned in circles.

"Star?" He called as loud as he could.

No response. There's no way she could hear him from up here.

"Where the hell is it, Simon?" He gnawed at his lower lip.

The bracelet beeped. A blue light glowed as symbols spun to their zero position. Running his fingers through his hair, he looked up at the moon and paused with his hand over his mouth.

He spun around and reached into his pocket for the letter. Wind rattled the edges of the paper when he held it up in the moonlight.

Turning it over to the word 'MOON', his eyes widened. He positioned it in front of the moon creating a backlight that highlighted a hidden message. Squinting at it, the faint image of five symbols appeared embedded in the fibers of the paper.

With the bracelet held up, he spun and matched the five symbols. It flashed green, and the familiar sultry voice spoke from the bracelet. "Oh yeah."

A blue plasma beam sparkled from a three-foot-wide line in the rock. A rectangular portal slid up from the slot and formed a paper-thin doorway, trimmed by the blue light.

Great. Another damn portal. He licked his lips and took a step through it, but he was still on top of Chimney Rock. Still night. Everything the same except...a staircase of floating stone platforms spiraled out over the cliff's edge high into the night sky.

"You've got to be shitting me." He leaned forward and pushed the first platform, but it didn't move.

Drifting his foot from the ledge to the platform, he stepped onto it and leaned forward.

When his full weight went onto the platform, it sagged and he gasped. The stone wobbled in the air and then stabilized. A disorienting nausea washed over him. The drop had to be over a hundred feet. *Don't think about it. Just do it.*

After a quick glimpse back at the portal, he approached the second platform and stepped up onto it. Fixated on moonlight that glistened off each stone, he continued the spiraling ascent.

At the top platform, the wind ripped at his jacket. He glanced at the stairs descending into darkness and shook his head. *Maybe going down will be easier.*

No time to think about that.

He stood before two four-inch-diameter metal columns that rose from the center of the platform. Atop one column sat the third ring of the Empyreax key. A silver tube with a red button on its end, rested on the other column.

Jack hovered his hand over the key but stopped. He paused, then grabbed the cylinder.

The metal column sank into the platform and disappeared. He lurched back with his hands up and stood still.

Nothing else happened. He flipped the cylinder over in his hand. The word '*Boom*' had been painted down its side in red. Placing it in his back pocket, he turned his focus to the other column.

Moonlight reflected off the glossy surface of the Empyreax key. He grabbed it, and the metal column retracted into the platform.

A loud buzzing from far below broke his attention. *Now what?*

The very bottom platform disappeared and a low-frequency electronic *thunk* resonated from the darkness. Jack shoved the Empyreax key into his pocket and ran down the first few stairs, but stopped in his tracks.

Another platform disappeared, and another *thunk* echoed in the dark void left behind.

He skipped back to the top platform and spun around.

Thunk.

The next platform disappeared, and he caught the flash of the bracelet. He grabbed the paper from his pocket and opened it in the moonlight. A gust of wind kicked up and snatched it from his grip.

"No, no, no!"

He thrust his hands over the platform's edge to catch it, but the paper floated beyond his reach and drifted into the darkness below.

Thunk.

Less than half of the stairs remained.

His fingers flicked the bracelet. Digits spun in random order. Nothing.

Thunk.

"Shit."

Three stairs remained. A blue light flashed from ten feet below the platform.

What was that?

The beam of light formed a square portal suspended in mid-air.

Thunk.

The platform just before his disappeared.

He stepped to its back edge and inhaled a deep breath, which he held as he ran forward and leaped.

Jack screamed with a last rush of air from his lungs when the main platform disappeared.

Thunk.

His feet slid into the portal and he plummeted through the opening. A narrow, blue tube of light tucked his arms into his sides. Unable to move, he slid and slipped, screaming all the way down through the corkscrew tunnel.

The slide stopped and spat him out onto the solid rock at the foot of the mountain, right where he began.

His back hurt. His feet hurt. His hands grappled at the stone as he rolled.

The '*No Rock Climbing or Rappelling*' sign wobbled in the wind as if to taunt him.

He smirked back at it and stood with a twinge of pain in his left thigh.

Dusting himself off, someone called out from behind him.

"Hey, Jack."

Jack froze. Simon stood on the dirt path with two cultists who held guns to his head. Four armed men stood behind them.

Two large, mechanical panther-like robots crept out of the shadows, reared their heads at him, and dug their claws into the earth.

Jack's gut clenched. "Simon."

"Fun ride, huh?" Simon laughed but it soon turned into a cough. Blood trickled from his nose mixing with sweat down into his white goatee.

A bald, heavily tattooed man stepped out of the shadows and waved his arm. "Get them."

Two men with guns approached Jack from behind but before they neared, he reached into his back pocket.

"You better get back." He pulled the cylinder out and hovered his thumb over the red button.

One man stopped in his tracks and chimed back. "Whoa, Rivera he's got something."

Rivera waved his hand and the men stepped back.

Jack sneered. "If you don't let him go, I'll—"

"You'll what?" A deep throttled voice grumbled from behind Rivera and a large figure dressed in black emerged. He stepped forward and into the light of the moon.

"I'll blow us all to hell."

A deep snarl trailed from the man.

"You must be Demi."

"Whatever you want to call me."

"Demi, let's just kill them," one of the men shouted.

Jack scowled. "You killed my father."

"If the human stood in my way, then so be it."

Fury raged through Jack, burning like fire in his veins. "Give me a reason not to kill us all."

Demi motioned his hand and two other men brought Star out of the shadows. "I don't think you'll do that."

"Star," Jack said, his fury now tempered with fear. "Are you okay?"

"I'm fine," she replied. One man shoved her forward with a shotgun.

"She appears to be a beautiful creature," Demi said. "Different from the others. One would say, special perhaps? Would be a shame to kill this one too. Give me the key." Demi held his hand out, tilting his head in expectation.

Jack's thumb trembled over the button and beads of sweat dripped down his brow.

Demi twisted his hand, thrusting it toward Jack, but nothing happened.

He leaned back then tried again.

The bracelet on Jack's wrist glowed and emitted a low-pitched buzz. Jack held it up with a quick glance.

Demi's eyes flared at the bracelet. "So, it appears you have help from the Calodox."

"Yeah, that's right," Jack said.

Demi motioned his hand toward Simon and swirled his hand clockwise. Simon's left arm rotated and twisted at the elbow forcing a pained look across the old man's face, but Simon contained his anguish while the cultist held tight. After several seconds of increased torque, Simon relented and let out an excruciating scream.

Jack pulled the Empyreax key out of his pocket. "Enough! You're looking for this aren't you?"

Demi's eyes rolled over to gloss black and his pupils slit open to reveal a bright red light. He released his grip on Simon who collapsed to the ground nursing his arm.

"So let's make a trade, huh? You let them go and I give you this key."

"Jack, no. Don't do it," Simon cried.

"Why not, Simon? I didn't ask to be part of this. Now people are getting killed. I'm done. We leave. What do you say, Demi? Let's trade."

"But Jack," Star tried to step forward but the cultist yanked her back.

"No tricks?" Demi asked.

"No tricks."

"Then we have a deal. But first you give me the key."

"No way. We swap at the same time."

The red in Demi's eyes flashed brighter, then faded. "Rivera." Demi motioned his hand and turned his back to Jack.

Rivera stepped forward and grabbed Star by the arm.

He tugged Simon up and led them both toward Jack who stood guarded with his arms outstretched. Bomb in his right hand, Empyreax key in his left.

Rivera stopped a few feet in front of Jack and released both Simon and Star who crept behind him.

Jack held the key out to Rivera who took it, turned, and carried it back to Demi.

Demi's eyes lit up while he examined the key, then handed it to a cultist. "Take this to the scientist." The cultist bowed then disappeared into darkness.

When Demi turned back to Jack, Star and Simon, he folded his hands behind his back and smiled. "Kill them."

Rivera stepped forward with his knife. "With pleasure."

The cultists raised and aimed their guns.

Jack pressed the red button on the cylinder and tossed it right when the cultists opened fire. It exploded in the air and formed a pulse of plasma that arced creating an orb-shaped protective shield. Bullets ricocheted off the shield and shot right back at the cultists, cutting through them, spraying blood in all directions.

The edge of the energy blast shaped a secondary ring of fire with an explosion that knocked Demi back and thrust Rivera over a stone ledge.

Two cultists behind Jack collapsed, their bodies riddled with bullets and flames.

Simon fell backwards, slid down an embankment, and disappeared into darkness.

Jack grabbed Star's arm and yanked her off the ledge onto a lower dirt trail. They landed hard, stumbling, but found their footing as cultists shouted from above.

Gunshots cracked through the air while the two robot panthers leaped over the ledge. The creatures crashed onto the trail, roars echoing against the rock walls as they gave chase.

Jack cast a quick glance over his shoulder at the mechanical beasts. "Shit. Run. Faster."

Star trampled through brush and branches, losing her footing at the top of a steep embankment. Jack grabbed hold of her waist to steady her, but momentum carried them forward, crashing through low scrub and tumbling onto the dirt road below in a cloud of dust and gravel.

Jack rolled to his feet, pulled out his 9mm handgun and racked the slide. "Keep running," he yelled.

The silver panther growled as it jumped, jaws stretched wide.

He pulled the trigger in rapid succession. Two blasts hit the beast's head and forced it to veer away. It landed on its side with a loud thud.

The panther scrambled back to its feet.

Jack turned and ran.

The rusty-black panther was already bolting toward Star. Jack snatched a spare magazine from his pocket and reloaded his gun.

The panther scampered up a rock ledge for higher ground, and as Star rounded a bend, the panther sprang. Moonlight glinted off its serrated metal teeth. The blades nipped at her arm as she slid under the bottom lip of the rock.

Jack fired every round at the beast.

Sparks flickered off its metallic hide as it landed, recoiling, and sliding back several feet.

Jack yanked Star up, and they dashed toward her car. She threw open the driver's door and Jack jumped across to the passenger side.

The rusty-black panther landed on the trunk of the car, bouncing the vehicle with a metallic thud.

"Hurry!" Jack said.

Star hammered the engine start button just as the silver panther pounced onto the hood, rocking the car from side to side.

The engine roared to life.

"Go! Go! Go!" Jack screamed.

Star shifted into gear and slammed her foot on the gas pedal.

As the car lurched forward, the silver panther smashed a paw into the hood, spiked claws shearing through the engine block. The car sputtered and rolled to a stop.

"No, no, no... Jack," Star said, and her eyes drifted to meet his.

The rusty-black panther smashed the rear window, glass spraying throughout the car. It tried to crawl inside, but its head was too large for the small window. It gnashed its teeth together like crashing cymbals.

The silver panther burst through the front windshield and tried to shove its head inside.

Jack threw himself over Star and shielded her from the beast that struggled to reach them.

It tried to push deeper and searing heat from its chomping, mechanized jaw nipped the back of Jack's neck.

A voice cried out from the darkness. "Hey, fuckers!"

A bright green plasma blast struck the panther snarling on the hood, exploding the creature with an electric arc of thunderbolts. It collapsed through the opening, its head smashing down onto Jack.

The panther at the rear of the car lifted its head and leapt away from them, but another green blast burst into the panther mid-air. Its body convulsed from the electrical hit to shatter into a pile of metal pieces that slid to a stop just in front of a pair of boots.

Jack tracked his eyes up from the boots to an older Black man standing in green army fatigues who held a large rifle by his side.

The man laughed through a whoop. "Now that's some crazy shit right there." He sprinted to the car and looked through the missing windshield. "You guys okay?"

"Barely," Jack said, moving to uncover Star.

"We need to roll." The man opened the door, helped them out, then led them to a rusted-out yellow-lime 1972 Datsun 240Z.

He pulled open the passenger door and guided them in. "It's only a two-seater. She'll need to sit on your lap." The man cast Jack a wide grin. "Your old man didn't tell me you'd have company."

"Wait, what?" Jack said, but the man threw the door shut.

He opened the hatch, dropped his rifle inside, slammed it closed, then jumped into the driver's seat. "Name's Dex," he said, firing up the engine. The car let out a pop, and its twin carburetors roared to life.

"Thank you," Star said.

"Don't thank me," Dex said. "Thank his father." He stomped

the clutch, shifted into gear, and full-throttled the Datsun away from Chimney Rock.

24

· DARK ENERGY ·

Roger Young pulled his blue Toyota Highlander up to a police blockade across the main highway heading into Stone Creek. He switched off the music in his car and rolled down the window to greet the officer. Several trucks filled with strapped-down luggage drove past him in the opposite lane, leaving town.

"Evening officer, what's going on?"

The State Trooper shined a flashlight into the vehicle. "Evening. Can I see your driver's license, please?"

"Wait, why do you need to see that?"

"I can't discuss that right now. If you don't want to show me your license, you can just go right ahead and turn around."

Roger stuck his head out the window and glanced behind him. No headlights. Why would he be the only car in this lane?

"Well, wait a minute. I need to get into town to see my brother."

"What's his name?"

"Do I have to give that to you?"

"Governor's orders. Nobody's allowed into town without proper identification, so if you don't want to show me your license, then you'll need to leave."

A soldier dressed in camouflage fatigues led a German shepherd on a leash toward the right front bumper of his car. Roger glanced at the soldier who led the dog sniffing around the vehicle in a circular sweep.

Did he get Jack's message too late? There's no way any of this could be related to him.

"Sir, I'm gonna need you to pull your vehicle to the side of the road."

"Huh? No, wait. Here." Roger reached into his back pocket and pulled his driver's license out of his wallet, handing it to the officer.

The officer shined his light on it, then back in Roger's face. "Do you know a woman named Stella Hopper?"

Roger shook his head. "No idea who that is."

"Damien Carver?"

"No, I don't know any of these people. Who are they?" The less he said, the better. At least he didn't mention Jack's name.

The officer studied Roger. "Any tattoos on your wrists?"

"Tattoos? No, none." He pulled his sleeves up to show the officer both of his wrists. "Why?"

"Wait right here." The officer headed to a man dressed in a black suit standing at the back of a black Suburban.

Roger strained to watch them from afar as best he could. The man swiped what appeared to be Roger's license on a card reader attached to a tablet computer. The suited-man stared at the screen and flicked his fingers up and down while a cold, white glow flashed against his glasses, then handed the license back to the officer as he spoke.

If this involved Jack, he'd better have a damn good reason.

The officer came back to the window and returned the license. "All right, you may proceed. But there's a midnight curfew in effect for the entire town, so make sure you're inside before then."

"Okay. Thank you."

Rolling his window up, Roger drove through the blockade and headed down the main road leading to Black Wolf Mountain. He dialed Jack on his cell phone, but the call went straight to voice mail for the third time.

As much as he didn't like it, he knew it would.

The person you are trying to call is unavailable. At the tone, please record your message.

"Jack. It's Rog, need you to call me back, little brother. You're making me nervous here. I'm almost to the cabin, where are you? Text or call me back. Bye."

Dex drove his Datsun with the lights off through an overgrown path, and parked behind a large, deteriorated gambrel-roofed barn. He shut the engine off and Jack and Star got out of the car.

"What are we doing here?" Jack asked.

"Pit stop," Dex said while dragging a large canvas tarp over the Datsun to conceal it.

Star crossed her arms. "Jack, I think it's time we go to the police and—"

"Nope." Dex shook his head. "You don't want to do that."

"Why not?"

"The cops ain't running the show anymore."

"What do you mean?"

Dex grabbed the barn door and slid it open with a grunt. Cobwebs and dust flipped off rotten wood slats when it rattled across the rusty track overhead.

As soon as the door opened, the dark shape of a man emerged from the entrance jolting Star to let out a shriek.

Dex and Jack jumped back as the figure stepped forward and yelled. "Surprise!"

"Holy shit." Dex flashed his light up at the figure to reveal Simon. "Goddammit, Simon. Don't scare me like that."

Jack pulled Simon forward into a hug, patting him on the back. "How the hell did you make it out of there?"

"Wasn't easy. That blast was a bitch."

Star aimed the light on a deep gash across Simon's collar. "Oh my god, you're hurt." Blood had run down and soaked through his shirt.

"Don't worry about me. I'm nobody special."

"Don't say that. Here, take off your shirt."

Simon laughed. "Jack, you hear that? She wants me to take off my shirt."

"We'll get him patched up." Dex pulled down a blue tarp hanging over a small enclosure. It fell to the ground in a cloud of dust and revealed a soda machine. "Jack, your dad and I go back a long time."

The picture from the bedroom flashed in Jack's mind and he mumbled at the realization. "Vietnam."

Dex nodded and flipped a coin at him that he caught with one hand.

It was the Lady Liberty quarter from the drone. His eyes widened. None of this could've possibly been planned. "But how...?"

"I made a promise to your dad, and here I am."

"We all made promises," Simon shouted from behind Jack.

"You thirsty?" Dex pointed toward the soda machine.

Jack paused for a moment, then stepped up to it and inserted the quarter into the slot. "He always loved Mr. Pibb." He pressed the Mr. Pibb button and a mechanical whir with several clanks rattled inside the machine. A can of Mr. Pibb fell into the dispenser tray that he reached in to grab. "It's cold—"

A pulse of red light flashed around the machine and a panel just above the dispenser slid open. Another panel appeared, this one glass, with the outline of a hand. Jack glanced back at Dex who jutted his chin at it.

Jack placed his right hand on the panel and a light scanned it. A loud, metal grinding sound grated from the floor of the barn and a sequence of clunking thuds vibrated the ground. A hidden two-by-two-meter square panel popped up several inches from the floor and rotated open nearly ninety degrees. A green light flickered several times then turned solid, illuminating a staircase to an underground bunker.

Star helped Simon sit up from the bench and the man staggered next to Jack and Dex.

The green glow from the bunker lit up their faces and Dex turned to them with a big smile.

"How did you guys get this here?"

"Your dad owns this place. In fact, he owns a bunch of abandoned farmland around here. You had no clue, huh?"

Jack shook his head.

Dex scampered down the stairs followed by Simon.

Jack let Star lead and helped duck her head under a support beam.

Dex grabbed a medical supply kit and sat Simon on a chair. Simon glanced up at an M1 rocket launcher on the wall and jolted up to reach for it. Before he could stand, Dex swatted the man's shoulder forcing him back onto the chair. "Sit."

"Oh. Make it quick." Simon rolled his eyes in annoyance.

Rifles, shotguns, and handguns lined the walls of the bunker. Metal shelves on the opposite wall held buckets of survival food with bottles of water. Jack smiled when he spotted cases of Mr. Pibb stacked against the wall. "Guess he was preparing for the end of the world, huh?"

"Pretty much." Dex spread a medicinal salve on Simon's shoulder.

"That's not funny," Star said.

Jack scanned the long workbench and found a cassette player sitting in the middle of it with a metal ring attached to a tag that read "Jack".

He pressed play as Dex looked up from Simon's wound.

The tape started and Bill's voice, accompanied by a static hiss, filled the bunker.

"Hello, Jack. If you're listening to this, then I'm dead and you've got a cold Mr. Pibb in your hand."

Deep warmth shot through Jack's body and he leaned against the workbench with his hand to his face. Star put her arms around him and laid her head on his shoulder.

"By now you've probably figured out there is some serious shit that's about to go down. For reasons I can't explain, I was the unlucky bastard who found the Empyreax device." He let out a sardonic three note laugh.

Jack remembered that laugh and it punched him hard, flooding him with memories. He let out a deep sigh as his father continued.

"I wish I'd never discovered the damned thing. But...if it wasn't me, all of humanity would have been wiped out by now. That, I'm sure of.

"No doubt you've also met Cà Rá. Feisty, isn't she? But she's my best friend, well, besides your mother, bless her soul. If she's standing next to you then everything is going according to plan, and you've found the three keys to open the Empyreax. Nicely done."

Dex shrugged and smirked through a puff of smoke.

"The rest is easy. Below the cabin I built a portal device that will complete charging on Friday September 13th. When this portal opens, Cà Rá will go through it to take the keys to a secret location only she knows. Dex will make sure you get safe passage back to the cabin. I know it must have been tough when Simon died..."

Simon's eyes lit up. "Wait, what?"

"...even though he was a little weird, I loved the guy." Simon grinned and gave two thumbs up to Dex.

"Dex, to say thank you, I've stashed some cash for you in a safe at the cabin. The combo is right two, left thirty-seven, right forty-two. Maybe give the Datsun a fresh coat of paint."

Dex choked on his cheroot and smoke shot out of his mouth. "Shit."

"And Jack, I just wanted to tell youee—ee...oo—"

Bill's voice cut off with a high screech and the cassette tape media spiraled out of the machine. It unwound into a tattered and ripped mess of black plastic.

"What the—what was the combo?" Dex pleaded to Star. "Right two, left forty-seven...right?"

Star looked back at Dex. "It was right two, left thirty-seven, right forty-two."

Jack grabbed the spaghetti mess of tape and pushed it aside. Could this have really all been planned? If so, did he screw something up? His mind raced like a Monday-morning quarterback at what had gone wrong.

Dex reached into his empty shirt pocket and patted his pants. "I need a pen, dammit." A puff of cheroot smoke engulfed his face and he glanced around the bunker while mumbling. "Right two. Left thirty-seven. Right forty-two."

He found a pen and scribbled on his matchbox. "You sure? Right two. Left thirty-seven. Right forty-two."

Star nodded. "Yeah, I'm pretty sure. Right two. Left thirty-seven. Right forty-two."

Dex looked at Jack, "Is that what you heard?"

Jack shrugged. "I thought it was left twenty-six."

Simon chimed in. "I heard left forty-six."

Star shot back, "It was definitely left thirty-seven."

"Well, which is it?" Dex asked.

"Whatever she said," Jack muttered. He turned his attention to the back wall of the bunker.

Dex sighed in relief and inked the numbers on the matchbox. "Okay. Right two. Left thirty-seven. Right forty-two. Good, thank you."

"Couldn't you just blow open the safe?" Simon asked.

"And burn all that money?"

"Right on. Didn't think of that."

Jack pulled a blue tarp off the wall revealing multiple bullpup rifles. "So what do we do now?" he asked Dex.

Shoving the matchbox into his shirt pocket, Dex walked to the wall and grabbed a rifle. "Well, you heard your old man. We've gotta kick some alien ass."

"Aliens."

"Damn straight." He pulled back the charging handle and released it, triggering a blue light that illuminated in sequence to the end of the handguard.

"And Jack," Dex said, "I've known your old man for fifty years. He was definitely batshit crazy, but he always knew what he was doing. He knew you wouldn't have that key. I guarantee it."

"What's that supposed to mean?"

"It means he trusts you."

"Still don't know what that means."

"Don't overthink it." Dex patted Jack on the chest. "We get the key, rescue Cà Rá, and save the world."

"And you get the cash."

"Damn straight," Dex said. He blew a puff of smoke through a snorting chuckle. "You get the cash, you get the women." He turned and winked at Star.

Simon reached for the M1 rocket launcher and held it to his eye. "I ain't dead yet motherfuckers." He stood and eyed a sign on the wall that read '*Danger*' hanging above a pen-light sized cylinder. "What's this?" He clicked the end of it and a solid, thin, red laser shot out, slicing through the workbench. The beam flicked around the room when he waved his hand, incinerating anything it touched.

Dex screamed and jumped out of the way before the laser passed by him, cutting his chair in half.

"Woops." Simon clicked the button and shut it off.

"Simon, what the fuck man? Gimme that." Dex snatched it from Simon's hand and clipped it to his belt. "I'll hold onto this."

"Sorry about that. Had no idea."

"Just stop touching shit," Dex snapped.

"I said I'm sorry." His cloudy eye drifted to a shelf filled with explosive charges and picked one up. He turned it over and flipped a red switch. A digital three-minute countdown timer appeared on the screen.

"We need these?" He spun around to the group and held the charge up.

The cheroot dropped from Dex's lips. "Whoa, shit, put that down. Do *not* touch the red button."

"This red button?" Simon's finger hovered over it. He giggled then flicked the switch and the charge's display went dark. "Just messin' with ya." He grabbed a black duffle bag and stuffed all of the charges into it.

Dex shook his head and racked the fore-end on a shotgun. "All right, load up, and let's roll." He yanked a dusty tarp off a red Datsun 620 pickup truck. "God, I love JDM."

Roger's Highlander reached the secondary road turn-off from the main highway. The vehicle kicked up dust as it rounded a grove of trees and crunched through gravel. Its headlights pierced into the darkness of the forest ahead, carving a path of light through the pine-tree-lined road. It rolled up over the knob and stopped at the pipe gate that led to the cabin.

"What the hell?" Roger mumbled, shifting the car into park.

The headlights shined bright on two men at the closed pipe gate, each holding a shotgun.

Roger paused and looked down at his phone. No signal. He hadn't thought to pack his handgun, and now he needed it.

Opening the driver's side door, he stepped out of the car and tried to act casual. "Excuse me, can I help you, fellas?"

They stood in silence and looked at each other. One of the men spit on the ground.

Roger closed the door halfway and stepped in front of it. "I hate to tell you guys this, but you're trespassing on private—"

One man racked his shotgun, interrupting Roger.

"Whoa, easy now. Look, I own this property with my brother."

"Not anymore you don't." The man pointed his shotgun at Roger. "All right. I'm leaving."

When he turned around, a third man blocked his path with a rifle. "You ain't going nowhere."

Roger slowly raised his hands. "Okay then."

Demi stood in front of the jump gate with his eyes fixed on a digital timer attached to it, counting down from *1:24*.

Two male and one female cultist stood behind him dressed in white robes.

Elena ascended the steps to the circular stage where Demi stood and presented the black box. He opened its lid and removed the energy sphere from within.

Demi's voice filled the temple. "In a few moments, these three brave souls will experience something very few ever will. Do not fear, for they will cross over into a new existence in a new world."

The sphere drifted from his fingers into a slot on the jump gate. When it clicked in place, it ramped into a spin of thousands of revolutions per second. As it rotated faster, and faster still, electrical sparks of plasma arced around the glowing rectangular outline of the gate.

As the timer struck thirty seconds, lights flickered in the room and an ambient sizzle of electricity surged. Wires sparked and sprayed electric radiance into the air. Monitors shattered and the jump-gate end-points rattled. The timer hit ten seconds and cultists raised their hands to shield their eyes from the intense light.

When the timer hit zero, the sphere stopped spinning and froze. After two seconds of weighted silence, a shimmering burst of light-refracting molecules rippled through the room and passed through everything.

Tarkos, Bruce, and Fletcher twitched when the wave of energy hit them.

"Did you feel that?" Bruce asked.

Tarkos nodded.

A black portal opened in the jump gate and everyone fell silent.

Demi smiled. "Behold. A Xurrican Wraith. A warrior unlike any you have seen."

A glowing, blue-translucent hand emerged from the portal followed by an arm, then a torso and a full body. It wore a metallic suit for protection. Electrons pulsed from the back of its head down through its body.

The Wraith moved to the center of the stage and scanned the room of cultists.

Demi spoke to it in a series of pulsating tones that mixed with digital screeches.

The Wraith snarled and turned to the cultist in front, towering over the man.

"Go on, child." Demi waved the cultist toward the Wraith. "Prepare to experience your destiny."

The cultist pulled off his robe and stood naked on the stage. He stepped forward, eyes in a daze. "Take me," he said.

The Xurrican grabbed the man and bolts of electric energy raged over him.

It swirled around their bodies and they morphed into an enormous creature born from the man's fears. It towered seven feet in the air.

As it took shape, another glowing entity appeared from the jump gate.

Demi clasped his hands in delight. "And now the Slayer. Mercenaries of chaos and despair. Feared across worlds."

Tarkos watched it step forward and approach a cultist. This one had a large white dot on its forehead that shimmered when it moved. It grabbed the cultist and their bodies stretched and elongated into an amalgamated demon spawn. Its black body sprouted tendrils of sharp quills and spikes. Razor teeth sat behind a forked tongue. No doubt a cultist memory-echo of the devil.

One by one the Xurrican soldiers stepped out of the jump gate and onto the stage. As each entity appeared, it reached into the souls of those in the temple and twisted into their nightmares, their fantasies.

A battalion of interstellar death.

"Is this the end of the world?" Bruce asked.

"I don't know what it is," Tarkos said.

Demi turned to Tarkos, Bruce, and Fletcher, motioning at two armed guards who stood behind them with rifles.

"Take them to the Empyreax and prepare it for my arrival."

Fletcher stood frozen and stared at Demi.

"You will soon meet your true god, priest."

"I'm a Reverend."

25

· NEURO COLLAPSE ·

Friday, September 13th, 2019

Meeks held his Timex wristwatch up to catch light from a nearby pole and squinted to read it. Thirty seconds to midnight. "Damn, would you look at that," Finn said, pointing to the night sky.

Meeks looked up just in time to catch the tail of two meteors that streaked across the dark horizon and flashed for a fraction of a second. "Friday the thirteenth."

Finn tilted his head down, looked at Meeks and turned his gaze to National Guard troops lining up trucks and gear. "I've got a bad feeling about this."

"You and me both."

The voice of a man boomed from behind them. "Nothing to worry about, Sheriff, we can handle a few doomsday nut jobs." Master Sergeant James Parker stepped up behind them.

Turning to look up at Parker, Meeks pulled an FDE plate vest marked 'Sheriff' over his head and cinched its Velcro straps. "Has Burke told you what's really going on here?"

Parker angled toward Meeks, crossed his arms and spoke in a heavy southern twang. "Sheriff, I respect you trying to protect your town. Just stay in the rear, let us handle it, and you can take all the credit. We don't keep score."

"This isn't a game, Parker," Meeks said. "Why do you think you're all here?"

"Domestic terrorists stole a weapon, killed about a dozen or so Feds and are planning a rendezvous with a foreign buyer."

"That's what they told you."

"That's right."

"And you believe them?"

"Look, Sheriff, I'm not gonna cry over a few lost government suits, but if this weapon gets in the hands of our adversaries, then who knows how many innocent Americans are gonna get killed. We know this isn't a Cub-Scout picnic, but we don't bullshit around."

"So you're just gonna go in there blasting?"

"No. We serve the warrant, we sweep, we clean, and if anyone gives us trouble, we deal with it."

"That simple, huh?"

"Like I said, just stay out of our way and you'll be interviewed as a hero before you can even say thank you." Parker patted Meeks twice on the shoulder, walked past him, and yelled, "Sergeant Braxton!"

"Yes, sir," Braxton replied from afar.

Meeks spun around as soldiers scurried and climbed into multiple trucks.

Parker snapped at the men. "Commence Operation Rat Nest. Roll out in fifteen minutes."

Finn held a combat helmet out to Meeks but he waved it away. "I'm not wearing that," he said. He pulled out a brown twill baseball cap marked 'Sheriff' in yellow and snugged it down on his head. "Helluva way to end the week."

∞

Jack and Dex crawled to the crest of a hill on the edge of the forest surrounding the Temple of New Hope compound. They held binoculars to their eyes while Star and Simon knelt behind them.

Jack whispered to Dex, "There's over a dozen buildings. What do you think?"

Dex paused and darted his binoculars left to right. "Well, the guards all seem to be focused on that big barn."

Jack swiveled his head. "Yeah, I see them." A pulsating blue light at the top of the barn caught his eye. "Do you see that light?"

"Yeah. She's definitely in there."

Star moved up between them. "What do you see?"

"You see that big barn on the backside with the light?"

"Yeah."

"That's where we're going." Jack turned to Dex. "Dex, you and Simon go around the left side and get those charges planted. I'll go find Cà Rá."

"I'm coming with you," Star said.

"No, absolutely not."

"You can't stop me."

Dex smiled. "You sure you two aren't married?"

Jack smirked then waved to Simon who crawled forward with the bag of charges.

"What's the plan, boss?"

"You and Dex need to plant the charges in that barn. Star and I will look for Cà Rá."

"What about the key?"

"We'll figure that out once we get her."

"Simon, on me," Dex said. "Set a ten-minute timer on those charges."

"On it."

Jack grabbed Dex's arm. "Good luck."

Dex winked at Jack then he and Simon crawled down the hill.

"Star, you don't have to do this."

She leaned in and pressed her lips against his. The sweet taste of her met the tip of his tongue. Pulling away she whispered, "I do."

Jack grinned, canted his head, pausing for a moment. "You do what?"

Without a word, she smiled, then turned down the hill, disappearing in the shadows.

"I do," he murmured. He glanced up at the starry sky and crawled after her.

∞

Two armed cultists led Tarkos, Bruce, and Fletcher out of the main temple theater and into the front corridor. Tarkos locked his eyes on a stream of robed figures passing them in the hall, each cultist carrying a different weapon.

"Seems strange you guys need so many weapons for the afterlife," Tarkos said.

The cultist behind him shoved the butt of his rifle into his back. "No talking."

Fletcher smiled. "I don't think guns are gonna help them where they're going."

Bruce whispered over them. "Guys, shut up."

"You don't know what you're talking about, priest," the other cultist snapped.

Fletcher stopped walking, and the entire scrum staggered to a stop.

"Here we go," Tarkos muttered, turning around.

Fletcher squared up to the cultist. "For the last time, I'm a *reverend*, not a priest." A huge grin spread across his face. "And you'll meet your maker soon enough."

The cultist snarled and stood his ground, towering over Fletcher. "It doesn't matter. Pretty soon, you'll be begging your god to save you from my god. Now move." He shoved his rifle into Fletcher's stomach.

Fletcher grunted, but straightened quickly. "Well, I guess we'll find out who's right, won't we?"

"Move."

Bruce shook his head. "I told you not to piss them off."

Tarkos turned forward and a hooded brunette woman walked past him. Her eyes locked onto his for a split second before a man behind her stepped between them, held Tarkos' gaze for a long moment, then ushered her down the hall.

"Well, let's just get on with it, shall we?" he said to his armed guard.

As the cultists pushed their group forward, Tarkos turned to look for the pair but they'd disappeared into the crowd.

Why weren't they armed like the others?

The cultists turned the men through a side door and exited the barn to a running pickup truck. A man opened the back tailgate and motioned them into the truck bed with his rifle.

Leaning on one hand, Tarkos jumped into the truck and then helped pull Fletcher up. Bruce climbed in and four armed cultists piled into the truck around them. A fifth man banged on the top of the truck's cab, and it drove away from the Temple, through an open field and into the forest.

Dex peered around the corner of a small shed and looked across the rear of the Temple. Two armed guards in black robes smoked cigarettes while sitting on a stack of wooden crates. One of the guards set his rifle down, stood, and walked to a trough at the far end to urinate.

Dex held two fingers up to his eyes, then pointed at the guards.

Simon gave the men a quick glance then showed Dex a thumbs up. He darted into the darkness and Dex snuck up behind the smoking guard, grabbing him by the neck. He shoved an injection gun beneath the man's jaw and pulled the trigger. Within two seconds, the guard passed out, and Dex dragged the body behind the crates.

He kneeled to disrobe the man but another figure in a robe walked up behind him, casting a long shadow from the light above.

He spun around with frantic eyes and raised his handgun ready to fire.

"Don't shoot, it's me." Simon pulled the hood back to reveal his face in the light. "What's taking you so long?"

"Quiet," Dex said. He pulled the robe off the cultist and draped it over his head.

They crept into the main pavilion of the temple where metallic structures, crystals, and machines gleamed all around them. They stayed on the perimeter of the massive room and kept distant from the other cultists, weaving behind plants and flowers.

Large creatures stood readying what appeared to be weapons while several drones stood watch, floating overhead.

Dex kept his head down and passed around several columns. When he reached the rear of the column, hidden from view, he attached a charge to it and pressed the button with a casual arm movement.

He glanced around for Simon, who had knelt against a far wall and placed a charge. Simon stood, nodded over at him as two cultists passed between them.

Dex pretended to scratch his face and pointed his finger at a structural support post that led up to the roof of the temple. Simon lifted his eyes to the beams high above and nodded.

Jack and Star pulled the hoods of their robes down to cover their faces from other cultists. He tugged on her arm to pull her back from the crowd. As soon as the others passed, they turned down a corridor and entered a small foyer with a split-level staircase. One flight led up, the other went down.

Jack peered around the corner and the cultists had gathered at the far side of the temple, where a yellow light strobed against their raised hands.

Star tapped and pointed her finger at Jack and motioned upstairs. She pointed at herself and motioned down.

Jack shook his head but she turned and left before he could stop her.

He glanced back down the corridor then moved up the flight of stairs. When he reached the top, he unholstered a handgun and rounded the corner of the stairs. He scanned the large, dark veranda, and a nearby moan froze him.

Squinting to adjust to the darkness, he made out a dark shape in the middle of the room. It moaned again and he took a cautious step forward while unhooking a small flashlight from his belt.

As he neared, he found a man bound to a chair facing away from him. Blood dripped down his tied hands and a bloody, white gag had been knotted around the back of his head.

Distant chanting from the cultists in the temple echoed throughout the space, and Jack stepped to the front of the man.

The flashlight hit the prisoner's face.

Roger. Drenched in blood and sweat. His right eye was bruised, and he glanced up at Jack and let out a loud muffled cry through the gag.

"Roger," Jack said, grabbing the gag and pulling it down.

"Jack, it's a trap, get out of—"

Bright lights flashed on, flooding the veranda with a burst of light.

The trauma to Roger's battered and bloodied face shocked Jack. His left eye had swollen shut, and his jaw was starting to purple from bruising.

"Jesus Christ." He knelt, grabbed the knife from the sheath at his hip, and sliced the rope binding his brother's hands. When Roger slumped to the floor, Jack cut through the rope around his ankles and helped him stand.

Robed cultists streamed onto the veranda, blocking both exits.

A monster of a man emerged from the stairwell, brandishing a knife, and walked straight at the brothers.

"Rivera," Roger whispered.

A loud clapping echoed across the veranda, and Jack turned with Roger to find Demi floating above them. A man wearing sunglasses stepped up from the stairwell.

Demi's voice boomed a sinister laugh. "Bravo, bravo. Well done, Jack. I just love family reunions. Don't you?"

Jack turned Roger toward each blocked exit before returning his focus to Demi. "You have what you want, now let us go."

"Not quite, my dear boy. After your trick last time, it seems you didn't give me the final piece of the key."

"I don't know what you're talking about."

"No time for games. Look." Demi turned and motioned to the far side of the temple where cultists and huge, deformed creatures stood around the portal of light.

"The Xurrican army is gathering before your very eyes. Soon, an entire armada will arrive. You may not understand this, but your father was a genius. To have unlocked the most powerful device in all the universe and keep it hidden all these years with that Calodox. Remarkable. It's too bad he had to die. He won't be able to save his boys now."

Tears welled in Jack's eyes, and he leaned forward to steady his brother.

The percussion of a distant explosion outside the barn rattled the walls, followed by an eruption of gunfire and loud screams.

Demi snapped his head to the windows. "It seems we have company. Friends of yours?" He cast a glance to his left. "Rivera, take care of it."

Rivera nodded and motioned several cultists to follow as Demi blocked Jack's view with a scowl. "Now, where is the key?"

Star entered a tunnel marked by green path-lights that led to a circular room with steel doors. The door to her left creaked open and she leaned behind a column, slipping into a dark shadow. A cultist emerged carrying a box, then started up the stairs. Star slid against the wall and turned the corner to the back side of a room with glass windows.

Inside, Cà Rá lay suspended in red plasma bindings beneath cylinders that created an energy cage around her. An armed cultist stood watch over her.

While Star had weapons, she needed a distraction. She looked down the hallway, spotting a thick pipe sitting atop a pile of junk on the other side of the door.

Star crouched low and crept under the windows. Upon reaching the other side, she grabbed a piece of metal from the floor and tossed it against the glass windows.

The rapping noise distracted the cultist, and he ran to the main doorway. He looked up the hall, and as he turned his head back, Star whacked him in the head with the pipe. His rifle fell to the floor, and he stumbled forward in pain. When he spun around, she swung again and cracked him across the face, throwing him to the ground.

She dropped the pipe, and dashed into the room, tracking a series of wires from under Cà Rá to the bank of electronics on the wall. Scanning the myriad buttons, she pressed one. Nothing happened. Every time she pressed a button, she glanced back at Cà Rá.

Nothing.

Grabbing a round dial, she turned it to the left, and the energy bindings on Cà Rá's wrists dissipated. She fell to the floor, and Star ran to help her sit. "Cà Rá. Cà Rá."

Cà Rá's head flopped back, and her gloss-black eyes drooped. A blue, sparkling light pulsed around her eyelids, and she muttered Jack's name.

"He's upstairs." Star said.

With a wheezing breath, Cà Rá mumbled again. "Jack. Trouble."

"I know, I know. What am I supposed to do?" She laid Cà Rá on the floor and stood, spinning around to scan the room.

Her eyes traced back to the energy cylinders that held Cà Rá captive and followed the connected wires to the main control panel.

More screams, followed by relentless gunfire, grew louder outside. Several Xurricans ran out of the main temple alongside an armed group of cultists.

Jack searched for a way off the veranda but found nothing. With a final downward turn of his head, the bracelet on his left wrist caught his eye.

"All right, all right." He reached up across Roger and unsnapped the bracelet with his right hand. Wriggling it off his wrist, he held it out to Demi, and the bands retracted into its silver chassis. "It's the bracelet. The final key is the bracelet."

Demi raised his eyebrows and spoke in a skeptical tone. "Why didn't the scientist mention it?"

"I don't know any scientist. Maybe he's hiding something."

Demi paused and looked down at the ground in thought. "Perhaps."

"Take it and let us go. I don't want to be part of this anymore. You win."

"Takashi." Demi motioned toward Jack.

Takashi hesitated, then stepped to Jack, grabbed the bracelet, and took several steps back. He handed it to Demi then stepped aside.

Turning the bracelet over in his hand, Demi examined its silver face and found several grooved slots at the end of it.

Roger slumped again in pain, and Jack struggled to hold him up. He looked back at Demi. "I don't know how it works, but that's it."

Demi peered over the bracelet and his eyes flashed gloss black. "Kill the wounded one, take Jack to the Empyreax."

"Wait—"

A cultist fired his AR-15, the bullet striking Roger in the middle of his abdomen. Blood sprayed up on Jack's face as he gasped.

Roger's limp body slid out of Jack's arms, down his legs, and crashed onto the floor.

Jack fell to his knees. "Roger. No..."

26

· THE SACRIFICE ·

Star grunted when she ripped an exposed wire out of an energy cylinder and pressed it into Cà Rá's neck. She sprinted back to the control panel and plugged the end of it in, along with three other thick wires. As soon as she turned the voltage knob to full power, a jolt of electricity shot across the wires and shocked Cà Rá's body into a frenetic convulsion.

An energy surge burst across the control panel exploding a shower of sparks and electric pops throughout the room that forced Star to duck. Smoke and fire billowed out of the machines and electronics in the room.

Cà Rá's eyes opened amidst the bolts and streaks of power, and she rose into the air. Flashing light and arcs of electricity shrouded her.

"Jack," she said and streaked out of the room with a trail of sparking electricity stretching behind her like a comet's tail.

Sparkles of energy jumped past Star. "Shit, Cà Rá. Wait for me."

"Takashi, bring everyone to the Empyreax." Demi turned to float off the veranda.

Jack knelt crying over Roger's lifeless body then screamed up at Demi. "You bastard!"

Demi paused and turned back to look at Jack.

Takashi stepped forward and as soon as he grabbed Jack's arm, the entire wall of windows exploded inward. Shards of glass and debris showered across everyone in the room, followed by a brilliant stream of blue, fiery light that blinded everything. Takashi flipped back and fell off the Veranda as Demi recoiled from the blast.

Cà Rá streamed into the room, enveloped in a strobe of wispy light that trailed behind her every move. She twirled and spun faster than Jack could follow, and within seconds, she had incapacitated every cultist. One near Demi fired his weapon at Jack but Cà Rá deflected the bullet and killed the cultist with a fatal strike to his neck.

She spun down in front of Jack, grabbed him, and pulled him up out of the temple, floating into the night sky above the forest canopy.

Dex moved closer to the main stage of the temple and let a charge drop from inside his robe to his feet. He kicked it under the stage and turned to find the cultists running toward the far end of the temple.

They pointed up to the veranda and ran up the stairs. As his eyes tracked them up, Demi floated through pulses of smoke and light that flashed above.

Dex turned back to the portal and another Xurrican entity appeared from it and stared down at a cultist. It contorted and morphed into a larger creature that amalgamated to the twisted form generated by the cultist's dazed mind.

"Not on my watch." Dex reached into his bag for another charge, and as he did, a metal pin fell out and hit the floor.

Everything fell silent.

A Xurrican turned at the sound, and a drone rotated toward him.

Dex turned his back on them, but the Xurrican walked up and tapped him on the shoulder. The drone floated down just in front of him.

The Xurrican flipped the robe's hood back and Dex smiled. "Hi."

A loud scream behind them stopped the Xurrican in his tracks. "Hey, assholes!"

Simon stood on the stage holding the bag of charges, one of them in his hand.

The drone spun around and emitted a warning siren that set off a chain reaction of alarms and flashing red lights throughout the temple.

Simon threw off his robe and grabbed a gun from his chest holster. He fired indiscriminately at the Xurricans and cultists, hitting one square in his chest that flipped the man off the stage.

A Xurrican jumped up onto the far end of the stage and sprinted toward Simon through the hail of bullets.

Spinning to shoot the Xurrican, Simon pulled the trigger and got a shot off but the blunt force of the Xurrican's shoulder pounded into him, sending him tumbling back, into the jump gate.

On the empty veranda, Roger lay on his side, his right cheek stuck to a pool of coagulated blood. He stared across the floor at rays of moonlight shining through the broken windows.

A quiet stillness enveloped his body, and an empty void filled his mind. He had no thought, no feeling. Everything he knew had vanished, and there he lay, locked in a moment of calm.

And then, as if a hand had reached inside of him, into his very soul, a soft tingling trickled across his forehead. Had something touched him?

A warm rush of blood filled his head, seeming to bring his brain back to life. His lip quivered in the puddle of blood, and he drew in a soft, weak breath. His eye twitched, fixed in a trance-like state while the synapses of his mind fired, replaying the last thing he witnessed in slow motion.

A cultist raising a rifle and shooting him. Collapsing to the ground while Jack screamed. An explosion of shattering windows hurtling thousands of shards of glass through the air.

A beautiful angel who burst into the room and slit the throat of the first cultist. She spun and grabbed the barrel of the next cultist's rifle, shoving it into the man's neck and pulling the trigger. One by one, she floated down the line, slaughtering every one of those bastards until she slid across the floor and shielded Jack from a bullet.

She turned to look down at Roger, locked eyes, and reached out to him. Her index finger pressed gently against his forehead, and a wave of energy rippled throughout his body.

As she carried Jack away, the trail of light from her body shimmered and revealed his father standing before him.

Bill knelt by his side and placed his hand on Roger's head. "Son, it's gonna be okay."

Roger choked on the pool of blood, gagging before drawing in a heaving breath.

The light faded, and the man called Takashi appeared directly through the apparition of his father.

He knelt by Roger's side and picked him up.

Simon crashed hard onto a gray, metallic floor, landing with a thud. Catching his breath, he pressed up off the floor, and rubbed the back of his neck, scrunching his face in pain. "Shit, that's gonna hurt tomorrow."

A flashing light caught his attention, and he turned for a closer look.

He traced it to a floating platform outside a glass wall. It was then Simon realized he was inside a hexagonal crystalline structure filled with a series of translucent, acrylic-like machines floating over a vast expanse of rippling lights that stretched into a dark sky.

The sky swirled with a neon-blue atmosphere that wisped into the outer reaches of a starscape. Several large ships floated in the sky and appeared to be docking next to the platform. One by one, more ships dotted the distant horizon—an entire armada of troops and machines stood by.

A flatbed transport craft left from the hull of a larger ship and flew towards his platform. As it neared, he counted at least twenty Xurrican soldiers in its open bay.

One of the Xurricans preparing to receive the transport on a level below, spotted him and sprinted to an elevator-like energy beam that ran up past his platform.

Simon leaned over the edge to follow the Xurrican riding the elevator to his position. He looked back over his shoulder at the jump gate then down at the fleet of arriving troops.

The ethereal and glorious sky tingled his spine, filling him with the warmth of cosmic wonder and fear. Having stood by the window of his room all these years, this was the view he'd been waiting for, and he knew what he had to do.

A humming grew louder, and the elevator stopped at his level. Right when the Xurrican stepped off the platform, Simon reached into the bag for a charge, flicked its red switch and smiled.

"Magnificent. Thank you, Bill."

The charge beeped in rapid succession and exploded in a violent, spectacular burst of volatile energy that shredded the machines, the Xurricans, and destroyed the jump gate.

The machines that formed the jump gate in the temple exploded, sending an electric shockwave that pulsed across computers and jolted several Xurricans.

The force knocked Dex to the ground, and he looked back at the stage. "Just had to be the hero, didn't ya?"

Sparks and fire forced everyone to duck for cover. Before Dex scrambled away, he activated a charge, dropped it in the bag and slid it to the Xurrican's feet.

Dex raced around the corner of a column, sprinting for the exit.

The bag exploded behind him, sending a massive, incendiary blast across the temple.

The other charges detonated and the entire structure blew, destroying columns that had the temple collapsing in on itself.

Cà Rá carried Jack over the front of the farm as the temple exploded beneath them. Several concussive blasts formed an enormous napalm-like ball of fire that collapsed the temple in a cloud of thick, black smoke.

Soldiers and cultists scurried about the farm, muzzle flashes and explosions dotting the ground through the darkness.

"Jack!" Star cried out from below, where she sprinted across the farm, dodging gunfire, and ran into the woods.

"Star!" Jack cried. "We have to help Star! Put me down!" Cà Rá landed in a forest clearing and set Jack down gently. Slivers of moonlight shot through the cove of trees.

He drew a stuttered deep breath and fought back tears. "They killed Roger."

Star raced into the clearing and Cà Rá spun around into a defensive position.

"Jack..." Star threw herself into his arms, hugging him tight.

Tears streamed down his face. "He's dead, Roger's dead."

"Your brother?"

"Yes."

Cà Rá tilted her head to the side. "No, he's not."

"Wha-what do you mean?" Jack asked, trying to stifle his tears.

"He is not dead. He will live."

"But...they shot him. I saw—"

"I promised William to protect you both." Cà Rá smiled.

"I don't understand."

"There is no time to explain," Cà Rá said. "I must help Dex and Simon. You two, get to the Empyreax chamber. We will meet you there."

"How?"

Cà Rá turned and pointed to the Lincoln Continental that sat at the edge of the forest.

"Holy shit," Meeks said while looking through a pair of binoculars at the exploded barn. A bullet whizzed past him and he ducked.

"It's an all-out war, Sheriff." Finn huddled behind the truck and Meeks crouched at his side.

"We're gonna need more than the National Guard." He spotted Burke and crawled back to his position.

"Burke, what the hell is going on?"

"Say again, say again!" Burke yelled into his headset and waved Meeks off.

"Burke, answer me! What the hell is going on?"

An agent stepped in front of Meeks and pushed him back.

"Don't push me, goddammit."

"Sheriff!" Finn yelled back at him and pointed to a far corner of the farm.

"A bunch of kids are in there!"

Meeks raised his binoculars and focused them on a group of young children yelling out the window of a stable. "Christ." Without hesitation, he sprinted to his Jeep and turned the ignition.

Finn jumped into the passenger side. "Punch it!"

Meeks revved the Jeep's throttle and tore past Burke who yelled, "You're gonna die!"

Jack floored the Continental and smashed through the cabin's main pipe gate, ripping the car's front bumper off. Several cultists fired at them and the bullets riddled the car, shattering its windows.

Star ducked and banged into the dash when the car's shocks bottomed out from a rut. Jack drove foot to floor up the mountain road, swerving to keep the back end of the car from fishtailing. They rounded the last bend, tearing up the main driveway to the cabin.

Several empty trucks sat in front, and two guards on the front porch opened fire.

Jack slewed the left side of the car away from the cabin and he and Star climbed out of the passenger door to crouch behind the tire.

Bullets ricocheted off the car, and Jack peered over the door's edge at the men.

Newt ran up behind the men, barking and growling. One of them turned around with his shotgun ready to fire.

A loud rotary sound filled the air and the bladed lawnmower-drone dropped from above. The cultist looked up at the noise, and the blades dropped onto his face, shredded it, spraying blood all over the second cultist.

The rotation of the blades forced the man's body to turn, and his finger twitched on the trigger, blasting the other cultist square in the chest, throwing him back dead.

"Nice," Jack said. "Two for one." He grabbed Star's hand. "Come on."

They sprinted across the yard and into the cabin. Newt ran in behind them, wagging his tail. Jack pressed the elevator button and ran into the kitchen to grab his handgun. "You okay?"

Newt let out a quick bark.

"Good. Wait here for Cà Rá, Dex and Simon."

The elevator door opened, and Jack ushered Star inside. He pressed the button, and the door closed, taking them down to the Empyreax chamber.

27

· RUMBLE ·

As soon as the elevator door slid silently open, Jack led Star at a crouch to the back of a workbench on the upper rock ledge. Demi stood on the lower platform with armed cultists across from three men—two of middle-age, and a much older man wearing a clerical collar. Several large Xurricans stood behind them, and the striped drone hovered above.

When the elevator door closed, it clicked, and a cultist turned his head up toward the ledge. Jack ducked and motioned for Star not to move.

Demi's voice echoed through the chamber. "It's time to prove your worth, Mr. Tarkos. Miles, bring him the keys."

Jack stood and aimed his gun at Demi's head. His finger touched the trigger but before he could squeeze off a shot, the cocking hammer on a double action revolver clicked next to his ear.

"Drop it."

Star called out to him. "Jack."

He turned and a man holding a revolver to her head blew a bubble and snapped his gum. "Demi, look what I found," the man said in a song-like voice.

Jack dropped his gun and raised his hands.

Demi snorted. "I know, Edgar. Bring them down here."

Edgar pointed his revolver down the path, forcing them to the stoop where Demi stood.

"I'm getting tired of you," Demi said with an exaggerated sigh. "But now that you are here, you can witness what your father hid from the world. The dawn of a new creation."

Jack didn't stop his laugh. "Is that what this is all about? Power?"

"Unlimited power," Demi said, glaring. "A power that is beyond your comprehension. The Empyreax created you. Me. Everything." Demi swooped his arms in a giant arc.

"If it's so great," Jack said, infusing as much scorn as he could into his words, "why did someone go to all this trouble to hide it?"

Demi's glare only deepened before turning to Tarkos. "Open it, now."

Jack yelled, "Don't do it, Tarkos! If you open that thing, we're all gonna die."

"I have to see," Tarkos said, then his eyes locked on Jack. "I'm sorry." He turned back to the group. "I need the final piece of the key."

Demi tossed the bracelet to Tarkos.

The scientist caught it, examined it closely then shook his head before dropping it to the ground. "This isn't it." He turned to the reverend. "Fletcher, I need your necklace."

"For what?"

"It's the final piece of the key."

"You knew this entire time?" Fletcher removed the necklace and handed it over, whispering, "I hope you know what you're doing."

Tarkos placed his hand on Fletcher's shoulder. "You're gonna be fine."

As Fletcher smiled and turned away, he made the sign of the cross.

The pendant clicked into the inner ring, and Tarkos stepped up onto the main platform where the Empyreax sat.

∞

In a dark tunnel, a metallic door swung up and Dex stuck his head through the opening. Cà Rá stepped past him and disappeared around the corner of a stone wall.

"Cà Rá, wait." Dex stepped into the room and shut the door behind him, sliding a large metal latch to lock it.

Stepping to the stone ledge, he peered across the room. A dim, white light shone down from above, casting shadows from rocky protrusions that formed a maze of pathways to the other side.

A flash of white from Cà Rá's body darted from the corner of his eye, and she jumped through the air from ledge to ledge.

"Dammit, will you wait for me? I don't move that fast anymore." He glanced around and found an angled slab of stone that he shuffled down.

He reached the bottom and tripped, falling face first, catching himself before he hit the ground. As he pushed himself up, a metal boot stepped inches from his face. He twisted his head and flicked his eyes up. A Xurrican stood over him, grunted, and charged a long plasma weapon.

"Oh, shit." Dex pushed himself up, then raised his hands.

The Xurrican spoke in a cryptic language—a deep voice enhanced with electronic frequencies.

Dex placed his hands behind his head. "I'm just trying to—"

Cà Rá's fist punched through the Xurrican's head, and a blue goo splashed on Dex. The alien's body twitched to the ground.

As she pulled her hand free, a door on the opposite side of the room opened and a horde of Xurricans rushed in. Dex grabbed the plasma rifle and pulled the trigger. A rapid-fire burst of lasers streamed at the creatures, killing several. Dex screamed as he held the trigger down, and the blasts continued in a torrential blitz of explosions.

The rifle ran out of energy, but Dex kept screaming.

Only six Xurricans remained standing and they returned fire.

Cà Rá jumped to an upper ledge as Dex threw himself behind a large boulder. "Where the hell?" Sparks singed his arm, and he crawled around the other side of the rock. "Cà Rá, need some help here!"

She jumped up to a third ledge and stood before a sealed metallic door. Cà Rá pressed a button, and a tray slid out from the door. A holographic ring of symbols swirled up from the tray and she touched one then spun it with her finger until she touched another. With each touch, her fingers moved faster and faster, rotating through the sequence of symbols.

Dex turned his attention to the Xurricans who were creeping toward him, their weapons shouldered. He grabbed his handgun and aimed for the controls on the opposite door. As it started to open, he fired a direct shot at the panel and the door collapsed shut.

Grabbing a grenade from his belt, he pulled the pin and tossed it at two of the Xurricans. They looked down at it just before an explosion ripped them apart. Debris from the blast showered across the room.

Four left.

"Cà Rá?"

No response.

The Xurricans aimed and fired their weapons. Sparks and rocks showered down on Dex as he covered his head. "Jesus!"

He pulled a hockey-puck device off his belt and slid it to the feet of the Xurricans. An electric pulse shot up from the puck and sent an EMP blast that disabled their weapons.

As they tried to recharge, Dex stood and creaked his neck, staring dead on at them. He yanked his hand down and a three-piece blade unfolded from its hilt, a yellow arc of energy spiraling around it.

"Bottom of the ninth, down by one," he said. "All right, you fuckers, let's rumble."

The Xurricans smashed their hands together and their eyes flashed red.

Dex roared a maniacal war cry, raised his sword, and charged.

The first Slayer swung its arm, and Dex bobbed like a boxer before taking two steps back "Swing and a miss."

He ran at the Slayer, sword ready to strike. The monster snarled and tried to punch him, but Dex fell into a sliding position and slashed the blade across its knee, hobbling it. He leapt to his feet, thrusting the sword into the second creature.

"Safe," he yelled.

The third beast lunged for Dex's feet and tried to pull him up. When it grasped his leg, he slashed its arm off and spun to stab the fourth in the chest.

"Oh, an error puts the tying run in scoring position."

Two Xurricans remained, and both glared at Dex.

He held the sword by his side and raised his left arm, pointing beyond the Xurricans.

The aliens looked at each other then one of the beasts charged.

Just before it reached him, Dex spun to his left, arcing his sword through the air. The blade sliced through the neck of the Xurrican, and its severed head dropped to the ground in a splash of neon-blue ichor.

"Oh my God! He called the shot. Dexter Mosely with the greatest swing of all time!"

Cracking his neck, Dex brandished the sword with both hands. "Come and—" The yellow energy field died, and the sword collapsed into its hilt. "Oops."

The last Xurrican took a giant breath and screeched into the air. The deep shrill reverberated in the cavern.

Dex screamed along with it, shifted his weight to his back foot, then leaped forward.

The beast ran at Dex, and their bodies smashed into each other. It punched Dex in the face, and although he held his arm up to soften the blow, the force of it spun him to the ground.

He pushed up from his knees and attempted to tackle the Xurrican, but the creature flipped him like a rag doll against the rock wall.

His body hit the ground, and something cracked inside his chest.

The Xurrican stepped forward and Dex grabbed a handful of dirt, throwing it into its ugly face.

Snatching Dex's arm, the Xurrican pulled him forward and wrapped its hand around his neck.

Dex scrabbled at the grip with both hands, gasping for air. He looked up at Cà Rá and tried to yell. "Cà Rá, a little help."

Without shifting her gaze, she replied, "You're fine."

His eyes widened at her response and the Xurrican squeezed harder while pushing him down against a boulder.

Veins popped from his sweat-drenched forehead. Stars sparked in his vision, blackness encroaching. He reached for his belt, searching for anything, and his fingers wrapped around the pen-light laser.

When he clicked the button, the laser pierced through the stomach of the Xurrican and it recoiled in pain, dropping Dex. He struggled for balance, and held the laser at the creature, slicing through it with each dismembering pass.

The laser soon died out and he dropped it to the ground.

Doubled over, hands on his knees, he sucked in lungfuls of air that scraped his throat like glass.

He staggered up the ledge to Cà Rá as she completed the coded sequence. The hologram flashed green and the door slid open.

She smiled at Dex. "I beat my best time by seven hundred and sixty-three milliseconds."

"Congratulations," he rasped, side-eyeing her as he jogged through the doorway.

"Thank you," she said, then followed him into the tunnel.

Meeks drove his Jeep through a swirl of black smoke and stopped just in front of the shed. He and Finn jumped out and ran inside to a group of children huddled in the corner. A little girl cried while staring at a dead woman with a gunshot wound to her forehead, her body sprawled on the ground.

"It's okay. Shh." Meeks picked up the little girl whose red face streamed with tears. Finn helped the other two boys stand, and they scampered out of the shed to the Jeep.

Placing the children inside, Meeks opened the driver's side door. "Finn, get these kids out of here."

"What?"

"I said get—look out!" Meeks spotted a cultist with a rifle aimed at Finn. The gun fired and he pushed Finn to the ground, both of them crashing into a pile of wood.

The bullet missed, but when Meeks hit the ground, his knee twisted and he cried out.

Finn rolled Meeks over. "Sheriff, you all right?"

"Yeah. Don't worry about me, Finn. You get those kids out of here."

"Not leaving your side, Sheriff."

Meeks nodded and peered over the wood. Another volley of bullets hurtled towards him and pelted the Jeep. Its windows shattered and rained glass on the children who shrieked from inside.

"Finn, I'll create a diversion. Get them out of here."

"Okay." Finn darted his face to the Jeep then back to Meeks. "I'll come back for you."

"Don't you dare. Get your ass to safety. Now go."

Finn shook his head in disgust. "Aw, shit."

Meeks cocked the hammer on his revolver and popped up above the wood firing at the shooter. He turned, ignoring the agony in his leg, dodging and weaving beneath a steady stream of bullets. *How could that asshole miss?* "Amateur," Meeks muttered, as Finn scampered into the Jeep, and sped away.

As Meeks ran for another building, a bullet hit him square in his chest with a metal ping that reverberated throughout his entire body, knocking him back to the ground. He turned and spotted the Jeep driving back across the fence line to safety.

Sitting up with a groan, he glanced down at the plate carrier. A shredded tuft of canvas and Kevlar material jutted from a hole. "Not an amateur." He grabbed his hat, fitting it snug on his head.

When he sat up, the cultist greeted him with his rifle aimed point-blank at his head. "Do what you need to," Meeks said, and closed his eyes.

A gunshot blasted through the air and Meeks flinched.

It missed. What the hell? He opened his eyes as the gunman's body fell to the side, finger on the trigger.

An automatic burst of bullets fired into the dirt.

A group of National Guard soldiers raced over, M4A1 rifles pointed at the gunman. "Shooter down, shooter down."

"You okay?" One of them helped Meeks to his feet and he hobbled to keep pressure off his busted knee.

"Thanks," Meeks said.

One of the soldiers yelled into his headset and turned back to the other men. "Let's go—"

A bright blue fireball struck the solder in the head and shredded his flesh. Blood pumped out of the wound in his neck and he dropped to the ground.

"Contact! Contact!" The soldiers turned, firing their rifles at a large Xurrican beast that shot plasma bolts at them.

A drone flew in behind the beast and fired back at the soldiers, hitting one in the head.

It lifted high into the air and flanked the other soldiers.

Meeks shifted his stance and aimed his revolver at the drone. He pulled the trigger right as his knee twinged, causing the bullet to miss.

The drone spun around and shot a dart that whizzed past just as Meeks' knee buckled, the shot striking the wall behind him. The silver drone reflected the fiery glow from the burning buildings and swooped toward him.

Meeks wouldn't miss this time. Firing again, the round struck the drone, shattering its front eye. The drone spiraled away and crashed in a ball of fire.

Turning back to the melee, Meeks fired at the Xurrican but the bullets didn't do any damage. The beast grabbed a soldier by his head and thrust a glowing metal spear through his chest.

"Shit." Meeks glanced around the yard and spotted a bucket tractor.

He limped over, climbed in, fired it up and lowered the front bucket.

The remaining two soldiers kept sustained gun bursts on the Xurrican as the spiked teeth of the bucket speared deep into the monster's lower back.

It wailed, turned, and pounded on the tractor with heavy punches that shunted Meeks off the side. A soldier unpinned two grenades and shoved them into its open wounds.

They exploded and ripped the beast apart in a shower of glowing blue blood.

One of the soldiers ran and stood over Meeks, offering a hand. "Thanks, Sheriff."

"I need to thank you guys first." Meeks took the hand, and when he was pulled to stand, the sound of a wet balloon bursting ripped through the air. Blood showered over him, and the next moment Meeks fell backwards, hitting the ground with the soldier's severed arm in his hand.

He sat up and wiped blood from his face. Two large feet stomped to a halt before Meeks, and he followed them up to a Xurrican that towered over him. He raised his revolver, and pulled the trigger.

Click.

"Holy balls."

The Xurrican raised its rifle, but a large metal pole exploded from its head and pulled its aim away. The plasma blast shot across the courtyard and demolished a nearby van.

Meeks turned to find a man dressed in black wearing sunglasses squaring up against the alien. The man spun the pole several times and folded it under his arm. Calm as hell.

A wounded man lay nearby, coughing.

Meeks crawled over, examining the bloodied and bruised face.

"Jack," he muttered

"I'm not Jack, but I'm gonna get you out of here. Alive."

Takashi flipped the pole up under his arm and strafed to the side. When the Xurrican lunged at him, he leaped and smashed the pole across its head.

The Xurrican yanked the pole, tossing it away. Takashi spun mid-air, landing a series of tornado kicks that knocked it farther back.

It shook its head then rushed at Takashi

From his periphery, Takashi spotted a sharp metal bar jutting from the tractor, and stepped back, waving the beast toward him. When it lunged, Takashi backflipped, and the beast fell forward. The spike pierced through the bottom of its jaw, momentum driving the metal bar up through its head.

"Hey, Takashi!" Rivera slid to a stop, waving his knife. "I knew I didn't like you. I'm gonna slit your fucking throat."

Rivera swung his blade, but Takashi leapt clear of the tractor. With a growl, Rivera slashed again. Missed again.

Takashi moved into the open and stood ready, waiting for Rivera to strike.

The knife handle flitted between Rivera's hands, and he gnashed his teeth. Swinging the blade, he swiped left and right, the blade singing through the air.

Takashi bobbed and weaved before stepping in to swat the strike away.

Rivera grinned, landing an uppercut to Takashi's jaw.

Takashi danced back and Rivera rushed him, turning to drive his elbow in as a feint only to stab toward Takashi's head. But Kaze Baku grabbed Rivera's wrist, stopping the blade inches from his face.

Rivera drove an elbow into Takashi's chest, while pressing the knife forward as hard as he could. Takashi grabbed the blade with both hands, and blood streamed down his palms. Rivera screamed with a last burst of energy, but Takashi kicked the man's feet out from under him. The knife fell from Rivera's fingers, and Takashi dropped onto his enemy's chest, pinning Rivera's arms with his knees. He wrapped his hands around the big man's neck and squeezed.

Precision pressure on the carotid arteries cut blood flow to Rivera's brain. The man gagged, twitched, face red and eyes bulging.

Rivera's head jerked before his eyes rolled back and his body fell limp.

Takashi gave a final squeeze then stood, and walked to the Sheriff.

"Thank you," Meeks said as the man beside him coughed.

Takashi pointed at the man.

Meeks looked down. "Yeah, we need to get him to..." Meeks turned back but Takashi had disappeared. "...a hospital."

Finn's voice rang through the radio. "Sheriff. Sheriff, come in. Tom, you still there?"

Meeks grabbed his radio. "Finn, I'm still here. Did you get those kids out? "

"Yeah, they're safe."

"Good. I've got a wounded man here. I need a medic asap."

"Sheriff, Burke says the cult is falling back and heading up to Black Wolf."

"Black Wolf?" He turned to face the silhouette of Black Wolf Mountain against the moon.

Meeks looked down at the wounded man with grave concern, who spoke through a bloodied cough. "Jack."

28

· ANNIHILATION OPERATOR ·

Tarkos stepped toward the Empyreax with hesitation, and held the key up to the main port on its front face.

"No!" Star screamed.

Fletcher closed his eyes and prayed.

"Andre," Bruce yelled. "You promised me."

Tarkos slid the key into the round-toothed hole, and it latched with a smooth click.

A blue light pulsed inside the pendant and the inner-most ring started to spin. The second ring spun slower than the third while the outer ring rotated even slower.

The rings spun oscillated in a sequenced order for about twenty seconds then stopped when the pendant turned green.

Tarkos looked to Demi who stared at the Empyreax with wide open eyes.

"Let it begin," Demi said.

The chamber fell silent, all except Fletcher who mumbled an Our Father with closed eyes.

A loud horn blared through the chamber, and a series of red lights flashed on the upper perimeter of the Empyreax, staining the room crimson.

The sound of an analog-phone dial tone filled the chamber followed by twelve beeps.

Tarkos frowned. "What the...?"

A whirring modulation stuttered varying octaves—digital birds chirping to each other.

"It's a dial-up modem," Bruce said.

The sounds rang familiar and nostalgic throughout the chamber.

Tarkos backed down the steps to stand by Fletcher and Bruce.

"What's happening?" Demi yelled.

Edgar and Miles cast hesitant glances at each other.

When the static ended, a small door at the front of the Empyreax slid open. Nobody moved.

Demi pointed at the Empyreax. "Edgar, go."

"Me?" He looked at his brother, who nodded.

Edgar edged down the ramp, crept up the stairs and hesitated before looking into the opening with a flashlight. "There's something inside."

Tarkos took another step back.

Edgar leaned closer to the opening and reached inside. "It's some kind of toy."

Tarkos yelled, "No, don't!"

Edgar retracted his arm from the box and pulled out an eight-inch-tall doll. The toy had a white outfit with a red cache around its waist. Its hair was white and frizzy, and a cigarette stuck from its mouth "It's just a doll," Edgar said, holding it up with a grin.

Miles pointed at it from the upper ledge and laughed. "It's a fucking Jobu doll. You know, from that baseball movie."

A series of clicks sounded from within the device, and Edgar flicked a nervous gaze at it.

The chamber filled with a loud buzzing from overhead, and everyone looked up at the ceiling.

"Get down," Jack yelled, pushing Star to the ground and covering her with his body.

Large cannons slid in from the top of the curved walls and fired multiple laser bursts in scattershot directions. Explosions ripped across the floor, hitting several cultists.

Bombs detonated beneath the ground, shaking the entire chamber. Large cracks formed in the stone floor, giant slabs breaking apart. Debris from the destruction floated upward, defying gravity.

The ground split and everyone found themselves separated on floating stone platforms. Laser blasts ripped and shredded the chamber into fragmented chunks of rubble, and the ceiling collapsed upward in a fiery molten blast.

An explosion near Fletcher slammed him to the ground, knocking him out cold.

The walls of the chamber crumbled as fire and smoke choked the air.

Edgar wobbled on his floating rock, dropping the Jobu doll. Instead of floating upward, the doll plummeted into the black pit below. "Miles," Edgar shouted to his brother. "Don't fall off the stone."

"Jack!" A familiar voice called. "Up here!"

Jack looked up to see Dex just above them at the edge of a tunnel. He lifted Star to an upper ledge that still clung to the chamber wall. "Dex, get her out of here! I have to get the key!"

Star shook her head. "No, Jack!"

Dex reached down for her. "Star, let's go! There's no time."

Star climbed the ledge and Dex caught her hand just before the stone crumbled beneath her feet.

Then Cà Rá appeared, lifting Star to safety. "Go. I will help Jack."

"Jack!" Star shouted as Dex ushered her into the tunnel.

Jack ran down the main ledge, a splintered fissure in the rock chasing him. He jumped just before the stone platform crumbled away and landed on a floating boulder that tilted when he hit it. Clinging to the edge, he steadied himself onto it.

Smoke filled the chamber, masking the floating boulders. Glancing over the edge, he spotted the Empyreax key on a platform near Tarkos and Bruce. Tracing a path from his rock down to that platform, he stood and readied to jump but was bowled over when Demi careened into him. He fell, crashing onto a slab that rotated on its center axis.

Jack struggled to hold onto the edge, straining against his own weight. He slipped.

The initial momentum of the drop sank into his stomach but he was jerked to a stop when Cà Rá grabbed his wrist and pulled him to another platform.

Demi sneered. "Ah, the Calodox. It won't be able to save you this time."

Several stone boulders smashed into each other and crumbled, revealing a metal object floating in mid-air. As the rubble drifted away, a dark cylindrical object appeared, hovering above the platform.

Demi's eyes locked on it and he screamed. "The Empyreax!"

Tarkos looked at the device that floated above him. "Soulgazer."

"Andre," Bruce called out. "Help."

Tarkos glanced down at Bruce, who dangled off the edge of a rock platform next to him.

Demi pointed at Cà Rá and yelled for the Xurricans. "Capture the Calodox."

Jack hopped onto a ledge and balanced himself, trying not to stare into the abyss of darkness below. Finding the key again, he jumped down onto its stone, dropping low when it bobbed beneath him.

He grabbed the key but a Xurrican landed on the opposite edge of the rock, teetering it back and forth.

Jack kept his center of gravity low, steadying his balance.

Demi floated down in front of him, a smirk on his face.

Before he could attack, Cà Rá smashed into him, driving him through the crater opening above.

Jack darted his eyes to an overhead platform and reached for it. When his feet left the platform, the weight of the Xurrican flipped the rock over and it tumbled into darkness.

Just like Chimney Rock, Jack leapt from slab to slab, zigzagging until he reached the top of the crater, only to have a cultist smash a rifle into his head. The key flung out of his hands. He clawed after it, but it bounced off the edge and into the chamber below.

Tarkos tried to tug Bruce up onto the platform. It wobbled, and he lost his balance. The weight of Tarkos' body pulled Bruce a little farther off the edge.

"Andre," Bruce cried, "don't let me fall!"

Tarkos dropped to the ground and squeezed Bruce's wrist with both hands.

Bruce's eyes widened, and his glasses fell off his face, tumbling into the void. "Please don't let go of me."

An object flashed in the corner of Tarkos' eye followed by a loud metallic ping. The Empyreax key sat on the ledge just below him, a few feet within his reach. "The key."

Glancing back, Tarkos pulled with all his might and looped his elbow around Bruce's right arm. The platform that held the key started to flip, and Tarkos stretched for it with his other hand.

"What are you doing?" Bruce's eyes darted to the key. "Forget the key!"

The tip of Tarkos' middle finger touched it, and he tried to pull it to him. "I can get it." The stone continued to rotate, and the key slid another inch away.

"Andre! I'm slipping."

Tarkos strained and stretched farther for the key. "I can reach it."

The platform flipped up, and the key slid off. With a lunge forward, Tarkos tried to grab it, but it slid over the edge.

Bruce's arm slipped from his grip, and he flipped back off the rock. His wide eyes locked on Tarkos and cut right through him.

"Bruce!" Tarkos lunged but Bruce's scream echoed into pitch black.

Tarkos closed his eyes until Bruce's scream faded away. When he opened them, his focus was on Fletcher lying face down on a slab below. Beside the reverend, sat the Empyreax key.

"Fletcher! Fletcher!"

Nothing.

"Hey, priest!"

Fletcher didn't move.

The rock Tarkos sat upon, floated to the upper ledge where stairs rose into the cabin.

He stared down at Fletcher's motionless body.

"Shit." Tarkos turned and ran up the stairs.

A cultist flipped off a rock and fell past Edgar, who clung tight to the boulder he lay on. He shouted for Miles. "How you doing, little brother?"

"Little brother? Mom always told me I came first." Miles gripped his rock and it began to slowly rotate upside down. "Shit. Not sure I'm gonna make it."

"Hang on, I'm coming." Edgar jumped from his stone onto another then leaped onto the platform where Miles clung below. He stretched his body across it and swung his arm underneath.

Miles hesitated, then grabbed onto his brother's arm. Edgar pulled with all his might, lifting his brother up onto the platform.

They both let out a hoot and Miles hollered up at the sky, "Holy shit, I thought I was a goner there for a moment." Their laughter stopped when the platform started to rotate again.

"Uh oh." Edgar scrambled up but the platform flipped too fast. Miles lodged his foot into a crevice and grasped his brother's hand. Edgar's body fell away from the rock, only his brother's hold keeping him from falling.

He looked up at Miles. "Bro, don't let go."

"I got you man, hang on."

Edgar's hand slipped down to Miles' wrist. "Ah, man no, no."

Their fingers clawed at each other, but Edgar's hand slipped away. "So long, Miles." He slid into the pit and disappeared.

"So long, Edgar." The platform tipped over, and Miles fell into the darkness behind his brother without a sound.

Dex and Star climbed up from an outcropping of rocks on a trail down the far side of the cabin. Fire and smoke engulfed the forest. Dex grabbed Star's hand and helped her up from the rocky ledge.

He paused and looked around the forest perimeter. "The grid." His eyes followed a massive wall of electric-blue lasers that spread around the yard of the cabin. Each wall connected at a mirrored column and diverted its energy to the next, forming a protective shield.

Xurricans tried to get through the shield but when they touched it, a shockwave of electricity jolted across their bodies.

"Damn, it worked."

"We have to get back there and help," Star said through several deep breaths.

"I know." He winced and grabbed his stomach.

"Are you hurt?"

"I'll be fine. There are more weapons in the cabin." Dex's breaths came fast and sweat poured from his brow.

"Well, let's go."

"Just give me a second," Dex said holding his hand up. "You're half my age."

"We don't have a second." Star turned and bolted away from him.

"Star, wait, you need the code." Dex shook his head and muttered to himself, "No rest for the weary."

He grabbed his stomach and limped up the trail toward the back corner of the cabin. As soon as he reached Star, a Xurrican appeared, stopping them in their tracks.

Dex let out a frustrated groan. "Oh, come *on*."

The Xurrican eyed Star then turned to Dex who shouted, "Star, go!" He charged the Xurrican while she took off running.

As the alien raised its rifle, Dex dropped, the plasma blast nicking his left shoulder. Despite the wound, he lunged forward and snatched the rifle away from the creature.

With a scream borne of rage and hate, he pounded the butt of the rifle into the Xurrican's head, over and over again until it split open and neon-blue ichor sprayed up on him. The creature stilled, and Dex took deep panting breaths as he dropped the rifle.

He staggered and glanced at the wound on his shoulder.

With a heaving sigh, he fell back against a wooden fence post on the main trail and slid to the ground.

Fletcher awoke on a hard stone platform and wheezed to catch his breath. His hand rested off the edge of the rock and it tingled from a flowing wave of energy that rose from the black pit.

He sat up, squeezed his temples and adjusted his vision to the room. Glancing around his immediate space, he locked onto the stone platform where his bible lay open next to the Empyreax key.

The stone platform bumped into something and jostled him to the side. He leaned down on the rock's smooth surface to steady himself and looked up.

The Empyreax hovered before him, and diffused lights reflected off its matte-gray surface, casting an ethereal luster around it.

Blood dripped from his brow down his cheek, and muffled voices screamed from below as if buried in a shallow grave at his feet.

His vision blurred, but he collected his bible, the pages fluttering in some unknown breeze, then snatched up the key.

A bright light burst down from above, and Fletcher shielded his eyes. He couldn't see or hear anyone.

The light from above lit up the bible's red-edged pages and he held it close to his face to read its passage.

Romans 8:18 – For I consider that the sufferings of this present time are not worthy to be compared with the glory that shall be revealed to us.

He looked at the key in his right hand and dropped his bible. It rolled over the edge of the platform, its pages rippling through the air as it disappeared.

Fletcher locked the key into the Empyreax and a beam of light streamed out from the pendant. The rings spun in opposite directions and a loud whine followed by a low percussive boom reverberated through the chamber.

Stepping back on the platform, a laser of pure white light shone from it and drew a rectangular outline in mid-air.

Millions of particles of light scattered across the rectangle and seemed to reflect the image of Fletcher back at him before flipping to a void of darkness.

Fletcher peered around the backside of the paper-thin portal but found nothing.

Voices screamed from above, and he looked up but was blinded by white light. Everything around him had disappeared and he stood on a wafer-thin, rippling surface that reflected sparkling light.

As he peered into the darkness of the Empyreax portal, a tiny flick of light spiraled out from it, and he lurched back. The light stopped in front of him, and a brighter light replicated from the spark until a shimmering entity of luminescence appeared.

The entity morphed and molded into the shape of a young boy wrapped in a glow of pearlescent light.

Fletcher gaped. "Daniel." A single tear streamed down his face, and he reached out to his son. Could this be him? Had he died and gone to Elysium? Tears streamed down Fletcher's face as the brilliant light cast a crystal blue glow in his eyes.

The boy walked up to Fletcher, smiled, and took his hand. Daniel turned back to the Empyreax and tugged.

Fletcher paused, but Daniel took another step forward.

His son looked back at him and waved him forward with his other hand.

The reverend took three steps forward and passed through the black void.

His foot landed on a cobblestone street at the entrance of a Parisian café. A man on a bicycle rode past and when Fletcher turned, he found his wife sitting at a small round table. She sipped from a cup of hazelnut espresso she held over a plated prosciutto crepes.

Daniel ran up behind her, holding a red balloon, and she turned to greet him with a smile. The sun bounced off her bronze hair and she tucked a lock of it behind her ear then guided Daniel to his seat.

When the boy sat, she looked up from the table and her eyes locked on Fletcher. A radiant smile of affection stretched across her face.

Fletcher closed his eyes, and every fear, each moment of anxiety and tragedy that plagued his life, disappeared.

29

· CREATION OPERATOR ·

Star raced through the cabin's back door and ducked behind the kitchen counter. Ear-piercing gunshots blasted through the air. Crawling along the floor into the hallway, she kept her eyes locked on a group of cultists huddled in the living room, firing their weapons out the windows while bullets streamed back into the cabin, filling the room with shattered glass and shrapnel.

A bullet struck one cultist, who fell back and cracked his head on the floor. His bloodied face fell into her line of sight and his lifeless eyes stared back at her.

Star crawled into the office and jumped when PO floated in front of her face and startled her.

"PO, we need to help Jack," she whispered. "Where are the weapons."

His glass eye beeped green and rotated with a red laser that pointed at a cabinet against the wall. She threw the door open and shuffled through clothes hanging on the rack. At the back of the cabinet she found a lever and pulled it down to reveal a cutout in the wall. A modified M40 grenade launcher sat inside with white, scraggly paint down its side that read, 'Black Widow II.'

She grabbed it and threw open the window. "Let's go."

PO beeped and followed.

The earth's crust above the chamber blazed with fire and molten magma, dripping down the chasm's edge. Jack scrambled across the stone rock section leading to Black Wolf's upper slope. Looking back across the pit, the cabin's outer wall rested just above a sharp precipice.

National Guard troops shouted in the distance and shot at cultists lined up at the front of the cabin. Xurrican Slayers and Wraiths fanned out through the woods, attacking anything that moved.

Cultists streamed through the perimeter of the yard, yelling in maniacal drivel while returning fire. Smoke poured across the landscape and fire crept along treetops, engulfing the back edge of the forest.

A stray bullet whisked past Jack.

The ground shook behind him with a concussive thud and he turned to find Cà Rá and Demi had crashed into the ground. Spider-like cracks splintered across the earth, the impact creating a large plume of dirt and rocks.

Cà Rá sat on Demi's chest and landed blow after blow across his face, each strike slicing a beam of light that morphed and folded back into his head.

Demi swiped his hand to the side and its energy lifted a boulder that smashed into Cà Rá. Her body flipped away, and he rolled onto his stomach, but she rebounded and rammed down on him.

"Jack," Star called out, and ran around the back corner of the cabin, sprinting toward him along the outer edge of the pit.

"Star, no." He waved her off but an explosion masked his voice and threw her to the ground. Jack ran to her. "You need to leave," he said, lifting her to her feet.

"No, we need to help Cà Rá."

Jack picked up the Black Widow.

The blunt force of a Xurrican Wraith bashed into his chest and tossed him away. The Black Widow flipped across the ground and slid down an embankment.

When he rolled over and reached out to grab it, a Slayer stepped on his hand.

Gazing beyond the beast's craggy foot, Jack watched the Xurrican Wraith tower over Star. Jack screamed and smashed the Slayer's foot with his fist but it didn't relent.

Star took a step back and tripped on a rock and fell on her backside. She looked up at the Xurrican.

Jack struggled to free himself, but the Slayer had him pinned.

The Wraith engaged a glowing light sword and lifted it to bring down on Star.

Jack screamed again.

The blade sliced through the air but before it met her flesh, red lasers blasted the alien's hand, and the blade fell to the ground.

PO swooped in, firing a small cannon from its belly and the Xurrican swiped its arm at him.

The Slayer holding Jack lifted a spear above its head and thrust it down. He rolled to his side, contorting his body under the foot of the Slayer. His hand twisted and a sharp crack of pain tore through his wrist.

Freeing himself, he scrambled down the embankment and grabbed the Black Widow, charging it with his good hand. The Slayer turned and angled over him with the spear, but Jack fired up at it, disintegrating the monster into thousands of light particles.

Jack glanced at Star who had scrambled away from the creature while PO kept a volley of shots directed at it. Before he could stand, the striped drone flew out of the sky and fired a rocket that hit PO, sending him into a downward spiral crash.

The Xurrican grunted, picked up its spear, and turned to Star who stood cornered by the edge of the cliff.

Jack raised the Black Widow and pulled the trigger. The plasma projectile spiraled at the Xurrican and struck its head. This time, the particles spread down through its body and shattered in a burst of brilliant light just above Star.

He turned back to PO who had bounced off the ground and back into the air with a shake and a wobble.

PO straightened his glide and jetted across the burning pit high above the Empyreax chamber. He pitched, rotated, and rolled through the air, dodging bullets and plasma blasts in the line of fire between soldiers, cultists, and beasts.

The striped drone was in close pursuit, firing energy bursts to add to PO's obstacles.

He darted through a window in the cabin, passing by cultists who fired in random patterns at the soldiers. Bullets, shrapnel, and the chaotic micro-debris of war whizzed by him. He exited through the front door and the striped drone fired a shot from behind that nicked him.

He almost reached a clearing in the front yard when a vehicle exploded in front of him, and a large piece of metal smashed into his fin. PO flashed red and jerked sideways, spinning to the ground. He bounced and landed in a smoldering pile of rubble near a truck.

His red light beeped non-stop and he rotated with electric sparks that shot from his body.

The striped drone descended just in front of him, and without hesitation thrust a metal spike through PO's chassis above his glass eye.

He quivered and let out a series of final beeps and digital whines that ended with an electronic sizzle.

Jack spun around to find Cà Rá swarmed by four Wraiths. She whirled around, striking one with a rip to its gullet, spraying neon-blue blood into the sky. Her body contorted to free from another and with a twist in the air, she tore its head off.

A rush of wind hit the back of Jack's neck and he turned only to be struck in the face. Demi laughed as Jack smashed to the ground.

Star screamed from behind.

Jack's eyes fixed on Cà Rá as she rushed toward him, but more Wraiths and Slayers dropped into her path.

She picked up an energy blade and somersaulted over one Wraith slicing it in half. Touching off the ground, she rotated and hacked through a Slayer, but a Xurrican smashed into her, knocking her off-balance.

A relentless line of creatures and cultists swarmed over her.

Two Wraiths wrangled her legs and forced her to her knees. An electric baton zapped her body, stunning her into a submissive trance that forced her to the ground.

Tarkos sprinted up from the basement and made for the cabin's front door but a hail of bullets from an M2 machine gun burst into the space, striking several cultists and cutting large splatters of blood through the air.

He dropped to the ground, panting as he crawled over bodies scattered along the floor.

Grabbing a rifle from a dead cultist, he kept low as bullets whizzed overhead, wood splinters and glass raining down on him.

Right when he located an open window, a man screamed behind him. He turned to find the man sprinting down the hallway, revolver in hand. Tarkos raised the rifle and pulled the trigger. A volley of shots exploded from the barrel and struck the cultist throwing the man into a small table.

"Shit."

As shadows appeared on the far side of the hallway, Tarkos slid to the window and crawled outside. He hit the ground, eyes drawn to a satchel in a tuft of tall grass near the front deck. Tarkos scampered over, grabbing the bag.

He pulled out the Moleskine journal and Bruce's phone.

A boom ripped through the air and he ducked. He glanced across the pit at Demi and then down at Bruce's phone.

The sim card.

Patting his pockets, he located the sim, scrounged a piece of scrap metal, ejected the sim tray and clicked the card inside.

Demi had been wrong about one thing. The real power of the Empyreax was in its key. Maybe Jack's dad knew what he was doing. Whoever held the key, held its power. And he now held its blueprints.

A loud bang and whine of twisted metal broke his focus. A Xurrican smashed a column that had formed the grid shield. Waves of energy arced across the yard, hitting the house, shredding through a propane tank.

The tank exploded, gaseous flames setting off a series of thunderous detonations behind him. The fiery shockwave blasted him across the front yard, and he flipped through the air in scalding flames, away from the cabin as its side sheared off and fell into the chasm.

He landed on the edge of the woods, bones snapping as his body erupted in agony.

Claws from the Slayer pressed deeper into Cà Rá's throat, and she kicked her legs into the ground for leverage.

A Wraith clamped an energy collar around her neck and she convulsed.

Electric sparks sizzled from a strand of red plasma that spread from the collar and draped over her body. She flicked her eyes at a boulder and drew it toward her, smashing it into the Slayer. The blunt force knocked it back and it growled then fired a taser-like device into her leg.

Energy pulsed through her core, fragmenting her foot into shimmering particles. Sensory fibers through her body crackled, but she made no sound—her expression carried the weight of the trauma.

A large oak nearby caught her attention, and she strained to topple it, crashing it down on top of a Wraith. Its body flailed beneath the tree, giving off a deafening screech.

Two more Slayers kicked Cà Rá and rammed electrodes into her thighs. Another tied her up with a halo of red plasma and flipped her over, face down. It pulled on the energy cord around her neck and jerked her head back. A Slayer stepped up behind her with a large spear and rammed it through her back. Her body jolted.

The Slayer motioned at two Wraiths, who nodded and picked her up.

As her cheek lifted off the ground, she spotted Jack fending off a horde of Xurricans. The blue light in her eyes dimmed and her bottom lip quivered.

Dark claws from the two Wraiths grabbed her shoulders and lifted her into the air.

Her head flopped down but she kept her eyes fixed on Jack.

They passed through clouds of smoke and disappeared into the dark sky.

Star grabbed the energy sword and ran up behind Demi, swinging it as hard as she could down on him. "Leave him alone!"

Demi turned and dodged the blade, flicking it into the air where it hovered just behind him. He stretched his fingers at Star and rotated his hand, lifting her into the air, defenseless.

"Why are you doing this?" she cried out.

Demi didn't respond, just squared his body, and closed in on her. His skin glowed and seemed to twist, rotating as if contorted by some form of energy beneath it.

Jack lifted his head and moaned, "Star." He tried to push up, but his broken wrist betrayed him.

Her eyes locked on him. "I'm not leaving you, Jack."

"Pathetic creatures." Demi thrust his hand forward, and the energy sword flew through the air.

The blade crunched into Star's chest and cut straight through her back.

A single gasp of air escaped her, and her eyes widened, rolling into the back of her head.

Everything fell silent.

Jack let out a blood-curdling scream and reached out for her.

Her head fell back, and Demi released her limp body. She smashed to the ground, and the energy sword electrified through her before burning out.

Jack clenched his teeth at Demi and pressed up from the ground.

Dex gritted his teeth and propped up against the rotted wood fence post, shifting to the least painful position. The prick of a sticker bush scraped against his lower back, but he didn't mind, it distracted him from the pain of his sprained ankle, and the two or three ribs that had cracked. Sweltering heat streamed sweat down his neck and chest that reflected the orange glow of the surrounding fire.

The screams of cultists and soldiers blended with a cacophony of gunfire and bombs—a front-row seat to a theatrical performance. About fifty yards to his right, down a sloping trail of fire, the dark silhouette of a cultist rounded a tree and smashed a soldier with a bat.

Scampering bodies dotted the fiery backdrop, but this particular one caught his attention. The cultist grabbed the soldier's rifle and cackled with a demented screech, spraying bullets in random directions.

A stray bullet whizzed past Dex's head and struck the fence post.

The magazine emptied and the cultist turned around coming face to face with a Xurrican Wraith. The creature brandished a glowing white blade and sliced the cultist in half.

Unfazed by the macabre scene, Dex pulled a mangled cheroot from his shirt pocket and snarled his lips around the end of it. He pulled the matchbox out of his pocket and flicked a match, cupping his hands to light the cheroot.

He inhaled the earthen wood fused with the tang of cocoa, leather, and spice, savoring the flavor before exhaling a large plume that swirled into the sky.

Turning the matchbox over in his hand, he glanced at the safe combination and laughed at the spectacle before him—an apocalyptic symphony of doom. He shoved the matchbox back into his pocket and drew his focus to the silhouette of the Xurrican Slayer headed his way.

An explosion rocked in the distance that sent flames billowing black ash into the sky. A meteor streaked overhead, and he chuckled past the cheroot that now dangled from his lower lip.

With no fight left in him, he unholstered his Browning Hi-Power and racked the slide. Dex chawed down on the cheroot. "Check out time." At least he got in one last smoke.

The Slayer moved up the embankment, the sword brandished by its side, creeping closer and closer.

Dex propped the base of the gun on his knee and steadied his aim straight at the Xurrican.

The loud bark of a dog broke his focus. "Newt."

Newt stood next to Dex with a loop of rope in his mouth.

"What's this?"

Leaning in, Newt dropped the loop in Dex's hand.

He wrapped his arm through the rope and squeezed tight. "Now what—"

Newt snarled and leaped into the air at the Xurrican. The rope tightened and yanked Dex back, pulling him at a high speed away from the post.

His body slid through tall grasses and splashed through a mud puddle. He crashed through a small wooden fence and rolled to a stop inside the main door of the barn. The winch that pulled the rope wound to a stop and he knelt on all fours trying to sit up.

With more effort than he cared to admit, he stood and pulled a canvas tarp off an armored Ford F550 truck.

Letting out a bellowing laugh he winced in pain. "Haha. Bill, you son of a bitch."

He climbed into the cab, fired up the engine and listened to it rumble to life. A Cubs bobblehead on the dash vibrated. Lighting another cheroot, he pushed an 8-Track tape into the radio and cranked the volume.

Flipping a switch on the dash, a light bar switched on and cast a powerful beam into the forest. When he pressed a red button, two side panels with 50-caliber guns slid out from the quarter panels of the truck.

Grinding the clutch, he mashed the throttle and sped out of the barn. The guns pulse-fired bullets and tracers throughout the forest, hitting cultists and Xurrican creatures. He turned sharply, making his way up the hill blasting anything in its path.

Something ran in from the side of the trail and jolted him to slam on the brakes. The cheroot popped out of his mouth.

The side guns spun to silence with smoking barrels, and he jumped out of the truck.

Newt stood in the bright headlights, the severed hand of a Xurrican in his mouth.

"Good boy." Dex laughed while opening the passenger door.

Newt wagged his tail, dropped the hand, and scampered into the truck.

The striped drone angled in on PO, capturing its reflection against his glass eye. It opened a door on its main body and an armature with a welding torch emerged and lit up a white-hot flame.

The blade sizzled and moved in on PO's glass eye.

PO lay cold and silent, unaware of the looming threat.

Deep inside his circuits, amidst the transistors, diodes, and chips, a single 1.5v capacitor flicked a tiny erratic spark. A drop of electrolyte gel had leaked from its seam onto the circuit traces, and it struggled to maintain a charge. Just before the final spark of energy faded, it broke through the gel and powered the next circuit. The circuit took over from the backup capacitor bank. Power swarmed through the circuits and the main logic board reset.

Just before the striped drone's flame touched PO, his glass eye flashed red, and he jerked back to life.

PO opened his own trap door and fired a tethered hook that attached to the evil drone and spun it with a hard jerk.

Stripe tried to cut the cord, but PO ejected a large, spiked, micro-missile that slammed into the drone's eye spinning it away. It exploded in a burst of fire and electricity before plunging into the Empyreax pit, leaving a trail of smoke behind.

PO's eye flashed green with a beep and he pulled himself up from the pile of rubble. He teetered and wobbled in the air, but oriented himself and floated back across the pit.

A massive blast ripped across the edge of the forest. Flames engulfed trees that swayed against violent winds.

Demi passed through fire and smoke to the pit's edge and glanced at the Empyreax. His eyes widened. "Yes." He leaned forward over the pit and screamed. "It's open!"

Three Xurricans and two cultists looked across the pit at Demi, then down at the open portal.

He stepped off the ledge, but his forward momentum stopped, and he froze, unable to move. A laser lasso spiraled up from his right foot and zapped around his right arm. He followed the energy trail to Jack, who dug his heels into the ground and pulled hard on the electric whip.

Another lasso spiraled down his leg, his body weakening from the zaps of electricity. Demi staggered, losing his balance, and fell to the ground. He lifted his eyes to a drone holding the second beam.

"Pull hard, PO," Jack said.

PO yanked back and dragged Demi forward, turning his body around.

Demi glanced into the pit and smiled when a group of Xurricans and cultists jumped down across stone platforms, making their way to the Empyreax.

"You're too late, Jack. Once they're inside, it begins."

"Not before I kill you, you bastard."

Demi's booming laugh echoed through the forest.

PO's glass eye zoomed in past Demi at the Xurricans nearing the Empyreax. It rotated back at Jack who had turned to reach for the Black Widow.

"We need to pull him just a few more feet," Jack yelled.

PO turned to the Empyreax and flicked one last glance back at Jack.

Jack turned, and PO let out a green beep. A booster rocket fired from his backside, thrusting him down into the pit.

"PO!" Jack's voice echoed throughout the chamber.

He weaved in and out of the floating stone rocks and platforms, spinning past the cultists, his eye fixed on the Empyreax portal.

A Xurrican jumped off a platform to enter the portal and PO flew beneath it.

A trap door on his side opened and his claw arm reached up, yanking the Empyreax key out of the lock.

PO rotated with the key into the portal and disappeared just before the border collapsed inward on itself, rippling to a close.

30

· QUANTUM SOUL ·

With the force of PO's lasso gone, Demi jumped to his feet, eyes flaring red, and unleashed a wrathful cry. "Ah, fuck." Jack scrambled backwards to grab the Black Widow.

Demi raised his arm and Jack jerked into the air, then was pulled to Demi's hand, which closed around Jack's throat, squeezing tight.

"Time to join your father."

Jack strained against Demi's strength but with his oxygen running out, his head tilted back and his eyes closed.

Meteors streaked across the night sky while Wraiths carried Cà Rá higher and higher away from Black Wolf Mountain.

She opened her eyes and scanned the distant ground below. As soon as she found Jack, she rolled up under the Wraith and a burst of white light shot from her core. The bindings fractured away and she grabbed one of the Wraiths, severing its head.

A Slayer fired a plasma cannon, but she pirouetted through the air, avoiding each burst of energy. The second Wraith reached for her, but she arched her back, creating a swirling plasma vortex that cut through it. It shattered into thousands of particles that dissipated into the sky.

She paused against the backdrop of the moon and glanced down at Jack.

A horde of Slayers and Wraiths shot through the sky toward her, but she leaned forward and dove down to the mountain.

Jack opened his eyes with a jolt. Bright light from the afternoon sun forced him to squint. He stared up at the trunk of a tree that rose high into the blue sky. He lay flat against the ground and he tried to wiggle his legs.

"Jack, don't move." A gentle voice echoed from above, and his father appeared leaning over him.

"What happened?" Jack muttered.

"You had a pretty bad fall, kid." Bill placed his hand on Jack's forehead and Roger leaned in over his shoulder.

"Is he gonna be okay, Dad?"

"He'll be fine, son. Just give him a minute to clear his head." He turned his head. "Beth?"

Jack's mother called from the distance. "Ambulance is on the way."

"What happened?" Jack asked.

Roger replied, "You fell out of Star Nest."

"I did? Well, help me get up."

Bill pressed down on Jack's chest. "Don't move, son. People are on the way to help. Just breathe and listen to my voice."

When he tried to sit up, a deep pain shot through his lower back and he winced, tears gathering.

Roger sniffled and wiped tears from his own face.

Jack's head fell back on the grass. "I'm sorry. I didn't mean to."

Bill's eyes welled up. "It's okay, son. I'm not mad. You're gonna be all right."

His mother appeared behind his father and she cupped her right hand over her mouth. "Is he gonna be okay, Bill?"

Bill paused. "He's gonna be just fine. I promise."

"It hurts, Dad."

"I know." He squeezed Jack's hand and smiled. "I'd do anything to take your pain away." His smile faded beneath teary eyes and a choked breath. "I'm here son. I love you, Jack."

"I love you too, Dad."

Bill leaned to his left and rays of sunlight hit Jack's face. A distant object, high in the sky, glinted in the sun and seemed to be in a freefall straight at him.

It shimmered and he tilted his head with a curious squint at the object.

The shape of a woman draped in showering streams of white light streaked down toward him.

The beaming light filled his face and he blinked.

Jack opened his eyes and a burst of light filled the night sky. His eyes locked on tendrils of glimmering rays that streaked behind Cà Rá.

She turned and looked at him as he tracked her trajectory toward Star.

Like an incoming missile, she streamed down and exploded into the ground behind Demi.

A blinding dome of electric energy and purple plasma flashed from the ground and grew with a burst of power that pummeled Demi and Jack.

Wraiths and Slayers that had been in pursuit recoiled from the blast.

Jack's body flipped out of Demi's grasp and landed near the cliff's edge.

Demi staggered back and pressed his feet into the ground, spinning to confront Cà Rá.

She had disappeared into a swirling pool of light around Star's body, bending and refracting the space around her. Energy vapors collapsed upon cackling sparks and waves of radiance that beamed into the sky.

Jack struggled to pull himself up as heavy gusts from the energy wave blasted his face.

Demi regained his footing and tracked the silhouette of a figure rising from the light, its back arched, arms and legs dangling in the air.

Jack crawled up from the ledge on his knee and tracked the body rise into the sky, only it wasn't Cà Rá.

"Star."

Electricity rose from the ground and crackled all over Star's floating body.

She twitched to life, opened her eyes, and rotated upright.

Demi let out an unhinged roar as the Wraiths and Slayers swooped in behind him. He hurled a massive blast of dark energy toward her and the Xurricans fired every weapon they had.

Star moved to the side and reached both arms behind her. With a head tilt, she threw her hands forward, unleashing a devastating arced wall of energy that destroyed a Slayer in its path.

The beam passed through Demi and he tried to move through its resistance toward her.

Jack crawled to the Black Widow and snatched it up, launching into a sprint toward Star. He pulled back on its charging handle and fired into the back of a Slayer.

The pulse hit the beast, shattering it into a million particles.

Demi raced at Star and swung his arm back to strike. A red stream of fire trailed behind his hand hurtling toward her, but she disappeared.

His arm swiped through the air, and he spun off-balance, stumbling as he glanced around searching for her.

As he turned, Jack blasted a Wraith and charged at Demi with a frenzied scream.

Demi reared back to attack Jack, but a hand grabbed his arm and yanked it back. Another hand appeared and gripped his left wrist. A third arm wrapped around his neck and Demi rolled his eyes up as four holographic apparitions of Star clung onto him.

Demi struggled against Star's restraint. Muscles and veins in his neck bulged and rippled like cords, pulsing with strength. His skin glowed an intense red iridescent, desperate to break free. He grunted ragged gasps as he refused to give in, straining with all his might.

Jack thrust the end of the Black Widow's barrel into Demi's chest.

"Say hi to my dad."

He squeezed the trigger and an energy bolt pierced into Demi, unleashing an intense, frenetic strobe of light that spread through his body.

Thousands of light particles broke through his skin and melted away his human form to reveal a skeletal figure of light under a translucent glowing body. His gloss black eyes flickered and he let out a demented shriek that mixed man, beast, and digital chaos. The particles ate away his remaining body, shooting sparks into the sky, and Jack grinned into Demi's face as it fractured, grinned wider as the last of the alien ruptured into nothingness.

The multiplicities of Star merged, and she collapsed to the ground.

Jack rushed over, gathering her into his arms. "Star. Star, look at me."

She groaned and tilted up at him, opening her eyes. "What happened?"

"I don't know. But it's over," he said. "Thank you."

"For what?"

"Never mind." He leaned down and kissed her. Drawing her in tight, her body pressed against his broken wrist, and he winced in pain.

"What's wrong with your hand?"

"Don't worry about it. Time to go."

Straggling gunshots echoed in the distance and smoke billowed through the night sky.

As he helped her stand, Jack glanced back at the cabin that had been consumed by fire. A photo of him and Roger curled and smoldered in the flames. Logbooks that now made so much sense, burned to hot ash. The recorded memory chips from his father were nothing but a molten pool of hot liquid metal. The framed picture with Dex, incinerated by the heat. The penguin. Surely, the penguin with the pink bow had already been destroyed.

Every trace of William Young lost forever.

The sound of an incoming helicopter caught his attention.

He glanced up at the sky then ushered Star down the trail.

∞

When Tarkos regained consciousness, he gagged on ash-laden and smoky air. Lying in a ditch at the forest's edge, he rolled his head to the side and gazed at the cabin burning in the distance.

A deep sting ran across the left side of his face and the smell of cooked flesh filled his nose. Blood pooled in his mouth from busted teeth. His left eye was swollen shut.

He groaned in pain and tried to orient himself to his surroundings. The intense heat from nearby flames crept toward him and he lifted his head. His left arm was charred and oozed blood. Drawing in a deep breath, his eyes fell upon the leather satchel near the edge of the fire line.

He rolled onto his stomach and cried out from the pain. His broken femur jutted from his thigh, and the gaping wound on his shredded left cheek scraped on the ground when he tried to drag himself forward.

Moving to mere feet from the satchel, he reached out, but the flames caught its strap.

With heavy groans, he clawed at the dirt and tried to pull himself along faster.

The satchel caught fire and burning embers spread along the ground at him. "No," he muttered through his bloodied mouth.

Fire consumed the satchel while the line of flames flared up and spread around him.

Darting his head to the side, he pivoted his body away from the encroaching fire and moved to a low-lying gully. Tarkos was nothing but pain as he rolled down into the runoff of a natural spring and crawled away from the fire's leading edge. Dragging his busted leg behind him, Tarkos hit a steep section of ground, gasping as he rolled down an embankment, his mind swallowed by darkness.

When he came to, he found himself next to a large boulder. Blood poured from his shattered jaw, and he gurgled for air.

He pressed his cheek against the cool boulder and caught a faint blue glow in the darkness ahead of him. Squinting with his one good eye, he made out the form of the alien entity that had a white dot on its forehead; the same one he'd seen at the temple.

It sat slouched over, pulsating with feeble breaths of pain. Wheezing through digital static gasps, it turned to Tarkos.

It reached out its hand and slapped into the ground, pulling itself toward him.

Tarkos didn't make a sound. Nothing at this point mattered.

The entity moved in front of him and grabbed his leg.

With one last strain of energy, it latched onto Tarkos' arm and a pulse of blue light merged into him.

Jack and Star reached the base of Black Wolf Mountain and hobbled down an overgrown path. The *thwump* of helicopter blades, sirens, and screams echoed down through the blazing forest.

They reached a wooden bridge spanning a narrow section of Stone Creek. Before they crossed, the rumbling sound from a vehicle crunching over gravel grew louder and lights appeared over a hill behind them.

The beams aimed right at them toward the bridge, drawing closer, its diesel engine grumbling through a clutch grind.

Jack turned and shielded Star behind him as the vehicle ground to a stop. He held his hand up from the blinding lights as the driver's door opened.

A silhouetted figure stepped out of the truck and moved toward them carrying a rifle.

"Don't say anything," Jack whispered to Star.

A dot of red-hot ash lit up through the dark and smoke puffed into the air. "You guys need a ride?"

Newt jumped out of the truck and ran toward Jack.

"Newt!" Jack smiled and knelt to pet him with his uninjured hand.

Dex stepped forward into the light and Jack staggered upright to hug him.

"We thought you died," Jack said.

Dex groaned in pain from the hug and took a puff on his cheroot. "Can't keep a good man down."

"What about Simon?"

Dex shook his head. "Didn't make it. But he saved our asses."

"Damn."

Star hugged Dex. "Are you hurt?"

"Nothing that can't be fixed. When's the wedding?"

Star turned to Jack and smiled then raised a brow at Dex. "You do know we just met Tuesday."

"Uh huh," he replied with a wry grin. "We better leave before they lock this place down."

"Yeah."

"Just one thing though, Jack." Dex placed his hand on Jack's shoulder. "Your old man would be proud."

Jack paused then smiled. "I hope so."

After helping them into the truck, Dex took a long drag on his cheroot and flicked it away.

Dex slammed the driver's door and looked back. "You guys strapped in back there?"

"Yeah," Star said. "Did you know there's a big safe back here?"

"You bet your ass I do," he said, pulling the matchbox out of his pocket and kissing it.

The truck rolled across the bridge and through an open field of high grasses. As they cut onto the main road, lights from several police and military vehicles rounded a distant bend behind them.

A large crowd of spectators, reporters, and military gathered outside of the main road leading to Black Wolf. Soldiers yelled into bull horns, demanding the crowd move away.

NQCO agents in hazmat suits scrambled from large vans carrying cases and equipment, passing beyond a fence erected by the military.

Meeks helped load a wounded man into the back of an ambulance and turned with a limp. Gazing up at the burning mountain, he scratched his neck and took his hat off to rub his hand through his hair.

He spotted Linda Fox speaking into her microphone with an excited expression. No doubt ready to shine for her big story.

"Officials are not saying much but what we do know from sources who spoke to us off the record is that a military cargo plane transporting radioactive material crashed up on Black Wolf Mountain sometime after midnight. They won't acknowledge if it was a bomb, but the entire area has been sealed off and residents are being warned to stay away. In an unrelated incident, a hostage situation at a nearby farm took place earlier in the evening and caused a number of casualties. It's been a busy night here in Stone Creek and we're going to try to get you more information as soon as we can."

Finn stepped up to Meeks and handed him a cup of coffee. "You sure you don't need a doctor, Sheriff?"

"Not sure what I need, Finn." He sipped the coffee and turned to a rumble where a column of black Suburbans drove past a group of guards with German shepherds before making their way up the mountain road. A soldier zip tied a large sign to the fence: 'Danger Radiation Exposure'.

Meeks flitted the bill of his Sheriff baseball hat between his thumb and forefinger and held it up to Finn. "How about a retirement party?"

"Sheriff." Finn shook his head and waved the hat away.

"Take it. You've earned it."

Finn stared long and hard at the cap then finally took it and pulled it onto his head.

They shook hands and Meeks looked over Finn's shoulder, spotting a familiar face mixed in with the crowd.

Takashi stood with his sunglasses tight to his eyes and stared back at Meeks.

A small grin creased on Takashi's face. He nodded and turned, disappearing into the crowd.

Meeks lifted his eyes to the heavens, his mind filled with

burning questions.

Meteors streaked through the dark abyss of the universe, and it gazed back at him with answers he didn't quite understand.

· EPILOGUE ·

Friday, September 13th, 1985

"Look, another one," Jack said. His finger tracked a shooting star across the firmament. "It's so cool..."

"Yeah," Roger said.

The brothers lay on their backs staring into the night sky from the plywood observatory of Star Nest. It gave them a front-row seat to the cosmic meteor shower.

"Jack, Roger, time for bed," Bill shouted from the back of their house.

Jack called out to his father, "Dad, come check this out."

Bill stepped into the dark backyard, wiping his hands with a towel that he then threw over his shoulder. Dozens of meteors shot across the dark horizon.

He jumped back up on the steps and cracked the screen door open. "Beth, come here a second. Quick." He flicked the kitchen lights off and thrust the yard into complete darkness.

Beth stepped outside and stood by his side. "What's up?"

"Meteor shower."

"Wow, that's beautiful." She leaned into him, and he placed his hands on her shoulders.

The voices of their two boys echoed from the treehouse.

"It's so awesome."

"Totally."

Beth looked up at Bill. "They say when you see a shooting star, you're supposed to make a wish."

"Yeah?" He tilted his gaze down while wrapping his arms around her.

She pressed her head into his chest and he squeezed her tight. "And sometimes they come true," she said. She looked up at Bill with a gentle smile. "So, what will you wish for?"

A white rabbit dashed from the shadows.

Bill looked down at his wife, then lifted his head with a smile and cast his gaze straight through this page at you.

Out of the darkness, a blue dasher dragonfly skimmed past Bill's shoulder and lifted you high into the sky along with it.

The rotors of a UH-60 Blackhawk helicopter chopped its blades through a billowing cloud of smoke and forced you to pivot and spiral left.

The dragonfly swooped down in a wide arc and dove through the clouds, emerging onto the backside of Black Wolf. Fire had consumed the mountainside and dark figures of firefighters and military personnel worked to extinguish the flames.

The dragonfly weaved amongst humans and machines.

Dodging...ducking...spinning—and rose higher and higher into the sky with you in tow.

It fluttered above the giant crater that exposed the hull of a crashed ship buried in the earth. Soldiers rotated large spotlights into the pit and illuminated the Empyreax floating in stoic silence.

Men in white protective suits surrounded the upper edge of the crater with cameras, weapons, and drones.

One of the drones buzzed past the dragonfly and it strafed to its right.

It flew back into the sky and lifted you higher…farther and farther away until you both nosedived into the dark canopy of a forest.

It rolled in and out of beams of moonlight, cutting between branches and the still of night.

You soared in tandem…hooking…skimming—through, over, and under rock ledges and hollow logs.

Easing into a final descent, you slowed to a hover then landed on a flat rock.

The dragonfly twitched and stared back at you. Moonlight reflected off the geodesic pattern of thousands of lenses in its compound eyes. A vibration, a buzzing, cut through the silence and a cold light illuminated its body.

You both turned and there, half buried in the mud, rested the glass screen of a phone with a glowing message.

The dragonfly tilted its head and the phone's light reflected off its eyes.

'Incoming Call from Lily Hon'.

THANK YOU

Dear Reader,

Thank you for spending time to experience EMPYREAX. I enjoyed creating it for you to read. I understand not everyone will have a paid copy, so if you liked it, please consider purchasing a copy - maybe for a friend. Please also share it on social media so the story can travel far and wide across the universe. Your support enables me to expand this world through sequels.

For those who purchased my book, I am truly grateful.

Warmest regards,

Scott

Check out more stories at
www.SCOTTFROST.com

ACKNOWLEDGMENTS

I am deeply humbled by those who have inspired, taught, and motivated me. Writing is impossible without an amazing network of support.

Thank you to my family for their belief in me.

Thank you to the AutoCrit community including Gareth Jones, Daniel Kaplan, Katherine D. Graham, Bekah Brinkmeier, Geoff Brown, and my editor Amanda J. Spedding. I have learned so much from you.

Thank you to my fellow authors for their support: Cage Dunn, Toni King, Jim Tully, Tim Barrett, Eric Hull, Josh Conley, and B. Griffin Meiling.

And special thank you to author Ceci Li for her encouragement and motivation. Without her, this book would not exist.

"The best is yet to come!"

PREPARE YOURSELF

EMPYREAX

COMING SOON

JOIN THE MAILING LIST

www.EMPYREAX.com

ABOUT THE AUTHOR

Scott Frost is an award-winning author who writes Gothic Horror and Dark Sci-Fi stories that highlight the Cosmic Wonder of Humanity. He works in technology leadership and was named CIO of the Year in 2023. He collects movie soundtracks, autographs, movies, and owns a complete Fangoria collection.

Follow his writing journey at
www.SCOTTFROST.com